ALL THE SACRIFICE OF SHADOWS

HILLARY RAYMER

❀ Created with Vellum

*For the ones who discovered the darkness
was within them all along*

CONTENT WARNINGS

- Voyeurism
- Adult Language
- Explicit Sexual Content/Sexual Themes
- Attempted Murder
- Brief on page attempted SA
- Blood
- Violence
- Death

Havnokk Deep

Dragnatt
Lair

CHAPTER ONE

*E*ighteen days.

Creslyn Starstorm had been living in Brackroth for eighteen days. Not once had she seen the sun shine through the dense wall of gray clouds that seemed to shroud the entire city. Not once had she slept through the night—the shriek of dragons always woke her with a racing heart. And not once had Prince Drake Kalstrand, her betrothed, spoken a single word to her.

But she knew he watched her.

She sensed his presence between the shadows of the dreary halls of Castle Brackroth. His scent followed her, and the long stretches of darkness moved in perfect cadence with her as she walked. He kept her locked in a private wing with her own bedchambers, her own maids and servants, her own loneliness. She had yet to meet the king. Stars above, she hadn't even been allowed to explore any other part of the castle. Creslyn was a prisoner in what was supposed to be her new home. She took her meals in silence, and it was a rare occasion if she could get more than a few words out of one of the servants. Though she supposed that had everything to do with the fact that she was fae and they were all humans. She imagined it must've been quite the shock for their beloved prince to return with a faerie for a bride instead of a mortal princess. Not that it was any excuse for them to act as though she didn't exist. For the most part, she spent her days fuming in idle boredom, so much so that she'd taken to tracking the constellations in a journal. Hidden away from court affairs and any other possibilities of excitement, she remained exiled to her wing like she was nothing more than a bargaining chip from a deal gone sour.

But she knew Prince Drake remained in the shifting darkness, patiently waiting for her to scream, to cry and weep, to beg him to return her to Aeramere. Where she belonged.

Creslyn scowled.

She would not give him the satisfaction.

Freshly annoyed by her own downtrodden mood, she peeled herself up from the sumptuous bed and sighed.

Her personal chambers were nothing to complain about. In fact, they were quite lovely, save for the lack of color. She would've preferred brilliant hues of gold, pink, lavender, and teal. Something reminiscent of the magic coursing through her veins. Yet nearly everything here was doused in shades of black, gray, and silver. Though the silver she didn't mind at all because it reminded her of the stars.

The walls were papered with black velvet roses, tipped with specks of glitter. The canopy of her four-poster bed was pale gray silk and the sheets were midnight satin. White fur rugs were spread across the ebony hardwood floors, and the hearth, with its glowing fire to ward off the constant chill, was lined with dark marble. Even the draperies hanging from the arching windows were a gossamer fabric that reminded her of a starless night.

Creslyn swung her legs over the edge of the bed, bundling her rosy pink fur robe around her. At least her gowns and shoes weren't as drab as everything else.

Once Drake had deposited her in this room upon their arrival, her personal effects from House Celestine had been delivered a few hours later. She had no idea how he'd managed that, nor had she been given the opportunity to ask. The moment the trunks full of her belongings had shown up, he'd disappeared again without saying anything.

The man was absolutely maddening.

She raked her fingers through her mass of hair, untangling the strands of silver streaked with icy blue, soft pink, and pastel purple. The loose waves fell to nearly her waist and while her lady's maid—a petite woman with plump cheeks and kind eyes —arranged her hair daily, by lunchtime Creslyn had already taken down her fine handiwork. It was useless to have her hair done so beautifully when there was no one around to see it.

Standing, she padded across the soft rug, shivering when her bare feet touched the chilly hardwood floor. She pulled open the glass doors to her balcony, grateful the prince had not seen fit to lock those as well, and stepped out onto the ledge jutting high above all of Brackroth. A gust of brisk air cut through the fur of her robe, causing her skin to pebble with goosebumps. She shivered against the assault, wrapping her fingers around the ornate bronze railing to steel herself in the stiff breeze. Though it had been near the end of summer when she left Aeramere, she had no idea if the kingdom of Brackroth followed the same seasonal patterns, or if it had any change in weather at all. It was always damp and overcast with a steadfast bite in the air.

Creslyn stared out over the vast city of spires and misshapen dwellings to where angry mountains slashed across the inky horizon. Only in the dead of night were the skies of Brackroth clear, and it was then she could see the hundreds of twinkling stars embellished like diamonds across a canvas of black satin. Here, the constellations were not the same as they were in Aeramere. They were scattered about, as though the Mother

Goddess herself had flung them into the sky with haphazard care. Creslyn sought Vespira the Druid, the star sign she was born beneath, searched the skies for her radiant staff, but found nothing.

Vespira could not be seen in Brackroth.

The moon was barely a sliver in the sky, its illuminated crescent a small reminder of home. In the far-off distance, she could see the silhouettes of dragons soaring above the steep mountaintops.

A shiver trekked down her spine.

Cupping her hands together, Creslyn called to the magic flowing inside her. A tiny drop of sunlight formed in her palms, filled with dozens of iridescent rainbows. Her power wasn't quite the same as that of her seven other siblings. Whereas each of them possessed some form of celestial magic, she controlled sunshine and rainbows, a pretty kind of magic that was hardly useful. Even her twin sister, Caelian, was blessed with the ability to create falling stars and grant wishes upon them, despite their souls mirroring one another. Creslyn always assumed it was a product of being the last child born into the Starstorm family line. Perhaps the gods and goddesses had simply run out of stellar powers to grant.

She didn't mind, though, not really.

She loved being able to fashion showers of rainbows and beams of sunlight. Her magic suited her.

Behind her, there was a shift in the air, like a weighted looming presence, and she couldn't shake the sensation of being watched.

Which could only mean one thing.

Prince Drake was here.

Snuffing out her magic completely, she spun on one heel and stalked back into her bedroom. She caught the scent of him first —frosted pine and cold mountains, the fragrance of the earth right before the first promise of snow. Her gaze slid around the space, focusing on the play of shadows against the far wall, how they seemed darker, more sinister, than the rest. The only light source came from the hearth, where orange flames wavered and sparked, as though they'd been recently stoked to life.

Creslyn's mouth pulled to the side in disdain.

So, the mighty Prince of Brackroth wanted to ensure she was warm but didn't have the decency to show his face. How thoughtful of him.

"You know," she drawled, closing the balcony doors behind her, "I don't appreciate being made to feel like a captive. I'm quite certain Ariesian would be none too pleased to learn the truth of my current predicament. Especially considering the terms of your contract."

Her eldest brother, Ariesian, had negotiated for her to marry the prince in exchange for Brackroth's protection. Though why House Celestine needed the promise of safeguarding from someone like Prince Drake was beyond her. Either way, she had been part of a carefully arranged deal. One that involved her becoming the wife to a prince, not his prisoner.

"Still ignoring me, I see." She curled her fingers around one of the bedposts, swinging casually. "And why is that, I wonder? Perhaps we should make a game of it..."

Creslyn snapped her fingers, a smile tugging at the corner of her mouth. "I'll try to guess the reason why you keep me secluded in this wing of the castle. If I'm wrong, you can continue lurking in the darkness and acting as though I am nothing but a thorn in your side. However, if I am *right*, then you will show your face and explain exactly what is going on here."

Sensuous laughter, deep and rumbling, spilled from the far corner. The sound of it chilled her blood while sending a spear of heat straight through her. She'd never heard him laugh before, even if it was at her expense. To make matters worse, she *enjoyed* it.

No matter, she was well-versed in the art of whittling away her opponent's willpower until they caved and gave in to her demands. She had years of practice with her older siblings.

She fiddled with the satin sash of her robe, running her fingers over the soft fabric. "Maybe it's that you had no intention of taking a wife, and I'm nothing more than a significant means to an end."

Silence, but the shadows continued to lurk.

"I take it I'm incorrect in that assumption?" Slowly she paced the length of her quarters, considering each word with care. She would get his attention, one way or another. "Very well. I suppose it's possible that you intend to offer me up as some kind of sacrifice. Could it be that your dragon, Svartos, has a taste for magical blood?"

Creslyn pinned the far corner of the wall with a pointed look. Again, he said nothing. But the shadows were crawling with tension, nearly pulsing with irritation.

Good.

She sauntered back toward her bed, then sat on the edge, crossing her legs so that her robe fell open neatly on both sides all the way to the top of her thighs. She couldn't be certain, but she could have sworn a guttural noise came from the corner and it sounded much like a growl. Planting both hands behind her on the cushioned mattress, she leveled the pressing darkness with a glare of her own.

"But I think the real reason you keep me hidden within these walls is because you're ashamed of me. You wanted Novalise and you got me instead, the younger, spoiled sister who lacks any kind of social decorum and who doesn't give a damn about being a lady." The words hurt far worse when she said them out loud, but sometimes the truth was painful to hear. "Not only that, but it's been terribly obvious since the moment I arrived that you're disgusted by the fact that I'm fae and not a human.

I'm sure your court is in an uproar with unpleasant jokes and vicious rumors."

The fire in the hearth fizzled, dying to nothing more than a few spitting sparks and burning embers. Already her bedchamber was drastically colder, as though all the warmth had been leached from her room. She fought against the urge to tremble and locked her jaw to keep her teeth from chattering. Without the glow of the flames from the hearth, the shadows devoured every wall, every window, every breath of space.

Still, he did not show himself.

Agitation clawed at Creslyn, and though she knew it was likely an awful idea to goad him further, she no longer cared. Rolling her eyes to the painted ceiling, she shoved up from the bed and stood.

"Fine," she ground out, yanking on her sash. "If you will not speak to me, then I am going to bed."

She dropped her shoulders, allowing her robe to fall to the ground in a pile of rosy fur at her feet, leaving her fully nude. She pointed to the door. "You can see yourself out."

Creslyn spun back toward her bed, but she wasn't fast enough.

The prince was on her in an instant.

One minute she was reaching for the plush comforter, and in the next she was in the air, then flat on her back, pinned beneath him.

A startled cry pealed from the back of her throat, but she swallowed it when his face came into her line of vision and all the shadows bled away. Dark hair tumbled forward, slanting across half of his face, falling lightly onto her forehead. She longed to reach up and tuck it behind his ear, just like she wanted nothing more than to trace his chiseled jawline with the tip of her finger. Unfortunately, he snared her arms above her head and held them in place with one hand.

The feel of his palm against her skin was like ice, and this time she couldn't stop herself from shuddering.

His mouth curved at the corner. Slow and intentional. Those dark green eyes of his, with the mesmerizing gold rings around the outer edge, held her in place. "I rather like it when you shiver beneath me, *wife.*"

The audacity.

"I am *not* your wife." Creslyn strained against him, then immediately regretted her actions. Her bare breasts scraped against the leather of his vest, causing the sensitive peaks of her nipples to ache.

"Not yet." Prince Drake's mocking smirk remained in place. He adjusted himself above her, nestling one knee on the mattress directly between her thighs while the other pressed close to her hip.

He bent forward, lower so that his nose almost touched her own. His lips were so close, if she angled her head to the right, she could kiss him. She imagined he tasted of dark winter nights, of forbidden desires, of everything she should never want. She dragged her gaze from his mouth back to his eyes, then tipped her head back, determined to remain defiant.

"Not ever at this rate," she snapped, and a tiny thrill of delight sent her cheeks flushing when those damning eyes of his followed the curve of her neck to the swell of her breasts.

Her entire body ignited beneath the heat of his gaze.

She knew she should fear him. After all, he was capable of killing her in less time than it took to breathe. He was the Shadowblade Assassin, lethal and cunning, a deliberate mastermind of death. He moved with shadows, had stolen more lives than she could count, and was beyond violent in nature. The prince lacked any morals, his soul long ago tainted by unknown demons, and yet she'd been selected to marry him. Of course, she'd never witnessed any such atrocities, but she had every reason to believe they were true.

Despite being malicious and cruel, Prince Drake was also devastatingly handsome, which made it all the more difficult to resist him. That…and there was something about the darkness haunting him that enticed her. Something about the brutal monster skulking beneath his surface that called to the deepest, most secretive part of her soul.

With his free hand, he gathered a few strands of her hair, his scarred knuckles just grazing the valley of her breasts.

Creslyn's blood hummed, and she held her breath.

He twirled the pieces of her hair around his fingers, the starlit hues a harsh contrast to the tan of his skin. The sleeves of his black shirt were rolled, revealing muscled forearms that strained as he kept himself propped up above her with one hand, her wrists still tight in his grasp.

"Tell me, *solysa*." Drake's thick Northernlands accent coasted over her, and she found it impossible to look anywhere else but into the depths of his intense gaze. "Do you often sleep naked?"

She huffed. "Yes, Your Highness. Though you've watched me often enough, I would assume you already know the answer. I prefer sleeping in the nude to nightgowns as I find myself tangled up in the middle of the night. Though I don't see what that has to do with—"

"I was merely curious." He ran his thumb back and forth through the strands of her hair. Then he let them fall away and slid two fingers beneath her chin, his lips brushing along the corner of her mouth as he spoke. "Let me be clear on one thing."

Creslyn stilled, waiting for the reprimand.

"Everything I do is for a reason. King Marius hates all that is more powerful than himself. And you, my pretty little faerie, are *powerful*. More so than a pathetic human king." He slid his hand around her neck but applied no pressure. Instead, his thumb stroked lazy lines up and down her throat. "I will make you my wife, but only when I choose to do so, and not a moment sooner."

His mouth moved to her cheek, then hovered above her ear. "Do you understand?"

A line of frustration pinched her brow. "So, you intend to keep me confined to this part of the castle for what? Weeks? Months?"

He pulled back so she could once again see his face, and this time, shadows danced around him. "Are you so eager to bed your prince?"

"I am eager to have a life." Her scowl deepened. Of course, he would think so little of her. But she wasn't accustomed to spending her days alone, wallowing in a state of tedium. She preferred to be outdoors or wandering through gardens, and she enjoyed parties and sharing bits of gossip. Stars above, she would accept being relegated to the library to read if it meant she didn't have to sit in this room one more day.

Creslyn peered up at him from beneath her lashes and sighed softly. "Please."

Prince Drake stared at her. His jaw clenched, but his grip on her neck remained easy as he continued his smooth caresses. Then suddenly, he released her completely. With his shadows swarming, he sat back on the bed. His voice was cold when he said, "Fine. But you will have an escort."

"Really?" Creslyn jolted upright and launched herself into his lap. She threw her arms around his neck, grateful that freedom was finally within her reach. Tomorrow, she would leave this godsforsaken wing and see as much of the castle and Brackroth as possible. "Thank you."

Icy cold fingers grabbed her waist, and she almost jumped out of her skin. It occurred to her, albeit belatedly, that she was fully nude while straddling him.

"You tempt me with your graciousness, *solysa*," he murmured into her hair before plucking her off his lap and depositing her back onto the bed. His stony gaze devoured every inch of her, lingering on each dip and curve. "I've yet to decide if you will be my destruction...or my salvation."

Creslyn shook her hair back and crawled beneath the heavy velvet comforter. Then she flashed him her most flirtatious smile. "Please, Your Highness. It will take more than a few flowery words to get me on my back."

He smirked, then stood and stepped into his mass of shadows. "I already have."

CHAPTER TWO

*D*rake remained in the darkness, ever vigilant.

He didn't leave Creslyn's room right away, choosing instead to melt into the shadows as she slept. He watched the steady rise and fall of her chest, the way she flung one arm out across the bed as though reaching for something just out of her grasp. She was an interesting creature when she slumbered—sometimes peaceful, sometimes fitful. Every so often she made these soft little noises, like a sigh of contentment. In some strange way, it was comforting to see her at ease, so Drake stayed in her room long after she went to bed, the same thing he'd done every night since he brought her to his castle.

For him, sleep was a useless endeavor. He had no need for it and even if he did, he refused to do so. Not while Creslyn was constantly in a state of danger. He preferred to ensure she remained safe and protected, even if that meant rarely leaving her side.

Though most of the time he never made his presence known to her.

She wasn't aware of the guards stationed along the entire

perimeter of her wing, more specifically, dragon riders who were loyal to him and not their bastard king. She didn't know the servants reported to him hourly, any time he was forced to leave her general vicinity. He'd taken every precaution necessary, but he was not a fool.

Drake knew he wouldn't be able to keep her locked in this wing forever.

Eventually, Creslyn would become his princess, and then his queen. She would have to be introduced to Brackroth, welcomed and accepted. His main concern was the men that would undoubtedly leer at her with lascivious eyes and the waspish women who wielded words like daggers. But he had no problem cutting out the tongue of anyone who spoke ill of her.

Despite his better judgment, he'd granted Creslyn a boon.

He would allow her a shred of freedom to move about the castle, but only if she had an escort. Doing so meant entrusting her care to his general, Kjeld Holtstrom. Granted, Kjeld would much prefer to be training his soldiers and dragons than babysitting a faerie. But Kjeld was the only person Drake trusted with his life.

A breath shuddered out of Creslyn, and Drake's gaze was instantly drawn back to her.

She rolled over, revealing a sliver of her smooth backside.

Without warning, his mind drifted to images of her naked body when he'd had her pinned to the bed. It was the first time he'd seen her fully nude. He'd caught glimpses before and while his morals were often lacking, he'd had the decency to look away. But tonight, she'd disrobed in front of him...*with purpose*. He'd been overwhelmed by her, desperate for her. She possessed shoulders capable of a careless dismissal, a narrow waist and hips that swayed when she walked. Her long legs were positively flawless, and he knew without a doubt that her breasts would fit perfectly in his hands.

She was all lush curves and satin skin, and he wanted to worship every inch of her.

Whereas the touch of winter seemed to emanate from him, she was the kiss of summer's breath. Warm and inviting.

And when she'd leapt upon him, straddling him, it had taken the entirety of his self-control not to bury himself inside her right then.

Drake's cock thickened, and he swallowed a groan.

He wanted to ruin her. Shatter her.

He longed to see those sapphire eyes of hers glaze with lust, to witness her full lips part as she cried out his name over and over. Then maybe, if she was good, he'd kiss each one of the freckles that dotted her nose and cheeks like constellations.

His shadows unfurled, straining for her, but he kept them in check.

All in good time.

Yet his desire for her did not subside.

Damn it.

He couldn't very well find release while Creslyn was sleeping in her bed, barely a breath away. Knowing the sun would be up in less than an hour's time, he retreated to his private quarters, moving like a wraith through the darkened corridors.

Once inside his room, he removed his clothing and strode into the bathing suite. He'd lost track of the number of times he'd stood within the black opal enclosure beneath a spray of icy water and gripped his cock with an image of her in his mind. He'd wanted to fuck her from the moment he first saw her. It had only been some kind of terrible omen that her brother, Ariesian Starstorm, chose her to be his bride.

Drake stepped into the glittering stall, pulling the glass door closed behind him. Frozen beads of water pounded his shoulders and back, but he didn't care. He'd lost the ability to feel much of anything long ago. For him, there was only pleasure and death. Nothing else.

Already his erection ached with anticipation.

Today would be no different.

Leaning against the shimmering black wall, he jerked his hand up and down the hardened length of his shaft, watching as shadows flared and coiled around his cock, pulsing and squeezing. A twisted smile curved at the corner of his mouth. He couldn't wait to see Creslyn's face when she saw him—all of him—when she realized she was not marrying a man, but a monster forged from the darkness. He closed his eyes, imagined himself spearing her into oblivion as she unraveled around him.

Drake came hard and fast on a groan, gradually opening his eyes. He let his head fall back against the shower wall, then reached over and adjusted the handle so the hot water sluiced over his battered body. It soothed his numerous scars yet did little to ease the growing knot of tension forming at the base of his neck.

The king had requested his presence at first light, which meant it was time to pay Marius a visit.

DRAKE STALKED toward the throne room with purpose, his boots echoing loudly. Generally, he might be stealthy and discreet, but this time, he wanted to instill fear into the soul of every curious servant and insolent noble he passed. If they thought him to be furious, they would be more inclined to stay the hell out of his way and less likely to eavesdrop.

Listening in on royal conversations was a crime in Brackroth, but that didn't sway anyone from dispensing rumors.

He shoved open the doors to the throne room with excessive

force, so the ancient wood rattled on its hinges and the courtiers milling about the opulent space scattered like rats. They darted behind pillars of mirrored obsidian, their panicked gazes reflecting in the polished surface. He could hear the erratic beating of their terrified hearts, the noise sounded like a beating drum, reverberating up into the cavernous ceiling where oak beams stretched overhead. A few of the courtiers rushed to either side of the throne room, choosing instead to cower by the murky windows, where deep red curtains fell to the ground like a waterfall of blood.

Sitting upon a throne of silver crafted to look like crawling vines decorated with thorns was King Marius Kalstrand.

Over the years, he'd lost his hair, and his silver crown embellished with garnets was set atop his bald head. Half of his long, white beard had been braided, the rest of it hung loose in coarse, scraggly strands. Beady eyes were set beneath bushy dark brows streaked with silver. His nose was crooked from having been broken one too many times, and his lower jaw jutted outward so that he always looked like a snarling beast. He was a rotund man with gnarled knuckles, and his temper was shorter than his lacking stature.

Drake strolled toward the throne, adjusted the cuffs of his black leather armor, and the spiked chains dangling from his shoulders softly clinked together.

He stopped a few feet from the raised dais and tucked his hands behind his back.

The hushed silence was almost deafening, save for the patter of rain against the windows and the low howl of the wind.

Drake inclined his head. "You wished to see me?"

Marius stroked one hand down his beard, but Drake didn't miss the way his mangled knuckles whitened with barely contained rage. "I hear you brought a fucking fae into my castle."

"She is not a fucking fae." Drake's hands coiled into fists

behind his back and his gaze sharpened on the king. "She is Lady Creslyn Starstorm of House Celestine, and she will soon be my wife."

Marius's mottled cheeks flushed with anger, and he sat forward, damn near ready to combust. "You really intend to take a faerie as your future bride?"

"I told you my intentions when I left for Aeramere, a land ruled by a fae queen, where all five noble houses are dominated by fae bloodlines." Drake dipped his head, and a few pieces of dark hair tumbled into his face. He looked up at the king from beneath a narrowed brow. "I'm not sure I could have been any more clear on the matter."

"I won't allow it!" Marius boomed, rising from his throne. He shook one knobby finger in the air. "Fae are wretched creatures. They're filthy. Violent and ruthless."

Drake scoffed. "Not this one."

"She must've spelled you, then." Marius paced the dais, his large stomach jiggling with each uneven step of his gait. Then he turned and pointed to Drake in accusation. "She lured you into her snares with her overly sexual nature."

An understatement, to say the least.

"She's using you," he continued, shaking his head. "She's charmed you into thinking she's harmless. The witch did the same to me." Marius's wild eyes darted back and forth, and he gnawed at his bottom lip, a testament to the instability of his mind. "She'll worm her way into your bed, then distort your mind until you're promising her a crown and your kingdom."

Already done, Drake mused silently. "Hardly."

Marius hobbled down the obsidian steps of the dais. "The moment you let your guard down, she'll kill you."

Drake offered the barest of smiles. "Nothing can kill me."

"Damn you!" he raged, his large body trembling with madness. With his own paranoia and fear. "This faerie will be a pestilence. A disease. A blight upon the entirety of Brackroth!"

Drake spoke in low, clipped words. "Her name…is Creslyn."

"I don't give a dragon's left eye what her name is, do you hear me?" Marius ambled forward, stabbing his fucking finger into Drake's chest. "You will keep her, and her foul, tainted magic, under control. If I so much as catch a glimpse of her power, if she so much as *dares* to use her godsforsaken magic within these walls, I will erase her very existence."

Drake caught the king's wrist, squeezed until the frail bones nearly snapped. "Are you threatening my wife?"

Marius's tiny eyes bulged, but his mouth contorted into a sneer. "She is not your wife."

"*Yet*," Drake growled, furious that he'd had to repeat the same words to both this wretch of a man and to Creslyn. He would need to remedy that. Quickly.

He tossed the king's arm aside. "Might I remind you of what I am, of what I'm capable of doing?"

His shadows appeared then. But this was not a quiet summons. No, the tendrils of sinewy darkness exploded from him, absorbing every fiber of the light, drowning out all sound. They crawled and seethed like heathens of his own making.

Marius paled, but then a slow smile stretched across his face. His lips peeled back, revealing uneven, yellowed teeth. "And might I remind you, Shadowblade Assassin, that I'm the one who hands you the names of those you're forced to kill."

Drake didn't flinch, he didn't even blink. But the king's words tarnished his already blackened soul. It was the one thread of control Marius held over him. It had been a mistake to give the king ten vials of his own blood in exchange for the Shadowblade. Whenever the king handed him a name in red ink, Drake was compelled to assassinate the person selected on Marius's behalf. In the beginning, he'd delighted in the bloodlust. But now, each kill was becoming more senseless, as though Marius wanted him to end lives for the sheer and brutal joy of it.

"Keep her in line," Marius warned, "or it will be her name I hand to you next. Creslyn, was it?"

"If you touch a single hair on her head, I will find a way to end your life. Slowly." Drake would've killed the prick already if it wasn't for one vicious little detail.

If Marius died by Drake's hand, then Drake would die as well, a regrettable oath he'd taken upon accepting the Shadowblade.

The king chuckled, his sinister laugh grating like dragging rocks against glass. "You think you can threaten me?"

"That is not a threat." Drake inclined his head, checking his own wrath. "It's a promise."

He turned on his heel, heading back for the doors of the throne room that were still thrown open. Then he paused, glancing over, ensuring the cruelty of his gaze met that of the king. "And I always stay true to my word."

He strode out into the hall, his fury seething, when a scrawny servant handed him a folded piece of parchment sealed in wax with the king's crest.

Drake ripped it open.

Inside was a single name, scripted in his own blood.

His next kill.

The fucking bastard.

CHAPTER THREE

Creslyn stared out the door of her balcony as gray mist obscured the mountain peaks in the distance and droplets of rain slid down the glass like fallen tears. Today she was finally leaving the wing and had hoped to at least tour the castle grounds—with an escort—but going outside into the steady drizzle would ruin her gown.

She glanced down, admiring the way soft, rosy pink chiffon shifted to gold when she moved. The bodice was low, revealing the constellation tattoo of Vespira's staff across her heart, and was embellished with rows of tiny pearls around the waist. Sleeves of the same fine material draped off her shoulders then tapered at her wrists, and the voluminous skirt flowed around her like sheer, candy pink clouds.

Again, she glared out the window.

Still, it might be worth it.

But the minutes continued to tick by and there was no sign of her apparent escort.

Heaving a sigh of discontentment, she rummaged through her jewelry box, searching through the velvet-lined drawers, and decided on a pink sapphire choker with a pair of earrings that twinkled like roses covered in stardust. Adjusting the clasp of the necklace, her gaze landed on her unmade bed.

For a brief moment, she considered the satin linens.

Creslyn supposed if she really wanted to, she could tie the linens together into a makeshift rope and attempt her hand at a daring escape. Besides, it had worked for her eldest sister, Novalise.

Originally, Ariesian had chosen Novalise to marry the Prince of Brackroth. It had been her name on the contract Ariesian signed in blood, but a mating bond had formed between Novalise and Lord Asher Firebane and nothing, not even the Shadowblade Assassin, could keep them apart. So, Creslyn's hand had been offered instead.

Second best.

She wondered what it would be like to share a bond like that, where she could hear her mate's thoughts if his mind was open to her, where she could sense his emotions, and perhaps always know if he was thinking of her. It must be quite wondrous to be so in love, to be completely infatuated with the other half of one's heart.

Creslyn snorted, a most unladylike noise.

She held no such illusions with Prince Drake. He hardly seemed like the type to profess his undying devotion.

She flopped onto the bed on her back, staring up at the canopy of gray silk that reminded her of a storm cloud. There was no way of knowing how long she would remain trapped in her quarters until she was allowed some semblance of freedom. If she wanted to pass the time, she could always attempt to draw, or try again at needlework. Both terrible hobbies had been forced down her throat by her mother. Not only that, but they were painfully dull, and she was far from proficient.

A sudden knock sounded on the door, jarring her from her thoughts of melodramatic boredom.

She jumped up off the bed and darted across the room, half

expecting to find the prince standing on the other side. The moment she yanked the door open, she faltered, and a faint blade of panic wedged its way into her spine.

There was most definitely a man on the other side of her door.

But he was certainly not Prince Drake.

He was dressed in rich brown leathers, the same ones she'd seen the prince wear when he rode atop his magnificent dragon, Svartos. Except this man didn't wear gloves. His boots were polished yet scuffed from use and unusual runes were carved into his vest and the cuffs at his wrist. A strap lined with daggers was slung across his waist, and an ornate silver pin in the shape of a dragon was fastened to his chest. He wasn't quite as tall as the prince, but he was obscenely muscular, and she had no doubt he was capable of crushing windpipes with his bare hands.

The man towering above her had hair the color of rustic gold with half of it pulled back into a knot, while the rest of it fell down past his shoulders. His eyes were as blue as the summer skies in Aeramere and though his beard was well-trimmed, she could just make out a scar along his bottom lip, as though someone had attempted and likely failed at ripping open his mouth.

"Can I help you?" Creslyn asked, wary.

She hated the slight wobble of her voice.

He bowed, tucking one arm in front of him and the other behind his back. "Kjeld Holtstrom, General of the Brackroth Dragon Legion. At your service, my lady."

She edged back a bit, preparing to slam the door in his face and lock it, though she sincerely doubted it would hold against him. "At my service for what, exactly?"

"Your escort, my lady." He arched a brow, eyeing her curiously with those cool blue eyes of his. "At the request of the prince."

Oh.

She'd been expecting a female escort. Or a guard. Certainly not a general.

"I see." Creslyn rubbed her lips together, not quite ready to let down her defenses. Just in case. "So, General Holtstrom—"

"Kjeld, my lady," he interrupted smoothly.

"Kjeld," she repeated, rolling his name off her tongue, mimicking his Northernlands accent. "Do I get to choose where we go today, or are you choosing with the intent to make me think it's my idea?"

The corner of his mouth lifted. "The latter, my lady."

Oh, that was going to get annoying rather quickly.

"Very well." She clasped her hands together and rolled her shoulders back. If she was eventually going to be a princess, she might as well start acting like one. "You may choose on one condition."

"And what's that, my lady?"

"That you stop calling me 'my lady.' I much prefer my given name." She dropped into a practiced curtsy. "You may call me Creslyn."

Kjeld offered her his arm. "As you wish, Lady Creslyn."

She rolled her eyes to the door frame separating them. There would be no swaying him to change his mind.

Creslyn accepted his arm and allowed him to guide her out into the hall and down the corridor. She glanced over at him, tucking some strands of her lavender and pale pink hair back behind her ear. "I take it you're under strict orders to keep me out of trouble?"

Another almost-grin. "More or less. I follow my prince's instructions without hesitation or question."

Ah. So Prince Drake trusted his general.

Creslyn filed that information away in case it became of some use for later. "Loyalty is an admirable quality, Kjeld. I hope to earn yours one day, without the prince demanding it."

Considering she was in a foreign realm and hundreds of miles away from her friends and family, she could use any alliance she could find.

Kjeld inclined his head in acknowledgement. "You already have."

She smiled in return, not entirely sure if she believed him or not. But for now, she would allow herself to think she wasn't completely alone anymore.

"You know," she continued as they reached the end of her wing, "you're one of the only people who have spoken to me since my arrival."

There was a shift in his demeanor then, and his arm stiffened where her hand rested. "Again, Lady Creslyn, we follow the prince's orders."

Her mouth fell open, and she stumbled to a halt. Tilting her head back, she glared up at the mountain of a general. "He told everyone to ignore me?"

Kjeld ducked his head, reaching for the door. "I'm not at liberty to say."

"Can't?" Creslyn asked, removing her hand from the crook of his elbow and crossing her arms like a scorned child. "Or won't?"

He flashed her a quick smile that illuminated the whole of his rugged face. "Both."

Was every man in Brackroth so infuriating?

"Fine," she snapped, huffing out a breath of annoyance. "Then what does my agenda consist of today? I'm assuming my time has already been scheduled according to the prince's demands?"

"It has indeed." He yanked open the door, allowing her entry. "First, a tour of the castle."

$$\supset\!*\!\subset$$

C ASTLE B RACKROTH WAS…UNDERWHELMING.

Creslyn wasn't foolish enough to expect something lavish and glittering like the houses of Aeramere, but she had secretly hoped it wouldn't be so drab. Most of the walls were made of stone and the long planks of hardwood creaked beneath her every step. It was well-lit with arching windows reflecting the dismal skies, all of them echoing the constant patter of rainfall. Kjeld showed her the dining hall, the throne room, and a library that was vastly larger than most of the other rooms. There were long corridors and some grand halls, including a ballroom which looked as though it hadn't welcomed the rhythmic foot-falls of dancers in far too long. Gilded chandeliers dropped from the ceiling, covered in a fine layer of dust, and a piano stood in the far corner of the ballroom, draped in a worn white cloth.

Kjeld continued to guide her through the castle, and she listened to his stories intently, ever curious about the ways of a human land. Their warriors were chosen at a young age, taken from their families so long as their parents agreed, and then rigorously trained in the art of warfare. There were forges where weapons of steel were crafted—swords, axes, and daggers —the thought alone made her skin crawl with unease. She would have to be mindful to keep her distance from any sort of weaponry made of cold iron. Though steel would make her bleed, cold iron was lethal to all fae. The metal would dull her magic, confound her senses, and eventually…kill her.

Kjeld told her how both men and women joined their ranks, how only the most elite were chosen to fly on the backs of dragons and mentioned some mystical world of the afterlife. He seemed rather intent on being destined to die a warrior's death, if it meant he would be granted entrance into this otherworld of esteemed heroism. And while she enjoyed his story about the eternal resting place, all the while she couldn't help but notice that he never once mentioned the late queen—Prince Drake's mother. There were no portraits of her, nothing at all to commemorate her honor. It was as though she simply ceased to exist.

A number of servants scurried by them as they passed, some of them plastering themselves against the wall to avoid being noticed. Not one of them dared look in her direction. As much as she imagined Prince Drake had warned them against it, she couldn't help but wonder if the true reason for their avoidance was because she was fae.

Nearly everyone was dressed in some monotonous shade of gray or brown, and Creslyn became acutely aware of the fact that she stood out among them like a glowing beacon. Her rosy pink gown that glinted like it had been kissed with gold swirled and swooshed around her as she walked. She was a Midsummer sunrise amidst the doom and gloom of Brackroth.

Finally, Kjeld paused in front of a large set of bronze doors which looked as though they led outside. Two floor-to-ceiling windows were positioned on either side and though she couldn't see out of them clearly, the distinctive gray hue of the outdoors beckoned her.

Hope sparked deep within Creslyn, a tiny little flame waiting to combust. Perhaps she would get to see some of Brackroth after all. If not the city itself, then maybe even a glimpse of the gardens.

Assuming they had gardens.

She smiled up at him, excitement causing her magic to stir. All she wanted to do was send dozens of sunbursts and rainbows up into those dreary heavens. "Where to next, Kjeld?"

The corner of his mouth twitched. "Now it's time for training."

"Training?" Creslyn gaped at him, as though he'd insulted her very birthright. "Do you mean training in etiquette? Because in case you have forgotten, General Holtstrom, I *am* a lady, albeit not a very good one. But I have been trained in the rules of decorum and proper manners since—"

"Not *that* kind of training, Lady Creslyn." Kjeld shoved open the door. "Welcome to the Trench."

Creslyn gasped, clamping one hand over her mouth.

She was going outside for certain, but it looked like she was walking right into a war zone. The Trench, as Kjeld called it, was filled with soldiers squaring off and battling one another. Men and women alike fought side by side with swords, bows and arrows, daggers, and an otherworldly number of weapons she couldn't name. Their movements were precise and measured, the slick mud beneath their boots never hindered their stances. The clang of metal and the sound of painful grunts echoed in her ears as she took in the sopping field littered with soldiers whose rigor and accuracy caused her knees to tremble.

Or perhaps it was simply the gust of cold wind blasting through the thin material of her skirts.

Kjeld held out his hand. "Are you coming with me, Lady Creslyn?"

Her gaze darted to his, but there was no mischief to be found in his eyes. They were steady. Keen.

This was a test.

Surely, it had to be some kind of test.

"I…" She swallowed, slowly accepting his hand. "I'm not sure what I'm supposed to do."

"Never mind about that." Kjeld led her out into the Trench where walls of ancient stone rose around them. "I'll teach you."

Icy rain pelted her skin, plastering her gown to her legs. She clamped her teeth together to keep them from chattering as the howling wind raised goosebumps across her flesh. With each step, her shoes sank an inch deep into the thick, mucky grass. She locked her fingers around his firm grasp, certain she'd already lost feeling in her toes as he led her further into the fray. Her entire body was trembling from the wet and cold, but she steeled her spine, refusing to cower from whatever it was she would be forced to endure.

"But Kjeld, I'm not dressed like…" she hesitated, glancing around her. None of the soldiers spared her a glance. To them, she was a phantom. A brilliant wraith they couldn't see. Invisible. "Everyone else."

"Brackroth can be dangerous at times. Not only the city itself but also within the castle walls." He shoved some damp strands of fallen hair back from his face, and she caught sight of a series of rune tattoos crawling up the side of his neck. "When you learn to fight in a gown, it will be even easier for you in leathers."

Creslyn bobbed her head in understanding, but in truth, none of it made sense.

This had to be the prince's doing, if for no other reason than to simply humiliate her.

She inhaled a deep, shaky breath, trying to catch the scent of him. But only the smell of fresh rain, wet grass, and lingering sweat clung to the air. Shivering, she focused on the tiny ball of heat, the rise of anger building inside of her. She was going to hate every minute of this, and as soon as she saw Prince Drake again, she was going to slap him across his face.

Kjeld took her hand and curled it into a fist. "Oh, and one more thing, Lady Creslyn."

Creslyn blinked the raindrops from her lashes and squinted up at him, preparing for the worst. "Yes?"

He winked. "No magic."

CHAPTER FOUR

*D*rake lounged against the wall of one of the darkened exterior corridors outlying the Trench with his arms crossed over his chest, watching Kjeld train Creslyn. He didn't mind that his most trusted general was holding her hips, enforcing her proper stance, because Kjeld's eyes reflected strict discipline. He would demand the very best from her and settle for nothing less. And Creslyn would give it, if for no other reason than her stubborn pride.

Whereas if Drake was in his same position, he likely wouldn't be able to keep his hands off of her. So, Kjeld would train her in the art of combat, while Drake would withhold his lessons for the bedroom…or anywhere else he deemed fitting.

At first, he almost pitied her.

She was too delicate, too demure.

He'd seen her body, had memorized every perfect dip and curve. But she was without muscle and strength where it mattered. Her arms were weak, her core lacked definition, and her thighs could use some plumping. Especially if she ever wanted to ride a dragon. But that was discussion for another day, as she was nowhere near ready to venture down to the lair.

When Kjeld coaxed Creslyn to throw her first punch, he dodged it easily. She threw her entire body into it and sailed past him, careening face-first into the muddy ground. And Kjeld had allowed her to fall, exactly as Drake had instructed. She would not be shown favoritism in the Trench, nor would she be given a shred of sympathy.

After she pulled herself up from the muck, the slashing rain slowly washing some of the grime off her face, she glared at Kjeld. Fury radiated from her, and the sapphire in her eyes burned with the fire of a thousand suns. She was a quick learner, and Drake knew speed would certainly be in her favor, especially when she wasn't wearing a dress that likely weighed an extra fifteen pounds when it was soaking wet.

In retrospect, he would suggest she wear a slightly less revealing gown tomorrow.

One of her sleeves had torn and she'd ripped it off completely, discarding the ribbon of fabric like it was an utter nuisance. Her water-logged beaded bodice sagged dangerously low, and she continually yanked it back up, huffing in annoyance as her breath misted before her. The rain had plastered her sheer skirts to her legs, the hem covered in mud as she slogged through Kjeld's rigorous demands. Even with her hair drenched, clinging to her neck and shoulders, with smears of filth covering her cheeks, she made Drake positively ravenous.

He scanned the Trench, eyeing the rest of his soldiers. More specifically, the men. Not a single one of them looked her way.

Good.

They were doing exactly as they'd been instructed to do as well. Though Drake had promised to gouge out the eyes of anyone who considered stealing a glance in her direction.

Creslyn kicked off her shoes, apparently annoyed by the way they sunk into the sludge beneath her. Drake smirked when she tossed one at Kjeld's chest in frustration. He caught it with one hand, and Drake didn't miss the slight twitch of his general's lips before she launched the second one in retaliation.

Already she was improving. She was faster. Sharper.

All because she was *angry*.

He wanted her to channel that rage. To wield it like a weapon. If she wanted to survive in Brackroth, she would need to be able to defend herself in his absence.

Kjeld said something, and Creslyn whirled around to face him. Drake couldn't be sure, but he was almost positive she fired back with an enthusiastic "fuck you." She reared back and swung upward, in damn near perfect form, landing a solid punch on the underside of Kjeld's jaw. His head snapped back like he'd taken a hit from one of their best dragon riders. Creslyn's eyes rounded, and she clamped both hands over her mouth. But Kjeld's booming laughter exploded throughout the Trench, and he flashed her a blood-stained grin.

He placed his thumb and forefinger at the corners of his mouth and loosed a loud, piercing whistle.

At once, the soldiers ceased their training and stood at attention, their gazes homing in on their general and not on the mud-caked fae standing next to him.

Kjeld offered Creslyn his arm. She scowled but accepted, gathering up her ruined skirts as she stomped out of the horrendous weather.

Drake stepped back into his shadows. The cold surrounded him as he moved with stealth through the stretches of darkness, causing a shiver of fear to race down the spines of anyone he passed. His power was a vice, an addiction he craved. To most, it might be damning, but he thrived on inciting terror and panic—his cruelty knew no bounds. He enjoyed the way people whispered desperate prayers and pleas to their gods whenever he crossed their paths. He possessed no heart, no soul, both had been lost to him years ago. For Drake, there was only the thirst for more power.

Except now there was Creslyn.

And his desire for her was deeper and darker than even the most poignant sensation of bloodlust that coursed through his monstrous veins.

He remained in the furthest corner of her bedchamber, slinking into his shadows, when the door flew open and she stormed inside.

Creslyn slammed the door behind her, barreling toward the bathing suite without noticing him. A trail of muddy footprints followed in her wake. "Of all the foul, vulgar things."

She faced the long, mirrored wall, its onyx frame carved with whorls and painted with silver swirls. Shoving her damp, filthy hair back from her face, she gripped the edge of the wide white marble counter and screamed.

Creslyn ripped off her gown, a torrent of obscenities erupting from her pretty mouth. Drake grinned, admiring the ferocity with which she tore at the bodice, her fingers clawing at the ruined fabric as she yanked the laces undone. Shreds of sodden pink cloth landed in a heap at her feet and when she stood in nothing but a scrap of triangular gold lace, his blood heated. Drake drifted closer to the bathing suite, withdrawing his shadows and morphing into his full form. He reached up, gripping the top of the door frame with both hands, his nails biting into the hardwood to keep himself from touching her.

If she sensed him watching her, she made no show of it.

Instead, she stalked toward the glass-enclosed shower and turned on the faucet, silent as ribbons of steam slowly fogged the room.

"I swear to the stars," she mumbled, fisting her hands at her side, "as soon as I see him again, I'll—"

"You'll what, *kearsta*?" he purred.

Creslyn shrieked, spinning around so fast her bare feet slid out from under her. Drake moved like lightning, snaring her by the waist with one arm to keep her from falling.

She righted herself and tried to shove him off, her palm smacking soundly against his chest.

"How dare you?" she spat. "How could you possibly do such a thing? You threw me out into the Trench with no preparation. No warning!"

He kept his hand firmly around her waist, his thumb running back and forth along the thin string of lace, strumming lightly. "I knew you'd refuse."

"You know *nothing* about me." This time she swatted at his hand, but he refused to release her. "I am only a lady, Your Highness, not a warrior. And I am even quite terrible at that! You can't expect me to fight. I'll never be able to throw a dagger or carry a sword. I cannot be what I am *not*."

"Then you will learn." Drake pulled her closer, tipping one finger beneath her chin so she looked up at him with piercing eyes full of stars and fire. "No wife of mine will be left defenseless."

She crossed her arms, her lips pursing in displeasure. "I suppose it was your idea to make me train in a gown?"

"Yes. And you will continue to do so until I have you fitted for leathers." He trailed his finger down her neck, hooking it beneath the collar of pink stones at her throat. Her pulse jumped at his touch and the corner of his mouth curved. "Do you enjoy sparkly things, *solysa*?"

"You know very well that I do." Creslyn jabbed him in the shoulder with her finger. "But you're changing the subject."

He was indeed, with purpose.

"Then perhaps I know something about you after all." Drake bent his head low, letting his lips trail across her flesh, and whispered his next words along her neck, just to see. "Tell me what it is you desire most. Sapphires as blue as the ocean? Emeralds that glitter like the northern forests? Moonstones that shimmer like your pretty rainbows?"

She shivered in his arms, goosebumps pebbling over every inch of her satin skin.

He was getting closer to his answer.

Pressing a faint kiss to her fluttering pulse, he moved to her ear. "Or perhaps you'd like me to please you with a strand of pearls between your thighs? Or devour you while diamonds drip from your ears, neck, and even your breasts?"

The scent of her arousal slammed into him, and he swallowed a groan. Oh, yes. She would like that very much. His little faerie would take all he offered her. The hunger inside him roared to life, awakening his shadows. He clamped down on his urges, he couldn't risk scaring her. Not yet, anyway.

"My breasts?" she asked, a tremble in her voice. "How—"

"There are ways," he murmured, easing back.

"No." Creslyn planted her hand on the solid wall of his chest, where his heart pounded with greed. "You're doing it again. We are not discussing jewels, my breasts, or anything else. Do you have any idea how difficult it is to move, much less fight, in wet silk?"

Just hearing her say the word wet almost snapped the last of his control.

"No. But I must say." He flicked his tongue along the tip of her ear. "You looked rather ravishing in it."

"It's..." Her gaze narrowed and a scowl pulled her brows together. "I...you *watched* me?"

Drake grinned. "The entire time, *solysa*."

"You bastard!"

She raised her hand, and he caught her wrist right before her palm connected with the side of his face.

"Have you learned nothing?" he growled, no longer caring if the truth of his nature reared its ugly head.

But Creslyn didn't shrink away from him.

"Arrogant ass!"

She moved so fast, he barely had time to react. In one fluid movement, she hoisted her knee high, preparing to make direct contact between his legs, forcing him to hunch over to avoid the blow. But then she twisted, raising her arm so her elbow struck him right in the throat. Sudden pain left him gasping until he felt the sting of her palm against his cheek.

Drake coughed, choked, then laughed. He pounded his fist against his chest in a valiant effort to catch his breath. When he looked back over to her, she was enveloped in a cloak of steam and her lacy underthings were discarded on the floor. Creslyn stepped into the shower, shutting the glass door soundly behind her.

As though she could ever dismiss him.

He sauntered over, propping his shoulder against the wall, and watched in silence as she washed away the sweat and grime. She shampooed her hair and scrubbed her body, the rain scented bubbles gliding over her bare skin. Every so often she sent him an absolutely scathing look, but he was far too impressed with the pain ricocheting from his throat down to his chest to care.

Drake folded his arms, intrigued by how...*comfortable* she seemed around him. For some reason he couldn't quite place, it left him unsettled.

"You did well today, Creslyn."

Her gaze shot to him and held, recognizing the slip of intimacy he'd given her.

He'd called her by her name.

Agonizing seconds ticked by while he waited to see if she would accept his lack of an apology.

"Thank you...Drake." She rinsed the soap from her body, her eyes never leaving his. "Is there something else you wanted to discuss, or are you simply going to stand there and stare at me?"

Drake bit back another grin. He rather liked it when she was feisty. "I have something you might find of interest."

"Oh really?" she drawled in disbelief. "And what's that?"

He waved his hand through the air and an envelope appeared between his fingers, the silvery gray wax seal indicative of two flaming swords.

Creslyn swiped at the glass, rubbing away the condensation, and he'd never seen anything quite so radiant than the look on her face. "Is that from House Emberspire?"

Emberspire, one of the five houses of Aeramere, was also the home of Lord Asher Firebane. The fae lord was bonded to Novalise, Creslyn's eldest sister, and last he heard, they were set to be married. Drake and Asher had a somewhat complicated past in terms of bargains, but it was only made worse when they were bound by some ridiculous fae law to fight to the death for Novalise's hand. Even though Drake didn't particularly want to kill Asher, he would've done so out of duty had Novalise not chosen that exact moment to reveal she possessed the magic of the starstorm—an ancient power thought to have died out from her family's bloodline entirely.

Either way, her daring interjection served Drake well.

He never wanted to marry her, anyway.

Drake flipped the envelope back and forth. "Perhaps."

Creslyn squealed, shut off the shower, and he handed her a fluffy black towel. She wrapped it around herself, knotting it just between her breasts, then looked up at him from beneath her damp lashes. "May I see it?"

Gods, why did she have to be so damned perfect?

He handed it over.

Creslyn tore it open, her eyes flitting over every word.

"It's a wedding invitation! For Novalise and Asher." She skimmed the contents, her smile widening. "Can we go? We will go, won't we?"

Drake tucked his hands behind his back. "I'll make the necessary arrangements."

It wasn't as though he could ever deny her. Anything.

"Thank you!" She leapt up, throwing her arms around his neck, and her towel slid to her navel.

Torture.

She was torture in the purest form.

She leaned back and he adjusted her towel, wrapping it back around her.

"But," he amended, "there are matters we must attend to first."

"And?" Creslyn prompted.

"And what?"

She tilted her head, shaking out her hair so it glamoured dry, the silver strands dusted with shades of pale pink, purple, and blue falling around her like a hidden waterfall. "There's something you're not telling me."

Drake clicked his tongue. She was incredibly perceptive. "It's nothing that needs to be discussed now. We can talk about it after breakfast tomorrow...with the king."

Because now he and Creslyn both had been summoned by Marius. The last thing Drake wanted to do was subject Creslyn to the king's heinous behavior, but he had to pick and choose his battles.

"Breakfast with the king." She was bouncing on her toes. "How exciting."

Drake grabbed both of her shoulders, hauling her against him. "No. No Creslyn, it is *not* exciting. King Marius is vile, a cold-hearted bastard of a man with a temper."

She arched one brow, the corner of her mouth lifting. "The apple doesn't fall far from the tree then."

He knew her remark was in jest, but this was not the time for games. When he responded, a chill swept through the bathroom, and she shuddered in his arms. "We are not the same."

She searched his face, looking for an answer he could not give. "But...but he's your father."

Drake stared at her and said nothing.

She stiffened. "You make it sound like I won't be safe with him."

"Which is why Kjeld is training you." His hands coasted down her arms to her wrists. "Which is why you must be on your guard. Always aware. Trust only myself and Kjeld, no one else."

Creslyn nodded slowly, but wariness clouded her eyes.

He would explain in more detail when he could, but all she needed to know right now, in this moment, was that so long as she was in the company of him or his general, then she would be safe.

Drake took her hand, pressed his lips to her knuckles in a fleeting kiss, and then released her. "Goodnight, *solysa.*"

"*Solysa,*" she repeated softly. "What does that mean?"

He didn't move when he said, "Sunshine."

Creslyn refused to break eye contact, watching him with the same collected evenness as he gazed upon her. "And *kearsta?*"

"Darling."

Her brows lifted, and Drake considered her a moment longer. "Do you prefer one over the other?"

"No." She clasped her hands together, looking quite pleased. "I rather like them both."

He nodded. "Then both it shall be, *sjellhert.*"

"Wait!" She reached for him, but he stepped away from her grasp. "What does that one mean?"

"That," he said quietly, "means something you do not yet understand."

Drake left her then, vanishing into the shadows of her bedroom to stand watch.

CHAPTER FIVE

hen Creslyn woke the next morning, she found she couldn't quite shake the unease settling around her shoulders like a cloak. She'd replayed her conversation with Drake over and over in her mind, always circling back to his one cool, detached statement.

"We are not the same."

It seemed that no matter what she knew about Drake's sordid past, which admittedly wasn't much, his father was apparently far worse.

The only way to distract herself from the growing sense of disquiet was to reflect on some other, more fascinating snippets of their discussion the night before. She wondered what exactly he intended to do with a strand of pearls, and how he planned on using them between her thighs. A delicious shiver of anticipation coursed through her when her thoughts drifted to his mention of diamonds. Lifting her hair from her neck and piling it on top of her head, she imagined the desired gemstones dripping from her ears, from her neck, and finally...her breasts. She had no idea what he meant by that promise, but she was more than curious to find out.

Creslyn rummaged through her drawer of jewels and opted for dangly moonstone earrings and a necklace to match. The rainbow-hued stones were shaped like stars, a perfect complement to her gown for breakfast. She'd chosen a dress of shimmery gold velvet embroidered with decadent pale pink lace along the bodice. The sleeves were long and belled near her wrists, while the neckline was more modest, just lightly showing off her curves.

Her lady's maid had entered her room nearly an hour prior to help her dress, fashioning her hair into one thick braid with a series of tiny smaller ones woven into it. The hairstyle was lovely, a Northernlands style she'd seen once or twice, yet unnecessary. Even if she was to dine with Drake and his father this morning, it still seemed useless to even bother with her hair. It would be ruined in seconds if she was sent out into the Trench again.

Her magic hummed in her veins, longing for some kind of release.

Creslyn considered creating an explosion of rainbows just for the fun of it when a jarring knock sounded from the other side of her bedroom door.

She crept over, her footfalls silent, and slowly opened it.

On the other side stood Drake, and she nearly melted into a puddle at his feet.

He wore his usual regalia of solid black riding leathers, with silver chains hanging from each shoulder. The faintest stitching could be seen on his chest—a mighty dragon encircled by a wall of flames. His boots were polished and his pants were trim, his broad, muscular body taking up nearly the entirety of the door frame. A lock of dark hair fell in front of his face, while half of it was twisted into a knot at the back of his head.

He looked incredibly handsome.

Positively breathtaking.

Gripping the knob for support, Creslyn leaned one hip

against the door. "You know, you don't have to knock, considering you rarely ever leave."

Drake smiled, but it didn't reach his eyes.

It was something she noticed about him. His smiles weren't quite real. They were practiced with an intention of being convincing. Never genuine.

"Would you prefer if I just walked in then, *sjellhert?*" he asked, his deep voice coasting over her, the new pet name rolling off his tongue with ease.

She accepted his proffered arm. "I might."

He guided her down the long corridor that would lead them from her wing into the heart of Castle Brackroth. As they neared the door, Creslyn loosed a shaky breath in a desperate attempt to calm her rattling nerves.

Drake noticed immediately. He glanced down at her, a line etching its way across his brow. "Are you well?"

She highly doubted he would believe her if she lied. "I am simply wondering, is there anything I should be made aware of before breakfast?"

He patted her hand the way one might subdue an anxious child. "Not while you're with me."

"But you won't always be with me," she asked, angling her face for a better view of him. "Will you?"

His jaw tensed, locking into place.

"I just want to know what I'm getting myself into, Your Highness." More than anything, Creslyn wanted to be prepared. She didn't want to be thrown into the Trench again, metaphorically speaking. If King Marius was as wretched as Drake claimed, she wanted to know what to expect.

Drake stopped as they reached the door, then inhaled. Deeply. When he looked at her, the green of his eyes had darkened to that of a forbidden forest. The gold ring around them looked cold.

"King Marius is…*corrupt.*"

Creslyn stepped closer to Drake, ignoring the shiver of apprehension needling along her spine.

"Remember what I told you, he hates anything with more power than himself. And you are powerful." Drake reached for the door and pulled it open. "He hates witches, faeries, any being that might pose a threat to his own greatness. Anyone capable of overthrowing him."

"You?" she asked, taking in his commanding presence, his daunting stature.

Drake's gaze flicked back to the door.

"Does he hate you, Drake?" Creslyn pressed, worried she might already know the answer.

"Yes, *kearsta*." He led her through the opened door and out into one of the main castle halls, refusing to meet her penetrating gaze. "He does."

Swallowing her shock, Creslyn allowed Drake to guide her through the maze-like corridors. She couldn't imagine what it must be like to have a father like that, to have her entire existence be filled with abhorrence. Her father had been good. Loving. But he'd died sooner than planned, and she'd been too young to fully comprehend her grief.

The doors to the dining hall swung open and Creslyn stumbled.

Drake carefully pulled her to his side right before they entered.

"He will be offensive. Disrespectful. He will be cunning and cutthroat. Insulting and vile. But do not cower. Do not let him think he can scare you." Drake's warning caused her blood to rush in her ears. "And no matter what, do not use your magic."

A rush of air escaped her lungs. "Okay."

She didn't sound nearly as confident as she hoped. Looking up, she stared into Drake's eyes, searching for something to ground her. Then she caught sight of it. Strength. It was a flash, solid and steady. That was what she needed from him. Strength.

"Are you ready?" Drake asked, looping her arm through his own.

"Yes." Creslyn rolled her shoulders back and lifted her chin, defiance ricocheting through her. "I'm ready."

☽✶☾

THE DINING HALL was as lackluster as the rest of the castle.

Crimson draperies hung from rain-splattered windows and though a low fire bloomed in the hearth, the space was drafty and cold. The stone walls were all bare, there were no paintings or tapestries, nothing which might suggest the castle was actually a home. Old wooden beams stretched upward on either side of the ceiling where a black chandelier housed a dozen or more half-melted candles. With each step she took, the aged floorboards creaked beneath her feet. A long oak table stood in the center of the room, draped in plain black linen, and seated at the head of the table was King Marius.

The King of Brackroth did not stand when she entered, and in turn, Creslyn did not sit.

He lounged in the embroidered high-back chair, rapping his misshapen knuckles against the hard surface of the table. A silver crown studded with garnets sat atop his shiny head, and he watched her from beneath a severely drawn brow. Glassy eyes tracked her every movement, her every breath, while he stroked his wiry white beard. His bottom lip stuck out in a snarl, revealing yellowed teeth, and the wide expanse of his stomach seemed to perch on the edge of the table.

Creslyn slid her gaze elsewhere to avoid his harsh stare.

But there was no one else in the dining hall, only the three of them. The silence was agonizing, save for the occasional screech of a dragon from beyond the castle's walls.

Drake's hand moved to the small of her back. "May I introduce you to Lady Creslyn Starstorm Celestine of Aeramere, my *betrothed.*"

She didn't care for the way he enunciated the word, as though he was driving the point home. He spoke like a threat. A dare.

King Marius's dark, cynical eyes roved over every inch of her, looking most pointedly at her ears.

"So," he drawled with condemnation, "this is the faerie."

Drake stiffened and Creslyn became all too aware of the fact that his movements were forced. His rage seethed just beneath his surface. She could tell by the way his knuckles whitened when he pulled out her chair and softly muttered, "Sit down."

Creslyn obeyed, sitting in the seat directly next to his own.

"Breaking protocol already, assassin?" King Marius barked, his sneer focused on her. "Your future wife should be sitting across from you, not right beside you."

"I have no intention of leaving her side." Drake eased back in his chair, strumming his fingers lightly on the curving arms. "Ever."

"Well." The king's voice echoed through the vast hall, and he snapped his fingers, all the while his gaze never left her. Servants shuffled in and out of the dining hall, offering platters of smoked salmon, warm biscuits with berry jam, a spread of various cheeses, and bowls of fresh fruit. "Your prince won't always be around to keep you in line."

Keep her in line?

Did he consider her some kind of feral beast? A creature in need of taming?

Creslyn remained silent, appalled by the king's insinuation, as a servant piled a variety of food on her plate. The mouthwatering scent of blackberry jam teased her, but she'd found her appetite had suddenly vanished. No matter what she ate, it would taste of ash and bitterness, thanks to this prick of a king.

"Tell me, Lady Creslyn." King Marius shoved a forkful of salmon into his mouth and chewed loudly. Her stomach revolted. "What sort of magic curses you?"

She stared at him, sickened, yet unable to look away as he sucked the food from his teeth with his tongue.

Swallowing the burn of bile, she blinked back at him. "I beg your pardon?"

"Beg. Such a lovely word." He lifted a goblet of frothy ale, gesturing to the dining hall. "You're here, are you not?"

"I am." Hesitant, she folded her hands in her lap. Drake slowly reached under the table with one hand, his palm coming to rest on her thigh. He squeezed once.

"Then you must suffer a kind of magical affliction," the king continued, oblivious to her discomfort. "There's no other possible way you could've tricked the Shadowblade Assassin into marrying one of *your* kind."

Again, Drake's grip tightened on her thigh. Bruising this time. He directed his attention to King Marius. "Be very careful with your next words."

His voice was a warning. An omen.

Fury radiated from him.

Creslyn, however, was finished. Oh, Drake had warned her about the king's abusive behavior, about the possibility of his disparaging remarks. But she would not sit idly by while he attempted to humiliate and sully not only her magic, but her birthright.

"I am afraid I don't know what you're talking about, Your Majesty." She intentionally kept her tone light and airy, border-line dismissive. "My name was written in blood as part of a deal between the Prince of Brackroth and my brother, Lord Ariesian Starstorm. We didn't even court one another. I am the product of a contract and nothing more."

This time, she held his damning gaze.

He looked like he was going to combust, like all the food he stuffed himself with was finally going to implode. She hoped his veins would burst open, that he would bleed from the inside out.

"Mind yourself, Lady Creslyn." King Marius pointed his fork at her, waving it through the air. "Eventually, the prince will need to sire an heir, and if you attempt any sort of magical trickery or any type of business where the future of my kingdom is concerned, trust you will pay with your life."

Drake jerked forward, ready to launch himself across the table, but Creslyn took hold of his hand and didn't let go.

"Oh, you needn't worry about that, Your Majesty." She flashed a vicious smile of her own. "I am perfectly capable of fucking your son and bearing his children without the assistance of magic."

King Marius erupted, his face turning a hideous shade of muddled red.

Drake, on the other, almost choked.

The king slammed his fist on the table, rattling his plate, and the goblet of ale set before him sloshed over the rim. "You watch your tongue, witch."

"Faerie," Creslyn interjected smoothly, with another callous smile.

"We have chains of iron for dirty creatures like yourself." King Marius's eyes glazed over, as though he was crazed. Corrupted, just as Drake claimed. "Another word from you and I'll have you whipped for—"

"*ENOUGH!*" Drake roared. He lurched to a standing position, heaving the massive table onto its side. Plates and glasses shattered, food toppled to the ground, crashing against the stone floor. Shadows swarmed, violent and predatory. The sinewy tendrils curled around Creslyn, dragging her from her seat and pulling her to his side. When Drake spoke again, his voice was low. Menacing. Disembodied. "You *dare* threaten her?"

The king had paled slightly, but he did not seem to fear Drake like most who witnessed his wrath.

"I'll do what I must to protect my kingdom!" he shouted, then pointed an accusing finger in her direction. "You think the people of Brackroth will bow to a half-breed heir?"

Drake's arm coiled around Creslyn's waist. "If you so much as look at her again, I will kill you."

"Go ahead, assassin. Just try to end my life." King Marius chuckled, sinking back down into his chair. His cruel gaze was once more focused on Creslyn. "We both know what will happen if you do."

In the next moment, before Creslyn could catch her breath, Drake stole her into the shadows. She gasped, clinging to him as they moved through long stretches of darkness. Endless pitch surrounded her, chilling her until she lost feeling in her fingers and toes. The first time he'd done it, back in Aeramere, she'd been too stunned to process what was happening. But now she felt everything, the way her body almost seemed to drift between the length of the shadows. As though she was a wraith, in possession of a beating heart yet non-existent all at once.

When Drake's shadows finally dissipated, Creslyn found herself standing with him on one of the treacherous cliffs over-looking the sea. Tiny waterways snaked between the rugged mountains that extended straight upward before plateauing to a damp, grassy knoll. She flung both of her arms out to catch her balance once he set her down, and Drake snatched her by the shoulders.

"Are you mad?" His voice boomed, sending rocks beneath the cliff tumbling into the churning sea below. "Are you trying to give him a reason to kill you?"

Anger ignited inside of her, burning bright.

"Apologies, Your Highness." She smacked his hands away, but he didn't release her. "I didn't realize that me wanting to perform wifely duties would be so offensive to you."

Drake snared her by the chin, jerking her face up to him. "You provoked him on purpose."

She answered with a ruthless scowl. "You expected me to sit there and take his cruel judgment?"

"Until you are fully capable of defending yourself, you will keep your mouth shut in the king's presence."

Creslyn pulled away from him, yanking herself from his grasp. "That could take months. Years, even. If my life will constantly be in danger, then why did you even bring me here?"

His hands fisted at his side and his face was devoid of any emotion when he said, "I needed a wife."

Wind gusted into Creslyn, and she tossed her braid over one shoulder, annoyed by the tendrils that had already sprung loose. "Need or want?"

"What difference does it make?" he countered.

Damn the stars, he was infuriating. "I don't even know why I came to this bleak, blasted kingdom. Oh, wait. That's right. I was given no choice."

"Creslyn..."

Her name was a growl on his lips, but she didn't care.

"You brought me here, locked me away like a prisoner, then ignored me. For eighteen *days*, Drake!" She paced through the sodden ground, her heels sticking in the soft grass. The frigid wind tore through the velvet of her gown so goosebumps riddled her flesh. She sniffled against the chill and crossed her arms, whirling on him. "Now, I'm expected to learn how to fight—"

"I will not always be around to protect you." He reached for her arm, but she dodged his hand, avoiding him.

"And why not?" she demanded.

Again, his jaw locked, and what little warmth was left in his eyes bled away. "There are places I must go and things I must do that I prefer not to discuss."

"Oh. Oh, I see." She drew the word out. A pang pierced her

heart, but she was so cold, she could no longer feel its pain. "Who is it then?"

He stared at her, then angled his head. "Pardon?"

"Is there some other female, some other *woman*, whose company you'd prefer to seek?" Because if there was, she would find Kjeld and demand he return her to Aeramere at once. It was one thing to be a wife to an assassin, it was something else altogether to be neglected while Drake gallivanted around with his favorite whore.

"No." He spoke through clenched teeth, his chest expanding. "There is no one else."

"I find that incredibly difficult to believe." Creslyn sniffed again, the frigid air causing tears to well at the corner of her eyes. Her chest heaved, her soul ached. "You rarely talk to me. I know absolutely nothing about you except for the fact that you're both assassin and prince. You hardly touch me. You've left your general to train me. Stars be damned, Drake, you've never even kissed me."

She threw both of her arms out to her sides, exasperated. "How am I to possibly believe anything else?"

There was a shift in his demeanor then. A change she couldn't quite pinpoint, yet it was somehow obvious to her all the same.

Drake closed the distance between them in one stride. He towered over her, his scent of frosted pine and cold mountains, the first hint of snow, wrapping around her like a comforting blanket.

"And is that what you want then?" His foreboding green gaze dipped to her mouth. "A kiss?"

More.

She wanted *so* much more from him than a kiss.

"Yes, actually." Creslyn bit her bottom lip, sparks of anticipation firing through her. "I would very much like to be kissed."

He moved in closer, yet kept his hands tucked behind his

back. "I do not touch you, because I know I will never want to let go. I do not train you, because I know nothing will stop me from taking you in front of my soldiers, not even your pleas. And I do not kiss you, because I know it will never be enough."

Drake captured her waist, hauling her against him. One hand stroked idly up and down her spine, sending tantalizing shivers of longing through her, until all she wanted was every inch of him touching every inch of her. She squeezed her thighs together as his other hand slid around her neck, dragging her mouth dangerously close to his own. He nipped her bottom lip with his teeth, tugging gently, then swiped the bitten area with his tongue.

Cautiously, she wrapped her arms around his neck.

"Now, *sjellhert*," Drake whispered against her cheek. "Tell me exactly what you want."

Creslyn gazed up at him, knowing she would never want anything else. The darkness inside of him called to her, owned her. She would willingly take whatever he gave, and this monster of a man would be her undoing.

"I want you to kiss me."

CHAPTER SIX

$\mathcal{D}$rake knew it would be a mistake to kiss her.

The moment his lips touched hers, every fraying thread of his self-control would unravel. There would be nothing to hold him back, nothing to stop him from devouring her. Unless she asked him to stop.

His fingers pressed into the soft flesh of her neck, his thumb sliding under her chin to tilt her face up to him. He kept his other arm wrapped tightly around her, his hand stroking her hip as he silently wished the fabric separating his touch from her skin would vanish. The echo of her wild pulse thumped loudly in his ears, his blood heating in response. A splash of freckles was scattered across Creslyn's nose and cheeks, and he'd already memorized the location of every single one. He didn't know what god or goddess had seen fit to curse him with the beauty in his arms, but her brother's words reverberated through his mind.

I think you'll find her a suitable match.

Match.

That one word would be his ultimate demise.

Ariesian Starstorm had offered up his youngest sister to

Drake on a silver platter, as though he somehow knew Creslyn was more than a simple bargain. She would be the one to bring him to his knees.

Her pale pink lips parted in anticipation, the softest of sighs escaped her, and Drake submitted.

His mouth crashed against hers in a brutal, punishing kiss. He was not romantic, nor was he gentle. She wouldn't swoon or fall lovesick, but she would know the intensity of his possession.

Creslyn's entire body went rigid in his arms as he pried her lips open with his tongue. He half expected her to pull away, to shove him off for being so demanding. But as he'd recently come to realize, she surprised him yet again.

Rising on her toes, she angled her head, granting him access to the delicious taste of her. The warm sweep of her tongue danced across his own, and her fingers tangled in his hair, drawing him into her. She tasted of raw temptation, of his darkest desires come to life. He angled her then, deepening the kiss, while the hand that once remained steady on her hip gradually slid down and around over the curve of her bottom. Gripping firmly, he squeezed, and the noise she made nearly caused his knees to buckle.

His cock thickened, strained against the confines of his pants, and Creslyn's gasping breaths roused the deep, primal desire he kept locked away.

She was desperate.

Longing for him.

And he fucking loved it.

Drake broke their kiss, then reached down and grabbed her thigh, not caring if bruises were left in his wake. She would wear his mark proudly, of that he had no doubt. He shoved her heavy velvet skirts out of the way and hoisted her leg up. Her nails scraped against the leather he wore as she struggled for purchase, her breath coming in gasping pants. She melted into him, her soft lips skimming his jaw and cheek, setting his teeth on edge. She was not his first kiss, but she would be his last. There was something about her, a likeness that called to the shadows of his soul. It was hidden beneath her pristine exterior, waiting to be discovered. She was a storm of violent sunbeams and catastrophic rainbows. A disaster in the making.

Holding her steady against him, he carefully slid one hand beneath the fabric of her gown. Her legs trembled as his fingers brushed along her thigh, then higher still. With painstaking slowness, he swept his knuckle along the delicate lace barricade protecting her from his touch, and found it damp. He hooked one finger around the fabric and tugged.

Creslyn's head fell back, and she arched into him, a silent plea.

He lowered his head, swiping his tongue along the swell of her breasts, leaving behind a faint trail of steam as the frigid wind of the cliffs barreled into them. Clutching her against him with one arm, his knuckles grazed her swollen center. She clawed at him then, her nails scouring his neck as she rocked her hips forward.

"Drake, please."

The way his name fell from her lips, the way it sounded like a prayer to the gods, was enough to drive him mad with lust.

He pressed a kiss to her neck, his mouth slowly moving toward the elegant, pointed tip of her ear.

"Tell me to stop," he whispered.

She shook her head, whimpering. "No."

Damn her.

Then he did the one thing he swore he wouldn't do, he slipped into her mind.

"If you do not tell me to stop," he murmured, and her sapphire eyes flew to his, wide with shock, *"I will ruin you."*

"You..." Her chest heaved as she searched his face for something she would not find. "I can hear your voice in my head."

"Do not get any fanciful ideas, *kearsta*. I am not your mate."

With painstaking slowness, he removed his hand from beneath her skirts and placed it on the small of her back instead. "I can enter anyone's mind so long as their guard is down."

The silver flecks in her eyes danced with a gleam he didn't recognize. "You can hear my thoughts, then?"

"Hear them. See them." He shrugged, bouncing her in his arms. "The two are not so different."

"Are they not?" she muttered, and then her sweet mouth was devouring him.

Images slammed into Drake's mind, vivid and colorful. Her imagination overwhelmed him. Her daydreams set him on fire until the scorch of them charred his already blackened soul. Creslyn tore through the walls of his own mind, until he was flat on his back in her bed, with her seated atop him. Naked and glorious, she rode him relentlessly, taking every inch of his cock while his shadows crawled all over her bare skin. Her orgasm drove him over the edge, exploding in a rush of blinding sunbeams as she fractured his darkness with a thousand rainbows.

Drake grabbed a fistful of her silky hair, gently yanking her head back, and broke the connection. He scraped his teeth down the column of her throat.

"Wicked little faerie."

"You might not be my mate." She smirked, and he wanted those lips of hers all over him. "But you will be my husband."

"All in good time, *sjellhert*."

A screech pierced the sky, as familiar to him as the pounding of his own heart, and Drake looked up to see Svartos cutting through the overcast skies. In Brackroth, the dragons were revered and feared like gods, and Drake commanded all of them. His legion was vast and powerful, with each of his riders being hand-selected by him. It was the dragon, however, who chose its rider. Their trust was earned, their loyalty never given freely. They could be trained, yes, but the intuition coursing through their veins spanned centuries.

He soared closer, the beating of his wings like that of a steady drum, sending a surge of wind rushing into them. Drake snared Creslyn's hand, lest the intensity of Svartos's landing blow her off the edge of the cliff.

The dragon pawed at the ground, his sharp claws sinking into the soft dirt. He tucked in his majestic wings and his numerous scales shone like polished obsidian in the muted morning light. Svartos craned his long neck, then tossed his head once, the striking yellow of his eyes fixated on Creslyn.

She didn't even flinch.

With practiced caution, she held out her hand, palm up, and approached the dragon. His thin, vertical pupils dilated, gauging her, and when she neared even closer, Svartos inhaled deeply. A rumbling sound emitted from the back of his throat, and his nostrils flared as he breathed in the scent of her. She was nothing compared to the magnificent creature, practically the size of a sprite against the backdrop of a mighty dragon. Drake watched as Creslyn's chest rose and fell, unwavering, while she reached up and gently touched the rough patch of scales right along his snout. He blinked once, lowering himself closer to her. From Drake's vantage point, it almost looked as though Svartos was *nuzzling* her open hand.

Fucking traitor.

Svartos lowered himself to the ground, another huff of warm air ruffling Creslyn's skirts.

"Come with me, *solysa*." Drake scooped her up off the ground and set her atop the wide leather seat strapped around Svartos's back.

"Where are we going?" she asked, smoothing her skirts and crossing her legs over one side of the saddle.

"For a ride."

Drake vaulted up behind her, tugged on his riding gloves,

then situated her securely against his lap. He kept one arm around her waist and took up the reins in the other, threading them through his fingers. Creslyn tucked a lock of silver and icy pink windswept hair behind her ear, then peered up at him.

He clicked his tongue, nodding once. "Say the word."

Pure exhilaration highlighted the gentle planes of her face, illuminating her from within. She'd only heard him speak it once, on the night they left Aeramere, but he knew she would remember.

"*Vaeja*." She spoke in hushed tones, mimicking his accent perfectly, and Svartos rose, stretching his vast wings.

A moment later, they were sky bound. Creslyn squealed, throwing her arms out to either side, tilting her face up to the invisible sun. Tendrils of her hair whipped in the frigid breeze, tickling Drake's cheek and chin. She dipped to one side, leaning back, and he locked her in his grip to keep her from sliding further. But in his arms, she was relaxed, as though she had not a care in the world. Her trust humbled him, her smile was brighter than the northern auroras that awoke during winter's coldest nights. She swung her legs freely, and one of her heels slipped loose, tumbling toward the earth.

"Oh!" She eased up and peered over, her cheeks flushed pink from the cold. "I lost my shoe."

The corner of Drake's mouth twisted into a wry smile. "Must run in the family."

Her elder sister, Novalise, had a habit of losing her shoes as well.

Svartos carried them high into the thick gray clouds, gliding far above the uneven cliffs that dropped off into the dark icy waters of the Havnokk Deep. Here, away from Castle Brackroth, away from King Marius, Creslyn could be free.

"Show me your magic, *solysa*."

She looked up at him, the blue of her eyes more endless than he'd ever seen it. "What?"

"Your magic," he repeated with a pointed look at the staff-like constellation marking her heart. "Show me."

Creslyn sat up straight and rolled her shoulders back. Without another word, she raised her arms, and for the first time since Drake could remember, beams of radiant sunlight shattered the leaden skies of Brackroth. The golden rays swirled and danced, splintering through the clouds as ribbons of rainbows coasted alongside them like colorful waves. Prisms in the shape of eight-pointed stars reflected the sunbeams, cascading over and around them in a shimmering iridescent sphere.

She was artistry in the skies.

Splendor in the flesh.

After what seemed like an eternity of feeling nothing, her power washed over him. A touch of warmth. Of life.

Creslyn sighed heavily, her magic gradually receding as she leaned against his chest, resting her head upon his shoulder.

As much as he didn't particularly care to ruin the moment, thus far, she'd asked only one thing of him—she wanted to be prepared. To know what she was getting herself into...and he could not deny her that request.

"I must leave you tonight." He guided Svartos back toward the castle, easing lightly on the reins to slow his speed.

Awareness spread through her, and he sensed the muscles in her body grow tense. "Leave me?"

"Only for a night, *sjellhert*. There is something that requires my attention." Drake lowered his head, brushing his lips lightly across her temple. "Duty binds me."

"Duty." She gnawed on the corner of her bottom lip, her intent gaze fixating on him. He could hear her thoughts, her doubts, her questions. She sorted through them, debating what to say, what to ask. The one she chose would haunt him. "Are you going to take a life?"

"Yes." Drake nodded solemnly. He would not lie, but nor would he expose her to the bloodthirsty reality of his nature.

"Is that what you meant before?" A tiny line of worry marred her brow. "When you said you had somewhere to go?"

Drake kept his expression neutral, admiring the stones dangling from her ears. "Yes."

Creslyn twisted to face him, stretching her legs out on either side of him, planting her hands on his thighs.

Gods, this female would be the end of him.

"Could I go with you?" she asked in earnest.

Blinking back his surprise, Drake chuckled. That had been the last thing he'd expected her to say. "The risk is far too great, Creslyn. As much as I'm loath to leave your side for even a minute, where I'm going…it is not suitable for you. It's dangerous. My reputation precedes me. If word gets out that I've brought my future bride, those who fear me would come for you."

She raised one eyebrow, her lips pursing. "So, are you saying I'm your weakness?"

Drake's hold on the reins tightened, and the silence that stretched between them was damn near deafening.

When he spoke again, he ensured his voice was cool. Detached. He could never allow her to be his weakness, it would be an omen for them both. "You are not a weakness, but you are not yet a weapon. You are not my Shadowblade. You are not the sharpened edge of a sword, nor are you the finely honed tip of a dagger."

Creslyn shifted again, tugging on her gown, dragging her legs higher to eliminate any space between them. She scooted forward, seating herself on his lap, and draped her arms around his neck. Drake eased back, uncertainty digging into the base of his spine.

"Fine then." Resolution and something darker burned in the depths of her eyes, and the soft features of her face hardened with steadfast determination. "Make me your weapon."

Fucking gods.

Drake almost groaned.

Those words falling from her lips sent a bolt of desire straight to his cock.

He grabbed her neck, kissed her hard, and when her teeth sank into his bottom lip, he knew he'd met his match.

"I will," he murmured into the delicious heat of her mouth, slowly breaking the kiss. But he didn't pull away. Not fully. "While I am gone, Kjeld will train you. And when I return, we will fly to Aeramere for the wedding."

Creslyn leaned into him, trailing her lips along his neck to his ear. "I will not fail you."

Drake never doubted it, but he could not erase the fear of knowing he would be the one to fail her.

CHAPTER SEVEN

Drake was gone when Creslyn awoke. She knew, because she could no longer sense his presence in her bedroom. Despite the glowing warmth of flames flickering in the hearth, the air was cooler. And she missed the scent of him. That intangible sensation of traversing through mountains as snowflakes tumbled from a blanketed sky, clinging to branches of evergreen. He'd told her he would return by tomorrow, but after the slight altercation with King Marius at breakfast the day before, Creslyn was already bracing for the longest day of her life.

To make matters worse, she longed to release her magic once more.

But instead of dazzling her surroundings with beams of sunshine and sparkling rainbows, she found herself back in the Trench with Kjeld.

Cold mud and damp grass squashed beneath her feet. At least this time she'd been prepared and had made the more sensible choice to wear a pair of flats as opposed to heels. Though her movements were slightly less hindered, she still slipped and slid through the muck. She'd also opted for one of her less fashionable gowns, choosing one in a deep plum-pink shade that would hopefully disguise most of the soiled hem. It was velvet with large sleeves that ballooned over her arms, then cuffed at her wrists. The scooped neckline was embellished with tiny rainbow moonstones and the back was cut low, exposing her to the elements.

Though she was grateful there was no rain this afternoon, she supposed it was only a matter of time. She'd been out here for hours already, and the skies of Brackroth were bleak again, roiling with heavy clouds of gray that appeared ready to break and unleash another downpour.

Only Kjeld and herself were in the Trench. The other soldiers she'd seen fighting the day prior had all gone down to Dragnott—the lair of the dragons. She squinted up at the sky in haste, spying outlines of shadowy wings as the dragons and their riders soared overhead, their screeching calls igniting a tiny spark of hope inside her.

Maybe she would have a dragon of her own one day.

The sting of a wooden sword smacked her arm hard, and she winced, glaring at Kjeld.

"Ouch." Creslyn rubbed the sore spot right below her shoulder, a line furrowing between her brows. "What was that for?"

He swung his sword out again, tapping her lightly on the top of her head. "You're distracted again, my lady."

"I cannot help it," she muttered, casting her gaze to the darkening skies once more. "Training is dull."

"Dull?" Kjeld lowered his practice weapon and stalked toward her. Wind stole through the Trench, strands of his long, dark gold hair fluttered across his face, and he shoved them back in annoyance. His summer blue eyes narrowed. "It'll save your life one day."

"But it's the same thing over and over again. Parry. Step. Dodge. Attack." She sighed, rolling her neck, then suffered him a look of boredom. "It's tedious."

"It's a drill." He spoke to her with all the patience of an adult scorning a child. His patronizing tone set her teeth on edge. "To make sure it becomes second nature to you."

Creslyn planted one hand on her waist, cocking her hip to the side. "I've already memorized every move."

His roughened, windswept features hardened, and he arched one brow in disbelief. "Have you now?"

She readied herself in a starting stance, kept her shoulders down, and raised her arms in defense. "Try me, General."

Kjeld lunged and they fought, Creslyn blocking his every attack, dodging his attempted blows. He held nothing back against her, and she pivoted through the movements he'd taught her, motions that had swiftly become muscle memory. She spun away from him, coiling her hands into tight fists as she avoided his relentless assault. It made no difference if she had no armor, if she was without a blade and was forbidden from using her magic, she would become a weapon. She'd never been any good at the typical accomplishments of a lady. Needlework was a thorn in her side. Drawing and painting were the very bane of her existence. But for some reason, hand-to-hand combat reminded her of music. Each strike was a chord, every motion a part in a great melody, the musical composition of battle.

Finally, chest heaving and his eyes widened in awe, Kjeld staggered back. He shook his head once, tucking a lock of hair behind his ear. "How?"

Creslyn shrugged. Her muscles were on fire, burning from exertion, but she relished the feel of achievement. She sucked in a deep breath, inhaling the misty air, and smoothed her heavy skirt. "It is just the way I am. I learn exceptionally fast, so long as it's something of interest."

"So...you enjoy training?" he asked, tossing the wooden sword onto the table.

She stretched her arms overhead, then let them fall to her sides. "It's not so different from music, I suppose."

Kjeld mulled over her response, roughing a hand over his beard. His blue eyes flicked to her. "Well done, my lady. His Highness will be quite impressed with you upon his return."

"It's possible." But she would accept his compliment either way.

The general sorted through the weapons spread on the table, drumming his fingers lightly upon the surface. "Perhaps we should move on to daggers. Or would you prefer a sword?"

She might be a quick study, but defending herself was not quite the same as swinging a sword. "I think I'd like to try—"

"General Holtstrom!"

Creslyn whipped around as two soldiers barreled into the Trench. Sweat dripped from their brows, and their faces looked to be covered in ash or soot. They were dressed in the traditional riding leathers with an onyx dragon emblem pinned to the collars of their vests. Both of them rushed past her, not even sparing her a glance.

One halted before Kjeld and snapped to attention. "General Holtstrom, sir, you're needed at the Dragnott Lair immediately. One of the whelps has gone rogue, he's setting fire to the stables and slaughtering the horses."

"Shit." Kjeld hesitated, locking his gaze onto Creslyn.

A tremor of alarm raced down her spine, and she wrapped her arms around herself.

"Take Lady Creslyn to her quarters immediately and stand guard outside of her door until my return," he ordered, stalking closer to both riders. "Do not leave under any circumstances."

The soldiers nodded in unison. "Yes, general."

Kjeld walked through the damp grass to Creslyn, gripping her shoulder. "I will not be long, I promise."

Before she could respond, he started running, vanishing into the castle and out of sight.

Creslyn whirled around and faced the two guards who

averted their gazes, taking up a sudden interest in their scuffed boots.

"My lady." One of them bowed his head, gesturing toward the door leading from the Trench and into the castle. "If you'll come with us."

Creslyn fiddled with the sleeves of her gown, uncertainty warring with rational thought. It would be foolish of her to refuse and stand out here in the Trench where King Marius could easily discover her alone and without Drake's protection. At the same time, he'd warned her to only trust himself and Kjeld. Granted, she could probably make it back to her wing all by herself, but she'd rather not take any chances. And since these two guards were refusing to even look at her, she assumed their allegiance fell to Drake and not necessarily King Marius.

Left with no other choice, Creslyn followed the dragon riders through the great hall towards her wing. Their heads swiveled at the faintest noise, one hand hovering above the hilt of the swords strapped to their waists. They moved with great stealth, their footfalls near silent as they stalked through the castle, and Creslyn found herself hoisting her skirts to keep them from swishing too loudly as she attempted to walk as quietly as possible.

She breathed a sigh of relief when the door to her bedchamber came into view.

One of the soldiers reached out and opened it for her, allowing her entry, then bowed his head. "We'll be just outside if you need anything, my lady."

Creslyn nodded, not that it mattered. He never even looked up before shutting the door soundlessly behind him.

She stared at the closed door a moment longer, unsure of what to do now that she was yet again locked inside her bedroom. Chilled, she rubbed her hands up and down her arms, her gaze lingering on the hearth where the fire had all but gone out completely. There were a few embers left, lumps of gray coals that glowed bright with the remnants of a flame. She would summon one of the maids to light it again as soon as she changed out of her mud-stained gown.

Kicking off her filthy shoes, she padded lightly across the floor, the soft fur rug cushioning her bare feet. She slid one arm out of her sleeve completely, when she caught sight of her reflection in the elaborate floor to ceiling mirror.

Another pair of eyes watched her from the far corner of the room.

Creslyn opened her mouth to scream when a rough hand clamped over her, muffling her cries for help. She struggled, clutching at her gown to cover herself, as arms swiftly wrapped around her, pinning her against a solid chest. The stench of sweat and stale tobacco overwhelmed her to the point of gagging, and though she tried to free herself from his beast-like hold, whoever held her captive only tightened his grip. Her feet lifted off the ground and she kicked, thrashing wildly, when another figure stepped out from within her closet.

He was a gangly man dressed in the black and silver of the king's guards, and a sneer peeled back his too thin lips, revealing a set of yellowed teeth. Sharp cheekbones only high-lighted his gaunt face as he stared down his hooked nose at her. He sauntered closer, and though he was positively hideous, it was the lecherous look in his eyes that sent a spike of fear into her heart. His tongue slid out, wetting his papery lips like a snake.

"By all means, don't stop undressing on my account." His raspy voice grated against her ears, and his mirthless smile widened as he approached. "Here, let me help you."

The vile man reached out and grabbed her bare breast, squeezing hard, his nails digging into her flesh.

Tears sprang to her eyes, threatening to spill down her cheeks. But this man's audacity, his cruel insolence, unleashed a rush of cold rage from within her.

Creslyn's magic exploded with blinding fury, more raw and powerful than ever before. Streaks of scorching sunbeams enveloped her in a sphere, and the arms holding her hostage fell away as screams of pain echoed throughout her bedchamber. The pungent scent of burnt flesh hung in the air as rainbow prisms morphed into shards, flying around her like sharpened blades poised to strike. She threw her hands up in front of her, barely controlling the violent beauty of intense sunbursts and shattering rainbows. The storm engulfed her as magic pumped through her veins, ripping through the room in spears of brilliant light and color, awakening the sliver of darkness locked away in the most cavernous part of her soul.

Banging and shouts sounded from outside of her bedroom door. Drake's soldiers on the other side fought to break it down, but the solid wood held, and the handle didn't budge.

"Put the shackles on her already!" the gangly man yelled, his gravelly voice resonating throughout the room.

Creslyn spun to face the man who ran up on her other side, and her mouth fell open in horror.

Half his hair was singed off his head, falling to the ground in burnt clumps. His face was bleeding, the skin charred and peeling away.

Her shock was the only opportunity he needed.

He lunged for her, and when she lifted her arms in defense, something like ice clamped snugly around her wrists. The sensation was jarring, causing her to yelp in pain as the cold iron snuffed out her magic like a flame in the wind. The metal bit into her flesh, pulling the air from her lungs on a gasp. Her knees wobbled, her vision blurred. Like a swallow of poison, the iron dulled her power until it was nothing more than a faint thrum in her blood. She swayed once, her strength giving out as she collapsed onto the hardwood floor, pain ricocheting through her. Rendered weak and defenseless, she could do nothing as she was tossed over the scorched man's shoulder like a sack of grain.

"I got her, Stygg." He headed toward the balcony.

"Good." The rasping voice sounded distorted to her ears, but there was no mistaking the venom spewing from his hideous mouth. "That'll teach the fae bitch."

Creslyn whimpered as they threw open the doors of her balcony. Frigid wind swept through the room, chilling her body, and without warning, the man holding her tossed her over the ledge. Her shriek was silenced as she landed hard on her stomach, all the air pushed from her lungs. Something cracked, splintering inside her, each breath becoming more agonizing than the last. She'd broken a rib, maybe two, and with her magic dampened by the iron, the chances of her injury healing were entirely too slim.

She rolled her head, a glimpse of silver scales glinting out of the corner of her eye.

Dragon.

The word reverberated through her mind. But her thoughts were muddled and incoherent, the iron making it nearly impossible to focus. Why would a dragon be working for the king's men? She could've sworn Drake was their master. He'd told her as much.

Biting gusts of wind slapped her cheeks as she soared through the sky and frozen drops of rain pelted her arms and legs. Her chest ached fiercely, her body stiff and broken. And she couldn't be certain, but it felt as though one of the men, likely the lanky one named Stygg, had his boot firmly planted in the center of her back.

The dragon finally landed, and bile scaled the back of Creslyn's throat as she was dragged off its back and shoved before none other than King Marius.

He stood on a cliffside that stretched out over the roiling sea. A gray fur cloak was pinned to his shoulders, billowing around his wide frame as he ambled forward, tugging his belt up over his excessively large stomach. The king scraped his gnarled knuckles along the side of his face, then stroked his unsightly beard once. Twice.

Stygg pushed her forward again, and she stumbled, the iron cuffs around her wrist clinking noisily.

King Marius chortled, his black eyes zeroed in on her, lingering heavily on her still exposed breast. He reached down, adjusting the bulge in his pants, and Creslyn nearly retched. She grappled with her gown, tugging it up to cover herself from his lascivious glare.

"It was foolish of you not to heed my warning." He closed the distance between them and bent down, his hot, rank breath smothering her. "When I said no magic, I meant it."

Creslyn refused to cower before this wretched excuse of a ruler. She was a Starstorm of House Celestine, a fae of noble birth and rank, and she would only ever obey the stars. Kings and crowns be damned.

She rolled her shoulders back, clinging to the fabric of her gown. "I was defending myself against those two bastards you call guards."

King Marius shook his head, tucking his hands behind his back. "Your excuses will not sway me. Much like your shadow prince, I always keep my word."

Again, her knees quaked, the iron weakening her further. She fixed him with a knowing look, her voice entirely too calm when she said, "He'll kill you for this."

The king's boisterous laughter sent her head spinning. "No, he won't. Because if Drake kills me, he will forfeit his own life as well."

Creslyn blinked, unsure if she'd heard him correctly.

He grabbed her chin, jerking her face upward. "And we both know he'd never sacrifice his power for you."

"Liar," she hissed between chattering teeth.

"Tell me," King Marius mused, crowding her so she was forced to step back, closer to the dangerously high cliff. "Do you have wings?"

"N-no." She shivered, realization settling in the pit of her stomach. Casting one desperate, fleeting look around her, she locked gazes with a set of startling blue eyes with onyx slits for pupils.

The dragon.

Help me, she pleaded, her voice hollow to her own ears. *Please, help me.*

But her shadow prince couldn't hear her pleas. And neither could the dragon.

King Marius gestured to the vast expanse of empty horizon behind them, where the gray sea churned and frothy waves crashed against a jagged slope. "Then I suppose it's time you learn how to fly."

"No!" she cried as Stygg grabbed her, scooping her off her feet. "No! Please!"

And then he threw her off the cliff.

Creslyn screamed as blurs of slate flashed by her. A piercing screech cut through the heavens as she tumbled through the air. She would die. This is how she was going to die. Drake's face appeared in her mind, his roguish smirk fracturing her heart. The last thing she saw was the faint outline of wings before she was swallowed by the ocean.

CHAPTER EIGHT

The kingdom of Lyrithia bordered Brackroth, its steep stretch of mountains carving up the rugged terrain, dividing the two land masses in half. Whereas Brackroth was bleak and bitter, constantly under overcast skies and frigid rain, Lyrithia was quite the opposite. Once Svartos soared over the magnificent mountain peaks, so high they were still dusted with snow, the gloomy mist of Brackroth dissipated and Lyrithia came into view.

Late afternoon sun splashed across the sky and thin ribbons of clouds cast long shadows on the ground below. Even on the back of his dragon, the beams of light never quite touched him. He couldn't remember the last time he felt the warmth of sunlight upon his skin, save for when Creslyn used her magic. Somehow, her power had reached him, and the thought of it left him slightly on edge. Sunshine and rainbows shouldn't be able to penetrate the darkness of his soul, and yet...

He shook his head, tightening his hold on Svartos's reins.

Sprawling towns dotted the lush green landscape. Many of them were nestled in valleys, situated by flowing river ways with crystal clear water that spilled down from the mountains.

Shops and homes were painted in rich, vibrant hues—deep red, navy blue, forest green, and burnt orange. From Drake's vantage point, he could just make out the castle in the distance, set against a backdrop of dense pines and sloping hills.

But he would not be paying the king a visit.

The piece of folded parchment tucked into his vest caused his bloodlust to stir, and he grit his teeth against the mounting pressure pounding against his skull. Each time King Marius gave him a name, it awoke the slumbering darkness inside him. He'd made a choice long ago. In exchange for a weapon of deadly force, he would become the king's assassin. The deal had only required a few vials of Drake's own blood, and he'd been so consumed with greed, he'd readily accepted the offer without realizing the full extent of the truth. That damn witch his father lusted after had made it so the weapon would end a life upon its first strike, but if he ever turned against the king, his own life would be taken as well.

Otherwise, Drake would have killed him with his shadows long ago.

He wondered how much Marius had given her in exchange for that bit of trickery.

The bastard must've known Drake would one day want him dead.

In the beginning, Marius sent him off to kill anyone who posed a threat to Brackroth—enemies, rebels, even those who had wronged him in the past. But now it seemed as though Marius was simply giving him names for sport.

Drake sneered at the notion, guiding Svartos to a patch of shaded overhang in a thicket of trees.

He wasn't above killing someone. In fact, there had been many times he'd enjoyed watching the life drain from his victims' eyes. Those who had been on the receiving end of his blade often deserved their demise. But Marius had begun taking lives for no other reason than the fact that he *could*, and even that caused Drake's shadows to hiss and recoil.

He swung off Svartos, adjusted his leathers, then yanked off his riding gloves, tucking them into his back pocket. The trees rustled on the breeze, disguising the annoyed huff of Svartos when Drake tossed him a chunk of raw meat.

"I'll be back just after nightfall." He rubbed his hand along the dragon's roughened black scales. "And then we can return home."

To Creslyn.

Svartos tossed his head once before settling down in the sparse patch of forest.

Drake wasted no time heading toward the village. The sooner he got this over with, the better. Moving through the elongated shadows of the setting sun, he found his way to the heart of the village square, then stalked out of an empty alley that reeked of urine and tobacco. He scowled at anyone who passed him, but his reputation was widely known in Lyrithia, and most of the inhabitants avoided him anyway, giving him a wide berth. He could sense their fear, the way icy panic slid down their spines, how their breathing grew shallow the moment they laid eyes upon him. While most of the villagers would pray to their gods as he strode past them, silently begging to be spared, he knew a select few would be bold enough to search him out.

He strolled through the village on his way to the local pub, pausing only when a display of sparkling jewels in the window of a storefront caught his eye—the diamonds in particular. The necklace was a collar made of four separate strands, each one graduating in size, and the stones along the bottom row were about as large as river pebbles. Matching earrings were paired with the necklace, and then there were the silver bars, where the gemstones dripped like a sparkling waterfall.

Perfect.

Drake made his purchase and continued to the pub, choosing a secluded table in the far corner where the grimy lighting couldn't quite reach. The stench of stale alcohol hung heavy in the air, coupled with a haze of smoke. Burnished sunlight angled in through shuttered windows and every so often the door would groan open as a few more patrons entered the pub, the end of the day drawing near. Three musicians were set up on the other end of the space, across from the scuffed bar, their instruments strumming out an off-key folk tune that grated against his ears.

He ordered a whiskey, biting back his grimace when they served it in a glass that looked as though it had never been washed.

The liquor was mediocre at best and lacking any real flavor, but Drake didn't really care. He was merely biding his time, waiting for his unsuspecting target to stroll into the pub.

Minutes ticked by as more villagers crammed into the run-down establishment, crushing tables together and fitting themselves into any open space at the bar. None of them looked his way, but then the distinctive click of heels echoed in his ears and a scent he'd all but forgotten heightened his awareness.

Drake's head snapped up, and he found himself staring at Ingrid, a tall blonde woman with keen eyes and a pair of lips that had taken his cock more times than he could count. She wore Lyrithia's traditional dress, a dark blue skirt with colorful flowers embroidered along the hem, and a corset that laced up the front, so the fullness of her breasts was on display. Her hair was twisted into two plaits, bound with the feathers of a raven, and she'd lined her eyes with kohl.

Her red mouth curved into a smile. "It's been a long time."

"And it will be even longer," he answered coolly, finishing off the foul drink.

Ingrid pulled out the empty chair next to his, its legs

scratching against the wooden floor. Then she plopped down, her hand reaching for his thigh.

Drake snared her wrist, digging his fingers into her flesh. "Don't even think about it."

She stuck out her bottom lip in a pout, seizing the opportunity to move closer to him.

"I haven't seen you in months. You came all this way from Brackroth, the least you can do is give me a few hours of your time. Preferably in my bed." Ingrid tilted her head, angling to kiss him. The heady scent of her flowery perfume was nauseating. "Let me show you how much I missed you."

Drake released her then, shoving her back with such force she nearly toppled out of the rickety chair. "I owe you nothing. Not my time. Nor my attention."

"I know why you're here." Her whisper was harsh, and she leaned back, drumming her nails along the table's uneven surface. "You think you've come to kill my father. Wait until you find out you've been made a fool, that you coming here was nothing more than a trick to—"

Drake moved with excessive speed. He yanked the parchment from the pocket of his vest and slammed it on the table in front of her, forcing her to see the name scrawled in blood. "Does this look like a trick to you, Ingrid?"

The rouge on her cheeks faded, and she turned pallid, her throat working tirelessly to swallow all the vile, hateful things she would never have the courage to say.

She reached for the parchment, but he was faster, snatching it up before she could rip it to shreds.

Like that would do anything.

Ingrid bared her teeth, the desire in her eyes replaced by cold loathing. "You can't do this."

He debated placating her with a sarcastic response when the bloodlust stirred. Inhaling deeply, he tracked the scent of the day's fresh catch from the fish market mixed with cherry tobacco smoke from a pipe. Halvor, Ingrid's father, was about to walk through the doors of the pub.

Her eyes flew wide, recognizing his intent.

"No!" she cried, clambering out of her seat and darting toward the entrance.

Drake watched her scramble through the crowd, cursing under his breath as she plowed into her father and dragged him out the door.

Damn Ingrid for getting involved. She would only serve to make things messy on his end, either with blood or tears.

He crumpled the parchment, cramming it into his pocket, and slipped into the shadows. They swarmed him, their cool caress a balm to the heated rush coursing through his veins. The compulsion to kill was raging, and he pulled the Shadowblade from its sheath. Its midnight blade pulsed with power, the hilt throbbing in his grip, summoning him to fulfill his long-standing bargain. The magic it possessed had become an obsession, a calling, serving only to intensify Drake's desire for death.

But there was something else. Something more prominent that prodded at the back of his mind, digging into his subconscious.

Shaking off the odd sensation, he moved like a wraith from the pub to the village square, clinging to the expanse of darkness coating the cobbled streets. The sun sank low in the western sky, so streaks of crimson bled against the approaching hues of twilight. A blonde head ducked around a corner, and he tracked it, following Ingrid and her father into a cramped alley littered with crates and piles of days-old rubbish.

The Shadowblade hummed against the grip of his palm, ready to sing with blood.

Drake slinked past Ingrid in a blur of shadows, prepared to strike, when her father laughed loudly and swatted away her hand.

"Don't be ridiculous, Ingrid. Prince Drake won't *actually* kill me." Halvor ran a hand down his beard, smoothing the wiry gray strands. "I'm nothing more than a ploy. Marius needed a reason to distract the prince so he could get rid of some blasted faerie."

Drake's blood ran cold.

"I saw your name inked in blood!" Ingrid shouted, grabbing at his arm.

Halvor paled. "That double-crossing bastard…"

But their words were nothing more than garbled nonsense, lost to the frenzy of hostility ravaging Drake's mind. His shadows seethed, fueled with vengeful wrath. They poured from him like a venom of darkness, stealing every shred of light and encompassing the alley with a gust of frozen air. So cold, Ingrid's panicked breaths puffed out in front of her and turned to icicles.

Creslyn was in danger. *That* was the unsettling grip of unease he could not shake.

Drake snarled, his arm arcing through the air as he drove the Shadowblade into his target. The dagger seemed to hum in satisfaction, its blade glistening with the blood of his victim. Ingrid screamed, but her cries fell on deaf ears.

He didn't care.

Sheathing the blade, he stole through the falling night toward the line of trees where Svartos waited for him. He swung up into the riding seat, his hands and veins turned black from the mass of shadows lashing out around him.

Drake's gaze narrowed. He would kill whoever hurt her.

"Vaeja."

DRAKE STALKED TOWARD DRAGNOTT LAIR, dusting off his hands.

Upon his return to Brackroth, King Marius gloated like an imbecile, dancing around the subject of Creslyn's whereabouts while his scathing remarks lingered in the back of Drake's mind.

"What did you do to her?" Drake demanded.

"I got rid of a pestilence upon my kingdom."

And when Drake threatened to slay every guard in the throne room, the bastard had only laughed.

"They're easily replaceable," the king chortled.

"Just like you," Drake replied before unleashing his power upon every soul in the room.

Their screams were drowned out by the piercing crack of thunder from an approaching storm. Shadows erupted from Drake in a relentless wave of terror, feeding off his own rage. Painful cries and pleas for mercy shuddered through the throne room as impenetrable darkness strangled each soul. As the thrashings subsided and the shouts of agony became nothing more than dying whispers, an unnatural calm took root in Drake, branching out to even the balance between man and monster.

Only when Kjeld ran in, claiming Creslyn was safe in the lair, did Drake cease his torment. But by then, it was too late.

He almost pitied the servants who would be forced to clean up the mess he left behind.

Slashing rain pummeled him as he traversed the crumbling cliffside toward the belly of the mountain where the dragons resided. Kjeld came with him, his hand constantly hovering over the hilt of his sword.

"This is all my fault," he muttered, slicking back his soaked hair from his face. "I never should've left her alone, Your Highness."

Drake stiffened at the formality between them but kept his pace clipped, ducking into the heart of the lair and out of the violent weather. "Besides myself, you are the only one remotely capable of controlling the whelps. You did what had to be done."

They walked through the winding tunnel in silence, their footfalls echoing off the cavernous walls as steady droplets of spring water dripped from the spires lining the ceiling. The dark was penetrating, but flaming torches were ignited every few feet, dousing the lair in a soft orange light. Dragons of varying size dozed in some of the caves set back off the main path, but every so often he caught the glint of glowing eyes watching him as he passed.

Deeper into the mountain they trekked until they came upon the den of Astrylys. She was a beautiful dragon, with piercing blue eyes and silver scales coated with an iridescent sheen. She also happened to be Svartos's mate, a coincidence that was not lost on Drake.

Astrylys inhaled, breathing in his scent, and he swore the dragon narrowed her vivid eyes as he approached. Just beyond the curve of her tail, he spied a muddied gown and the tip of a pointed ear.

Creslyn.

Astrylys snapped her mighty jaws once in warning and stretched her wings, ready to protect Creslyn the way a mother would her young.

"Careful, Your Highness." Kjeld drew up short, lowering his arms to his side to show he meant no harm. "She won't let any of us near Lady Creslyn."

Good.

Drake took one slow step, then another. "Easy, Astrylys. Easy."

The female dragon hissed, her growl deepening.

"Yes, I know I never should've left her alone. It was my mistake." He moved closer, maintaining eye contact with Astrylys the entire time. Her skinny pupils dilated in the faint light, wary.

"She is mine." Drake placed one hand over his heart and bowed low before the dragon. "Mine."

There was a snort, intense enough it nearly caused him to stumble, but Astrylys eased back, allowing him access to Creslyn.

As soon as he saw her, he knew the deaths of those guards would never be enough for retribution. Only when he had Marius's head on a stake, would he rest easily knowing Creslyn was safe. His gaze roved over her, his fingers clenching into fists at his side.

She was curled on a thatch of hay, protected by Astrylys's winding tail. Her dress was damp and torn, her face was entirely too pale, and her eyes were closed. He listened for her heartbeat. It was steady, but her chest rose and fell much slower than it should have. She was weak. Possibly unconscious. But what rekindled his rage were the iron cuffs clamped around her wrists.

Drake took a steadying breath and carefully stepped toward her, aware of Astrylys watching his every movement. He grabbed the metal chain, wrapping his hand around the links joining the two cuffs, and faint tendrils of shadows slithered from his fingers. Darkness met iron and the shadows devoured the metal bindings, dissolving them completely.

Creslyn whimpered and something inside of Drake fractured.

"Prepare our bags," Drake called out to Kjeld, scooping Creslyn into his arms. "We leave for Aeramere immediately."

She needed a healer. And not just any healer, one of fae blood.

Clutching Creslyn to his chest, Drake bowed once more to Astrylys. "Thank you for saving her."

"We?" Kjeld choked out, his eyes widening. "You want me to travel with you?"

"Yes." Drake walked out of the dragon's den, cradling a

nearly unconscious Creslyn, and headed back toward the passage of tunnels with Kjeld on his heels. "When I return to Aeramere with Lady Creslyn in this condition, there's a very good chance her brothers will want to kill me."

Kjeld stared at him.

Drake jerked his head toward the entrance of the lair. "*Now*, General."

Kjeld nodded once and bolted down the path to ready their belongings.

Usually, the odds were always in Drake's favor. But it never hurt to have backup, just in case. Besides, he was quite certain he could handle Lord Solarius on his own, and definitely the two younger ones, assuming they'd already returned to House Celestine from their seafaring travels. Lord Ariesian, however, could end his life.

CHAPTER NINE

here was a pull inside Creslyn's chest. A calling. A glimmer of recognition, like an invisible thread binding her through the stars, gently tugging, urging her to waken from her slumber. A presence hovered nearby, as familiar to her as the beating of her own heart, full of wishes and starlight.

Caelian.

Creslyn's eyes fluttered open to find gossamer panels of pale gold and soft blush falling around her on both sides. A stained glass ceiling arched overhead, depicting a small sunburst set against the background of the night sky, surrounded by dozens of eight-pointed stars. Crystal prisms were suspended in the air by a touch of magic, reflecting iridescent rainbows throughout the space. There was warmth here. Love, here. And something darker, like a shadow that lingered just out of reach before vanishing under the threat of the sun.

She was in Aeramere.

She was home.

Rolling her head to the side, she saw Caelian perched on the edge of the bed, humming to herself as she toyed with the ribbons of her violet gown. Her gaze flicked over to Creslyn, and she startled, nearly falling off.

"Cres!"

There was a blur of movement and Creslyn blinked as her twin sister's face came into view.

"Oh, Cres. I've missed you." Caelian knelt at the bedside, cupping Creslyn's cheeks with both hands, a sheen of tears glazed her eyes. "We've been so worried."

"We?" Creslyn croaked, wincing. She sounded as though she'd swallowed a wadded-up piece of parchment and had attempted to wash it down with sand.

"Yes." A masculine voice that caused her heart to shiver sounded from the far corner of the room. "We."

Creslyn glanced over to see Drake rising from a pale blue chair. He was a harsh contrast in the most magnificent of ways, darkness and leather against the shimmer and silk of her bedroom. He moved with lethal grace, his steps silent as the fractured beams of sunlight pouring in through the window shifted, avoiding the looming shadows.

Only when he approached the other side of her bed did she see the blotch of discolored skin beneath his eye where a bruise had formed, and there was a rather nasty looking cut along his bottom lip.

She eased herself up and Caelian helped her, gently fluffing the pillows behind her so that she could sit. But Creslyn's gaze remained focused on Drake.

She frowned, taking in his busted lip and beaten face. "You're hurt."

Caelian snickered, plopping back down on the edge of the bed and smoothing the satin layers of her ruffled skirts. "You missed quite the altercation while you were resting. Solarius was not at all pleased to find you unconscious when Queen Elowyn lifted the Veil for your arrival."

Of course her brother and his stars-cursed temper would

riot. He was incredibly protective of his younger siblings. Still, she didn't think Solarius would actually be foolish enough to start a fight with Drake. Much less live to tell the tale.

She peered up at him. "He *hit* you?"

Drake smirked, running a thumb along his swollen bottom lip. "I let him."

"I knew you were holding back." Caelian folded her hands in her lap, her sapphire eyes twinkling with mischief. "No one could possibly take on the shadow prince and survive."

"Cae," Creslyn admonished her sister's lack of decorum, but Drake merely shrugged, adjusting his sleeves.

"She's not wrong." He rolled the cuffs, revealing tanned forearms laced with sinewy muscle.

Creslyn clamped her mouth shut. It would be entirely too improper to drool at the sight of a man's arms, but she couldn't help but wonder what the rest of him looked like beneath all the leather and chains.

"I'll go let everyone know you're awake. But don't worry, I will be sure no one bothers you. Just come downstairs for dinner after you do whatever it is you're going to do." Caelian shoved off the bed and winked, her teasing laughter echoing in her wake.

Drake lowered himself next to Creslyn, taking Caelian's place, the sheer ribbons of fabric from the canopy framing him. He took her hand, sweeping his fingers back and forth along the underside of her wrist.

She flipped her hand, interlocking their fingers together. A sigh escaped her. "You left me."

He lifted their joined hands, placing a kiss along each knuckle. "Never again."

"I was chained in iron, pushed off a cliff, and left for dead." She watched him, the dark, mysterious depths of his evergreen eyes remained intent on her. "You were right. I am not at all ready nor prepared to face the dangers of Brackroth."

"You will not be harmed by the king's guards again." Drake's tone was icy, hardened by a sharp edge of finality.

Creslyn searched the chiseled planes of his face, absorbing the hard lines, seeking out the cruel vengeance lurking within the depths of his reserved exterior. There was the faintest glimmer in his eyes, a bewitching sort of sparkle that belied the truth of his ruthless nature. But she saw past it, she saw through his controlled composure to the shadows of his soul. They called to her, summoning her curiosity, awakening that tiny sliver of darkness that shifted between the sunshine and rainbows. His shadows filled her with a twisted thrill, a desire to be tainted by him, to watch him burn the world for her.

"You killed them." The words fell from her in a raspy whisper. "For me."

Drake said nothing, the callus of his fingers scraping over the smooth flesh of her hand as studied her.

Creslyn leaned backward, her head coming to rest against the mound of pillows behind her. The strap of the silky nightgown she wore slid from her shoulder and she pulled it back up, but not before Drake tracked the movement.

"How many?" she asked, and his eyes flicked back to her face.

"However many were standing in the throne room at the time of my wrath."

"Only three took me." She tilted her head, arching one brow. "How many?"

His jaw ticked. "Twenty-three."

Twenty-three.

He'd killed twenty-three men for her.

Drake reached out, sliding one hand around her neck. His touch was cool, a possessive caress. "And I would do it again."

Of that, she had no doubt.

He eased back, and she shoved the velvet comforter away, climbing out of the bed. She padded across the glossy hardwood floor toward the bathing suite, to scrub her face and brush her teeth. Drake joined her, leaning against the door frame with his arms crossed. Always silent. Always watching. At least this time she could actually see him, and she much preferred it this way, as opposed to him waiting in the shadows. A bolt of pleasure shot through her, even though he was merely observing her perform the most mundane of tasks.

"I will keep you safe, *sjellhert*. You needn't worry." He followed her as she moved from the bathing suite to her wardrobe to choose a gown for dinner. "And from now on, even when I must leave Brackroth, you will be by my side. Though I will do whatever is necessary to spare you from the horrors of my deeds."

"Spare me?" Creslyn whirled on him. "You are the Shadowblade Assassin, you think I don't know what it is you do? You do not have to hide that part of yourself from me, Drake. I see you as you are."

"And how exactly is that, *kearsta?*" he asked, his Northernlands accent thickening on each word. "As a cold-blooded killer? As a monster with no heart? As a man whose soul has been blackened by greed and power?"

"Yes. All of those things." She turned back toward her wardrobe, selecting a gown of heavy gold silk to combat the chill in the air. Autumn was settling into Aeramere, but at least here, the warmth of the sun made the cooler temperatures somewhat tolerable. Knowing he watched her, she slowly shimmied out of her nightgown, letting it pool in a puddle of silvery blue at her feet. "You are a killer. A monster. A man whose soul is darker than the pitch of night. However..."

Creslyn stepped into the gown, pulling the sheer beaded sleeves over her arms. "I know you can *feel*. I know you feel for *me*. The depth of those feelings, however, remain unknown."

She tugged up the bodice, the dazzling gemstones reflecting the fading hues of the setting sun, and he moved closer, coming to stand before her. "But I do not need words of adoration to know that you desire me. That you care for me. The proof of your devotion is evidenced by the twenty-three men you slayed on my behalf. All I ask for, all I want, is your heart. I do not care if it is tarnished, if it has been blackened by lack of morality, if it is nothing more than stone and ash."

Creslyn stared up at him towering above her. His intimidating stature loomed over her, and she'd almost forgotten that without a pair of proper heels, her head barely met his shoulders in height. She rose up on her toes, capturing his cheek with one hand.

"I want your heart, Drake." She brushed her lips lightly across his, a thrum of power humming between them. Then she whispered, "And I want to wear it like a crown."

Again, he remained quiet.

To most, his silence would be a sign of refusal, but to her, it was a promise. A sacrifice, even.

She turned slightly, pulling her long hair over one shoulder, then glanced back up at him. "Will you tie my laces, please?"

There was the sharpest of inhales as he expertly laced up the ribbons of gold adorning her back, and the cool touch of his knuckles grazing her skin as he knotted them into a bow at the base of her spine. When she faced him again, he was holding a black wooden box in his hands.

"I have a gift for you."

His finger unhooked the bronze latch, and her breath caught.

It was entirely too large to contain a ring, but when he lifted the lid, her gaze landed on a sparkling necklace of diamonds cushioned in dark red velvet. And two pairs of earrings.

Creslyn's heart hammered. It constricted against the tight walls of her chest as he lifted the necklace and fastened it around her throat. The collar of gems held her captive, and she touched them lightly with the tips of her fingers, the stunning stones gliding like icicles across her flesh.

Slowly, she reached for the earrings with silver bars, where diamonds tumbled like a tiny waterfall. "These don't have a clasp."

The corner of Drake's mouth lifted in a slow, sensual smile. "They're not for your ears."

Her head snapped up at the realization of his words.

They were for her *breasts.*

She swallowed hard, and a shiver of delight spread across her shoulders and down her back. Unable to break his knowing gaze, she collected the other set, the ones for her ears, and put them on.

Drake closed the lid, setting the box on one of the shelves in her wardrobe. "Those are for later. When I've made you my wife."

Creslyn slipped on a pair of heels, rising to nearly his chin. "And when will that be?"

His hand took its familiar place around her throat, his thumb sliding along the column, lifting her face. "Sooner than you think."

She smiled then, grabbing a fistful of his leather vest, and tugged him toward her. Drake's mouth slashed across hers in a demanding kiss, and all the while, he kept his eyes open. The deep green of them darkened further, shaded by lust. His shadows stirred—she wanted them crawling all over her, exploring every inch of her. He watched her as their tongues tangled, as she took everything he offered. Her blood heated, restless and frenzied. She'd never had anyone kiss her with their eyes open before. It was riveting, a shameless display of power.

Drake's teeth sank into her bottom lip, tugging lightly, and she arched into him. His free hand slid down her satin skirts, capturing her thigh. He dragged her leg up to his hip, dipping her, deepening their kiss.

"Tell me you're mine, *solysa*," he murmured against her mouth. "Only mine."

"I'm yours." She clutched at him, fearful that if she let go, she would tumble into oblivion and never recover. "Only yours."

He broke their kiss, pulling her back upright, and she missed the cool press of him, for now she burned far too hot.

"I never thanked you." She ran her fingers through her hair, then looped one hand through his arm. "For saving me."

"It was not me who saved you." Drake opened the door of her bedroom, leading her out into the hall.

She angled her head, looking up at him. "Who did?"

"Astrylys."

"Who is Astrylys?"

"A dragon."

She stumbled to a stop alongside him. A dragon. The silver one with the radiant sheen and piercing blue eyes. A *dragon* had saved her.

"Will I be able to meet her?" she asked.

"Eventually."

"When?"

"So many questions." The corner of Drake's mouth curved, and he bent down, pressing a kiss to her temple. "Come, let us join your family for dinner. If we take much longer, I have reason to believe Solarius will take our tardiness as a personal offense. And I do not care to fight your brother again, because this time, I will not let him win."

She did not want to think about the pain Drake was capable of inflicting upon her brother. Instead, as they walked the glimmering halls of House Celestine where moonstone stars were embedded into the walls and crescent moons crafted from selenite floated overhead, she redirected her focus to the heavy collar of diamonds hanging from her neck. Heat blossomed through her, so great she could feel the flush staining her chest and cheeks. She was fire, the diamonds were ice, and she longed for nothing more than to be dripping with them, exactly as he'd promised.

Her nipples pebbled, the fabric of her gown rough against the sensitive peaks, and her breasts ached.

Without warning, the frigid cadence of Drake's voice whispered into her mind.

"If you do not cease those thoughts immediately, I will be forced to bury myself so deep inside of you that the diamonds you're wearing will not be the only thing to shatter."

A shiver raked down her spine, and she leaned into him, keeping her voice even when she said, "And what is stopping you from doing such a thing, Your Highness?"

There was a low rumble, and the muscles of his arm tensed beneath her touch. "Only a single, fraying thread of control."

Creslyn had no idea what to expect when that thread of control snapped. But she wanted him. All the shadows. All the darkness. All the sharp, jagged pieces of his heart.

CHAPTER TEN

The dining hall of House Celestine was alive with chatter and soft laughter, except for the moment when Creslyn entered the room on Drake's arm.

Stilted, painful silence befell the space.

Her family was seated at the long, oval table, and every pair of eyes flicked to her. Ariesian was positioned at the head of the table, elbows propped on its smooth surface, fingers interlaced together. A scowl of disapproval marred his brow. Their mother, Trysta, was right beside him, and though she offered a tight-lipped smile, it didn't quite meet her eyes. Her expression was one of calm poise. Creslyn had been absent from Aeramere for less than a month, and her mother had seemed to age greatly in those fleeting weeks. The lines around her eyes were deeper and the skin beneath them was discolored, as though she'd been worn by exhaustion. Strange, considering Trysta never seemed to tire.

Sitting next to Trysta, however, was a new face. Well, not entirely new. Creslyn had known Narissa Seaborne for a number of years, though it was more than a little shocking to see her as an invited guest, and seated right by Solarius, no less.

As far as Creslyn knew, and could remember, Sol and Narissa absolutely despised one another. Caelian beamed from her place beside Solarius, and across from them were Sarelle, Novalise, and Lord Asher Firebane. Creslyn was even more surprised to find that Kjeld had apparently joined them as well. She didn't realize Drake's general had made the trip, but she was more than pleased to have him accompany them.

Only her other two brothers, Tovian and Nyxian, were missing. She supposed they were both still off sailing on some seafaring adventure with the High Prince from Faeven.

Creslyn stepped forward and Kjeld stood immediately, bowing slightly. Asher did the same, followed by a disgruntled Solarius, and a fuming Ariesian. Neither of her brothers smiled upon her, instead their frosty glares were pinpointed on Drake. If she could pluck the invisible daggers they were throwing at him out of the air, she would do so. The tension between the lot was practically suffocating.

Drake led her to the opposite end of the table from Ariesian and pulled out the chair for her. She sat next to Novalise, while Drake took the empty seat beside his general. Servants filed into the dining hall, filling the table with a spread of platters, and the delectable scents flowing through the room caused Creslyn's stomach to grumble. She couldn't remember the last time she ate, she was practically famished. There were dishes overflowing with spiced meat and stewed vegetables, bowls of fruit and baskets of freshly baked rolls coated in garlic and butter. More importantly, however, was the tiered tray showcasing an assortment of desserts. Including Creslyn's favorite, star-shaped chocolates filled with popping candies that crackled across her tongue.

Gradually, everyone began filling their plates, but hostility hung in the air like the humidity from summer's hottest day. Sticky and positively miserable.

Refusing to suffer through more menacing stares and

uncomfortable silence, Creslyn plucked her glass of starberry wine from the table and nodded toward Kjeld.

"You clean up quite nicely, general." She smiled at him from over the rim of her glass. Half of his rustic gold hair was pulled into a knot, bound by a leather strap. He wore a shirt the color of bronze that strained across his muscular frame, as though it was perhaps a bit too small, and the insignia of a dragon was carved into the collar of his leather vest. The top button was undone, revealing the swirls of inky runes crawling up his neck. "I almost didn't recognize you without your riding leathers."

Though his blue eyes twinkled, he shifted in the high-back chair, as though he'd never been more on edge. "You flatter me, my lady. I'm glad to see you're back in good spirits and health."

Creslyn caught it then, the twinge of remorse in his voice.

She shook her head, speaking softly. "None of that, general."

"Nova," Caelian piped up, her twin easily picking up on the need for more pleasant conversation. "You simply must tell Creslyn all about your wedding plans."

Novalise's face illuminated, her cheeks pinking with the blush of a proper bride. She launched into the details, gushing about how the wedding would take place at twilight beneath the stars. It would be held in the gardens of House Celestine in three days' time, there would be floating lanterns of captured starlight, dozens of miniature cakes from Moonbeams—a darling little bakery in Celestine's city center—and dancing until dawn broke the horizon. As Novalise described the flowers she chose, moonstar orchids with silvery purple petals that only blossomed under starlight, Creslyn couldn't help the twinge of longing pinching between her shoulders.

Her own wedding would be nothing of the sort.

Not that she desired pretty flowers and a star-dusted ceremony, because she most certainly did not, but she couldn't help but wonder if her wedding would possess its own kind of magic.

Eventually, conversation slowly carried on, and when there was the briefest lull, Creslyn didn't let it settle.

She turned her attention to her second oldest brother. "Sol, I was not aware you were courting Lady Narissa."

"Alas, sweet sister, I am not." Solarius flashed her a hard smile, and from the head of the table, Ariesian cleared his throat. Solarius's glare shot to him. "Lady Narissa is my *betrothed.*"

He spoke the word with such spite, he nearly spat it out.

"Oh." Confusion clouded Creslyn's mind. When she left for Brackroth, Solarius had been decidedly single, a bachelor on all counts. Though she knew Solarius and Narissa had a falling out some years ago after a rather brief courtship, she was too young at the time to make sense of it and could no longer remember why. "How lovely for you both."

Again, Drake's voice filled her thoughts. *"Ariesian made the arrangement."*

Creslyn glanced over at him, her brows knitting together in concern. *"But why? They've hated each other for quite some time."*

Drake shrugged, lifting his glass of wine to his lips. *"I would imagine an alliance was far more important than a squabble from their youth."*

Creslyn looked at Lady Narissa Seaborne. She was a fae of House Azurvend with sun-kissed skin and a naturally rosy blush that shimmered on the apples of her cheeks. Her golden hair fell to the middle of her back in waves twisted by the salty tang of sea air, and her eyes were a pale green, like an ocean touched by frost. She wore a gown of turquoise and the bodice was lined with delicate pink pearls. Thin gold bands were on almost every finger, including her thumbs, and a strand of crushed shells hung from her neck. With one hand wrapped around the stem of her wineglass, she looked composed, elegant, and positively raging.

The glass of water in front of her swirled, spiraling and sloshing like a small whirlpool.

Solarius snatched one of her hands, clamping it tightly. He pressed a hasty kiss to her knuckles, his silver hair with black tips falling into his face. "No tidal waves at the dinner table, Rissa love."

The look Narissa sent her brother would have made even the most seasoned of warriors balk.

She looked absolutely cutthroat.

Drake fisted one hand in front of his mouth to disguise his chuckle.

"Creslyn, darling." Trysta waved a hand through the air, bracelets jingling, as she dismissed her son and his furious future bride's subdued quarrel. "How fares life in Brackroth?"

Ariesian slammed one hand onto the table, rattling the dishes.

Creslyn snatched up her wine before it spilled.

"Is that a serious question, Mother?" he demanded, his words clipped.

"It's wonderful, really." Creslyn sipped her wine, attempting to override her brother's anger.

"Aside from the fact that you almost *died*?" Solarius drawled, his silver gaze zeroed in on her before flicking with contempt in Drake's direction.

"Aside from that, yes." She shook off his churlish demeanor. "I was rescued by Astrylys, one of Drake's dragons. Quite exciting, I should think, though I wish I'd been coherent enough to remember it. And Drake killed twenty-three men on my behalf."

Deafening silence befell the room once more. So quiet, she could almost hear the sound of her own heartbeat.

"But other than the drab weather," she continued, as though she hadn't stunned all of them with mention of his violent tendencies, "Brackroth is fine enough."

A beat of measured stillness passed. Then another.

"Stars above," Novalise murmured, and Asher's shoulders began to shake. Then he was laughing fully, shaking his head in disbelief. Novalise smacked him soundly on the back.

"I had no idea my nefarious ways were so amusing to you, kearsta." Drake's crooning voice reached into her mind, and she spared him a glance before pouring herself some more wine.

"On the contrary." She swirled her glass, watching the bubbles dance. *"I find your vengeful nature most provocative."*

"Is that so?"

Something cold slid around her ankle, and Creslyn startled.

"Only a shadow," he whispered. *"You're safe."*

She wasn't entirely certain she would have used the word *safe*, not when that particular shadow slinked beneath her skirts like a phantom hand coasting along her leg and over her knee... then higher still. She clutched her glass of wine, taking a rather large gulp as the shadow hovered at the apex of her thighs. It teased her skin, its touch like ice. Her chest heaved and she squirmed in her seat, but there was nowhere to go. No means of escape. Drake had her trapped, and he wasn't even *looking* at her. He was speaking to Kjeld about one of the dragons.

Creslyn frowned.

He wouldn't dare.

The shadow slid past her undergarments with ease, and she tensed, trembling against the cool touch. Heat bloomed low in her belly as it brushed across her folds before sinking into her. The sensation was both fascinating and terrifying as his power moved within her like a ribbon of velvet. Frozen, she didn't dare move as the shadow swirled, thickening, taking on an all too familiar shape. It stroked her gently, delving deep until she was wet with need. Spasms of pleasure ricocheted through her, and though she attempted to keep her serene expression in check, her legs fell open in a silent plea for more. Drake's shadow pulsed, throbbing, and she planted one hand on the table to keep herself steady, her nails biting into the hardwood.

"Cres?"

Creslyn's gaze shot to her twin. She gripped the stem of her wineglass so tightly she thought it might shatter.

"Are you alright?" Caelian asked. "You seem a little tense."

"Mm. Fine. Completely fine." She thanked the stars her voice didn't waver, but gods, if Drake didn't stop teasing her soon, she would come undone right here, at the table, in front of her entire family.

Creslyn finished her wine, but it wasn't nearly enough to take off the edge. The darkness inside her continued to build, pushing in and out, driving the coldness deeper with every icy thrust. She bit her tongue to keep from crying out, her thighs shaking as the sweet pressure reached the deepest part of her core.

She was close.

Stars above, she was *so* close.

"Your Highness." Ariesian's firm voice cut through the air, and the shadow withdrew, vanishing completely.

Creslyn swallowed her whimper of disappointment.

"My lord?" Drake replied, his tone smooth and unruffled, as though he hadn't almost just brought her to orgasm.

Ariesian stood, adjusting his blue coat so the silver sheen glinted in the low light. "Might I have a word?"

"Of course." Drake pushed back from the table, then he bent toward Creslyn, pressing a kiss to the tip of her pointed ear.

"I'll finish you later, *solysa*," he murmured.

Creslyn shuddered as she watched him follow Ariesian out of the dining hall.

If the Prince of Brackroth held such command over his shadows, there was no telling how capable he was in the bedroom. And if one thing was for certain, Creslyn's imagination never failed her. She spent the rest of dinner daydreaming of how exactly he planned on finishing her.

CHAPTER ELEVEN

rake seated himself in the chair across from Ariesian's desk. The Starstorm lord's study was quiet, save for the crackling of orange flames in the hearth. Shelves of books lined one wall and there was a rather impressive tapestry with shimmering thread depicting a stag leaping into the night sky. Sitting on a three-legged pedestal was a silver statue carved to resemble a hand. Above its open palm and outstretched fingers, an astrolabe floated and whirred, its golden globe encircled by watercolors of turquoise and midnight blue. Gilded constellations swirled around it as an eight-pointed star flanked by two crescent moons hovered over the sphere like a shimmering crystalline orb. Four large windows framed the hearth, and hanging behind Ariesian was a painted portrait of the Starstorm family. His parents stood in the background, surrounded by all eight children.

Curiosity got the best of Drake, and he found his gaze drawn to Creslyn's youthful face. Though her twin, Caelian, was seated next to her in the portrait, there was no mistaking the stark differences between them. For most, the only noticeable distinction was the dusting of constellation-like freckles across

Creslyn's nose and cheeks. But Drake saw more—the slight tilt of her head, as though she'd rather be anywhere else. The distinctive curve of the corner of her mouth, the sort of smile one would offer when they were harboring a secret. The darkness in her sapphire eyes, the ones that seemed to drown him every time he looked into them too closely. They were not the bright and bold blue of Caelian's...no, Creslyn's eyes were full of cunning intrigue, a complexity she kept well hidden beneath the façade of her perfectly angelic exterior.

Wicked little faerie.

Across from him, Ariesian drummed his fingers on the edge of the desk. Its surface was glossy and free from clutter, each piece of parchment had its place in a tidy little stack.

Tension stretched taut between them, a constant strain, a pull of who held more power. Of who would be the first to let go.

"I noticed there is no ring on Creslyn's finger." Ariesian's jaw popped, and his dark brows drew together. "You have not yet made her your wife?"

"I have not," Drake replied evenly, though that would change soon enough.

"Is she not up to your standards?" Ariesian's words were curt. Threatening. He sat forward and steepled his fingers together, the silver of his eyes as hard and as cold as steel.

"Lady Creslyn suits me fine." More than fine, though he highly doubted her brother wanted to hear the sordid details of all the things Drake wanted to do to her. He ran his thumb along his bottom lip, over the abrasive cut left behind by Solarius's fist. "But with all due respect, my lord, marriage rites in Brackroth differ vastly from those in Aeramere."

Ariesian edged back into his seat, shifting uncomfortably. He pressed his lips together, considering. Then finally he asked, "How so?"

"I imagine the fae perform a hand binding ceremony or use

some other magical means to form a union." Drake's brow lifted in question, and Ariesian nodded.

"Correct." He rocked back in his seat, stretching out his legs, and crossing one ankle over the other. "Though it varies with each couple. When two mates are fated and a bond forms between them, such as in the case of Novalise and Asher, when they seal their vows with a kiss, their magic will bind."

"You're saying they will share each other's power?" Drake asked.

Ariesian shook his head. "Not quite. In the instance of mating bonds, the magic must choose one another. It's a joining of sorts, but Asher will not gain the starstorm, and Novalise will not acquire his frostfire. I suppose it's more like a formality, a union of their magic for show and nothing else."

"I see." Drake considered this information. "Then not every fae in Aeramere will ever find a mate?"

"A mate, certainly." Ariesian lifted one finger. "But a mating bond, finding the one who is fated for you, is not always guaranteed. As I said before, the magic must choose, but even then, a fae can deny the bond. Just as such bonds can be broken. Though I've heard it's the most atrocious kind of pain imaginable."

"Indeed." Drake held out his hand, palm up, mimicking the slice of a blade. "In Brackroth, we seal our lives to one another through blood."

Ariesian paled. "What, like blood magic?"

"I wouldn't call it *magic*. More like a ritual. The combination of blood is tradition, it's the joining of two souls." Drake lounged in his chair, his mind drifting to the moment when he would cut his palm and press it against Creslyn's. To the moment their blood would mingle. To the moment when he would have to make a gut-wrenching choice. "Lady Creslyn may think she is ready to be my wife, but she must first accept all of me. Every shadow. Every secret."

The Starstorm lord glowered, the sharp lines of his face highlighted by the rigid flashes of warmth from the hearth. He inhaled, his shoulders rolling back with the same calm fury Drake had witnessed a thousand times before.

"You intend to corrupt her." His accusation was harsh, though not altogether erroneous.

Drake wouldn't ever admit to corrupting Creslyn. It was more like an awakening. Though he kept those thoughts to himself.

He offered a calculated smile instead. "Without the darkness, a star can never shine."

Ariesian slammed his fist on the desk, rattling a small jar of ink. The dark liquid spilled over the side, staining the wooden surface. Power emanated from him, a mighty throng of vast shadows and piercing starlight.

Ah, there was the potent magic of the Lord of House Celestine. The violent tempest he kept so tightly under control.

"And with the exception of her being thrown from a cliff in your absence," Ariesian ground out, "you intend to keep her safe?"

Intend was such a fickle word.

Intentions could always be swayed.

Drake was no such man.

He leaned forward, leveling the lord with a menacing glare. "I will end the life of anyone who attempts to harm her. Creslyn is *mine*."

Ariesian's eyes expanded, the lines of rage set against his forehead easing. "You love her, then?"

"Do we truly love anything?" Drake asked with a hint of amusement. He rolled his wrist, gesturing to nothing and everything at once. "Many have done foolish things in the name of love."

He ignored Ariesian's scoff of arrogance.

"If you're asking if I will shower her with affection, appease her on a daily basis, and write poems in her honor, the answer is no. But if you're asking if I will defend her name, remain faithful only to her, and slay all of her enemies without hesitation, then yes."

Ariesian studied him a moment longer before expelling a gruff breath of frustration. "Fair enough."

"I assume you didn't ask me here to discuss your sister." Drake rested his elbows on the arms of the chair, his boot tapping a slow, measured rhythm against the hardwood floor. "What's on your mind, Lord Starstorm?"

Ariesian ran both hands through his silver hair, but the pieces fell back in front of his face. "I took heed of your advice during Midsummer and formed an alliance with House Azurvend."

"So I noticed," Drake mused, roughing his knuckles along his jaw in an effort to disguise his smirk. "Solarius seems thrilled with the betrothal to the water faerie."

Ariesian grunted in response, rolling his eyes to the beams of dark wood stretching overhead. "He could do far worse. Lady Narissa is amicable, attractive, and more than tolerant of his roguish manners. If anything, she'll help him get over that miserable human who repeatedly ripped his heart out for fun."

"Indeed." This conversation, however, brought up another matter entirely. Drake inclined his head. "I do hope you realize the likeliness of Creslyn and I returning to Aeramere for *every* sibling's wedding is slim."

"Trust me, Your Highness." Ariesian rolled his neck from side to side, his bones cracking slightly during the adjustment. "There are many days I wish I were able to leave myself."

Drake nodded, understanding the need for escape. "Has the situation changed?"

"You tell me."

He reached under the table and pulled out a decanter of whiskey and two glasses. Filling them both to the rim with the golden liquid, he passed one to Drake. He lifted his cup and Drake followed suit, the glasses clinking before they each downed the alcohol in one gulp. Ariesian twirled his empty glass in his hand, eyeing it as though it might refill on its own.

"The last time you were here, you offered House Celestine protection in exchange for the hand of one of my sisters. To which you were granted Creslyn." He set the glass down. "However, the details you provided were incredibly vague. So much so that it made me wonder what the Prince of Brackroth could stand to gain from such a contract, unless something was in it for him."

Drake lifted one shoulder, then let it fall. "Yet you agreed."

"I have seven siblings whose wellbeing falls to me. Four of whom are female, which makes it much more…agonizing. Thanks to you and Lord Firebane, I'm down to two. That being said," he paused, tugging at the collar of his shirt, "I am not one to take a threat lightly. Rumors have been circulating about Prince Aspen's involvement in rebellions to the north near House Galefell. If the prospect of any such perils endangers my house and my family, I will stop at nothing to end it. Even if it comes from within Aeramere."

Drake stared at him from across the desk, his gaze unwavering. "I said the threat could come from *within*, I never specified Aeramere."

Ariesian straightened. "What are you insinuating, my lord?"

"Only that you should be mindful of the company you keep." There was only so much Drake could reveal, only so much he *knew*, for dark magic came with its own kind of binding rules. He could not alter the fates' design no more than he could weave the pattern of destiny. "Three very specific constellations aligned for Lady Novalise during Midsummer, did they not? The Great Stag, Aedes the Fae Warrior, and Vespira the Druid. If I recall, Novalise mentioned them being a sign of war. Which is curious, considering the stars never lie."

Almost instantly, Ariesian sobered. His expression morphed into one of practiced composure, entirely unreadable. "You truly think a war is coming to Aeramere?"

"I think it's already here." With that, Drake rose from his seat and straightened his vest. "Though the grass remains still, the serpent does not rest."

Ariesian stood, nodding once. "I will remain vigilant."

"As you should."

Drake left Ariesian's study then, his footfalls silent as he walked the sparkling starlit halls of House Celestine.

His mind drifted to thoughts of war. It was always such a grueling process. The battles and bloodshed. The terrors, the screams, the wading through mountains of bodies and burying the dead. Aeramere was pristine, a picture-perfect realm of magic and beauty. It would be a shame if it crumbled under the brutality of battle. Drake was prepared for such an instance though, and he would not hesitate to offer Creslyn's family the support he promised when the need ever arose.

He continued his slow, leisurely pace through the majestic house, but something prodded his thoughts, begging him to take notice. To acknowledge. It was something Ariesian said to him earlier on in their conversation.

Unless something was in it for him.

Of course something was in it for him.

He chose to strike an accord with the Starstorm family for a *reason*. Granted, Creslyn had been a wondrous surprise, but now, he planned on marrying her for a *reason*.

Drake wanted her blood.

CHAPTER TWELVE

Creslyn sat on her bed after dinner, the gown she wore spilling around her like liquid gold. She'd kicked off her heels and drew her knees up to her chest, twisting the tiny gold beads on her sleeves between her fingers. Caelian was sprawled on her back on the opposite end, skirts of violet and cobalt silk fanned out around her, with her legs hanging over the edge. Her tumble of silver hair with the same pale pink, icy blue, and lavender strands as Creslyn's was unbound and loose. She rolled onto her side, propping her elbow on the bed and cradling the side of her face with one hand.

"Did he really kill all those men for you?" Caelian asked, the blue of her eyes glinting with curiosity in the warm glow of firelight.

Earlier, they'd been discussing Novalise and Asher's wedding, and both of them had agreed it was bound to be absolutely lovely. That conversation had quickly descended into speculation about Solarius's engagement to Lady Narissa. Creslyn pitied Solarius for not being able to choose his own wife, but on that topic, Caelian did not agree. Her sympathy lay with Lady Narissa for being tied down to their brother for the rest of her days. Now, it seemed, Caelian was keen to learn about Creslyn's relationship with Drake.

"Yes." Creslyn nodded, suppressing a shiver. "He did."

As much as she loved her twin, and as much as they talked about everything together, Creslyn suddenly found herself not wanting to share this part of her life. It wasn't as though she didn't trust her sister implicitly, because she did, but revealing her feelings for Drake and the intricacies of their relationship seemed wrong. Like a betrayal of his trust and a stain upon her character. If she opened up too freely to Caelian, there was a terrible chance she'd be unable to stop the admissions longing to pour from her.

Like the fact she found his lack of morals alluring. That a thrill of sinful delight enraptured her each time he wrapped his hand around her throat. That she was painfully aware of being dangerously close to making the mistake of falling in love with him.

All things she worried her family would possibly disown her for admitting.

"How terrifying," Caelian murmured, then her lips twitched, and she grinned. "Though you must admit, it's also strangely exhilarating."

Creslyn forced a light laugh, hoping her twin couldn't see through the carefully crafted wall of glass she'd constructed around herself. It was too close to shattering. "Indeed. It is much more impressive than a bouquet of flowers."

Or even jewelry.

"Could you imagine finding yourself a male willing to go to such extremes for you?" Caelian sighed, already dreaming up all the ways she might find a male ready to make such a noble, if not bloody, sacrifice for her.

"In my defense," Creslyn countered smoothly, "I was almost killed."

Caelian lurched upright and grabbed her hand, squeezing tightly.

"I am so sorry, that's not at all how I meant for it to sound. Not in the least. I am quite glad you survived." She swung her legs over the edge of the bed and scooted closer. "I could not bear to live without you, Cres. It's hard enough being separated from one another, what with you now living in Brackroth. I miss you tremendously."

"I miss you, too." Creslyn leaned forward, pressing her forehead against her twin's. The bond they shared stretched, as though being pulled taut across a great chasm. "Daily."

It was not a lie, nor was it the total truth. She missed Caelian often, and the rest of her family, but there was a distinctive divide taking place. One that pulled her toward the cold, rocky shores of Brackroth, and away from the glimmering mountains of Celestine. Aeramere would always be her home, but Brackroth was the beginning of her new life. Where she would become more than simply a Starstorm of House Celestine. She would be a princess, perhaps even a queen, and the world would know her name.

"You know," Caelian drawled, oblivious to Creslyn's innermost thoughts. "That general is quite handsome, in a rugged, beastly kind of way."

Creslyn's brow quirked.

She never would've imagined Caelian found Kjeld attractive. He didn't seem like her type at all. She was usually courted by males who were suave and smooth-shaven. They were proper lords of noble birth, charismatic and debatably charming, but in comparison to General Kjeld Holtstrom, they were simply...*less*.

"Perhaps he's in need of some company." Caelian's eyes sparked, her mouth twisting into a coy smile. "I could come stay with you in Brackroth for a season or two."

"No!"

Caelian startled, her lashes fluttering back at Creslyn's sudden outburst.

"That is," Creslyn amended with haste, "I would love for you to come visit me, truly I would, but…"

"But it's not safe," Caelian interjected, and the excitement illuminating the planes of her face dulled.

"Exactly." Creslyn sat up from the mound of pillows and crossed her legs beneath her. "And I would never forgive myself if anything happened to you. Once Brackroth is no longer dangerous, I promise you can stay for as long as you like. And I'll come back to visit as often as I can."

Caelian blew out a disappointed breath, her shoulders dropping.

"Maybe," Creslyn ventured, drawing the word out, "I can convince Drake to let Kjeld come with us."

"That, *kearsta*, might take quite a bit of convincing." A smooth, frosty voice coasted through the room, sending chills down Creslyn's back, and Caelian yelped.

Drake emerged from the shadows, not bothering with the door. He leaned against the post of the bed, his arms folded across his broad chest. A hint of a smile danced along the corner of his mouth and though Creslyn was rather accustomed to him seemingly appearing out of thin air, Caelian gaped, her mouth hanging open in surprise.

Creslyn nudged her elbow into her sister's ribs, and she snapped her mouth shut.

"But if it would please you, Lady Caelian," he drawled, angling his head so a few wisps of dark hair fell across his handsome face. "I will see if General Holtstrom would be willing to take you on a dragon ride tomorrow."

Caelian swayed, and for one fleeting, panicked moment, Creslyn thought she might faint.

"Dragon?" Caelian repeated the word quietly, wrenching the

fabric of her skirt between her fingers until it wrinkled. "He would take me for a ride on the back of a *dragon?*"

The slant of dwindling sunlight cut through the space, but Drake remained standing in a swath of darkness, untouched by the hazy beams of gold. "I had planned on taking Creslyn out anyway, I don't see why you and General Holtstrom shouldn't join us."

"I would love nothing more!" Caelian leapt off the bed and spun in a circle to face Creslyn, her crinkled skirts twirling around her. "A dragon, Cres! I'm going to ride on a *dragon!*"

She drew up short in front of Drake, as though suddenly remembering she was in the presence of a prince. Caelian gathered her hair over one shoulder, weaving the ends through her fingers.

"Forgive me, Your Highness." She lowered herself into a proper curtsy. "I would be honored to accompany you, my sister, and General Holtstrom tomorrow."

Drake's face remained impassive, but there was the briefest glint of amusement in his eyes. "It would be an honor to have you, Lady Caelian."

"And, um…" she hesitated, tilting her head with feigned innocence. "Is your general available? What I mean to ask, is he quite…single?"

"Cae," Creslyn admonished, stunned by her sister's boldness.

But Drake smirked and said, "Quite."

Caelian curtsied once more, then bounded out the door with the slightest spring in her step. As soon as the door closed behind her, shadows spilled from Drake, devouring the last shreds of sunlight until the only glow that remained was from the wavering flames of the hearth.

Trepidation skittered across Creslyn's shoulders, and she shivered, glancing over at him. "Drake?"

A dark look passed over his face, the deep evergreen of his

eyes frosting over like a forest succumbing to winter's first breath. "You and I have unfinished business, *solysa*."

Anticipation sent waves of heat spreading through her, the sensation settling low in her belly, and left her aching for his touch. But she peered up at him from where she sat on the bed and settled back against the mountain of pillows behind her. "Do we?"

He moved toward her with slow, deliberate movements. "You know damn well we do."

She tapped her finger against her chin, then pursed her lips. "I do not seem to recall this supposed *business*."

"Really?" His brows arched. "Perhaps I need to remind you."

Drake pulled a dagger from the sheath on his thigh, lifting it so the blade flashed hues of silver and gold in the low light.

Dread curled inside her, cooling the earlier warmth.

His gaze flicked from the blade to her. "Do you trust me?"

Creslyn could only nod, any smart retort she might have been holding onto died on the tip of her tongue.

"Then lie back," he ordered gently. "And be very, *very* still."

She obeyed, stretching her legs out and sinking down into the mattress of her bed. Sweat dampened her palms as she curled them into the blankets, clenching her fists until they ached.

Drake grabbed the hem of her skirt, draping the fine fabric over the curved edge of the dagger. It moved with ease, slicing through the satin as though it was nothing more than air. Thin strips of gold fluttered around her as the gown unraveled, cool air assaulting her bare legs. He inched the blade higher, using his finger as a guide so his knuckle gently scraped along her stomach and between the valley of her breasts. Creslyn sucked in a harsh breath as the bodice split apart, sending beads scattering like golden raindrops.

She was entirely nude, splayed open for him, and everywhere his eyes lingered, she burned. She melted beneath the intensity of his gaze, soft and pliable, like wet clay ready to be shaped by his hands.

He flipped the dagger into the air, catching it by the blade. In one swift movement, he pulled his arm back and launched it, the sharp tip sinking into the wooden frame of her door with a resounding thud.

Creslyn stared at the dagger sticking out of her bedroom door, but her shock dissolved quickly as Drake bent over her, pressing kisses to her abdomen and hips. His hand disappeared between her legs, his thumb lazily stroking her clit, sliding up and down until she thought she would die of sheer ecstasy. His mouth coasted toward her breasts, the warm air of his breath causing her skin to prickle in heightened awareness. Sucking one nipple into his mouth, his teeth sank into the soft flesh, then he laved the pain away with the comfort of his tongue. His thumb continued working her, and she arched off the bed, panting, pleading for more.

"Tell me, *kearsta*," he purred against her skin. "Do you remember now?"

"Yes." The word escaped her in a strangled gasp.

He peeled the remnants of the dress away, snatched her by the waist, then dragged her onto his lap as he sat down on the edge of the bed. His calloused palms skated up her thighs, dipping behind her to grip her backside. Jerking her forward, he rocked her against him, grinding her against his stiff erection. She clutched his shoulders as he repeated the motion, the abrasive leather of his pants rubbing the tender area between her legs. Desire blossomed inside her, filling her with urgency, with a desperate need to touch him.

"Wait," she breathed, and Drake stilled, his dark eyes keenly focused on her.

Carefully, Creslyn reached for the top button of his vest, and he snared her wrist.

She drew back, unable to keep the hurt from being written all over her face. "You don't want me to see you?"

A moment passed between them. His sharp inhale. Her weighted exhale.

"I am not without flaws." Slowly, he unbuttoned his vest and removed it. He yanked up his black shirt, pulling the hem from the waistband of his pants. "Everything you see on the outside is exactly as I am on the inside. Scarred. Ruined. Permanently marked by the choices I've made in my life."

She watched as he gradually removed his shirt, revealing the expanse of his beautifully carved body. His abdomen was solid, chiseled to perfection, and a long, jagged white scar marred the left side. There were other, smaller scars along his arms, and his shoulders were covered in inky runes. Despite the lack of sunlight in Brackroth, his skin was surprisingly tan, as though at one point he might have worshiped the sun. Her gaze slid to the mirror on the opposite wall, where his back was on full display. Dragon wings were tattooed there, wide and intricately detailed, and beneath them was a pile of skulls.

Creslyn sucked in a breath.

"One for each life I've taken." He captured her wrists again, placed her palms flat against his chest. "Now, you see me as I am. A monster."

"My monster," she whispered, tracing the runes with the tips of her fingers. He let her explore his arms and shoulders, hissing slightly when her touch feathered the rigid planes of his stomach. She hooked one finger into the waistband of his pants and tugged.

A low chuckle rumbled through his chest. "Wicked little faerie."

Creslyn scooted herself closer, her breath catching when her breasts finally met the cool press of his skin. She wound her arms around his neck, her hair falling around them like a curtain of silk, and then she kissed him.

His lips were cool, his tongue was hot.

Drake fisted a hand in her hair, angling her head, deepening their kiss. His mouth slashed across hers, his teeth scraping and nipping her bottom lip. Power thrummed between them, a steady hum of the dark and profane, of the shimmering and beautiful. She rocked her hips forward, longing for that feel of friction, silently asking for more.

He lifted her then, cradling her as he laid her back upon the bed, situating himself between her legs. She squirmed against the soft linens, attempting to pull him down on top of her. All she wanted was the feel of his hard body covering hers. Impatience fired through her when he sat back and reached toward her nightstand instead. Propping herself up on her elbows, she glanced over, her lashes fluttering back when he flipped open the small wooden box.

Creslyn's mouth ran dry. She swallowed, swiping her tongue across her lips as he lifted the silver bars dangling with diamonds. "I thought you said I had to be your wife first."

"I decided I couldn't wait." Drake rolled them in his palm, his dark eyes drifting from her mouth to her neck, then lower still. Her nipples hardened beneath the intensity of his gaze, and strands of shadows unfurled around him like the onset of nightfall. "Be still, *solysa.*"

Creslyn did as she was instructed, but her heart was suddenly beating far too fast, and it had absolutely nothing to do with the heat of lust coursing through her. His shadows crept toward her, brushing across her skin like feathers. They teased her thighs, flitted across her stomach, encircled her breasts. She bit back a sigh as her own magic was summoned, drawn to the surface, lured by the darkness. Prisms of rainbows and fractures of sunlight spilled from her, colliding with ribbons of midnight in a sensual dance.

"Will it hurt?" she asked, squeezing her eyes shut as an endless well of power poured from her and through her.

"Only for a moment."

An icy shadow slid down her stomach, then further to her core, pushing deep inside her. It filled her, gliding in and out with slow, languid movements. Her body pulsed with need, and she curled her fingers into the sheets, biting back a moan of pleasure. She imagined it was Drake instead, pictured him shoving into her with practiced, painstaking thrusts. She wanted him buried inside of her, she wanted him to be the one to bring her to release.

"Your imagination is most flattering, *kearsta*." Drake's words coasted over her like decadent velvet, and then there was a sharp pinch of pain in her left breast, as though a needle had pierced through her flesh.

Creslyn cried out but his magic stole her breath, pushing inside of her, delving deep so the twinge of discomfort was subdued by the rush of ecstasy. There was another pinch, on the right breast this time, and tears sprang to her eyes. She was torn between the waves of desire pushing her toward the edge of madness and the throbbing ache of her hardened nipples.

"Drake..." she whimpered, his name falling from her lips like a broken prayer.

"Don't worry." He palmed her thighs, and her eyes flew open, just in time to see him lowering his mouth to her. "I'll take all the pain away."

His tongue replaced the shadow and Creslyn was flying.

She soared, chasing after the high only he could give her. He devoured her, the glide of his tongue teasing and tormenting her until she came completely undone. He licked and sucked, tasting her, his fingers fanning out across her lower stomach to hold her in place as she squirmed and arched. Her legs fell open in an offering while his remained fused to her center. She was falling from the heavens, blazing through the night sky like a shooting star, and only Drake could catch her.

Release left her gasping and quaking.

Creslyn shuddered, trembling as he moved beside her, then pressed a kiss to the column of her neck.

"Look at you," he murmured, dragging one finger through her wet folds. "So beautiful. Sparkling and glistening."

Her chest rose and fell, and she struggled to glance down. But then she saw them—the silver bars piercing her nipples, her breasts dripping with diamonds.

She rolled over to face him, and he draped an arm around her, his hand settling at the small of her back. She placed her hand upon his bare chest, right over his heart. Its constant, even beat steadied her, soothed her. He propped himself up on one arm and she memorized the sharp line of his jaw, the fullness of his mouth, the slight cleft of his chin. She rarely saw him smile, at least, she'd never seen a *real* one. She wondered if he had dimples, if his grin illuminated his face. Pieces of long, dark hair slanted across his forehead, and she longed to smooth them away.

But she didn't dare move, worried that he might deem such a gesture too intimate, and then he would pull away from her. He would retreat to the shadows.

She would offer him something else instead. "Please don't make me wait."

Surprise registered in the depths of his eyes before it shuttered away. "For what?"

"For you."

The corner of his mouth quirked, his telltale smirk. Never an actual smile. "You would so quickly give your heart to an assassin?"

"No. To you." She laid her head on the pillow next to him but held his gaze. She would have to be strong, she could not look away from the eyes that seemed to stare into her soul. "Not your reputation. Not your title. Only to you."

"And if I break it?" he asked, his face devoid of any emotion.

"Then I shall break yours as well." She lifted her chin,

removing her hand from his chest. "And trust it will hurt you far worse than anything you could ever do to me."

Drake watched her a moment longer but said nothing. He adjusted the blankets, gathering the plush fabric and draping it over her naked body. For one terrible moment, she thought he might leave, but then he curled her into him, his arm locking tightly around her. She breathed in the scent of him—cold mountains, and pine, and the hint of winter's first frost.

"There's darkness inside of you, Creslyn Starstorm."

She peered up at him. "There's light inside of you, Drake Kalstrand."

He kissed her temple. "Perhaps."

Creslyn knew she was capable of withstanding many things. But if Drake broke her heart, she would find a way to cut him just as deeply. She simply hoped she would have enough strength to survive it.

CHAPTER THIRTEEN

Drake stood in the courtyard of House Celestine where slants of sunlight stretched across gray stone, the golden beams wavering slightly anytime they neared the shadows encompassing him. The entire space seemed illuminated with stardust, though he imagined that had more to do with the glittering specks shimmering in the stone walls and less to do with actual magic. It wasn't an ideal location for training. He'd done so once before, and Novalise had very nearly taken his Shadowblade to the heart. He'd chosen to meet Kjeld here, away from most of the Starstorm siblings who seemed to be everywhere at once, and out of sight of the matriarch, who was entirely too devious for her own good.

Trysta Starstorm was a force of reckoning, and Drake held no doubts that she was not nearly as benevolent as she let everyone believe.

The sound of boots clicking softly against stone echoed up the tall walls of the courtyard, and Drake turned to find Kjeld striding toward him.

His general looked...ill at ease. Kjeld was disheveled, his gruff appearance a far cry from the polished gentleman of last night. He roughed a hand over his face, trying to mask his bleary eyes. He'd twisted half of his blond hair back away from his face in a haphazard knot and some of the smaller strands were loosely, albeit messily, braided. There was a line of consternation that permanently creased his brow, and his eyes were shifty, as though he was constantly looking over his shoulder. Like he half-expected someone to jump out and attack him at any moment. Kjeld closed the distance between them, straightening his leather vest, and adjusting the folded cuffs of his sleeves.

He cleared his throat and rolled his shoulders back. "You wished to see me?"

"I did." Drake eyed him coolly, silently debating whether or not he should question his general and the edge of restless apprehension he balanced upon. "Is something wrong, General?"

Kjeld inhaled deeply and his shoulders dropped, his posture settled into a more relaxed stance. He stood with his legs apart, his hands tucked behind his back, while his alert gaze scanned the courtyard. "Nothing I can't handle, Your Highness."

A cool autumn breeze whistled through the courtyard, ruffling the leaves of some of the trees. A single branch bowed, then snapped back into place, and Kjeld nearly jumped out of his skin.

Drake arched a brow.

His general didn't reach for his sword, nor did he draw his dagger. But Kjeld was *startled*. It was most unusual, considering he feared practically nothing. Yet something...or someone...had frayed every last one of his nerves.

Drake ran his knuckles along his jaw, amused by the entire ordeal. "You're certain nothing is wrong, Kjeld? You seem rather anxious."

"Not anxious, Your Highness." Kjeld swung around, glancing back behind him. "Just cautious."

"Hm." It was also a rare occasion when his general and only confidant was bold enough to lie to him. Apparently, today was one of those days. "Very well, there are a few issues we need to discuss."

Drake moved about the courtyard, avoiding the bench positioned beneath the tree whose branches looked as though they were weeping. "First, I have spoken to Lord Ariesian on the matter, but my concern for the safety of House Celestine has not eased. It appears as though he did not take Lady Novalise's star reading seriously. With that being said, upon our return to Brackroth, I will need to prepare a journey to the Fenmire Bogs."

At the mere mention of the bogs, Kjeld visibly recoiled. He blinked twice, shoving a few loose strands of hair from his face. A new sort of tension rolled off him now, his large frame growing rigid with the strain of hostility.

"The Fenmire Bogs? Where the Runes of Callievan escaped to during King Marius's years of terror?"

"Correct."

Years ago, Marius fancied himself in love with Zaleria, a witch of the Runes of Callievan, an ancient coven with a lineage that predated most realms. Every witch alive could trace their bloodlines back to the Runes. Marius, the fool he was, thought he could seduce her and, in doing so, garner the favor of her magical spells and charms. But Zaleria was temperamental and jealous, and she did not care to be tossed to the side when Marius found a new object of his desires. His blatant infidelity left her seething with unfathomable rage, and when she refused to accept his apology, he ordered every last witch of the Runes to be slain. Many were burned at the stake—sometimes Drake could still smell the stench of burnt hair and charred flesh—but others were kept as pets, tortured and abused by Marius's guards.

Those who could escape his wrath did so by seeking refuge in the bogs.

Drake had no idea how many had survived, but Marius's revenge was one of many deplorable acts. Proof he could tolerate no one with more power than himself. If it was up to Marius, he would rid Brackroth, and every other realm, of magic for good.

"There is a powerful hag dwelling among the witches." Drake plucked one of the slender amber leaves from the tree, crumpling it between his fingers. "I need to speak with her."

Kjeld's brows pinched together. "A hag and a witch are not the same thing?"

"Shocking, I know. But no, they are not the same. At least, not in Fenmire. The hags are neither good nor evil. They remain neutral in most contests, though their intentions can be swayed if the offer is enticing enough. A bit chaotic, if you will." He turned to face Kjeld, shifting them further into the shadows to obscure the light and muffle the sounds of their voices. "Witches, on the other hand, are often less fickle in their alignment. In turn, they are much more difficult to influence."

Kjeld blew out a breath, rocking back on his heels. "I see. So, this hag…"

He lifted one hand, a quiet gesture for more information.

"This particular hag is not only a conduit of the sight, but she also creates an incredibly valuable gemstone called the *virdis lepatite*." Drake needed that gem more than he needed air to breathe.

"I recall you mentioning it before." Kjeld nodded in understanding. Another line formed across his brow, and he scraped his teeth along his bottom lip, where they snagged on the scar marring his mouth. "You witnessed it being used in the Faeven War."

"I saw the horrors it can bestow upon a realm, yes." He'd seen it used to control an entire horde of dark fae, watched as those hideous creatures of the night poured out from a void cut from the innermost circles of the Sluagh. Nightmares had been unleashed upon Faeven, and he had never seen anything more appalling in all his years.

Wariness crept into Kjeld's eyes, their vivid blue frosting over with caution. "And you *intend* to seek out this gemstone?"

That wasn't Kjeld's real question, of course. But Drake understood the underlying suspicion, the careful wording, all the same.

He had no intentions of using the *virdis lepatite* for his own gain.

"I *intend* to destroy it. And the hag." Drake folded his arms across his chest, his gaze flicking to where the blues of the sky were blurring into shades of crimson and gold. "I know the Runes of Callievan will not hand over the stone or the hag unless they are offered a rather significant benefit. Which is why I intend to give them the one thing they crave among all else—Marius's head on a stake."

If Kjeld was at all surprised by Drake's declaration, he concealed it well. Shifting his weight from one foot to the other, his gaze darted to the stone ground at their feet before finally focusing hard on Drake's face. "And what of Lady Creslyn?"

"My wife will be traveling with me."

Kjeld's mouth fell open, but he recovered quickly and snapped it shut. "Wife?"

He spoke the word as though it was foreign and unfamiliar.

Drake held his composure, keeping his face lacking any expression. His deal with Ariesian was not just parchment, ink, and blood. It was his written word. "That's the other thing I wanted to discuss."

Kjeld stared at him.

"I'm marrying Creslyn tonight, at the Moonfall Peaks." Drake reached out and clamped Kjeld's shoulder. "I want you to perform the ceremony."

"And…she's agreed?"

"She will." Drake's hand cut through the air, silencing his general. "I know what you're going to ask next, and the answer is, I don't know. I won't know until her blood mixes with mine."

Kjeld dipped his head in acknowledgement, the burdening weight of the unknown hanging between them.

An image of Zaleria, the witch who'd left Marius in a state of madness, appeared in Drake's mind. Her velvety voice flitted through his thoughts, her twisted riddle ever-present yet always just out of reach.

FORCED *to kill by the hand of a king,*
  Cursed in this life with a fate unseen.
  Bound to wield a blade of shadow,
  Break your oath on ground most hallow.
  Seek your freedom in the blood of stars,
  Sacrifice your heart, your soul, your scars.
  Son of rites, son of death,
  You are darkness, her final breath.

HE'D SPENT years trying to untangle the web of Zaleria's words, to make sense of her witchy, muddled divination. There were a few things he knew for certain. Marius was the hand of the king, and it was Drake who had been cursed. His own lust for power had bound him to wield the Shadowblade, and he imagined the oath he must break had something to do with the blood magic tying him to Marius. As far as sacrifices went, he'd surrendered his heart and soul long ago…his scars were another matter entirely. Rites and death meant very little to him, he did not fear his end. But the other pieces of Zaleria's spoken puzzle were falling into place.

Seek your freedom in the blood of stars.

Creslyn's blood could be the key to undoing the curse cast upon him. Not once had he come across anyone with celestial magic in their veins until Marius had sent him to Aeramere to learn more about Queen Elowyn. It was then he'd been approached by Lord Asher Firebane—the fire fae had wanted Drake to end his father's life. And it was then he'd met Lord Ariesian Starstorm, who just so happened to have four eligible sisters, and Drake set his own plan into motion.

Unearth the queen's secrets.

Form an alliance with Lord Ariesian.

Then wed one of his sisters in a blood rite in order to release himself from the curse. It had taken nearly two years to accomplish, and now he was mere hours away from knowing if binding himself to Creslyn through blood would free him from the monster lurking beneath his skin.

Of course, there was that bothersome last line that disturbed him more than all the rest…*you are darkness, her final breath.*

He'd refused to read too much into it, knowing there was a chance he would ultimately despise the outcome.

Drake shook away the troubling thought.

"Ready the dragons," he ordered Kjeld, who still appeared more than a little wary. "We're taking the ladies on a ride tonight."

"Ladies?" he choked out, his eyes widening. "As in, more than one?"

"Yes. Lady Creslyn and Lady Caelian. I can't very well marry Creslyn and not invite her twin sister to the ceremony." Drake paused, observing the way tiny beads of sweat dampened Kjeld's brow. The way he scraped his thumbs over his fisted hands in trepidation. "Is there a problem, General Holtstrom?"

"No problem, Your Highness." Kjeld's shoulders tensed, and he swept forward in a curt bow. "Just never imagined you'd be so full of fucking surprises."

Drake chuckled as the realization slowly slipped into place.

Kjeld wasn't riddled with anxiety or paranoia. He was *nervous.*

As Kjeld stalked away toward the opposite side of the courtyard that would lead to the gardens, Drake couldn't help but wonder if Kjeld's jumpy state had less to do with being in Aeramere and more to do with one Lady Caelian Starstorm.

For as long as Drake had known him, he'd rarely seen Kjeld fall into any kind of romantic relationships. There was the occasional courtesan or barmaid, but Kjeld was far too focused on the dragons and their riders to pay the necessary attention to any woman of interest. Then again, he'd never witnessed his general quite so flustered in the company of a female faerie before. Perhaps he'd taken a liking to her.

Drake spun on his heel to follow in Kjeld's wake, then stopped in his tracks.

Awareness fired through him, a prickle of warning that caused the hairs along the back of his neck to stand. He turned slowly to find Lord Solarius leaning against the entrance of the courtyard, the silver of his eyes frozen over like the most northern mountains in Brackroth. The star lord was propped against a rich blue pillar, his demeanor casual with his arms crossed and one ankle kicked over the other. But loathing hardened every line on his face, and his magic swam with hostility.

"Marrying my sister tonight, are you?" Lord Solarius asked, his voice seething with indignation.

Drake said nothing.

Lord Solarius shoved off the pillar and strolled toward him.

Rage billowed around him in violent waves. "Going to taint her soul that quickly?"

At that quip, Drake's composure pulled taut. "Her soul is already tainted, you're just too blind to see it."

Creslyn's brother lunged forward, and Drake's shadows unleashed, a warning to stand down.

"Mind yourself, Lord Solarius." Drake flicked his wrists, adjusting the cuffs of his sleeves. "I would hate for there to be a funeral right before a wedding."

The star fae grit his teeth, baring them so the slightly sharp canines were on full display.

"If you hurt her," he warned, lifting one hand and curling it into a tight fist. "I'll kill you."

The corner of Drake's mouth curved. "I would expect nothing less."

There was no doubt Lord Solarius would make a most valiant attempt. But he would not survive it.

Lord Solarius left then, muttering a stream of vile curses under his breath, and for a moment longer, Drake remained rooted in place.

Something was off.

He felt...discontent. Bothered. As though he'd misplaced something, yet he couldn't quite figure out what was annoying him, why he felt lacking. An emptiness had seized him from the inside, like he'd been pierced by the blade of a weapon that was tearing him open. Ripping him so the heated ache spread through his chest.

Drake sucked in a sharp, painful breath as understanding prodded the back of his mind.

Fuck.

He *missed* her.

CHAPTER FOURTEEN

Creslyn spent most of the morning and afternoon with Caelian in Celestine's bustling city center. They strolled arm in arm, browsing dazzling window displays filled with crystal moon catchers and bottles of perfume that shimmered like starlight. When their stomachs growled in unison, they stopped into Moonbeams, an adorable bakery with tiers of sweets, and chose from a selection of decadent desserts. Creslyn opted for a sugared sunrise cupcake. It had been ages since she had one and they simply didn't exist in Brackroth, while Caelian picked her favorite, starberry cheesecake. They flitted between shops, admiring gowns of silk and velvet, sifting through assortments of teas and chocolates, all the while on the hunt for the perfect wedding gift for Novalise and Asher.

Finally, after much deliberation, they settled on a crystal sphere filled with a drop of magic from each of them. A rainbow from Creslyn and falling stars from Caelian. The magic swirled together in the sphere, an illustrious blend of iridescent starlight that formed an image of Novalise and Asher in each other's arms as bursts of frostfire and starfire sparked around them. The shopkeeper packaged the beautiful crystal sphere, wrapping it in folds of tissue and tinsel, and once it was ready, the sisters made their way back home.

Already the sun was drifting across the early autumn sky, its warmth near fleeting, barely enough to ease the chill of the new season.

Creslyn knew Drake had promised to take them on a dragon ride, so she returned to her room to change out of her day dress into something more suitable, only to find a gown laid over her bed with a folded piece of parchment placed on top of it.

Scripted in fine lettering with black ink were the words *"wear the diamonds."*

Her heart thumped wildly as she inched closer, and her breath hitched in the back of her throat. The resplendent dress was unlike anything she'd ever seen before. Sunbeams spilled in through the far window, reflecting dozens of tiny rainbows throughout the room. Diamonds of every shape and size covered every inch of the gown, the clusters of them forming an array of constellations. The sleeves were long and fell off the shoulders, the bodice cut dangerously low, and there was a detailed slit up one side where the sparkling gemstones exploded like shooting stars. Navy blue silk lined the underside of the gown, and when Creslyn lifted it from the bed, it felt as though she was holding a thousand stars and the entirety of the night sky in her hands.

She slipped it on, fastening the sheer laces as best she could, and turned to admire herself in the mirror. The wind had blown her hair loose from its plait, so she raked her fingers through the waves, leaving the strands to fall around her. Her cheeks were already pink from walking around the city's square, so she dabbed a plum-colored cream from a pot of paint onto her lips. She rummaged through her drawers of jewelry, selecting the matching diamond collar necklace and earrings. The cold press of the stones against her skin sent a chill of excitement pebbling down her spine.

Again, her pulse skittered out of control, and her palms grew damp.

She was going to be married.

Tonight.

Shadows lengthened along the walls, obscuring the dwindling shards of light as twilight mingled with the fading sun.

Creslyn shifted to face them, her nerves settling as she breathed in his scent. "Drake?"

"Yes, *sjellhert?*" He stepped from the darkness, and her knees wobbled at the sight of him.

Drake was clad in his usual black attire, yet it was different this time. Sharper. More elaborate. He wore a sleek black shirt with the collar popped, and a longer overcoat of onyx that was lined with threads of silver. Dragon wings were stitched onto the shoulders, his pants were trim, accentuating his finely cut physique, and his boots were polished. He wore no gloves, revealing the small slashes of scars across his knuckles and the signet ring that reminded her of Svartos. Drake stood before her looking as though he encompassed the whole of the night, as though he'd absorbed every shred of light.

Pieces of dark hair fell loose from the knot at the back of his head, framing his handsome face, and the rest of the silky strands hung just above his shoulders. But it was his eyes that entranced her, that left her feeling as though he could see through her, to the depths of her soul. Their deep evergreen shade sucked her in, like she was wandering through a forbidden forest, drawn to the endless lure of enticement.

Her mouth had gone dry, words fled her.

By all counts, she should be accustomed to carrying on a conversation, but when he looked at her like *that*, like she was the whole of his universe, she couldn't remember how to speak.

"You are illustrious, *kearsta.*" He held out his hand and she accepted, allowing him to draw her into the darkness. "What need do I have for air? You steal away my every breath."

Drake molded her against him, pulling her close.

The shadows magnified, cool as they coasted along her skin. His magic enveloped her as the world melded into disoriented shades of gray. She clung to him, weaving her arms around his neck while they stole through glimpses of darkness. The shadow world was mesmerizing, an assault on the senses. Sounds were disoriented, movement was slow and weighted. It was like being swept away into a realm where she ceased to exist, where the world simply carried on without her. Further they ventured, slipping through the rest of the house unnoticed, then deeper into the gardens, past flowering arches and whispering fountains. Until finally, the ledge of the mountain came into view, along with two dragons. Svartos's black scales gleamed like moonlit obsidian, while the other had the coloring of violent storm clouds—menacing slate and moody gray.

Drake's shadows dissolved, and he stepped from the disguise of magic, bringing her with him.

Creslyn gripped his arm for support, her blood hummed, and her thoughts spun. If she could live with him between the shadows, between worlds, where it was only the two of them and no one else, she would.

"Be careful what you wish for," he murmured, bending down toward her so the warmth of his breath drifted past her cheek. "For anything that is given, the shadow realm takes."

Creslyn glanced up at him sharply, a frown tugging at her lips. She intended to ask what he meant by such a cautionary statement, but then Kjeld and Caelian were walking toward them.

"Cres," Caelian breathed, her eyes widening at the sight of her twin. "That dress…it's…it's magnificent."

A flush spread up Creslyn's neck, bleeding into her cheeks. "Thank you."

"General Holtstrom was just introducing me to the dragons." Caelian gestured behind them to where Svartos and the other dragon sat low to the ground, shifty and restless, as though they couldn't wait to stretch their majestic wings. "You likely already know Svartos, and this one is Odryss, General Holtstrom's dragon."

Kjeld tugged on the collar of his deep green shirt, loosening it. "I've told you already, Lady Caelian, you may call me Kjeld."

Caelian's sapphire gaze flicked to Kjeld, and she dipped her head, the tips of her pointed ears turning the faintest shade of pink. "Yes, I remember. But if you continue to call me Lady Caelian, then it seems only fair I should address you by your title as well."

Creslyn laughed, then almost snorted, and immediately covered her mouth.

"I am so sorry." Her apology came out muffled behind her hand, and she found Drake watching her, a glint of amusement in his eyes. "It's just General Holt—that is, Kjeld and I had almost this exact same conversation a few days ago."

Kjeld's scarred mouth twitched. "Indeed we did, my lady."

Then he held out his hand to Caelian. "Are you ready for your first dragon ride?"

She hesitated before accepting his hand. "Y-yes."

"Wonderful. Up you go then." He snatched her by the waist, and she squealed as Kjeld hoisted her into the seat on his dragon's back. In one swift movement, he hefted himself up behind her and took the reins.

Drake lifted Creslyn with ease onto Svartos, his movements fluid as he took his place behind her, curling her into him with one arm. With her legs hanging over one side, she twisted slightly to face him. He lifted a brow, his lips curving into a slow, sensual smile. Then he nodded once.

"*Vaeja*," Creslyn called softly, and Svartos rose at her command.

Wings stretched wide and claws scraped into the earth as the dragons clambered toward the edge of the cliff. Svartos kicked up fallen rocks and debris, the trees trembled in his wake, and Creslyn clutched onto Drake's arm as the dragon launched himself off the cliff face.

Then they were soaring.

Caelian's screech was pinched with terror, then followed by a bubble of laughter as Kjeld guided his dragon to glide alongside them. Creslyn glanced over at the two of them—where Caelian was positively glowing, Kjeld looked more than a little uncomfortable. He had one arm locked snuggly around Caelian's waist, as though he thoroughly expected her to fall off and tumble out of the sky.

Creslyn leaned against Drake's broad chest, her head resting just beneath his shoulder. She always forgot how much taller he was, how he seemed to constantly tower over her, even when sitting. He kissed the top of her head, steering Svartos higher through the clouds that floated past them like spun pink candy made of cotton. They flew past a number of carriages pulled by the Eponians, but the winged stallions were no match for the speed of dragon flight. Higher they went, over the jeweled forest of Emberspire, until the wondrous structure of House Galefell graced the horizon, its numerous balconies and open-air walkways crowned in violet and silver from the rise of twilight. Low-lying pillowy clouds always floated around it, drifting lazily around its base, as a flight of Eponians coasted between ivory pillars.

Eventually, they circled back around, and nightfall slowly descended upon them. Tendrils of silvery blue clouds unfurled across the heavens and stars winked against a backdrop of ink. The sharp rise of the Moonfall Peaks glowed in the wash of moonlight, and the dragons coasted downward, landing upon one of the steep mountain ledges. Here, the air was cold and the wind sent a chill through Creslyn that rattled her bones. But the stars...oh, she gazed up at them, lost herself to their vastness.

The constellations danced, their archaic power twinkling like drops of liquid silver against a canvas of indigo.

"Are you ready, *kearsta?*" Drake asked as Svartos landed.

She glanced up at him. "For what?"

Drake scooped her into his arms and abandoned his seat on the dragon's back, setting her gently upon the ground. His hand curved around her neck where the diamonds hugged her skin, as his thumb stroked the hollow of her throat. "To marry me."

"Here?" She twirled once, her gown clinking quietly like faerie bells.

"Yes." His hand slid to her bare shoulder, then fell away. "Right here. Right now."

Kjeld and Caelian joined them at the cliff's edge. Caelian's breath misted before her and she curled into her velvet cloak, but her eyes were alight with elation. Kjeld, on the other hand, looked more somber than Creslyn would have expected.

Doubt prodded at the back of her mind.

Perhaps he did not deem her worthy of marrying his prince after all.

"My lady." Kjeld bowed and when he straightened, his expression had softened slightly. She imagined it was often difficult for someone of his fierceness to not always look brash and intimidating. "The marriage customs in Brackroth are not the same as they are in Aeramere. We don't bind hands with ribbons or magic. Instead, we bind through blood."

"Blood," Creslyn repeated, her voice coming out as more of a squeak. She swallowed hard, pushing through the discomfort of such a notion, and stole a glance at her twin.

Caelian shifted on her feet, a line of concern furrowed her usually smooth brow, and her lips were pinched in displeasure.

Creslyn blew out a low breath and found Drake watching her. He pinned her with a gaze of provocation, a silent challenge. Waiting to see if she would stand her ground and remain true to her word or flee.

"It's an ancient tradition dating back hundreds of years," Kjeld explained, attempting to paint a picture in her mind. "When the bride and groom would join together through blood. A promise to one another. An eternal oath. It's a small slice across the palm, nothing to fear."

Creslyn's attention snapped to him, and she lifted her chin. "I am not afraid."

Kjeld smiled, but it was off. Perhaps even forced. It was a smile of disbelief. "Now, it might be a bit different with the two of you. Mostly because you're fae and Prince Drake is…"

Drake cleared his throat.

Kjeld ducked his head. "Well, His Highness is something else entirely."

"Meaning?" Creslyn pressed, his vague explanation needled at her rising wall of doubt.

"Meaning that once your blood fuses between the palms, there is a possibility it could alter things." Kjeld tugged on his shirt. It was far too constricting for a man of his size anyway, but Creslyn surmised it was not the fabric that bothered him. But his conscience. And everything he did not say. "There is a chance Prince Drake could gain some of your magic, and you may gain some of his."

Creslyn fiddled with the diamonds on her gown. She'd known from the beginning that marrying Drake was a risk, but this…this binding of blood and swapping of magic was not something she'd been prepared to handle. In fact, Drake had failed to mention anything of the sort to her at all. She lifted her gaze to him, and she caught the play of shadows crawling up one half of him while the rest was showered in moonlight, and she realized that not once had he spoken. He hadn't uttered a single word since this entire conversation began. He'd simply stood there, staring at her. Expressionless. Not a trace of emotion to be found.

She wanted to march right up to him and slap that impassive look of absolute nothingness right off his face.

Drake's brow lifted, and his mouth quirked.

Creslyn fumed. She was ready to open a verbal assault upon him when Caelian's voice cut through her frenzied thoughts.

"So, what exactly are you saying, General Holtstrom?" She planted both of her hands on her hips and glared up at him. "That the fusion of Creslyn and Prince Drake's blood could somehow *change* their magic? It could alter their current abilities?"

Kjeld stepped back, putting a safe stretch of distance between them. He shoved some fallen strands of golden hair back from his face, then winced, as though preparing for impact. "Like calls to like, my lady."

"But my sister is not shadows and darkness. She is beauty and light." Caelian shook her head, wrapping her arms around herself, and her velvet skirts of lavender billowed in the stiff breeze. She looked up at the wide, glittering night sky as though searching for an answer. But she could not read the stars, and she twisted her hands together, wrought with worry. Her shoulders slumped and tugged at her bottom lip with her teeth. When she spoke again, her voice was hollow. "Creslyn is the opposite of the shadow prince in every way imaginable."

"Are sunlight and shadow not two halves of the same whole?" Kjeld countered, finding his bearing against her storm of emotions. He reached out, cautiously placing his hand on her shoulder in an effort to soothe her frustration. "One cannot exist without the other, Lady Caelian. They are like magnets, two forces that are drawn to one another, much as the waves always return to the shore."

Caelian heaved a dramatic sigh, then faced her sister. "Are you certain you want to do this? To give up a piece of yourself to him?"

Creslyn found those frosty green eyes of Drake's and held them. This time, he was her captive.

"I already have."

Drake bowed his head.

Therein lay the truth of the matter.

Marrying Drake would not come without great sacrifice. She may not have been ready to admit it to herself, but Creslyn knew she would be giving up more than her home. She would be surrendering part of her soul. Yet despite it all, she still wanted him. She saw the good in him, that sliver of compassion, of tolerance, that wavering thread of his lost humanity. Even if she was the only one who would ever see it, who would ever feel it, that would be enough for her.

Caelian stepped back and Kjeld came forward, positioning himself between Creslyn and Drake as they faced one another. He pulled a small dagger from his pocket, the hilt wrapped in leather and the blade engraved with a dragon. Giving a small nod of encouragement, Kjeld reached for her. "Your hand, my lady."

Creslyn placed her hand, palm up, in his and while the beating of her heart seemed to thunder in her own ears, her breathing remained calm. Even and deep. She looked over at him. "What do I say?"

Kjeld's slight grin widened, and a kind of warmth filled his face despite the chill. "Whatever is in your heart."

Creslyn stared into the face of the man who would own her heart, whether she wanted him to or not.

"I take you, Drake Kalstrand, to be mine. From now until my last breath." She winced as the tip of the blade cut into her flesh, and then suddenly Drake was there, his arm latching around her waist, holding her so close she could hear the steady beating of his heart. He bent low, pressed his forehead to hers, and she melted into him. He held her until their chests rose and fell in unison, until the pain in her hand was all but forgotten. "You are the darkness to my light, the shadow to my sun, the night sky to my stars. I see you as you are, I accept you, scars and all. For as long as Vespira remains in the sky with her staff casting over us, my soul is yours."

Drake edged back, just enough to give Kjeld his hand, but he didn't spare the blade a glance. His eyes were only for her.

"Creslyn Starstorm. *Sjellhert.* You are the first blossom of spring, the seduction of summer's warmth, the chill of autumn's breath, and winter's final kiss." Again, Drake lowered his head, his lips barely a breath from her own, but he held her gaze, those eyes of his keeping her rooted in strength. When he spoke again, his accent was thick and tainted by an emotion she didn't recognize. "You are my compass. My star in the northern sky. You are my whispering tides, and I shall only ever worship your shores. You are the aurora in the midnight hour, that which beckons my soul."

Tears flooded Creslyn's vision, wrenched from some part of her she'd kept safely locked away for so long. Her bottom lip quivered, and she did not look away from him when she blinked and let them fall.

Drake's finger grazed the apple of her cheek, catching a single tear. Then he took her hand in his and laced their fingers together, so the sting in her palm met the cool touch of his own.

"Drown your secrets, your sorrows, in me."

With his other hand, he cupped the back of her neck and kissed her.

But this kiss, it was not like the others. It was imbued with magic, with wild energy, with fearless power. Crushing shadows and brilliant beams of sunlight collided in a chaotic whirlwind of midnight rainbows. His mouth slashed across hers, his tongue sought hers, exploring. Searching. Drake carved open that shadowy piece of her lurking deep within her heart. He exposed her. Left her raw. Bare. Creslyn tangled her fingers in his hair and pushed back, unleashing a storm of shattered prisms and sunbeams into the endless swath of his darkness. She dragged her teeth along his bottom lip, desperate for more, for all he was willing to give. Creslyn took. She claimed. And in that moment, Drake splintered.

He released her roughly, jerking backward, away from her, as he broke their kiss.

Creslyn gasped and Drake's chest heaved, the intense burning of his eyes setting fire to her skin. A fiery emotion flared to life, and he banked it, shuttering it away before she could focus on it for too long.

"General Holtstrom, take Lady Caelian home." Drake's gaze flicked to his bloodied open palm, then back to Creslyn's face. "I need to have a word with my *wife*."

"Wait, that's it?" Caelian asked, disappointment weighing down her tone as Kjeld guided her back to where Odryss waited. "It was a rather brief ceremony. Does something else happen next?"

"Trust me, my lady," Kjeld grunted and plucked her off the ground before depositing her onto Odryss's back. "You don't want to be around for what happens next."

At Kjeld's bold words, Creslyn's cheeks flushed as a blush crawled up her neck and spread across her chest. But when she looked back at Drake, his brows were drawn, his eyes were illuminated with a feral ferocity, and she could've sworn he growled.

Her new husband did not look like he wanted to rip off her clothing.

Drake looked positively *murderous*.

CHAPTER FIFTEEN

*D*rake tore his gaze away from Creslyn and stared at his open palm. The slice across his hand had sealed, leaving behind a shimmery thread binding the flesh together. He looked back at her, at the way she seemed to radiate starlight. His gaze skimmed her flushed cheeks, her lips still swollen from his kiss. Snaring her wrist, he flipped her hand over to inspect her palm. Where the blade cut her skin, there was now a scar of inky shadows.

His grip tightened, and he stared down at her.

"What the fuck was that?" he demanded.

Creslyn's brow crinkled, and she yanked her arm from his grasp. "What are you talking about?"

No, no, she wouldn't get away from him so easily. He grabbed her throat, careful not to be *too* harsh, and hauled her against him. Her lashes fluttered back, and her piercing blue eyes widened, shock flaring through them.

She reached up, wrapping her small fingers around his forearm in an attempt to shove him away. "I didn't do anything."

"Do not play games with me, *solysa*." He ran his thumb up the column of her throat, angling her face so she was forced to look him in the eyes. She set her jaw, and a line of mistrust marked her forehead. "You did something with your magic. I felt it."

"No, you were the one whose magic was scouring me, devouring me." Creslyn swallowed against his hold on her throat and her pulse fluttered. But she refused to cower. "Your shadows carved into me. They splayed me open. It felt like you were going to tear apart my soul."

"I was searching—" Drake cut himself off. He didn't need to explain himself to her, he didn't need to explain himself to anyone. He was the fucking Shadowblade Assassin. He did not obey the rules, he *made* them. Not that he would expect her to understand.

"Searching?" Creslyn repeated the word, her nails digging through his shirt into his skin. "For what?"

Drake let go of her. It was too late to reverse what had already been done. "Nothing."

"Do not ignore me, Drake." Creslyn grabbed for him, clutching the lapel of his coat. "What were you searching for? And what makes you think you can find whatever it is inside of me?"

Damn this female and her questions.

He didn't know how to explain it, didn't know how to convey that he'd made a grave mistake. He'd been rash in his decision. Time and again he'd replayed Zaleria's words in his mind, and he thought for certain the blood of stars implied that Creslyn, or any Starstorm female for that matter, would be the one to release him of his curse.

But he'd been wrong.

So wrong.

And now, there was no way to reverse it.

"Your sister, Novalise, controls the archaic starstorm." Drake pulled the tie loose from the knot at the back of his head in an effort to alleviate the dull ache throbbing through his temples, through his veins. His hair fell in front of his face, whipping wildly in the frigid wind, and he shoved it back with one hand. "The starstorm is a rare magic once thought to be dormant in—"

"I know what it is," Creslyn snapped, her temper rising. Sparks of sunlight and crackling rainbows erupted around her. "It is *my* bloodline. I do not need a history lesson."

Drake glared, his frustration with her incensed by her feisty attitude. "I was searching to see if you possessed some similar form of magic."

He ground the words out, hating that he was finding it increasingly difficult to shrug off her demands.

"Why?" she insisted, moving closer. Her infuriated gaze studied every plane of his face, lingering on his mouth before drifting back to meet his eyes. "To expose me?"

"No."

"To use me?"

"Yes."

The truth spilled from him before he could stop it, and Creslyn reared back as though he'd struck her.

An uncomfortable sensation wormed its way into the charred remains of his heart. It was unfamiliar and strange, this wrenching feeling that seized his gut and dug its claws deep into the uncharted, murky waters of his emotions.

Regret.

The word sliced through his thoughts like a blade forged from fire, its blazing heat burning him, scorching his anger.

He'd hurt her, wounded her, and it was the crushing weight of remorse bearing down upon his chest that made it seem near impossible to refill his lungs with air.

Drake moved slowly, and with painstaking awareness, he reached out to take her by the waist, pulling her flush against him. He half expected her to slap him again, or to spin away and avoid him, but she did neither of those things. Creslyn allowed him to wrap his arms around her, to draw her body into him, until the diamonds of her gown prodded against the fabric of his shirt. He wanted the gems to slash him, wanted them to pierce his skin. He would've taken great pleasure in the pain those sparkling rocks inflicted if it meant he could erase the hurt in Creslyn's eyes.

Her chest rose and fell against his own, their breaths coming in languid, measured intervals.

When she looked up at him, there was a sheen of tears in her sapphire eyes, and Drake's tarnished heart was skewered by another overwhelming emotion he couldn't quite name.

"I have been alive a long time, *kearsta*. I have seen realms rise and fall, I have witnessed magic disappear from history as though it never even existed." His voice was strained, the words more difficult to form each time he spoke. There was only so much he could say, only so much he could tell her, before he could no longer say anything at all. "I have seen the prophecies of fate, and I know what's to come. A piece of that ancient, slumbering magic lives inside of you and your siblings. But it is different with each soul carrying it. It's evolved over the course of its dormancy."

Confusion clouded Creslyn's face, it stole across her eyes like a wayward mist rolling in from Brackroth's coast.

"What do ancient prophecies have to do with anything?" she asked, sniffling. "You just admitted you want to use me for my magic."

A teardrop clung to her lashes.

Drake didn't dare reach up to swipe it away.

Let them fall, he told himself. *Let her realize the mistake she made for thinking she could find any good in me.*

Of course she cared nothing for prophecies or archaic magic. She was living in the moment they shared together, the one he'd ruined.

Drake rolled his neck from side to side, heaving a sigh as the bones cracked. "I only sought your magic because I thought it might break the curse cast upon me. The one fueling me with rage and bloodlust."

"Then why didn't you ask?" Creslyn shouted, her power so explosive that Drake lost his footing and stumbled backward. "You could have asked me, Drake. I would have given my magic to you freely! Without hesitation! All you had to do was *ask*."

Brilliant beams of sunlight whipped around her in a frenzy as streaks of shattered rainbows lifted her hair from her shoulders. The silver strands kissed by soft hues of pink, blue, and purple fanned out like ribbons of silk, amplifying her beauty. She held her ground as magic poured from her, ignited by her vexation. The mountain peaks trembled, the night sky shuddered, and the stars bowed before her sunlit storm. She was the heavenly wrath, the radiant darkness.

Drake's shadows expanded, craving her. He yearned for her, longed to be her undoing.

He stared at the magnificent creature before him, this celestial faerie who was both an alluring dream and his darkest fantasy.

Rarely did he ever ask for anything. He simply took what he wanted, consequences be damned. He'd grown accustomed to watching others cringe in his presence, to ignoring their pleas for mercy, to sneering with malice when they tried to hide or barter anything of worth in exchange for their lives. Yet here was Creslyn, the purest form of splendor, telling him he was wrong.

He did not have to take from her.

She would give, because she—*no.*

An agonizing pang speared through his corrupted heart once more.

Drake shook his head. Whatever it was they felt for one another—misplaced trust, tortuous lust, mutual respect—none of it mattered anymore.

Because when Creslyn's blood melded with his own, when

her magic collided with his, the joining bonded them somehow. And not in the sense of merely husband and wife. No, this ran far deeper than such a surface connection.

This was a binding of souls.

Creslyn had claimed him as her mate, and in doing so, unknowingly shackled herself to the curse he'd been so desperate to break.

She would belong to him for all eternity. Her heart. Her soul. The scar marking her hand.

Sacrifice your heart, your soul, your scars.

Drake shook the unbidden thought from his mind and dropped to his knees before her, capturing her hands. Gradually, her sunstorm ebbed, before fading completely.

"Forgive me, *sjlellhert.*" He lowered his head, dusting the faintest of kisses across her fingertips. "Next time, I will ask."

She scoffed. "If you are so lucky."

It appeared as though her fire had not yet dimmed.

Creslyn peered down at him, her lips pressed into a firm line. She arched one brow. "I might make you beg."

Arousal shot through him like a bolt of lightning, and his cock thickened at her brazen tone. He fucking loved that mouth of hers.

Drake stood, sliding his hands around her backside and squeezed, jerking her against him so she could feel the effect her words had on him. "And how shall I make it up to you?"

A wicked gleam sparked in the depths of Creslyn's eyes, but she did not smile. "By taking me to bed."

BY THE TIME they returned to House Celestine, Drake could not keep his hands off Creslyn. They crawled through the shadows together, her arms woven around his neck as his tongue meshed with hers. She tasted of every forbidden pleasure, of frozen winter nights and mist-fallen mornings. She enveloped him, and he lost himself to her scent of sweetened citrus and tantalizing fresh rain. Her body hummed against him, fizzling with tension and anticipation, a symphony only he could hear. Creslyn arched into him, grinding her hips against his throbbing erection, and he was half tempted to take her on the glittering staircase of the main hall for everyone to see.

"A room," she murmured against his mouth, dragging her leg up his waist while the chilling shadows engulfed them. "Find a room."

"Which one?" he growled, stealing her down a darkened hall, the sconces of faerie fire snuffing out as they passed.

"Any one." She was breathless now, and the pounding of her heart caused his blood to roar. "Just pick one."

Drake moved between the patches of darkness, slinking into the nearest room where dwindling embers clung to the last of their life in the hearth. He scanned their surroundings, taking in the walls of shelves lined with books, the glass ceiling revealing the expanse of the night sky, and the plush sofa set before the dying fire. A library in House Celestine wasn't exactly ideal when it came to finally being able to bury himself inside Creslyn, but he could no longer combat his excessive desire for her.

He had every intention of lowering her to the sofa, but then she sank those ever so slightly sharp teeth of hers into his throat, biting gently, and his control snapped.

"Fucking gods, Creslyn." He gritted the words out through a clenched jaw and spun into the darkness, pinning her against a wall of books. Grabbing her dress, he ignored the sting of diamonds cutting into his hands and yanked it up. He shoved it out of the way, molding his rough palms to the back of her thighs, and lifted her so she was forced to wrap her legs around his waist. Lowering his head, he trailed his tongue along the underside of her jaw to the lobe of her ear where jewels sparkled. "Bite me again and I will return the favor."

Creslyn leaned back against the shelves, angling her face up to him, and caressed the points of her teeth with her tongue. "Are you threatening me, husband?"

His fingers dug into her soft flesh. "That's a promise, wife. And I never break my word."

He bent down to kiss that vicious little smirk off her face, but right before his lips found hers, she turned her head to the side, denying him.

Drake chuckled, a deep rumbling sound. Despite Creslyn's unyielding countenance, he didn't miss the way she shivered in his arms. He let his teeth scrape just below her ear, applying the lightest sting of pressure. Her quick inhale was more of a gasp, and he smiled against her skin.

"Are you going to let me kiss you now?" he asked, easing back to drink in her flushed beauty.

"That depends," she replied, her voice tart.

He adjusted her in his hold, ensuring she felt the rub of his hardened shaft against her core. Her lips parted but no sound came out.

"On what?" he purred.

"On if you beg." Creslyn lowered her lashes and when she looked up at him again, her eyes were jaded with lust and twinkling with power. "Beg for me, Drake."

"Gladly, *solysa*."

He carefully set her down and peeled off his coat, then tossed it aside. One by one, he undid the buttons of his collared shirt, holding back a grin as she tracked his every movement, her heated gaze lingering on his body while he took his time letting it fall to the floor behind them. Reaching around to her back, he pulled on the laces of her gown, loosening them so the stones tinkled softly like bells. The dress slid from her, pooling around her feet like a pile of broken glass. Her body was a temple, all luscious curves and smooth satin, waiting to be worshiped. The diamonds hanging from her perked nipples sparkled, but he would pay them plenty of attention soon enough. He nudged her discarded dress to the side with his boot, then set his shadows upon her.

Creslyn's startled gasp filled him with satisfaction as tendrils of darkness swirled around her wrists, anchoring her arms above her head.

"Let me kiss you until your knees soften and your legs tremble." He leaned in, pressing his mouth to the base of her throat, then trailed his lips to the valley of her breasts. Running his hands from her hips to her ribs, he swirled his tongue around each of her nipples. Her head fell back and the noise she made left his cock aching to fill her. "Let me touch you, all of you, until you're wet for me, glistening like the diamonds you love so much."

"Drake…"

His name fell from her lips on a gasp, but it wouldn't be enough. He wanted her to scream for him.

He dropped onto his knees before her, raising her legs so her thighs rested upon his shoulders.

"Please, *sjellhert*. I beg of you." The tempting scent of her arousal slammed into him, and he moved his face closer, wanting just a taste. He flicked his tongue out, swiping along her slick folds. "Let me taste you."

"Yes," she whimpered.

Her consent was all he needed.

Drake delved his tongue into her center, and her cries of pleasure only spurred his hunger for her. He consumed her, committing her taste to his memory. She was an aphrodisiac, an addiction, an avalanche on his senses. Creslyn's moans filled his ears, and she writhed on his shoulders, clenching her thighs and arching her hips against his mouth. His shadows glided over her, thrumming in appreciation as they curled around her neck, holding her firmly in place while she whimpered and moaned.

He gripped his cock through his pants, stroking himself to alleviate the building pressure. If he wasn't careful, he'd lose control completely, and spend himself before he was even able to fill her with his seed.

Creslyn quivered, convulsing as the orgasm tore through her. Drake sucked her clit, his balls tightening, and he groaned into her sweet cunt, unable to wait a moment longer.

He stood abruptly, gathering her limp body into his arms, and carried her over to the sofa. He thought perhaps she might need a minute to recover, to regain her bearing, but she climbed onto his lap and reached for his pants.

Drake snatched her wrist. "I must warn you, *kearsta*. I am not like most men. Nor am I like most males."

She slid off his lap and smiled at him then, mocking. "Are you worried you won't fit?"

"Oh, I'll fit. And you'll take every inch." Drake eased back against the sofa and removed his pants, letting the full length of his cock spring free. The shadows ribbed around his hardened length seemed to pulse in expectation.

Creslyn's mouth fell open, then snapped shut. Her wide-eyed gaze darted to him, then back to his stiff erection.

Drake smirked and stretched out on the sofa, patting his lap. He glanced up at the glass ceiling above them, where the constellations seemed to burn with a fury. Then he pulled her on top of him, cupping her cheek with his hand. "Let me fuck you beneath your precious stars, so they can watch as you're ruined by darkness."

Creslyn heaved a breath, situating herself so her knees fell on either side of his waist. Her hair tumbled around her like an iridescent waterfall, and he tucked some of the fallen strands behind her ear. She grabbed his shoulders with both hands and gingerly lowered herself onto his shaft.

She barely made it an inch before her head rolled back and his name fell from her lips like a prayer.

Drake bit back a grin. "You are incredibly good for my ego, Creslyn."

Her nails bit into his skin in response, scouring his shoulders.

His hands moved to her hips, guiding her lower. "All the way down."

Her breaths came in heavy pants, and she clawed at him. The pain settled in his chest and he reveled in it. He wanted her to mark him, to claim him, just as he would do to her.

Gods, she was so tight. He could feel her stretching to accommodate his size, her slick walls gripping him as he pushed deeper, desperate for more of her.

"Almost there, a little further." He trailed his fingers up her spine, then back down. "Show me how well you're made for me. How perfectly your wet cunt can take my cock."

"The shadows…" Words failed her, and she shook her head violently.

"I'm going to fill you tonight, Creslyn. I'm going to brand you, so the world will know you're mine. Shadows and all."

"Yours." The word rolled off her tongue, and then she sank down onto his full length.

A strangled cry escaped her, and Drake wanted to empty himself into her right then.

Fuck, she was the best mistake he ever made.

"Take me," she whispered into the darkness surrounding them. "Take all of me."

"With pleasure."

Creslyn rode him with a fervor, breasts bouncing, diamonds twinkling, as he surged inside of her. Over and over, he rose to meet her blinding pace, grunting each time he slid out of her before driving himself home once more. Her skin was glowing, slicked with sweat, and with every thrust she grabbed at him, as though she couldn't get enough.

Drake was inclined to agree.

It simply wasn't enough.

He snared her by the waist and flipped them over easily, so she was splayed on her back and he was positioned between her legs.

The bond between them crackled and flared, and Creslyn's voice crashed into his mind.

"More. More. More."

He would give her everything.

Drake buried himself inside of her, driving so deep, she screamed his name. More shadows emerged, wraith-like hands that gripped her breasts and teased her clit, dragging her closer to the infinite spiral of climax. His cock expanded, swelling with the insurmountable need to find release. Her legs locked around his waist, her heels dug into his back. She thrashed beneath him, shuddering as waves of ecstasy crashed into them, drowning them both. He emptied himself inside of her, toppling off the dangerous cliff into a mist of eternal promises and lies. A churning sea of oblivion dragged them under and then Creslyn kissed him, breathing life and warmth into his tortured soul.

And Drake knew he would be lost to her forever.

CHAPTER SIXTEEN

$\mathcal{A}$t some point, Creslyn knew Drake had carried her back to her bedroom. He'd stretched out alongside her and kept one arm possessively slung around her waist. She'd fallen asleep in his arms, relishing the comfort of the way she fit perfectly against him. Her dreams had been filled with memories of his strong arms, his sculpted body, his wicked tongue.

And stars, the wispy shadows ribbed along his shaft?

Nothing would ever compare.

She rolled over, snuggling into her pillow, and reached out for him to see if she could entice him into taking her again. But when she flung her arm out, her hand landed upon cold satin sheets and emptiness.

Drake was gone.

Creslyn blinked, rubbing the sleep from her eyes.

A small fire crackled in the hearth, spitting flames and warming her chambers, but there were no lurking shadows, no swaths of darkness. Even though a gray autumn mist blanketed the outdoors and left tiny drops of dew upon her window, she knew Drake was not with her.

She was alone.

He'd left her…again. Without a word. Without a trace. So often it seemed as though he vanished into thin air, disappearing in such a way that she keenly felt his absence.

Flipping onto her back, she tugged the plush blanket over her naked form, then inspected the palm of her hand. The scar was still there, a smooth, even line, forged from Kjeld's blade. Though it healed fairly quickly, it was clearly visible, marking her with a pearly black ink like a tattoo.

Creslyn closed her hand into a tight fist, unable to ignore the pinch of guilt lancing through her.

She'd lied to Drake.

She knew exactly what she'd done.

When his dark power had torn through her, scoured her with an invisible blade, she'd pushed back with a vengeance. With fissures of sunlight and shards of rainbows, she had cleaved his shadows in half. She'd lured his corrupted magic, called to the darkness of his soul, and bound him to her with blood and a kiss. It was a heinous thing to do, to force a mating bond upon someone, but the shadowy magic he possessed did not retaliate. It didn't fight back or lash out. No, whatever lurked inside of him *yearned* for her.

Now, Drake was her mate, and the thread of magic tying them to one another hummed in appreciation.

She was tempted to reach out to him through his mind, to summon him back to bed, but a knock on her bedroom door left her startled and slightly annoyed.

Creslyn climbed out of bed, grabbed a shimmering robe of gold, tied it at the waist, and yanked open the door.

Only to find Kjeld standing on the other side.

He offered her a half of a smile in that ruggedly handsome way of his, then bowed. "Morning, my lady."

Creslyn wrapped her arms around herself, fully aware that she was not at all dressed appropriately to receive visitors. "Good morning, Kjeld."

He smoothed his windswept golden hair back from his face, then roughed his knuckles along his bearded jaw. His bright, summer blue eyes twinkled, and she took note that he was no longer in the same formal attire he'd worn upon his arrival but was now dressed in riding leathers. "His Highness had some business to attend to this morning and requested that I escort you to the courtyard."

Kjeld twirled the sword in his hand.

Creslyn groaned in frustration. "Kjeld, I was just married last night. Certainly that's cause for me to bypass a day of training?"

"I suppose you could try to explain your reasoning to the prince, but I have my orders." He grinned broadly, clearly evident that he had no intention of allowing her to evade his prince's instructions.

Creslyn glanced down, scowling at the sword. She knew it was heavy, knew her body would scream at her later once Kjeld was done educating her on proper form and every method of attack. She sighed. Heavily. "Fine. But at least let me change into one of my least favorite gowns. Preferably one I don't mind destroying."

He winked. "Be sure to dress warmly. It's overcast and chilly this morning."

She rolled her eyes and reached for the door. "Lovely."

"I'll see you in the courtyard, my lady." Kjeld's smile only widened as she shut the door in his face.

The last thing she wanted to do after her wedding night was go outside and be taught how to wield a sword should the need ever arise. But if there was one thing she was determined to do, it was to prove to Drake she was capable of handling herself.

Creslyn freshened up, and kept her hair down, despite the weather. She chose a gown of thick, silvery blue velvet trimmed in satin, then dug through her wardrobe in search of the supple leather boots she'd only worn once when her brother, Tovian, had attempted to teach her how to ride an Eponian.

She'd failed at it. Miserably. Much like everything else she attempted.

Creslyn tugged on the leather boots, lacing them up to her knees, then marched toward the courtyard like she was walking into battle.

)✶(

PAIN RICOCHETED through Creslyn's body.

Stars above, fighting with swords was so much worse than hand-to-hand combat. Muscles she didn't even know existed burned and ached. Her arms were on fire, her wrists felt as though they would snap off at any moment, and her legs seemed to be dissolving out from under her. There was an agonizing twinge in her ribs that throbbed every time she stole a breath, and though a fine mist settled over the courtyard, dampening her skin and hair, it was nothing compared to the sweat sliding down her neck and back. Her gown was plastered to her, an obnoxious hindrance she could not stand, and any time her elbows dropped, Kjeld smacked them with the flat edge of his blade.

The man was positively ruthless. He taunted her, ridiculed her, coerced her to keep fighting, to keep standing. She hated him for it, cursed his name more times than she could count, until his laughter provoked her to try harder. To work harder. To *be* harder.

He was gradually shaving away all of her soft edges so she was sharp and unbreakable. Fortifying her to become a force of reckoning. Molding her from satin into steel.

Creslyn stepped into the next movement, meeting his attack, and the clang of metal reverberated through her bones.

"Cres?" A feminine voice called out from the far side of the courtyard, and Creslyn recognized the concern in Novalise's tone. "What in the stars are you doing?"

Creslyn didn't turn, she didn't take her eyes off Kjeld. Because the moment she did, he'd use that opportunity to nick her arm or whack her leg with his blasted weapon.

"I feel as though...it's fairly obvious," Creslyn panted, dodging Kjeld's sword as he aimed for her elbow once more. She jerked it back into place, chest heaving. "I am in the midst...of training."

"Yes, I can see that."

Creslyn didn't have to look to know that her sister was frowning in disapproval.

"But why?" Novalise asked from the safety of the outlying corridor. "For what?"

"Anything." Creslyn whirled away from Kjeld, catching a glimpse of Novalise's lavender hair along the far outskirts of her vision. "Everything."

"But you're in a *gown.*"

"Am I?" Creslyn could not help the derision that fell from her tongue. She was too fixated on avoiding the sharpened point of Kjeld's sword. "I hadn't noticed."

"Now, now, my lady." Kjeld made a *tsk*ing sort of noise and lunged forward, the corner of his mouth curving in mirth. "There's no need to take your frustration out on your eldest sister. She's merely inquiring after your welfare."

Again, their swords met, but the blow was swift this time, and Creslyn's boots slid against the slick stone.

She grunted, biting her bottom lip against the assault as her arms spasmed in protest.

"I am quite well, Nova!" She glared at Kjeld, flashing him her most bitter smile. "Thank you so much for your concern, but if you wouldn't mind, I am significantly indisposed at the moment."

Creslyn stole a hasty glance at Novalise, gritted her teeth against the pain, and attempted another, though much less vexed, smile.

"Of course, Creslyn." Novalise stepped back into the corridor, her mouth still partially agape. "Um, do carry on, and forgive my intrusion."

Forgive, indeed.

There was no doubt in Creslyn's mind that as soon as Novalise fled their company, she would tell each one of their siblings what she'd just witnessed.

Creslyn huffed out a breath and her lungs seized.

"See?" Kjeld asked, gesturing toward the empty corridor with his blade. "That wasn't so hard, was it? Your concentration is greatly improving."

A scowl formed across her brow, and she glowered up at him. If he wanted a test of concentration, she would give him one.

She stiffened against a gust of frigid air that swept through the courtyard. Her teeth rattled and her bones trembled. She clenched the hilt of her sword, her fingers so cold she could no longer feel them, but she readied her stance anyway, taking aim. "Where did you say Drake disappeared to this morning?"

"Nice try," Kjeld teased, blocking her strike with ease. "I didn't."

Creslyn paced to the right, mindful of her footwork. Keeping her elbows lifted and her shoulders lowered, she rolled her neck, wincing when it cracked. "It's rude, is it not? To abandon one's wife the morning after their wedding?"

She twirled her sword and swung, the clash of metal ringing in her ears like distant thunder. Beads of sweat slid along her neck and over her shoulders, turning to drops of ice in the billowing wind. Autumn's chill sank deep into her bones, freezing her, as the mist from earlier bled into a steady drizzle.

Matching Kjeld's movements, she inched closer, staring up at him from beneath a drawn brow. She schooled her expression into one of impassivity as she asked, "You wouldn't be so quick to leave your new wife's bed, would you? Not without ensuring her needs were met first?"

A distinctive blush colored Kjeld's cheeks, and his blue eyes widened in surprise. He swiped the back of his hand across his forehead, not realizing that she was slowly backing him into a corner. Right where she wanted him.

His weapon lowered, the faintest of weaknesses. "My lady, I—"

"I mean surely," Creslyn interrupted smoothly, stalking toward him, "if you awoke next to your wife who was still naked and swollen from a lust-induced haze, you would snatch the opportunity to bring her to release again, would you not?"

Kjeld coughed loudly, stumbled, and tripped over his own feet.

Creslyn launched herself at him.

She leaned back and kicked one foot out, knocking his legs out from under him. Kjeld toppled to the ground like a fallen mountain, his back smacking soundly against the stone. He grunted, his face contorting into one of fleeting pain as his sword slipped from his hand. It clattered loudly, the sound of victory. Creslyn moved with practiced speed, leaping on top of him to prevent escape. Pressing the flat edge of her blade to his throat, she bent over him. His blue eyes flashed with surprise, then something that could have been mistaken for admiration.

"Now, I will ask you one more time, general," Creslyn crooned softly as the patter of rainfall sounded around them. "Where is my husband?"

Kjeld opened his mouth then snapped it shut, and a tiny vein pulsed along his forehead.

Darkness descended.

Cold shadows whipped around the courtyard, menacing and violent. They crept around her wrists and waist, snared into her hair, tangling in the wet strands. Her breath misted before her as the temperature plummeted, and the blade of her sword at Kjeld's neck frosted. She clutched the hilt tightly as white-hot pain seared her palm.

A low, threatening voice whispered past her ear, and pinpricks of awareness raced down her spine.

"Right here."

CHAPTER SEVENTEEN

Drake stepped from the churning shadows, where long inky tendrils curled like claws tipped with broken fractures of obsidian.

Fury pumped through him, freezing the blood running through his veins, amplifying the dark cadence of his magic so the nefarious tune struck in time to the steady beating of his heart. He popped his jaw and ground his teeth. Venomous rage twisted through him, imbuing him with hatred toward the only man he'd ever trusted.

The damn mating bond made him irrational.

Vengeful.

Envious.

Drake knew he should be proud of Creslyn for knocking Kjeld flat on his back. But seeing her straddling another man sent tremors of indignation coursing through him. If he so much as touched her…

Kjeld splayed both of his hands on the ground, digging his nails into the smooth surface, recognizing the dangerous look in Drake's eyes. His general swallowed hard and sucked in a shaky breath, as though he was trying to sink into the stone.

Drake's gaze shot to Creslyn, at the way she was hunched over Kjeld, with her blade pressed to his throat. She looked up sharply, and her wet hair fell in ribbons of glossy silk around her bare shoulders. Her cheeks were flushed pink, and her lips parted as she stared back at him. The dress she wore soaked her to the bone, the layers of moonlit velvet clung to her skin, highlighting every dip and curve. The hem was ripped, and the sleeves were snagged, as though they'd been caught by the tip of Kjeld's sword. Her bodice was heavily embroidered with crystals that looked like raindrops, and the weight of it sagged, gaping so that her breasts were precariously close to tumbling free.

He fisted his hands at his sides, clenching them so his nails bit into the skin.

Creslyn's gaze darkened, the blue of her eyes turning near black against the swarm of darkness.

"Hello, *wife*," he purred.

She looked up at him from beneath damp lashes, running her teeth along her full bottom lip. "Hello, husband."

Drake sauntered forward, determined to keep his composure calm despite the fact that he wanted to throw her over his shoulder and set fire to the fucking world. "Mind telling me why you're sitting on my general's lap?"

The mating bond flared, snapping and crackling with provocative tension. It fizzled through him, spiking his heart rate, blinding him with the impulse to possess her. To dominate her. To own her.

"Training." Creslyn bit the word out. She flicked her wrist, pulling the sword away from Kjeld's jugular, and the general heaved a breath in relief. But then she leaned back, seating herself across his waist even more. She raised her arms over her head and arched in a long, languid stretch. "Exactly as you requested."

Drake's nostrils flared. He glared down at her, hating that

his gaze was instantly drawn to the beads of rainwater cascading from her neck, then rolling and sliding over the swell of her breasts. Those breasts where diamonds lay hidden beneath the saturated fabric of her dress. Those breasts that were likely already swollen and aching, waiting patiently for his touch.

Creslyn's eyes widened, and the tips of her pointed ears turned pink.

"Get. Up." The words were a warning. A threat.

She crossed her arms out of spite, a delicate line pinching along her forehead even as her lips trembled from the cold. "Make. Me."

His shadows seethed as the rain increased, pelting them like tiny shards of ice. "In the mood for a lover's spat today, are we *kearsta?*"

"You are the one who left me without saying goodbye. You did not even possess the decency to tell me where you were going." Creslyn lifted her blade, aiming at him with malice. "You just *left.*"

"I have my reasons." Not that he had any inclination to tell her about them anytime soon.

"No, you have secrets," she countered, shaking her head once, and the damp strands of her hair stuck to her neck and cheeks. "Those are not the same."

He shifted his weight, studying her. She was a complexity he did not quite understand. Soft yet hard. Beautiful yet brutal. Whenever her tongue lashed out at him, whenever she scowled in his direction, he found himself more infatuated with her. He liked it when she was full of fire, when she was exasperated and temperamental. More than anything, he thoroughly enjoyed provoking her, exactly as he was doing now.

Drake adjusted the drenched sleeves of his shirt and held her gaze. "I did not realize I was now required to inform you of my whereabouts."

Creslyn scoffed. "Then you should not concern yourself with mine."

She fell forward over Kjeld's prone body, propping her elbow up by his head, and leaning close enough that the general received a full view of her cleavage.

Drake lost his damn mind.

He snatched her by the waist with blistering speed, yanking her off Kjeld, not caring if his fingers dug into her supple flesh.

"So, you think you can fight, is that it?" he asked, his tone mocking. "You think you have what it takes to defend yourself against anyone? Against *me?*"

"Put me down!" Creslyn shouted. She struggled in his arms, coiling her hands around his wrists, but he did not release her. She kicked her legs, attempting to disentangle herself from his hold. But her slight struggle was useless to the iron grip of his hands on her body. She smacked at him, the slap of her hands nothing more than an annoyance, like that of a bee sting. "I am *not* as weak as you think me to be!"

He dragged her against him, smirking at the little noise of shock she made when he crushed her to his chest.

Lowering his head, he nipped the bottom of her ear, tugging the delicate flesh between his teeth. Then he murmured quietly, "Prove it."

Drake dropped her abruptly and she staggered backward, arms flailing in a desperate attempt to keep her balance. Bitter wind swept through the courtyard, so the branches of the weeping tree lashed like whips, and the rain slanted downward, pouring from the miserable heavens. Lightning danced, scattering between the roiling gray clouds in a dozen different directions, and the angry rumble of thunder cracked above them. A torrent of wretched weather unleashed upon them, and Drake watched as Creslyn stood before him, shivering, freezing, but refusing to back down. To walk away.

"General Holtstrom." Drake spared his only friend a calculated glance. "If you know what's good for you—"

"Yes, Your Highness," Kjeld interrupted before Drake could get another word in, and he grabbed his fallen sword from the ground. Then he bolted across the courtyard, leaving Drake to deal with his indignant wife on his own.

Creslyn gathered up her soaking wet hair and twisted it into a messy, lopsided bun on the top of her head. Her chest was heaving, the steady rise and fall causing that damned bodice to dip lower with each breath. Silky satin draped off her shoulders and she tugged at the sleeves, yanking them up to her elbows. Her skirts were plastered to her legs, making her appear as though she'd stood beneath a waterfall of moonbeams.

He was torn between wanting to fight her and wanting to fuck her.

Drake ignored the stab of arousal and narrowed his gaze. Damp strands of dark hair hung in his face as the rain continued to drench them both. He removed his riding leathers, peeling them off over his head, and threw them on the ground. His black shirt was instantly assaulted by the storm, ruining the fine fabric. He rolled the sleeves, cuffing them, never taking his eyes off Creslyn.

She traced the outline of his wet shirt with her gaze, tracking the way the softly spun cotton molded to his arms, shoulders, and abdomen. Her eyes heated, like sapphires set on fire, lingering on his forearms.

He locked his jaw, clamping down on the urge to bend her over that forgotten bench beneath the weeping tree, and drive himself into her until the stars wept.

Creslyn's mouth curved at the corner, her face suddenly illuminated with smug satisfaction. As though she knew *exactly* what he wanted to do to her.

Damn it.

Drake pulled his sword from his sheath, the blade whistling

against the coarse leather. He swiveled it once, rolling his wrist, then pointed it in her direction.

"Ready, pretty faerie?"

"More than ever, shadow prince."

Irritation splintered through her, prodded by his ability to get under her skin. With the bond between them, he was incredibly aware of everything about her. The way her emotions changed like the ocean's tide, calm one moment, furious the next. He could hear every vile thought as it sifted through her mind as though it was his own, and he knew she would hear his as well, something he would have to be mindful of now.

She clutched her sword in her hands and raised it, keeping her elbows up.

He was in tune with the rhythmic beating of her heart, the way it hammered and skipped, the way it beat solely for him.

Creslyn's lips parted as though she was about to speak, and then she attacked.

Drake went easy on her at first, avoiding her strikes and sidestepping her advances. When their swords met above them, the familiar clang rattling in his ears, he was careful not to use too much force. Cautious not to hurt her. But she was far more skilled than he originally thought. Even though she had only trained with Kjeld for a handful of days, she moved through the courtyard as though she'd been fighting since she took her first breath. She spun in the downpour, with pink cheeks and wild eyes, deflecting him, dodging him, rising to meet him.

Together they sparred as thunder ricocheted through the angry sky. The storm devoured the clash of blades, deafening the sounds of their battle.

There was only him. And her. And the beating of their hearts.

For Drake, the rest of the world fell silent.

Creslyn lunged forward and Drake pivoted quickly to avoid

her assault. Then she twisted the other direction, her speed so unrivaled she was nothing more than a blur of smeared rainbows. She brought the hilt of her weapon down upon his wrist. Pain spasmed through his arm as his sword fell from his hand. Sliding one foot out, she kicked it away then took aim, bringing the tip of her blade to the base of his throat.

She leveled him with a look of superiority, adorable considering she stood nearly a foot shorter than him.

He shook his head, a deep laugh reverberating through him.

She thought she won.

Drake reached out and wrapped one hand around her blade. Blood poured from his palm, wet and sticky. It slid down his wrist, dripping onto the stone ground of the courtyard where the steady rain washed it away, leaving a small trail like a river.

Creslyn gaped at him, her mouth falling open in shock, and he ripped the sword from her grasp, throwing it to the side.

"Drake!" She rushed toward him, those pools of blue wide with worry. "Your hand!"

He grabbed her then, swinging her around to crush her between the outer wall of the courtyard and the solid barrier of his body. The beads of her bodice scraped against his shirt, creating the most delicious friction. His hand slid around her throat, his favorite place to hold her, as his fingers glided over her wet skin. Touching her was like capturing morning dew in his palm. Her pulse fluttered like the wings of a butterfly, chaotic and fierce, and Drake's blood hummed in response. He nudged his knee in between her thighs, enjoying the way her legs fell open for him. Like she knew where he belonged.

Creslyn brought her arms in close, curling them against his chest. Goosebumps riddled her flesh, and he pressed in, shielding her from the storm.

Drake lowered his head and kissed her.

Her tongue tangled with his, and he groaned into her mouth. She radiated heat, the kind that bit through the cold and seared him with a scorching trail of desire. Creslyn tasted of lazy summer mornings and sun-sprinkled roses. She was like walking through a field of wildflowers, a colorful expanse of endless beauty. He could *feel* her essence, her warmth soothed his bones, coaxed the darkness to lace with the light.

Drake drew back, breaking their kiss.

"Never show weakness." He moved his hand from her neck to her waist, gripping her. Droplets of rain rinsed away his bloodied handprint staining her skin. "Never show the truth of your heart."

"Fine." She blinked up at him, her eyes hooded, her lips swollen. She tucked a strand of his wet hair back from his face, her touch surprisingly gentle. The gesture was almost too intimate. "So long as you never abandon me."

His brow furrowed and he stared at her, searching her face. "You're still angry with me."

It wasn't a question but a statement of fact.

"You told me you never break your word. Just as you told me you would never leave my side again." Accusation lit her tone. "Yet when I awoke, you were gone."

Drake set his mouth into a hard line. "I had business."

Creslyn rolled her hips forward, rubbing against his groin. His cock sprung to life, and she slipped her hand between them, gripping his hard shaft firmly in her grasp. He groaned again, dropping his forehead against hers.

"Business that doesn't involve me?" she asked, squeezing tightly, eliciting a grunt of aching need from the cavernous walls of his chest.

She dragged her leg up the side of him, hiking up the hem of her soaked gown. His gaze fell to the swath of bare skin, where sleek leather boots rose up to her knee, and a lacy garter was strapped to her thigh.

He frowned.

Not a garter. A sheath.

Creslyn pulled the small dagger from its holder, running its blade lightly down Drake's chest so the soaked fabric of his shirt feathered and frayed.

"Tell me where you were, Drake, and do not lie." Her voice was a sensual cadence that spoke to his soul. She moved her hand lower still, positioning the dagger's tip right above the bulge in his pants. "Or I will cut off your cock. Which would truly be a shame, as I find I'm rather fond of it."

"Fuck." Drake slammed one fist into the wall of stone behind her, sending bits of debris crumbling around them. He snagged her bottom lip with his teeth, bit until she whimpered, then swiped his tongue across her pouty mouth to ease the sting. "Nothing arouses me more than when you're vicious."

Damn his faerie and her constant need for answers, for the truth.

She was entirely too wicked for her own good, and it filled him with a sense of immoral pride, knowing that the sliver of darkness inside her was expanding...because of him.

Drake reached into one of his pockets, felt the cool touch of metal against his fingertips, and pulled out a ring.

"I was buying you this." He held it out to her, and the black diamond solitaire sparkled with midnight rainbows. "As a token of my devotion."

CHAPTER EIGHTEEN

"*A* ring?"

Creslyn glanced down at the stone that sparked as though it had been heated with dragon fire. She blinked through the rain dampening her lashes and dragged her gaze back up to Drake. His mouth was set, the hard, chiseled lines crafted from stone. "You bought me a ring?"

"Ariesian mentioned you were without one." He reached between them, easing her dagger away from his groin. "I thought I ought to remedy that."

"I've never seen anything like it." It was smooth yet sharp. The band was silver and twisted around the gem, grasping it like a claw. Drake rolled it between his fingers and the stone glittered, the rainbow fire glinting to life only in the reflection of shadows. "Where did you get it? Surely there's nothing like this in Aeramere."

"There is…if one knows where to look." He pulled the dagger from her hand, then lifted it to his mouth, clenching the blade between his teeth.

The dark green of his eyes, ringed with fiery gold, held her, tempting and forbidding all at once, while he slid the ring onto her left finger.

Creslyn raised her hand, admiring the stone, the subtle promise of a thousand lives. Her brow arched as Drake seized her leg, his calloused palm raking along her flesh as he leisurely slid the dagger back into the sheath strapped around her thigh.

Rain continued to fall, soaking them, chilling her. She drank in the way his wet shirt stuck to his powerful frame, the way it seemed to accentuate his broad shoulders and solid abdomen. She liked how the veins running down his forearms seemed to bulge against the strain of hardened muscle, especially when he grabbed her. The small beads of water clinging to his skin only served to ignite the embers of longing inside her, pulsing between her legs.

Suddenly, she was no longer cold.

She reached for the dark, silky strands of hair that had yet again fallen into his face and twined them around her fingers. "Do not think for one moment that I will so easily forgive you, just because you've gifted me something pretty."

"Should I offer you something else then?" he asked, rocking his hips forward, rubbing his stiff length against her center. "Something more fulfilling?"

Creslyn tangled her hands in his hair, urging him down to meet her. His mouth was a breath from her own, and she whispered, "Yes."

His kiss was punishing, a violent clash of lips and tongues. Her magic roared to the surface, a spiral of sunbeams and broken rainbows, desperate to be devoured by the dark. Power thrummed between them, and the bond tying them together fused into an intricately woven pattern of slinking shadows and swirling prisms of color. He tasted of her deepest desires, of forbidden pleasures obscured by a moonless night. She vibrated against his touch, the feel of him evoking images of his hand fisted in her hair while he drove into her from behind, as he cupped her breasts, her hips, forcing her to watch her own reflection while he ruined her.

Not images, she realized.

Thoughts.

His thoughts.

The bond flamed hotter.

Creslyn tore at his shirt, aching to touch him, the ripping of fabric drowned out by the crack of thunder overhead. Stars above, he was beautiful. Not mortal, not fae, but something else altogether. Something dangerous and seductive, monstrous and powerful. She splayed her hands against his damp skin, roving over his shoulders, tracing his scars. Scraping her nails down his tanned chest, she left red scratches in her wake, marking him.

"There's my wicked little faerie," he murmured, unfastening his pants.

His cock sprang free, thick and full, and wrapped in sinewy shadows.

Her mouth went dry at the sight of him. Wetness pooled between her legs as Drake hiked up her sopping skirts, shoving them out of the way. He hoisted her legs around his waist, positioning himself so the tip of his shaft was nestled against her core. She squirmed, needing him to fill her. Wrapping her arms around his neck, she leaned in close, inhaled the intoxicating scent of wintry pine and frozen mountains, then she lowered her head and bit his shoulder.

Hard.

Until his blood coated her tongue.

It was like an aphrodisiac. Lush and velvety. Like drinking wine from the gods.

Damning.

"What the fuck did I say, Cres?" Drake growled in her ear, his voice tainted with untempered violence.

A shudder of delight trekked down her spine. She arched her

hips, pressing herself against his erection, laving her tongue over the mark she'd left behind on his shoulder. "I do not recall exactly."

His chest rumbled and that was all the warning she had before he surged forward, burying himself deep inside of her. He pushed into her, stretching her, and the shadows lining his shaft throbbed in time to her heartbeat, prying her open to accommodate his size. She cried out, her yelp of pleasure turning into a broken whimper when he dipped his head forward and sank his teeth into the top of her breast.

Creslyn laced her fingers around the back of his neck, holding him against her, as the searing pain of his bite sent a fresh bloom of heat straight to her core. Drake's fingers squeezed into the soft flesh of her backside, pinning her against the stone. He swirled his tongue over the bite, licking her, tasting her, and when he finally eased back to meet her gaze, his eyes were wild with unfathomable lust.

"You." The word was gravelly, grating. His expression was cruel, a tempest of volatile emotions. "You are my destruction. My salvation. My eternal damnation."

He pulled slightly out of her wet heat, then pumped himself back inside. Her head fell against the stone wall and raindrops trickled between the valley of her breasts, sizzling against the heat from her skin.

Drake claimed her then, shoving himself inside of her with a fierce and endless fervor. Her legs trembled and she held on, clutching him as each thrust sent him deeper than before, as the shadows slid along her inner walls, curling, guiding him toward the most intimate part of her.

"Take it." His warm breath tickled her cheek and ear. "All of it. All of me."

Darkness swirled around them as he pumped into her, luring her closer to the perilous tip of oblivion. She clenched around him, and he groaned, a guttural sound that caused her nipples to pebble and her stomach to tighten.

But there was something else…a distant chorus of voices.

Male voices.

Creslyn's gaze darted around the courtyard, and she spotted them through the misting wall of shadows. Three unfortunately very familiar figures.

"Drake," she gasped, as he lifted her higher, adjusting their angle so he sank further into her. Sweet stars, her eyes rolled to the storm-laden heavens. He was too much. Too thick. She wasn't certain she could take anymore.

But those voices drew nearer.

She struggled to get the words out, her body overcome with tantalizing pleasure. "Someone's coming."

"The only one coming is you."

She shook her head. "But it's—"

"Don't you dare say their names," he warned, beads of water and sweat lining his brow. "Not while I'm inside you."

Creslyn moaned then, as something cool crawled across her skin and teased the aching bundle of nerves between her thighs.

"Careful, *kearsta*." Drake's pace increased. "They'll hear you."

Frantic, her gaze shot to the entrance of the courtyard where Ariesian, Solarius, and Asher were about to stroll around the corner and discover them.

"Drake," she pleaded.

He clamped one hand over her mouth, and then his rumbling voice filled her mind, his accent thick and heady.

"Come for me and I'll keep my shadows in place. They will not see us, they will not hear us." He bent closer so his gaze stole into her soul. *"Come all over my cock right now. If you don't, I'll make sure they see me fucking you against this wall."*

Creslyn panted against his palm, chest heaving. Drake shattered her as the swell of ecstasy slammed into her, breaking her, blinding her. She crested, collapsing against him. A snarl tore from him on a final thrust as he emptied himself inside of her, filling her. He gathered her against him, keeping himself firmly inside of her, as he stroked one finger along the column of her throat.

"Still angry?" he mused.

"Furious." She mumbled the word into his chest.

He laughed, a low, throaty chuckle, then stole her into the shadows.

A moment later, they were in her bedroom, and she was flat on her back in her bed. Drake's hand moved beneath the hem of her dress, coasting up her leg, until he retrieved the dagger strapped to her thigh. He removed it carefully, then set to work, slicing through the wet satin of her gown, peeling the shreds of fabric away from her skin.

"That's the second gown of mine you've ruined." Creslyn feigned disappointment, pouting and crossing her arms.

"I'll buy you more." Drake dropped the remnants of her dress onto the floor, then stood. He grabbed the buckle of his already loosened belt, yanking it off with one hand. His pants fell, and he kicked them to the side. "And then I'll ruin each one."

Her gaze snagged on the mirror behind him, on the tattoos of a dragon and a pile of skulls painted onto his tanned skin. She skimmed his torso next, littered with scars, then traveled over the length of his rippled abdomen and sneaked a peek further, only to find him hard again.

Creslyn's eyes widened, and she propped herself up on her elbows. "Drake?"

"Yes, *sjellhert*," he crooned, stepping closer to the bed, that leather belt still in his grip.

"But we just, I mean…that is to say, I…and you—"

This time, his laughter was like velvet, and the smile almost reached his eyes.

"I recall you mentioning you are still angry with me." Drake crawled over top of her, trailing the belt up her body, the clinking of the buckle echoing softly in her ears as he planted a hand on either side of her head. Hovering above her, he kissed her chin. Her cheek. "I believe it is my duty as your husband to ensure you're thoroughly pleased."

Then he leaned back, and the look in his eyes told her he had no intention of leaving her anytime soon.

"Legs apart, *kearsta*," Drake ordered smoothly. "And eyes on me."

Creslyn obeyed.

CHAPTER NINETEEN

$\mathcal{D}$rake felt Creslyn's absence keenly.

She had gone off with her sisters to make the final preparations for Novalise's wedding, leaving him to his own devices. He'd spent the better part of the day on the cliffs of Moonfall Peaks with Kjeld, tending to Svartos and Odryss, generally avoiding the flurry of festivities. Now, he stood outside of House Celestine as fae from all five houses of Aeramere milled about, admiring the excessive decorations of stained glass stars that floated overhead and an abundance of overly fragrant flowers dusted in starlight.

It made his skin crawl.

Perhaps if he'd chosen another path, if he had not been bound to an immoral disposition, he might be more inclined to tolerate such idle revelry laced with potent glamour and fake smiles. But alas, his patience for enduring such atrocities was threadbare.

For years, he was trapped in between worlds, lost to the shadow realm. He moved between the darkness mindlessly with no purpose, watching as kingdoms rose and fell, as magic was both created and snuffed out of existence, as lands were renewed with life and touched by death. Prophecies came to him in the form of wakeful dreams, visions of fate not yet foretold. All the while, he traced the threads of destiny, curious as the woven tapestry unfolded before him, connecting lives and stories in one grand design. Eventually, his interest in the divine morphed into bitterness. For what gods or stars would seek to condemn him to a life of nothingness? To merely stand by as others endured love and loss, triumph and failure? Years bled into centuries, while he remained cursed to survive only in the shadows.

His existence was useless, one without feeling, without emotion, and it blackened his heart. The curse spread like a disease, rotting him, until he was nothing more than a hollow husk of a soul.

Drake vowed that if he ever broke free from the shadow realm, he would find a way to rid himself of the curse set upon him. But he lusted for power, he craved the wicked dark, and the cold, cruel grip that violent, vengeful nature held on him was inescapable. He was shadows, deceit, and death.

Until *her*.

Only her.

Creslyn claimed there was light inside of him, but she was wrong.

There was *only her*.

She was the cataclysm of everything he never wanted. She was a storm of sunlight and pearlescent rainbows fractured by a splintering shard of darkness—his endless obsession.

He was half-tempted to follow the tug of the burning mating bond, to seek her out and claim her again, when the thundering of wings jarred him from his thoughts.

A gilded coach pulled by two pristine white Eponians touched down along the main path to House Celestine.

Queen Elowyn had arrived.

She emerged from the carriage in a sweeping gown of

emerald with thin, tree-like embroidery that crawled up from the hem. Her earth-colored hair was piled high on her head, twisted into an elaborate crown that seemed to tug her eyebrows up across her brow. The Aeramere queen carried herself with lethal poise, her magic swirling around her like the Veil she kept in place over the whole of the realm. But it was different somehow. Like a carefully crafted enchantment he couldn't break.

Lady Trysta Starstorm possessed a similar type of magic, though hers was more like a spell, something she used to pretend to read the stars she so often misconstrued to her favor.

Drake scowled at the thought of the Starstorm matriarch and redirected his attention to the queen's arrival.

She was accompanied by a tall, lanky blond fae male whose nose was slightly upturned, and whose mouth seemed to curl at the corners as though he'd tasted something foul.

He wore the same green shade, a perfect match to Queen Elowyn's dress, except he was armed with a strap of vine-like daggers across his chest, and a sword at his waist. A cape of black billowed behind him in the steady breeze.

Drake stepped directly into their path, offering the queen a curt, if not hasty, bow. "Your Majesty."

"Prince Drake Kalstrand." She smiled, but it pinched her cheeks and she shifted uncomfortably. "Always a pleasure."

Drake arched one brow and looked pointedly at the blond fae.

He bristled, drawing himself up to his full height—which still required him to look up at Drake.

"Bastian Valewood." He inclined his head, his hair tumbling over one half of his face. "High Councilor to Queen Elowyn Willowblade."

"How curious," Drake mused, roughing his knuckles along his jaw. "I thought in order to be on the queen's council, one must be a lord or lady of one of Aeramere's five houses."

"Exceptions can be granted." Bastian pulled his shoulders back, though it did little to erase the fact that Drake continued to loom over him.

"Apparently." Drake bit back on his own growing dislike for this particular fae.

"Bastian has been in my confidence for many years, Your Highness." Queen Elowyn cut in, attempting to diffuse the animosity. "He has given me no reason to doubt his loyalty."

"Indeed." Drake cocked his head to the side, shoving his hands into the pockets of his more formal attire. "And does your counsel extend to Prince Aspen, Valewood?"

He sized up the councilor, his gaze analyzing him for any tells. But Bastian remained unwavering, his expression one of bland indifference.

However, it was Queen Elowyn who flinched at the mention of her son. The movement was nearly imperceptible, but Drake saw it all the same.

"My allegiance is to the queen," Bastian stated evenly.

Yet there was so much hidden behind all the words he did not say. It was clear Bastian did not support, nor likely trust, Prince Aspen. But then again, loyalty could easily be bought. The prophecy Drake had observed in the shadow realm surrounding Aeramere showed an impending war, which was validated by the star reading Lady Novalise conducted during Midsummer, but the vision itself was not entirely transparent. The images were hazy, coated with a sheen of melding colors. It portrayed a scene of royal versus royal, of toppled crowns and rotten earth, of celestial storms and destructive magic.

The only thing Drake couldn't discern was which royal would be the cause of such a war.

Queen Elowyn or Prince Aspen.

Another gilded carriage, this one emblazoned with a wolf-like skull adorned with horns, cut through the fading hues of sunset. The wings of the stone gray Eponians stretched like silver clouds, their hooves thundering against the ground, mist puffing out from their nostrils as they tossed their midnight manes.

"Ah, I see Prince Aspen has arrived as well." Drake cast his gaze upon the prince in question, who exited his carriage with a cool, lackadaisical air. "Lady Novalise and Lord Asher's wedding must be a rather special occasion indeed."

"Lady Trysta Starstorm is a dear friend of mine." Queen Elowyn stiffened, and her magic rippled around her as her gaze darkened. "It would be an insult if I—"

Bastian stepped between the queen and Drake, his mouth stretching into a sneer. "The Queen of Aeramere does not need to explain herself or her choices to a *prince*."

He practically spat the word out.

"No explanation was demanded." Drake's hands coiled into tight fists, and he ignored the thrum of the Shadowblade sheathed at his waist. It would be far too easy to grab it and slit Bastian's throat in one fluid movement. He inhaled slowly, determined to remain in control, to not give into his more villainous temper. At least not until he garnered more information. "I merely found it curious that Queen Elowyn would want to be in the same vicinity as her son, given the current rumors surrounding their volatile relationship."

Bastian bared his teeth, the tiny points of his canines gleaming in the wake of dimming sunlight. "Mind your tongue or else."

Drake moved closer and his shadows flared, crawling like tendrils of spilled ink. "Or else *what*?"

"That's enough." Queen Elowyn tugged Bastian to the side, pulling him from the confines of Drake's spreading darkness. "If Prince Drake has questions about the rebellions or my son's involvement with them, I am more than happy to discuss such matters with him elsewhere."

She smiled, but it was sharp and unpleasant. "And not during such a joyous occasion."

Perhaps Drake would take her up on such an offer.

Prince Aspen strolled toward them with his jaw set, a masked look of practiced boredom plastered on his face. His appearance was similar to his mother's in that they both possessed the same dark brown hair, high cheekbones, and angular chin. But whereas Queen Elowyn's eyes were brown, Prince Aspen's were a deep, interesting shade of green. Cold and dark, they looked almost black. He didn't wear the same emerald attire as his mother or Bastian but was instead outfitted in pants and a coat the color of a woodland forest. Around his neck hung a gold necklace with a replica of the wolf skull adorned with horns that was embellished upon his carriage.

The prince dipped his head in acknowledgement. "Mother. Bastian."

His cunning gaze slid to Drake. "Kalstrand."

"Willowblade." Drake arched a brow, gesturing to the company surrounding him. "We were just discussing the rebellions."

"Rebellions?" Prince Aspen rolled his neck, as though he'd rather be anywhere else. "I have no idea what you're talking about, I've received no such reports."

"No," Drake muttered, taking note of the way Prince Aspen seemed far less concerned about the apparent rumors shading his reputation and character. "I imagine not."

Just then, Lady Trysta Starstorm came bustling out of the front entrance of House Celestine, her obnoxious bangles announcing her untimely arrival. She had one hand clamped upon the wrist of Lady Sarelle, dragging her daughter down the steps. In her wake, Creslyn's sister struggled to keep up while attempting to maintain some sense of decorum despite her mother's hasty footfalls.

Lady Trysta barreled forward, drawing up short only when

she caught sight of Drake. She slowed her pace, barely, but continued to haul her daughter behind her.

"Lady Trysta, I am so delighted to see you." Queen Elowyn clasped her shoulders, planting kisses of air on Lady Trysta's cheeks. "And Lady Sarelle, you're looking as lovely as ever."

Sarelle blushed, a hue of pink spreading across her cheeks. She clasped her hands before her and lowered her head.

"Isn't she, Aspen?" the queen asked, swatting at her son with a flick of her wrist.

Prince Aspen's frigid gaze settled upon Lady Sarelle, and she froze beneath his scrutiny, the flush from before bleeding out of her. She fidgeted with the ribbons of her light purple gown, idly toying with the moonstone gems dotting the velvet fabric. Unease radiated from her, and she shifted on her feet before tucking a strand of her shimmery midnight hair behind one ear.

The prince clicked his tongue.

"Lovely." His tone was mild and lacking enthusiasm, his agreement in her appearance reminiscent of the way one might describe freshly papered walls.

Lady Trysta shuffled her daughter forward, and pieces of the unknown puzzle clicked into place. She and Queen Elowyn were trying to pair Lady Sarelle and Prince Aspen together, neither of whom looked too pleased by the forced suggestion.

The queen sighed dramatically, looking up to the sky where the heavens were blending like a watercolor, streaks of fiery orange and pink painted over with shades of violet and navy.

Her lips stretched into a tight smile. "It is such a fine evening for a wedding. And I recently received word that Lord Solarius is to be wed to Lady Narissa Seaborne."

"Indeed!" Lady Trysta replied, far more exuberant than necessary. "Solarius and Narissa will be wed in the winter. We are all quite thrilled with the arrangement. It will be the blessing of the stars to have House Celestine and House Azurvend united. And I can scarcely believe that after today, I shall finally have one daughter already married."

"Two," Drake corrected smoothly.

Lady Trysta's head swiveled in his direction, and a deep-set line creased across her forehead. "Pardon?"

"You will have *two* daughters married." Drake held up his fingers to emphasize his point, enjoying the way she immediately shrank back in fear. "Unless it has slipped your mind that Creslyn is my wife."

"Of course not." Her mouth opened and closed, her lashes fluttered wildly. "That is…I simply…"

Forgot.

The word reverberated through him, and Drake snarled at her lack of regard toward her youngest daughter.

"I was just telling Aspen it was time he took a wife." Queen Elowyn interrupted, shifting the strained conversation back to her own personal scheme. "Our realm is in need of an heir."

"Ah, yes." Drake rocked back onto his heels, chuckling at her foolish intentions. "Because an heir will subdue all forms of unrest."

"Will you not soon be in need of an heir yourself?" Queen Elowyn shot back, her ruthless guile sneaking out from behind her sophisticated façade. Challenge flashed in her eyes, and she lifted her chin in spite.

Stunned silence befell the group as Drake navigated the flood of unwanted emotion attempting to drown him. An unbidden image of Creslyn crashed into the forefront of his mind, her belly round and swollen with child. It caused something wretched to twist inside him, scouring him like a blade freshly heated over a raging forge. He blinked, erasing the vision from his mind.

"An heir is not of great importance to me, Your Majesty." Yet now, he couldn't quite escape the notion of Creslyn carrying his child. "There are more significant matters at stake."

"Agreed." Prince Aspen spoke with abrupt iciness dripping from his tone. Then his gaze shot to his mother. "If you'd excuse me, Mother, I find myself in need of a drink."

"Oh!" Lady Trysta flitted over to him, her hand pressed firmly against Lady Sarelle's spine. "Sarelle was just saying how she was terribly parched."

Drake made a derisive, scoffing noise. She'd made no such mention of being thirsty enough to have to withstand more of the prince's company.

If the color could leach more from Lady Sarelle's delicate complexion, it did. She looked aghast at the notion, swallowing hard, knowing exactly what her mother was trying to do.

"Aspen," the queen drew his name out with all the poison of a snake. "Be a darling and escort Lady Sarelle indoors for a beverage."

The lines of the prince's face hardened into stone. He inhaled deeply, barely sparing Lady Sarelle a withering glance. "Of course, Mother."

He held out his arm, his gaze latching onto Lady Sarelle's hand as she hesitantly curled her fingers around the crook of his elbow. A vein along the prince's temple pulsed and his jaw locked. Then he inclined his head.

"Mother. Lady Trysta. Bastian." Prince Aspen shot Drake a calculated look. "Kalstrand."

Drake tilted his head. "Willowblade."

When Prince Aspen departed with Lady Sarelle on his arm, Drake turned and bowed before the queen. "Enjoy the wedding, Your Majesty."

Her thin brow quirked. "Leaving so soon? You seemed rather eager to discuss the politics of my realm but a moment ago."

Bastian sneered, and Drake flashed the queen a bland smile.

"So I was, yet now with all this talk about marriage and heirs, I find myself in want of my wife's company."

Queen Elowyn startled at his blatant remark, and Lady Trysta blanched, her pallor fading further.

Drake turned to abandon them when Bastian's voice cut through the heavy silence.

"I'm watching you, shadow prince."

Drake smirked. "You can try."

He vanished into the darkness, melding into the shadows. Through murky shades of gray and garbled noises, the prophecies of the shadow realm made themselves known. They swirled before him like smoke rising from dying flames, eddying in and out of focus. The one that plagued him the most was the clash of stars and earth. They fell like a rain of fire, plummeting from the sky, scorching the ground, leaving nothing behind but a trail of ash. Oceans roiled, boiling and frothing in angry waves that lashed against a crumbling coast. The skies were a torrent of raging clouds and whipping wind, carrying the screams of battle and the stench of death.

A betrayal of royal blood, but with no clear outcome, and no way to determine friend from foe.

The fae of Aeramere were blind to the ways of the world. To them, war and other atrocities were learned through histories, stories, and ancient texts. Their world was its own kind of glamour, protected and held in place by Queen Elowyn's Veil. She claimed to keep them safeguarded, granting the five houses fragile promises of fraudulent freedoms in exchange for absolute loyalty.

It seemed most of Aeramere had forgotten that it was the Willowblade bloodline who, centuries ago, toppled the Starstorm crown and seized control.

Until Drake could determine who was the true enemy of Aeramere, he would trust no one.

The prophecy ebbed away, fading into nothing more than a fine mist, and Drake focused on the distinctive tug in his chest, following the thrum of the bond to Creslyn.

CHAPTER TWENTY

Creslyn folded her arms across her chest and stared up at her eldest brother. His silver hair was shorter than she remembered, and the longer pieces of the front were swept to one side and smoothed back from his face. He wore a suit of black with the crest of their house embroidered upon his lapel, and a lavender rosebud tucked into the front pocket. He mirrored her stance, arms crossed, though somehow he looked far more intimidating. His handsome features reminded her so much of their father, Zenos, and something cracked inside her, causing her breath to grow shallow. The painful stab of grief was not so easily forgotten.

Their father should have been there with them, watching Novalise get married. He would have loved the stars made of crystal that floated through the gardens, illuminating the petals of every flower with iridescent light. His boisterous laugh would've been heard above the music, and his endearing smile would have softened while he danced with Novalise before handing her off to Asher for the final time.

Instead, he'd been taken from them far too soon. Already, Creslyn could barely recall the sound of his voice. His image, once clear and crisp in her mind's eye, was beginning to fade at the edges, like a memory just out of her reach.

Cressie.

He'd been the only one to ever call her that, and she clung to the beloved nickname like a lifeline, refusing to let go. Worried that if she did, she would lose him forever.

Creslyn inhaled deeply, letting the cool autumn air alleviate some of her sorrow, and the knot inside her chest eased.

"I already told you, Aries." She cocked one hip to the side, wishing her brother didn't feel the need to have this conversation with her. Again. "I am perfectly fine. When you came to me with the contract drawn between you and Prince Drake, I understood I would be marrying him in Novalise's place should she find another suitor. I accepted my fate then, and I accept it now. You needn't concern yourself with my safety."

"You are my youngest sister. You are blood." Ariesian clamped both of his large hands upon her shoulders. The worry in his eyes had not yet diminished, but the line of displeasure furrowing across his brow had vanished. For now. "I will always be concerned about your safety."

Creslyn opened her mouth to object, but he shook his head, silencing her.

"You cannot expect me to not care when Novalise claimed she saw you training..." His hands fell to his sides, and the look on his face was one of utter defeat. Hopelessness. "With a sword."

"Yes, I am learning to defend myself." She grabbed his hand and squeezed tightly, wishing to the stars he would see her as confident and able, and not just his baby sister constantly in need of his protection. "But it's only because—"

A tremor raced down the bond, the faintest of caresses, as though Drake stood directly behind her and was trailing a single finger along her spine. Her skin grew hot and prickly, as awareness spread through her and goosebumps riddled her flesh. The scent of him came in layers. Frosted pine, then cold winter mountains, and finally, the promise of snow. She glanced to where shadows collected near a stone wall covered in ivy, to where the light of the harvest moon didn't quite reach. It was then she saw him, except…it was different.

Drake had not emerged from the darkness, he was still hidden, invisible to everyone but her. Yet she could *see* him, she could see *all* of it. The shadow realm expanded before her, revealing a world drowned in shades of gray, a haunting expanse of space that existed only in rare glimpses of time where light was never allowed.

She stood there, gazing at him, her mouth slightly ajar as he stared back at her, fully aware she could see through the shadows to him.

"Cres?" Ariesian's voice echoed through the fog of confusion clouding her mind. "Creslyn? Are you quite well?"

Blinking rapidly, she refocused her attention back on her brother. "Yes. Apologies, brother. I…I'm completely fine."

"Promise me this, Creslyn," Ariesian pleaded, squeezing her hand in return. "If you are ever in danger again or if you need help, promise that you will come to me."

"As much as I appreciate your kindness, my welfare is no longer your responsibility. I am more than capable of defending myself through any means necessary, be it magic or blade." She released her brother's hand, knowing her next words would rock the ground beneath his feet, break it open like a treacherous chasm. "Besides, I'm married to the Shadowblade Assassin. And Drake, well, he is my mate."

Ariesian's jaw went slack. He recovered quickly, but nothing he did could disguise the vein ticking at his temple.

"Mate." He repeated the word, his dark brows pulling together to form a small crease.

"Yes." Creslyn held out her hand, and Drake stepped from the fading darkness, pressing a kiss to her knuckles. "My mate."

Ariesian glanced between the two of them, bewildered. "Your magic *chose* each other?"

"More or less." Not quite a lie and not quite the truth, but it spilled from her lips easily enough.

Again, his skeptical gaze flitted to Drake, then back to her, as though he was trying to determine whether or not she told the truth. He must have settled on the former, for he sighed then, and his broad shoulders dropped.

"Very well. Then I suppose there is nothing more I can do."

Drake stepped closer. "There is one thing, my lord."

Ariesian sent him a questioning look.

"Your sister, Sarelle," Drake explained, sparing Creslyn a glance, one that spoke of warning and unfortunate news. "It would appear that Queen Elowyn and your mother think Lady Sarelle and Prince Aspen will…pair nicely with one another. He is in her company as we speak."

Creslyn's heart plummeted into the acidic pit of her stomach, and trepidation walked its icy fingers along the back of her neck. Sarelle deserved better than to suffer at the hands of the brutal, merciless prince. It was rumored he'd fought in far-off wars, none that ever graced Aeramere's shores, and that he kept tally of the number of lives he took. She didn't know if his number matched the count of skulls on Drake's back, nor did she want to find out. To make matters worse, she'd heard stories about some of his sordid affairs. Prince Aspen once threw one of his lovers out into the streets, half naked, during the middle of an argument. She was only wearing a cotton shift and was forced to make the shameful trek home during winter's first snow.

"Damn it." Ariesian shoved a hand through his hair, mussing it further. "I knew something like this would happen."

Shadows rippled around him, outlining him like spilled ink against the moonlight, and Creslyn stepped back. Bursts of starlight streaked through the oppressive dark as his magic throbbed in the air, like the intangible haze of a storm on the horizon. A storm of shadows and starlight.

"Ariesian, you must stop this." She clutched the front of her brother's coat, drawing his clouded gaze to her face. "You cannot allow Sarelle to marry Prince Aspen."

"Do not worry, dearest sister." He flicked his wrists, the cufflinks there snapping into place, then rolled his neck until it cracked. The power swarming him vanished as quickly as it appeared. "I won't."

He strode off, and Creslyn could only hope it was to put an end to whatever her mother and Queen Elowyn were planning. But the moment Ariesian was out of sight, Drake nuzzled her neck, his lips skating up the column of her neck while his fingers dug into her waist, pulling back flush against his chest.

"Now that we're alone," he murmured.

She swatted at him. "Don't even think about it."

Drake twisted her in his arms, spinning her so she faced him. His palm was splayed against her lower back, keeping her locked in place. The corner of his mouth curved.

"Oh, trust me, *solysa*." He reached up between them, tracing the outline of the constellation on her heart with one finger. "It is *all* I think about."

Creslyn rose up on her toes, wrapping her arms around his neck. Stars above, she'd forgotten how ridiculously tall he was. Even with her heels on, she barely grazed his shoulder. His hand slid around to her backside, cupping her firmly in his grasp.

"It is rather dangerous being alone with you in a garden." She let her gaze rove over him, drinking in the fine details of his attire. He wore a crisp black shirt and pants, with a sash of silver tied around his waist, one she couldn't wait to tug off later. His coat was trimmed with silky black thread and embroidered dragons detailed the cuffs of the sleeve. "Especially when you look so ruggedly handsome."

She twirled a strand of his midnight hair with one finger.

Surprise registered in the depths of his green eyes, but he shuttered it away quickly.

"You are mistaken, my lady." Drake folded his arms beneath her bottom and hoisted her up, keeping her positioned against his chest so they were eye to eye. "It is you who is dangerous."

He leaned in, his mouth a whisper from her own. "That dress is just an added benefit."

Creslyn smiled. She'd chosen her gown for no other reason than she thoroughly expected to have it torn off her by the end of the evening. The skirt was heavy satin, with two slits up each side, and the golden pink fabric shimmered whenever she moved. Gold floral lace made up the entirety of the bodice, draping off her shoulders and molding to her breasts, before wrapping around her and dipping scandalously low down her back.

She kissed him then, a gentle swipe of her tongue along his lips as her hands treaded lightly over the carved muscle of his shoulders and neck. She traced the dips, the ridges, needling the tips of her fingers into the solid mass of his body, massaging gently.

Drake groaned into her mouth. "I swear to any star or god that is watching, I will take you right here."

She eased back, and he slowly set her down, the bulge in his pants pressing into her belly as she slid down the length of him.

Creslyn grabbed his hand, leading him toward the gentle strumming of instruments. "If I miss Novalise's wedding, she may not ever forgive me."

"And what's more important?" Drake asked, twirling her into his embrace. "Your sister's forgiveness?"

He lowered his head, flicking his tongue along her ear, causing her nipples to harden.

"Or my cock inside of you?"

Her skin flushed at his words, and every sensitive part of her hummed in response. Her stomach tightened, the scrape of lace against her breasts suddenly too much to bear. Every nerve was heightened. Heat pooled between her legs, and she squeezed her thighs together, craving his touch, desperate for the release only he could give her. Her imagination spiraled, taking both of them with it, as she pictured him pinning her against one of the walls as stone bit into her back, as he drove into her, sending her soaring. Or he would bend her over as she clung to one of the flowering trees, and he would take her from behind, clamping one hand over her mouth to silence her screams.

"Creslyn..." Drake growled, the warning in his voice dragging her back from her thoughts.

His eyes were dark with lust, with power, and his large body pulsed with tension, as though he was ready to snap a neck at a moment's notice.

"Let's go, before I give into your explicit fantasies." He took her hand, pressing their scarred palms together so the bond burned hot, and led her toward the wedding.

She was half tempted to push another one of her daydreams onto him, one she'd kept locked in the darkest part of her, that place she wasn't quite ready to embrace. But then they rounded a corner of silver ferns and budding indigo winterblooms not yet ready to blossom, and Creslyn's lighthearted mood evaporated.

The ceremony for Novalise and Asher had not yet begun, resulting in lords and ladies from all five houses of Aeramere mingling with flutes of starberry wine while swapping landslide rumors and backhanded compliments. As soon as Creslyn came into view, with Drake right behind her, the buoyant conversations deflated, and every pair of disparaging eyes snapped right to her.

Her heart plummeted into her stomach, sinking into a bottomless pit of dread. They would see right through her in no time. Any moment now, they would break the wall of reflective glass she'd carefully constructed around herself to protect the truth of her character. The pieces would shatter around her, slicing her skin and flaying her open, so they could all bear witness to the gaping chasm of darkness lurking inside of her.

Whispers floated past her, muffled critics gossiping under their breath or from behind the back of their hands.

A gasp. "I cannot believe she was stolen away."

"I heard she was traded, a bargaining chip." A callous remark.

"She was sold off like a breeding mare." A vile notion.

Creslyn's confidence wavered. She wet her bottom lip, swallowing around the lump of worry that was making it more and more impossible to breathe. Her palms grew damp, her heart pounded. It felt as though she was walking upon a ceiling of glass, one that cracked and splintered with each step, and it was only a matter of time before it came crashing out from under her.

Then Drake was there.

He slid his arm easily around her waist, supporting her knees trembling beneath her skirts. His thumb stroked lazy lines of encouragement along the length of her ribs and when he glanced down at her, there was warmth hiding in his gaze.

His voice caressed her mind, soothing her, relaxing her. *"Let them see how brightly a star can shine in the pitch of night."*

She smiled, rising on her toes and planting a kiss at the corner of his mouth, and whispered faintly, "Thank you."

"Anything for you, *sjellhert*."

They took their seats, and with her hand clasped firmly in Drake's, Creslyn watched her eldest sister recite her vows.

Novalise and Asher's ceremony was decidedly dreamy. Lavender roses coated in starlight overflowed from cobalt vases while torches sparking with silver flames illuminated the garden like frostbitten moonlight. The pair of them stood at an altar crafted from selenite, swearing their love for one another as their magic soared above them in full display. Starfire swerved and sparked high into the air, followed by bursts of midnight frostfire. Their magic clashed over the rooftops of House Celestine, illuminating the night sky in a series of starlit flames.

It was wondrous.

Novalise was positively stunning. Her gown of silver fell off her shoulders and was fastened with moonstone buttons down the back. The soft fabric seemed to swirl around her like she was walking upon clouds. The drapes and folds of silk hugged her waist then billowed around her in ethereal beauty. But while Novalise's cheeks flushed and her eyes misted with a delicate sheen, it was Asher who held Creslyn's attention.

His gaze never strayed, not once did he ever look away from Novalise while they spoke their vows. There was a deep well of emotion in the dark gray of his eyes, and the slight ring of gold encircling them only seemed to burn brighter every time she was near. Asher looked at Novalise as though she was a goddess among the stars, like she hung the moon in the sky with her own two hands. He was fascinated by her, consumed by her, so fully and devastatingly in love with her that it left Creslyn breathless.

Everyone should experience that kind of love, everyone should have someone who looked at them the way Asher gazed upon Novalise.

When the newly married couple finally kissed, Creslyn sniffled once, wiping a single tear from her eye.

An hour later, she found herself at a round table draped with creamy linens while music and dancing carried on around her. The gardens of House Celestine had been converted to a makeshift ballroom, the chill in the night air just brisk enough to cool her skin from the warmth of so many moving and swirling bodies. Novalise and Asher danced to every song, unaware of any misgivings. Creslyn's gaze darted from where Ariesian stood protectively by Sarelle's side to their mother, who sent him a scathing look of reproach from the safety of the queen's table.

Creslyn knew she did not understand the depths of what was happening in her family. She was stuck in a web of lies and deceit, tangled in the threads of tension that seemed to tighten any time they were all together. She hadn't noticed it before, she'd been too busy dancing, too busy shopping and buying sparkly things to even pay attention to the undercurrents shifting beneath her feet, threatening to pull her under like a dangerous tide. Yet now, the smiles were strained. Words once spoken with honey were doused in vinegar. The foundation of trust, love, and respect her father had built was cracking, slowly crumbling. She just had to find the source of the damage.

She took a sip of starberry wine, unable to disguise her smile as the bright flavors played on her tongue and the bubbles fizzed in her mouth. Her gaze slid to Drake, who was staring at the piece of lemon and blueberry cream cake set before him as though it had personally affronted him somehow. Creslyn had already devoured her slice and if he didn't make a move soon, she was going to snatch it right off his plate.

Her knee bounced in anticipation.

Until Solarius yawned, excessively, slinging his arm across the back of the empty seat next to him. He ran one hand through his messy hair, rocking the chair back on two legs. He'd removed his coat, rolled his sleeves, and only half of his navy blue shirt was tucked in, as though it was an afterthought. His silver eyes were dark and glossy, and Creslyn thought perhaps he'd indulged in too many libations. Narissa sat on his other side, a stark contrast to the unkempt appearance of her brother.

She swirled her drink, eyeing Solarius from over the rim, tapping her nail against the glass. The pretty rings she wore glinted in the soft light. Her pale green eyes were subtly lined with kohl, and that signature rosy hue on her cheeks shimmered against her sun-kissed skin. Her hair fell in soft golden waves around her bare shoulders. The strapless gown she wore was the most beautiful shade of aquamarine Creslyn had ever seen. The bodice was covered in bits of crushed coral shaped like flowers, while the fine silk floated over her arms and tumbled down around her like cresting waves.

Her brow was knit together, and when she tapped her glass again, it was then Creslyn noticed only her ring finger was bare.

Perhaps Solarius had not yet given her an engagement ring. Or maybe he was simply delaying the inevitable.

Solarius took a lazy sip of his wine, hoisting the glass in Drake's direction. "When do you return to Brackroth?"

Drake inclined his head, studying her brother. "In such a hurry to get rid of me?"

Surely, he had to know Solarius was intoxicated. She could only hope that obvious bit of knowledge would keep Drake from engaging in what would only lead to another fight. One that Solarius would certainly not win.

"No," Solarius drawled, his gaze flicking over to Creslyn. "Only wondering how much time I'll have to spend with my sister before you steal her away again."

Drake stabbed at the slice of cake in front of him with his fork. "We fly at dawn."

Creslyn shot him a look. "So soon?"

He set the fork down and grabbed her hand, weaving their fingers together. "You wish to stay?"

Instantly, the gloom of Brackroth with its sunless skies and heavy, rain-laden clouds filled her mind. And an image of King Marius with his beady eyes, scraggly beard, and sinister smile caused her insides to sour.

She hastily took another gulp of wine. "Yes, I would like to stay. For a little while longer, if possible. I cannot say I am too keen to return to where my presence is unwanted."

"You are wanted." Drake kissed her knuckles, holding her gaze with his mesmerizing eyes. "Immensely."

"Yes," Solarius scoffed, slamming his glass down upon the table. "She's wanted dead by your piece of shit king."

Drake's power flared, and shadows crawled along his shoulders, slipping from between his knuckles.

"Solarius." Narissa's musical voice was laced with scorn. "That's enough."

She placed her hand on top of his, but Solarius jerked away like her touch was acidic. Narissa flinched, pressing her lips together.

"No, Rissa love, it is not enough." He lurched forward in his chair and faced her, leaning in so closely, the tips of their noses almost touched. "It is not enough that I am forced to sit here while my youngest sister is carted back to that shithole of a kingdom. All I can do is watch as my mother conspires with the queen to marry Sarelle to our insufferable prince, and Ariesian is caught between duty and honor while snakes whisper into his ear."

He slouched back, his gaze raking over Narissa in such a callous manner that even Creslyn shuddered. "Meanwhile, I can do nothing and help no one because I am saddled with *you*."

"Solarius!" Creslyn scolded, scowling at her brother. "For shame."

Humiliation colored Narissa's cheeks and her golden glow paled. A faint sheen flooded her eyes, and she stood abruptly, clasping her hands together.

Drake was on his feet a moment later out of respect as she fled from the table, while Solarius remained seated, his legs outstretched before him.

Mortification sunk its claws into Creslyn's neck. She could not *believe* her brother would be so disgraceful. She leaned forward, her hands curling into tight fists.

"Solarius," she hissed, seething at his complete lack of decorum. "How *dare* you? Have you no manners? What would Father say if he saw you treating her in such a way? You are a lord of

House Celestine, Narissa is a lady of House Azurvend, and you shall regard her as such."

Solarius ignored her reprimand, downing the rest of his drink.

Creslyn shoved back from the table, trembling with rage.

"Apologize to Narissa," she demanded. "At once."

Her brother leaned back, rolling his head in the direction of Narissa's retreating form. The anger and tension and frustration simply bled away as he slumped lower into his seat. "She doesn't want my apology, Cres. She wants a fight. She's looking for any way possible to break our future union."

Creslyn shook her head, folding her arms across her chest. "I disagree. She looked devastated. Embarrassed. No one enjoys being made to feel that way, Sol. If I didn't know any better, I would say she's crying right now and it's all your fault."

"Saltwater or pearls," Solarius muttered, lifting his glass and frowning once he remembered it was empty.

"Pardon?"

"That's how to tell if her tears are real or not." Solarius scraped his teeth along his bottom lip, tossing his disheveled hair out of his face. "She's a water fae, Cres. She can summon tears as easily as she can the waves. She can break your heart when she cries, like a siren's song. Saltwater stains her cheeks, but if her tears are tied to an actual emotion, they turn to pearls."

Creslyn placed one hand over her heart. "That is quite possibly the saddest thing I have ever heard."

"Sounds painful," Drake murmured.

Solarius shrugged, indifferent. "They only turn to pearls after they've fallen. I've seen it once. A long time ago."

Tears were tears, no matter the emotion, and Narissa was absolutely crying. There was no denying the way they pricked her eyes at Solarius's harsh words, and Creslyn knew for a fact she'd bitten her bottom lip to keep it from trembling. She glanced around the table, then checked the ground, scouring the smooth stone when a tiny glimmer caught her eye.

There, wedged between a single blade of grass and a small rock, was a perfectly round pearl. Its sheen was as iridescent as one of Creslyn's rainbows.

She snatched it off the ground, pulled her arm back, and launched it at Solarius's head.

"Shit, Cres!" He plucked it out of the air before it smacked him right between the eyes.

Drake sat back, then patted her bottom. "Fascinating."

Creslyn ignored the small display of affection, trying not to think too much of it, and pinned her brother with a hard stare.

Solarius rolled the pearl between his fingers, then pinched the bridge of his nose.

"Fuck." He jolted upright, shoving the gem into his pocket. "Excuse me."

Creslyn watched her brother sprint in the direction of Narissa's departure, then expelled a heavy sigh. Shoulders sagging, she lowered herself into Drake's lap instead of her own chair, finding herself in need of his comfort for the second time this evening. He curled her against him, wrapping his arms snugly around her waist, and she let her head come to rest against his chest. The beating of his heart matched her own, a steady rhythm that soothed her soul, and the bond between them warmed. His shadows calmed and that swath of darkness inside her yawned open a little wider.

Drake's hand rubbed her spine, moving in slow, easy circles.

"I hate to see them so unhappy." She tilted her head back, looking up at him. "Do you think she'll forgive him?"

His dark brows lifted. "Would you be so quick to forgive me if I claimed I was saddled with you as a wife?"

"It was awfully terrible of him." She winced, her teeth snagging on her bottom lip. "What do you suppose Solarius meant? By snakes whispering into Ariesian's ear?"

"I'm not sure, but I intend to find out."

"Should we be worried?"

He leaned down, pressing a kiss to her temple. "Not yet."

Creslyn settled into the safety of his arms. Her gaze drifted around the party, glimpsing Novalise and Asher looking so painfully in love it made her chest tighten. Ariesian was still standing watch over Sarelle, ensuring Prince Aspen kept his distance. But then her attention snagged on Solarius and Narissa.

They stood near a waterfall of flowers covered in stardust, likely Sarelle's doing, Narissa with her arms crossed protectively across her chest, and Solarius with his hands upon her shoulders. A tear slipped from the corner of her eye and her brother caught it, the drop of emotion turning into a pearl in his hand.

"If I cried pearls," Creslyn mused, snuggling against Drake, "would you catch them for me?"

His solid chest rumbled, a deep chuckle that sent tingles of awakening coursing through her. "I can think of other things I'd like to do with pearls."

Her lips twitched. "Oh, really?"

Drake stiffened, his muscles snapping into stone beneath her. He stood suddenly, drawing one hand to shove her behind him as his shadows unfurled like the tempest of night. Power radiated from him, a vengeful promise of death. He snarled, his massive body seeming to expand with otherworldly magic, nefarious and lethal.

This was not her husband.

This was not the Shadowblade Assassin.

This was something else altogether.

"Drake?" Creslyn whispered his name, her voice cracking.

And then the screaming began.

CHAPTER TWENTY-ONE

ovalise and Asher's wedding festivities descended into absolute chaos.

Drake had sensed the shift, a spear of awareness slammed into him almost immediately, but nothing could have prepared him for the sight unfolding before him. Monstrous tree forms with hollows for eyes and spindly branches for arms slashed their way through the delicate floral arches, crushing them beneath their trunk-like bodies. Grotesque vines slithered like serpents, overturning tables and crawling across the stone, cracking like whips with each strike. Gangly creatures with elongated limbs and animalistic skulls crowned with twisted antlers emerged from the gardens of House Celestine, smashing the floating crystal stars and gnashing their dislocated jaws, sending the noble fae who stood too close fleeing in fright.

Drake inhaled, his lip curling into a sneer.

The stench of rancid fruit, of tainted magic, permeated the air.

Whatever was controlling these fiends of the unnatural was corrupted, polluted by the desire of power. The magic of the earth had been sullied, defiled, and utilized to inflict terror.

Drake unleashed his wrath, his shadows unfurling, ravaging the gardens in vengeful ribbons of death. The darkness consumed him, erupting from the well of violence he kept tightly guarded, pouring from the tips of his fingers, and rolling off his shoulders in furious waves. Shadows whipped and hissed, attacking and lashing the depraved creatures, as the curse revealed the truth of his nature. He was a monster of shadow and night, of death and destruction. There was no sting upon his spine, no tattoo of a skull marked upon his flesh, as these vessels of soiled magic did not possess souls. But their lack of a beating heart did not stop the Shadowblade from thrumming with the call to kill, and it did not ease the intensifying need for bloodlust coursing through him.

He reached for the hilt of the dagger when a burning sensation cut through his palm, as though his hand had caught on fire. There was a push of power, a summons to his soul, as the bond flared hot and bright.

A storm of blinding sunlight and fissures of rainbows exploded in a rush of chaotic, familiar magic.

Drake glanced over and stared at the maelstrom of beauty beside him.

There was Creslyn, a sphere of radiant colors surrounding her as she took aim. She drew one arm back, stretching the other out before her as she gathered the glow of the sun in her palm. Fiery streaks of sunlight burst into devastating spirals, sparking and scorching the creatures rushing into the gardens. Her hair lifted from her shoulders, fanning out around her in a kaleidoscope of shimmering hues. The blue of her eyes deepened, a line of vexation marred her brow, and Drake swore he'd never seen anything more beautiful.

Even if she was holding back.

"What are you doing?" He meant it as a question, but she didn't blink when his tone conveyed it as more of a demand.

"The same as you." She didn't even spare him a glance. "Defending my family and my house."

Drake moved closer, his shadows mingling with the gleam of gold pouring from her. "Stay with me, do you understand? Do not lose sight of me."

Her hostile gaze flicked to him, but she nodded sharply.

Together, they assailed the volatile beings of the earth in a clash of dark and light that ricocheted throughout the gardens. Yet for each one they took out, another appeared in its place. It reminded Drake of when he'd been called to Faeven to assist in saving it from the dark fae, yet where those nightmarish beings were summoned through a portal, the ones they fought now seemed to reappear as though they were nothing more than illusions. But Drake could not detect a single trace of glamour, and the destruction they left in their wake was far from imaginary.

He'd grossly underestimated how ill-prepared Aeramere truly was in terms of defending themselves against any sort of attack. Many of the fae were running away, hiding behind flowering bushes, and shouting in fear, utterly useless at wielding their magic defensively. It was absolute madness, watching the disarray and panic unfold around him.

Besides himself and Creslyn, from what he could see, only two others held their ground.

Novalise and Asher.

They stood in the center of what was supposed to be the dance floor, protecting those who sought refuge behind them. Novalise in her wedding gown, a frenzied starstorm encircling her as bolts of starlight shot out in swift arches, like blazing shooting stars. Asher right by her side, his gray gaze banking the smoldering embers of rage, as he attacked with the cold, silvery black flames of frostfire.

Out of the corner of Drake's eye, he witnessed Creslyn jerk

violently. A tremor of fear sliced down the bond between them, and then his wife screamed.

"Caelian!"

If Drake's blood was already cold, hearing Creslyn scream like that turned it to ice.

He spun in the direction of her line of sight, only to find Caelian on the ground, those hideous vines wrapping around her ankles and waist, dragging her across the ground. She was thrashing against them, her nails scraping against stone as she struggled to get away.

"Calm." Drake spoke the word into Creslyn's mind. *"Stay calm."*

She whirled on him, eyes wild, the sapphire nearly as black as obsidian.

A moment later, Kjeld appeared, barreling through the mass of snared vines. He tore at the axe strapped to his back, swinging it into a wide arch, hacking at the leaves that stretched like claws. Kjeld slammed the weapon into the ground, severing the growth of vines, and the earth shuddered beneath Drake's feet. Black ooze spilled from the cleaved plants, spreading like diseased blood, the putrid stench of foul magic lingering in the air.

Kjeld scooped Caelian into his arms as though she were weightless, darting in long strides toward the safety of House Celestine.

One of the terrorizing tree fiends lurched toward Creslyn, and rage engulfed Drake. His shadows seethed with raw, feral energy, grasping the creature and snapping it in half.

Grabbing Creslyn by the wrist, he hauled her close, then grasped her chin.

Her eyes were orbs of midnight.

"Focus, *solysa*," he demanded, searching her face. "Never lose focus."

She blinked once, her gaze clearing, her expression hardening into solemn resolve. She whirled away from him then, lashing out, aiming with poise and striking with grace. Still, she did not unleash the depth of her potential. There was more there, something darker, hidden away beneath her surface. Something she refused to recognize, to accept.

But she would in time, for even the gods and stars could see she was fearless. A tempest of sun and shadow.

Drake scanned the gardens, his gaze landing on a small dais where Queen Elowyn stood with her arms spread, a halo of evergreen around her. She looked as though she was trying to summon something as a means to combat the attack. Her brow was furrowed in concentration and her eyes were closed, but nothing was happening. Again, her magic grated against his senses, though he could not pinpoint what it was that set his nerves on edge. Behind her, Lady Trysta cowered, her arms flung over her head in a means of futile self-preservation. And that bastard, Bastian Valewood, was nowhere to be seen.

Without warning, Ariesian sprinted across the gardens, directly into the battle, a storm of shadows and starlight churning around him. Exactly as Drake suspected.

Sarelle was rushing toward her brother, but her heels made no traction against the ground littered with vines and tree limbs. Her shoe caught upon one of the strewn branches and she tripped, stumbling forward. She cried out, attempting to break her fall, but even Drake could hear the snapping of the delicate bone in her wrist when she landed. Her peal of agony splintered through the night. One of the beasts with distorted arms and a misshapen skull loomed over her, its unsightly jaws grinding in crazed hunger.

Drake set his shadows upon the monster, but a blur of black and gray cut him off, launching itself in front of him. He pulled his power back as the beast took shape—it possessed the body of a dire wolf, the sleek fur glossy in the sparse light. Its head was nothing more than the wolf's skull, adorned with curving horns, and eyes that glowed like the sea set on fire. Drake had only seen such a creature once before, and only briefly…

The wolf-like creature growled, its menacing howl piercing the air as it hovered over Sarelle. She curled into herself, her broken sobs echoing through the gardens.

Ariesian bellowed.

Creslyn jolted forward, then froze as the dire wolf transformed, shifting into the one fae who'd been most notably absent during the entire attack.

Prince Aspen.

He gathered Sarelle with one arm, swiftly tossing her over his shoulder, then his fist collided with the ground. The stone cracked and fractured beneath the force of the impact, and Drake reached for Creslyn, lifting her off her feet.

Power blasted from Prince Aspen in a gust of magic that pulsed in steady waves. Decay spread across the earth from where the prince's fist met the stone, bleeding through the gardens like spilled ink across a messy canvas. The ground turned black, the fiends with sullied magic withered and died, crumbling into nothing more than piles of rotten ash as he took control of nature's elements, as he stole the entirety of their life force. Prince Aspen stood slowly, carefully lowering Sarelle back to the ground, but she clung to him, her face buried against his chest. He rolled his neck once, popping his jaw.

Silence befell the gardens of House Celestine.

Everyone stared at the prince, at Sarelle, whose muffled crying gradually ebbed. The shadows withdrew and the sunlight dimmed. The starlight faded and the frostfire dwindled. All around, the swell of magic subsided, until all that remained was an eerie, lingering quiet.

Drake set Creslyn down, linking their fingers together. He strode toward the prince, hauling her along with him.

Prince Aspen glanced over at Drake, his mouth pulling into a tight line, as he attempted to pry Sarelle off him.

At once, Drake shoved his way into the prince's thoughts. *"Explain yourself."*

Prince Aspen did not appear at all shocked to hear Drake's voice infiltrate his mind. He curled his hands around Sarelle's shoulders, looking back at him from over the top of her head. *"I owe you no explanation."*

But Drake refused to be deterred. *"Tell me, how does a fae prince of mountain, forest, and earth possess the ability to shift into the Eyrewolfe?"*

The prince's face held calm impassivity, his breathing remained even and steady, and the beating of his heart gave no signs of insecurity. *"Ask my mother."*

He held Sarelle out at arm's length. Her sparkling, midnight hair was tangled and fell around her in sporadic waves. Her blue eyes were rimmed with red, her pale skin splotchy from distress, and tears stained her cheeks. She cradled her broken wrist with her other hand.

When she spoke, her bottom lip quivered. "I owe you a life debt."

The prince scoffed, dismissing her plight with a wave of his hand. He straightened the lapel of his coat, then flicked his wrists, tugging on the cuffs. "You can keep your archaic traditions, Lady Sarelle. I care not for life debts."

Her mouth fell open, her damp lashes fluttering in shock. "But you saved me."

He clicked his tongue, annoyed. "I am not your hero."

Ariesian stepped forward, wrapping a protective arm around Sarelle's shoulders, pulling her into his side.

"If you will not accept a life debt on behalf of my sister," he stated, his voice low and threatening, "then accept it on behalf of me."

The prince merely lifted a brow, as though he might have been impressed for a moment but then thought better of it. He adjusted the gold chain of skulls hanging from his neck, effectively dismissing Ariesian with a singular look of disdain. "Unnecessary, my lord."

He cracked his knuckles and stormed off, casting one final glance of loathing in the direction of Queen Elowyn.

Sarelle shook her head, clutching her injured wrist to her chest. "What *was* that?"

Ariesian cocked his head, eyeing his sister. "Are you inquiring about the attack, or the prince's cheery disposition and rather interesting shapeshifting abilities?"

A blush colored Sarelle's cheeks, and she took up a sudden interest in the mucky hem of her dress.

"Solarius." Ariesian lifted one hand, beckoning over the second eldest Starstorm.

The glassy, alcohol-induced glaze in Solarius's eyes was gone, having been replaced by poignant determination. He moved toward their small circle, one hand firmly gripped around Narissa's wrist. Her face was ashen, nervous energy flowed off her in restless ripples, and there was a small slice along her left cheek.

Ariesian clamped one hand on Solarius's shoulder. "The queen will likely call her High Council to the palace to discuss tonight's events and hopefully uncover whoever was behind this attack. Mother and I will both be required to attend. Station guards at every entrance to the house and at the base of the mountain. No one comes in, no one leaves. The safety of our family is your responsibility until I return."

Solarius nodded, solemn. "Consider it done."

The eldest Starstorm had the distinct ability to command the attention of everyone around him. He wore his confidence, his demand for respect, like a crown. When Drake entered a room, people cowered. They shrank in his presence and avoided eye contact as much as possible. Ariesian, however, had quite the opposite effect. His demeanor reflected unshakeable resilience, composed power, and steadfast charisma. Rolling his shoulders back, he lifted his chin, garnering the notice of every fae in their general vicinity.

"Everyone shall return to their homes at once and take any necessary precautions." He pointed toward the main path leading out of the gardens. "Now."

Drake should have been concerned with who was leaving and who was loitering. He should have made it a point to keep an eye on Queen Elowyn and Lady Trysta, perhaps even have found a way to interrupt this supposed meeting of the High Council. But instead, he found himself facing Creslyn, finally able to truly look at her.

He didn't know what he expected to see.

Perhaps she would find him horrifying given she was finally afforded an opportunity to witness the depth of his curse. Or maybe she would loathe him for staining her blood with the shadows of his own. After all, when she'd been in the throes of her sunstorm, her eyes had been nearly black. Surely that was his doing, his fault, for binding her to his depraved soul. Not only that, but he'd seen the way she'd been able to look right through the shadows. She'd found him watching her while she was talking to Ariesian. Creslyn had known he was there, and he thought she'd always been able to sense him, but when her gaze had latched right onto him through the shroud of the shadow realm, he'd known with utter certainty that they shared more than simply a binding of blood. Unless...unless that shred of darkness had always been inside of her, just waiting to be discovered and coaxed to life.

In that case, he would be more than pleased to accept the responsibility of her potential ruin.

A sigh shuddered out of her, and he captured her cheeks in his hands, his rough palms gently tilting her face up to him.

He searched her, searched the bond, for any sign of injury.

"Are you hurt?" he demanded.

She shook her head, her hair shimmered like an iridescent waterfall. "No."

"Are you afraid?"

Her brows pinched together. "No."

"Are you—"

Creslyn rose up on her toes, wrapped her hands behind his neck, and pressed her mouth to his own. Her lips were soft, her kiss gentle, like a test of their intimacy, of the bond humming between them. She tasted him, explored him like it was the first time, and the quiet, barely audible noise she made caused his blood to stir. But this was not the pounding force of lust. It was different, a sensation that left his heart feeling like she'd wedged a dagger of promise into the wall of stone he'd built around it. One wrong move, and the entire thing would collapse. She was fracturing his defenses, breaking the foundation of his depraved soul.

She would be his undoing.

"Dearest sister," Solarius drawled, his bored tone laced with a hint of malice.

Creslyn broke their kiss, her expression smug as she glanced over one shoulder at her brother.

Solarius inclined his head. "Your Highness. If the two of you would not mind coming up for air, I would like us all to meet in the observatory. I believe there are matters we need to discuss."

He pinned Drake with a hard stare. "Some of which you may find rather beneficial."

"Certainly, my lord." Drake nodded. "We would be more than happy to join you."

He wove one arm around Creslyn's waist, fully aware of the power she held over him. Power that, if not mindfully controlled, could lead to his ultimate demise.

Drake glanced at the faint scar marring his palm, then clenched his hand into a fist.

Not only his demise, but hers as well.

CHAPTER TWENTY-TWO

Creslyn's entire body was humming, crackling with energy.

Her heart continued to thump wildly inside her chest, and her fingers still tingled from the magic pulsing through her veins. She'd never used her power like that before, never realized she was capable of creating a storm of her own, one that she could wield like a weapon. It was thrilling. Intoxicating. Empowering. A delightful kind of high, one that made her feel like she was standing on the edge of a cliff, leaning into the breeze, ready to leap and soar.

And when those terrifying creatures had emerged, wreaking havoc upon the gardens of House Celestine and ruining Novalise and Asher's wedding, Creslyn had not been afraid. She did not run and cry like so many others, no, she'd held her ground, defending what was hers. She wanted to destroy them for the fear they caused, for the pain they had brought upon her home. And when Caelian had been tangled in those wretched vines, clawing against the stone to break free of them, that crevasse of frozen darkness inside of Creslyn thawed, splitting wide open, ready to swallow her whole.

She had almost fully given into its demands for freedom.

But she'd held back, unable to let herself go. Because the moment she did, the second she succumbed to the tempting lure, she would be exposed. The raw truth of her essence would be on full display, and she would no longer be able to hide behind the façade of brilliant sunshine and dazzling rainbows. Her family, everyone she loved, would know she was tainted, a blemish upon her blood right. The darkness she harbored inside of her was a smear upon her family name, a flaw upon her character. If they caught a glimpse of it, they would undoubtedly blame Drake for corrupting her. They would claim he tarnished the good of her soul, and she simply could not allow them to think any more ill of him.

Not when the sliver of murky power had been within her all along. It was something she'd been born with, something that set her apart in the worst kind of way, something she'd discovered in her youth when she realized the whole of the world was not always painted with sunshine and rainbows. Like when her mother scorned her for not possessing magic of a celestial quality, or when Nyxian ridiculed her "pretty magic," claiming it would never be powerful. Or like the day when her father died, and all the color bled from her life, washing it in muted tones of lackluster gray.

So, she would keep the darkness locked away and whisper to the stars in the hopes that it stayed trapped inside of her, where it belonged.

The observatory was buzzing with muted conversations, the muffled words ringing in her ears.

Caelian stood near one of the glowing alcoves, where star-shaped fragments of moonstone, forming her constellation, the Tree of Life, sparkled over her head. Her gown was all but ruined, the hem was torn and covered in a layer of grime, and she twisted one of the frayed ribbons anxiously around her fingers. Kjeld was standing beside her, his golden hair hanging loosely around his rugged face, most of it having fallen free from the plaits once holding it in place. His rich brown coat was torn at the sleeve, and he swung his axe in his hands, the leather wrapped handle thumping against his rough palm.

Novalise was propped up against the dais, the back of her head resting against the molded fragments of blue goldstone and selenite. Her arms were wrapped around Sarelle, the top of her head tucked beneath Novalise's chin. Filth and a few crumpled leaves clung to Sarelle's dress, but Novalise didn't seem to care if the dirt transferred to her wedding gown. She just continued to stroke one hand absently down the length of Sarelle's inky black hair. Each time Sarelle took a shaky breath, stardust fell around her like scattered snow. Asher was beside them both, his arms crossed over his broad chest, his dark gray eyes heated with an emotion Creslyn couldn't quite pinpoint. He shoved a hand through his black hair, the silver lock streaking through the front tumbling forward across his drawn brow once more.

Creslyn's gaze scanned the dimly lit observatory, landing on Solarius and Narissa.

She watched in pained silence as her brother reached to touch Narissa's cheek, where a fresh cut sliced across her skin. But Narissa flinched, turning away from him, her golden sea-swept waves shielding her face from view. Solarius's hand fell to his side, his hands coiling into tight fists.

An arm slid around Creslyn's waist, and she leaned into Drake's comfort, into his cooling embrace.

Solarius cleared his throat, stalking toward the center of the observatory where the Faerie Star flanked by twin crescent moons was inlaid into the gleaming floor. He shoved his hands into the pockets of his pants, his silver gaze landing on each pair of eyes staring back at him.

"I intend to send word to Tovian and Nyxian about what

transpired here tonight. In no way am I expecting them to sail for home at once, but I do feel as though they should both be informed." He rocked back onto his heels. "Just in case."

The words he left unsaid hung between them, heavy like the boughs of an evergreen weighted with snow.

Just in case their brothers returned home to find Aeramere in the midst of a war.

"That being said," Solarius glanced around, his eyes flicking to the glass ceiling of the observatory, "what do we know?"

"That the fae of Aeramere stand no chance against any form of dark magic." Drake kept his hand positioned on Creslyn's waist as he spoke, his tone measured and calm. "With the exception of Creslyn, Asher, Novalise, Ariesian, and Prince Aspen, no one else used their magic to defend themselves or others."

Solarius's gaze narrowed.

"No offense, my lord," Drake added with a dip of his head, his mouth twitching slightly.

"None taken." Solarius pinched the bridge of his nose and loosed a hasty sigh. "And as much as it pains me to admit it, Prince Drake is correct."

He paced around the points of the Faerie Star, his boots clicking softly against the smooth stone.

"I fear that even if we had known this attack was coming, we would have been utterly defenseless. We have been spoon-fed into believing we are safe, that the Veil protects us from the dangers beyond our realm." Solarius tucked his hands behind his back, angling his chin, as though he knew whatever he was about to say next, bordered on the treacherous. "The Veil, however, is useless against any threats from within."

Creslyn shifted on her feet, uneasy. Apprehension dragged its cold fingers down the back of her neck. Though Solarius spoke true, there was an inflection of defiance in his voice. Such a connotation could be construed as treasonous. Disloyalty to

Queen Elowyn was a punishable offense, one where lashings were the sole form of penance.

She shuddered, unable to shake the vision of Solarius on his knees, head bowed, as a whip cracked through the air.

Asher stepped forward then, adjusting the lapel of his coat. He cast a fleeting look in Novalise's direction. She paled slightly, her grip tightening around Sarelle's shoulders, but then she nodded once.

"I believe the rebellions are being silenced for a reason. Someone within the palace wants us to believe that everything is fine, they want us to carry on as we always have, to keep up with the appearances of a society where all that matters is petty gossip and matched marriages. But our houses are more than simply a means with which to conduct frivolous balls and foster mundane courtship." The corner of Asher's mouth lifted when he found Novalise scowling at him. "Forgive me, Starlight. You know I would gladly suffer through all of it for you."

Novalise's expression softened, her eyes taking on the look of someone so sickeningly in love it made Creslyn's heart ache.

"But," Asher continued, his voice more threatening than before, "war is coming to Aeramere."

He gestured toward his new bride. "Novalise has seen it."

Creslyn gasped. "What?"

Sarelle reared back, putting space between herself and Novalise, a mixture of hurt and confusion swimming through her deep blue eyes. "Is this true?"

Novalise's skin flushed, and she floundered beneath the sudden attention, fiddling with the silver folds of her gown. "Yes...it's true. I conducted a star reading during Midsummer, after my own humiliating one."

Asher grabbed her hand, pulling her close to his side, his lips brushing lightly across her temple. Soothing her.

Novalise seemed to breathe him in, his very presence grounding her. Strengthening her. "I performed it here, in the observatory. Three constellations were revealed to me—the Great Stag, Vespira the Druid, and Aedes the Fae Warrior. By all counts, the three should not have aligned, yet they did, and what the stars showed me was a distant battle. A war. One that will take place in the very heart of Aeramere."

"Why did you not tell us?" Sarelle cried, clutching her muddied gown with one hand. She held out the soiled fabric as though it was proof of some kind. "We could have been more prepared, we could have done something!"

"Like what?" Caelian fired back, stomping away from the alcove, the remnants of her own soiled dress dragging along the ground behind her. "I suppose you can create little explosions of deadly stardust now?"

Sarelle huffed. She folded her arms across her chest and sneered at Caelian. "Explosions of stardust would be far superior to the impractical use of wishes upon stars."

"Caelian. Sarelle. That is *quite* enough." Solarius's low timbre cut through their argument, sounding so similar to their father that both sisters faltered before falling completely silent. "I did not ask all of you here just for the opportunity to bicker over the past."

"Besides," Asher interrupted smoothly, wrapping a protective arm around Novalise's shoulders. "My *wife* did exactly what would have been expected of her. She told those who are responsible for our safety, and they did *nothing*."

"That cannot be right." Creslyn shook her head in disbelief, a gnawing sense of dread needling its way deeper into her spine. Her thoughts were a chaotic whirlwind of information, none of which made any sense. How could she have been so blind to the world around her? "But why would Queen Elowyn ignore Nova's reading?"

The last person she expected to answer her was Drake.

"Novalise's warning was disregarded by Prince Aspen." Though he was addressing everyone, he looked only at her. His gaze was so intense, staring into the green of his eyes was like wandering through a dark, misty forest, lost and alone. "He refuted her claims. Disparaged her before the queen, belittling her to nothing more than a female whose only concerns should be finding a husband and admiring the weather."

Creslyn blinked up at him. "How do you know?"

His brows lifted with mild interest. "I was there."

"You…" Her voice trailed off. Oh. Right. Of course Drake would have been with Novalise. He had intended to court and marry her first. Creslyn was merely the secondary option. The last resort if his intentions with Novalise proved futile. Drake hadn't even noticed Creslyn until Ariesian had left him with no other choice but to marry her instead. The imperfect and inferior youngest sister who—

"Enough." Drake's cold voice penetrated her mind. He snared her by the chin, forcing her to look up into his face. *"Empty your mind of such thoughts at once."*

She tried to pull away, but his grip only increased, holding her in place. Envy was an ugly beast, one that always reared its head at the worst possible moment, but this was something deeper than trivial jealousy. It was *hurt*. Anguish over not being chosen first, despair over knowing she would never truly be loved.

His shadows fanned out, ensconcing them into a world of muted colors and eerie silence. The observatory, her siblings, everything faded away.

Drake yanked the Shadowblade from the sheath at his waist. He flipped it into the air, then shoved the hilt into her hand. The tip of its gleaming midnight blade bit through the fibers of his shirt, hungry for the flesh beneath.

Horror filled Creslyn. She tried to let go of the dagger, but Drake's strong hand closed around hers, making it impossible to break free of his iron-like hold. He leaned closer, so the blade frayed the silk of his shirt, the snap of each thread echoing loudly in her ears.

Sweat coated her palm as she clutched the smooth leather wrapping the Shadowblade's hilt. Power thrummed between them, a dark and sinister melody.

"Drake..." Her voice trembled in a harsh whisper.

"You asked for my heart. Here it is." He squeezed her hand until she thought the bones would snap. "Would you like to carve it out right now? Would that be enough to prove that you own my soul? That I would rather be a lifeless corpse at your feet with my still beating heart in your bloodied hands, than ever have you think I desire another? If that is what you need from me, then carve it out."

Her lungs hollowed, her stomach roiled. She couldn't tear her gaze away from the pointed edge of the blade that was mere seconds from sinking into Drake's skin. Creslyn stepped back, but he grabbed her by the waist, pulling her flush against him.

"You want my heart, do you not?" Drake bared his teeth in a predatory smile. "Take it. Carve it out."

"N-no. I did not, that is...I never meant to imply—"

"Carve it out!" he demanded, the hard planes of his chiseled face reflecting a void of emotion.

"No!" She shook her head, biting her bottom lip until it bled, the warm trickle of blood sliding down her chin. Tears sprang to her eyes. "I will not. I cannot."

Drake eased the Shadowblade from her limp grasp, and it hissed between them as he sheathed it once more.

"You are mine. Through life and death and centuries beyond." He cupped the back of her neck, drawing her face close to his own. His tongue darted out, sliding from her chin to her lip, swiping at the crimson stain on her mouth. "From now until eternity, you belong to me, Creslyn Starstorm Kalstrand."

He ran his thumb along the underside of her jaw, his eyes

conveying more than could ever be expressed through words. "And I belong to you."

The shadows vanished and Creslyn blinked. They were still in the observatory, and Solarius was watching her with one arched brow, his arms crossed over his chest.

He clicked his tongue. "Trouble in paradise?"

She swallowed, unable to find her voice.

"Not at all," Drake mused with an air of indifference, curling his arms around Creslyn so her back was pressed snugly against his chest. "I merely needed a moment to remind my wife of who she is."

The corner of Solarius's mouth ticked. "I see. Well, now that you have taken care of *that*, might I remind you that before you disappeared into a swath of darkness, we were discussing the matter of Queen Elowyn and Prince Aspen shunning Novalise's star reading."

"I still do not understand why they refused to take her warning seriously." Creslyn glanced up at the glass ceiling of the observatory, where a gilded wheel depicting all eight of Aeramere's most famed constellations slowly turned, its gentle creaking a kind of melodic symphony. "After all, the stars never lie."

"But they can be manipulated," Novalise replied softly.

Creslyn gaped at her eldest sister. "Pardon?"

"What?" Narissa, who had been exceptionally quiet, glided towards Novalise's side, her aqua gown crashing like waves at her feet. "What do you mean, they can be *manipulated*?"

"I...I never did such a thing." Novalise's eyes widened, lit with panic. She staggered back into Asher's arms, and he caught her by the waist, holding her upright. "I did not know, that is, I never realized—"

Narissa gathered Novalise's hands in her own, the dozens of gold rings she wore on her fingers glinted softly in the warm light. "I am not accusing you, Lady Novalise."

Her voice was gentle and lulling, like the call of the ocean.

"But your mother, Lady Trysta, has been the Reader of Stars for years." Narissa's frosty green gaze slid to Solarius. "Does that mean it's possible she could have...bent the readings to her will? Or even lied about them?"

"Yes," Solarius confirmed with a single nod of his head. "That is exactly what that means."

"But, Sol," Creslyn stepped closer, twisting her hair out of her face. The question she was holding onto, the one burning on the tip of her tongue, was the same question she wasn't entirely certain she wanted answered. Because she knew, once she heard the truth, everything would change. "How? How is Mother able to do such a thing?"

Solarius hesitated. He ran his knuckles along his chin, angling back, and met Asher's knowing gaze from over the top of Novalise's head.

Creslyn glanced between the two of them, trying to discern what sort of silent conversation they were having while keeping everyone else in the dark.

"Almost everyone." Drake's voice caressed her thoughts once more, and she whipped around to face him.

"You can hear their thoughts!" She gaped at him and his mouth curved. He slid a finger beneath her chin, closing her mouth.

She'd almost forgotten that Drake could hear everyone's thoughts, not simply her own. He'd heard hers *before* they were married, before she had forced the mating bond into place.

"Your brother requires your attention." He jerked his head back toward the center of the observatory, and Creslyn turned around to find Solarius watching her with feigned amusement.

"To answer your question, darling sister, star reading is the most basic form of celestial magic. It can be taught to anyone. In fact, it was our father, Zenos, who taught our mother how to read them." His shoulders slumped a little as he continued, rubbing one hand along the back of his neck. He paced away, then paused, turning back to face them all. "After our father's death is when I noticed Mother's star readings were going a bit awry. There were too many coincidences. Too many inconsistencies. Too many readings that seemed to be forged out of the ease of convenience as opposed to the actual stars. And after Novalise's star reading during Midsummer, I realized Mother was fabricating the truth."

"You don't trust her..." The unbidden words slipped from between Creslyn's lips. Now that she'd spoken them out loud, there was nothing she could say to take them back. They simply hung in the space between, and an unsettling sensation seized her stomach, causing it to flip. The realization of what Solarius was implying, of what he intended to say, was not lost on her. "Our mother, you think she is hiding the truth from us?"

"Yes." Solarius gestured toward Novalise and Asher. "What exactly she is hiding, well that, I do not know. But why else would she keep Novalise's starstorm magic a secret and lie to everyone, even Queen Elowyn, about Nyxian's injury? She kept it well-contained within the walls of House Celestine. She told everyone he was star-touched and then debased Novalise by relegating her power to nothing more than a star reader."

His voice was rising. He was balancing on the edge of calm rationale and explosive fury.

Solarius stalked toward the center of the Faerie Star and threw his arms wide. Magic ebbed and flowed, a cadence of power that seemed to magnify, drawing on the shards of moonlight pouring through the glass ceiling. "Novalise is more than a simple reader of the stars. She is *the* starstorm. As we discovered tonight, our Creslyn is the sunstorm. Her magic is more than just sunshine and rainbows. Ariesian made his power known as well, as he is the shadowstorm. And I..."

Beams of incandescent moonlight swirled around him in a frenzy, creating a sphere of glowing silver light as the radiant power of the moon encapsulated him. Solarius flashed Creslyn a wink, then shrugged, as though it was nothing out of the ordinary. "I'm the lunarstorm."

It was wild. Extraordinary.

Creslyn shrieked and rushed toward her brother. He caught her by the waist, spinning her around.

For so long they'd been told the ancient starstorm magic was dormant within their bloodline, that it disappeared and died out centuries ago. However, it appeared as though that power had adapted over the course of hundreds of years, exactly as Drake had suggested. Now, it seemed there was a storm within each of the Starstorm siblings. They just had to discover it, harness it, and most importantly, control it.

Solarius set her back down, and when Caelian and Sarelle began peppering him with questions, Creslyn looked for Drake.

She found him lounging against one of the pillars, a somewhat bemused expression on his face. Except he wasn't looking at her, he was watching Narissa, whose rosy cheeks were now flushed with tempered rage. She stood away from everyone else and kept fussing with her golden waves, like she was trying to cover her ears or hide her rather blatant sense of disappointment. Narissa did not appear pleased nor at all impressed by Solarius's lunarstorm, instead, she seemed somewhat aggravated by his display of power.

"Why is she angry?" Creslyn asked, sneaking into Drake's thoughts as she crossed the observatory toward him.

He smirked, then kissed her forehead. *"I do not make it a habit of sliding into the minds of others, darling wife. Despite popular belief."*

Creslyn's brow arched. *"And you, dear husband, are a terrible liar. Now, tell me. Why is she upset?"*

Drake draped an arm around her shoulders, the tips of his fingers playing along the column of her neck. *"Well, if I possessed the magic of the moon and you possessed the magic of the tides, would that not lead your fae heart into assuming the best, or quite possibly the worst, outcome?"*

An outcome…between the moon and the tides…

"Stars above," Creslyn breathed, ensuring she kept her voice very, *very* low. "Solarius and Narissa could be *mates.*"

She grabbed Drake's arm, rising on her toes to whisper into his ear. "Do they know?"

He turned his head, kissing her soundly on the mouth. "I'm sure they'll figure it out soon enough."

CHAPTER TWENTY-THREE

The next morning, House Celestine was preternaturally quiet.

Ariesian Starstorm and his mother, Trysta, had not yet returned from the palace, no doubt in the height of discussion over the previous night's attack, and while Drake intended to unearth more information as soon as possible, he instead received an invitation for a meeting from none other than Lord Asher Firebane.

He found the lord in question lounging in a high-back chair in the sitting room off the main hall, his ankle propped over one knee, with a book in his lap and a cup of tea in his hand. Asher's dark gray gaze lifted from the pages spread before him, tracking Drake as he entered the room.

"Fine morning, is it not?" Asher mused, turning one of the pages without so much as glancing at the book.

"Fine enough," Drake agreed, glancing at the large, arched windows where sheer indigo draperies detailed with beaded stars framed both sides. Golden sunlight spilled into the room, its warm beams stretching for the shadows in which Drake stood, just out of reach.

He lowered himself onto the navy blue sofa across from Asher, his movements formal and precise. The last time they spoke with one another, Drake had been trying to kill him in a battle to the death.

Drake's mouth twitched.

The fae and their ridiculous customs would never cease to amaze him.

Much to his surprise, Asher seemed more than willing to discuss their past agendas.

"Tell me, Your Highness," he drawled, closing the book and setting it on the small table next to him. "Have you yet traveled to the Fenmire Bogs?"

Drake stiffened, every muscle in his body tightening at the mention of the wretched, swamp-laden bogs. He knew he would have to venture there eventually, especially if he wanted to destroy the hag who created the vile *virdis lepatite*, but for some reason he could not quite fathom, the mere thought filled him with a sense of incomprehensible dread.

"I have been slightly preoccupied as of late."

Asher made a derisive sort of noise and sipped his tea, eyeing Drake from over top the porcelain rim.

Drake's shoulders bunched, the building tension between them palpable. "Something on your mind, fire fae?"

Asher canted his head to one side. "Not at all, shadow prince."

"If you have a mind to say something, then speak it now." Drake leaned into the cushions, casually throwing one arm across the back of the sofa. "I know you, most of all, are not one for idle conversation."

"Very well." Asher sat up straight, lowering his cup of tea. His gaze flicked to both entrances of the sitting room and when he spoke, he kept his voice low and laced with urgency. "You must make haste."

Drake blinked. "Pardon?"

A stern line pinched between Asher's brows, and he leaned forward, one silver lock of hair falling across his forehead. "You should have left for the Fenmire Bogs as soon as I gave you the location of the *virdis lepatite*."

"I do not take orders from you or—"

"Anyone else?" Asher interjected with a knowing smirk. "I wonder what your pretty new bride would have to say about such matters."

Drake's jaw clenched, grinding his teeth.

"Hear me out, Your Highness." Asher set aside the teacup, positioning his elbows on the arms of the chair, once more casting a cautious look about the room. "If what you've said about this gemstone is true, and I'm inclined to believe you given my own research, then you should aim to destroy it *and* the hag responsible for its creation as soon as possible."

His tone was too earnest, and he appeared on edge, his body taut with apprehension.

Trepidation gnawed at Drake's gut. "And what makes you say that?"

"Think of it this way, you saw the destruction it was capable of in Faeven, did you not?" Asher asked, already knowing the answer.

Drake nodded once.

"Imagine if that same kind of diabolical power fell into the hands of Prince Aspen?" The planes of Asher's face hardened into stone, and his voice was cold when he said, "Or Lady Trysta Starstorm."

Or Marius.

The absolute havoc King Marius would wreak upon Brackroth, or anywhere else, was unthinkable. There was no doubt in Drake's mind that he would use magic to erase magic completely if given the opportunity. The man despised anything more powerful than him. He'd been riddled with a kind of madness ever since Zaleria abandoned him.

"It is only a matter of time until word spreads," Asher continued quietly. "Until those who already hold great power seek even more."

Damn the fire fae for making such a valid point.

Drake stood abruptly, smoothing his usual attire of riding leathers, and pulled his gloves from his back pocket, tugging them onto his scarred hands. "If you would excuse me, Lord Firebane, I have suddenly become aware of more important matters I need to attend."

Asher merely inclined his head in acknowledgement, without an ounce of mockery. He plucked his book off the table and returned to reading, but there was no disguising the faint lines of worry etching the corners of his eyes.

Drake exited House Celestine through the main entrance, following the gentle tug on the bond that would lead him to Creslyn. It spiraled through him, wrapping around his heart and squeezing lightly, its soft pulse of life as familiar to him as his own heartbeat. He walked through the gardens, the brisk autumn chill slipping through budding foliage, until he discovered Creslyn sweeping the area near one of the gurgling fountains of liquid starlight, clearing it of debris. Beyond her, Caelian was collecting snapped twigs and shriveled vines, stacking them in a tidy pile in Kjeld's arms. Sarelle was there as well, along with Solarius and a handful of servants, each of them doing their part to clean away the disaster left behind in the wake of the attack.

Originally, Drake had planned to bring Creslyn to the Fenmire Bogs with him, but now he warred with uncertainty. After last night, he knew she could hold her own, but creepy tree creatures and crawling vines were nothing in comparison to the Runes of Callievan. The coven of witches was far more powerful than a blight of nature, and if Zaleria was among them, then he wanted to keep Creslyn as far away from her as possible. For now, even if another attack loomed on the horizon, Aeramere was the safest place for her.

He would have to make it swift, because she would not stay behind without a fight.

Strolling toward her, he tucked his hands behind his back, then planted a kiss on top of her head. "Morning, wife."

She paused, leaning her slight weight against the broom in her hands, her lips curving into a warm smile. "Good morning, husband. Have you come to join us in our efforts to clean up this mess?"

"I will soon enough." He nodded to where Kjeld stood with a stack of broken tree limbs and gnarled vines in his arms. "But first I must speak with Kjeld, and then I need to tend to Svartos and Odryss."

Mischief sparked in the depths of her deep blue eyes. "I can think of another who requires tending."

Gods curse him, he was going to miss that smart little mouth of hers.

He smoothed a lock of fallen hair behind the delicate point of her ear, letting one finger trail down her neck, pleased when she shivered. "Wicked little faerie."

Creslyn merely smirked, then continued sweeping the pathway, and Drake approached Kjeld, hoping he was far enough out of earshot that she would not overhear their conversation.

"General Holtstrom, a word?" He jerked his head toward the line of ornately trimmed evergreens, noticing the way Caelian's brow lifted in curiosity before she bustled away, pretending to gather more twigs and vines.

Kjeld followed him to the wall of trees whose spindly branches were shaped into miniature spires. His general blew out a breath, tossing a haphazard glance over his shoulder. "Whatever it is you need, Your Highness, consider it done."

It was a good thing Kjeld's loyalty knew no bounds, because

Drake had no doubt that if his general knew exactly what he was going to ask of him, he would have balked at the idea.

"Excellent." Drake glanced to the mountains looming in the distance, where Svartos waited. "Because I need you to stay here."

Kjeld's jaw went slack, then he snapped his mouth shut. Tension bunched along his shoulders, and he adjusted the heap of rubble in his arms. "Stay? Here? In Aeramere?"

"Yes." Drake eyed him coolly, waiting for the impending argument. "Here. In Aeramere."

"Your Highness, with all due respect, I am the general of your dragon legion. I belong in Brackroth, the Northernlands are in my blood. I should be flying with the riders, training the young whelps." He looked down at the bundle of sticks and vines he carried. "Not cleaning up the mess of a fae realm."

Drake tilted his head. "You could have told her no."

"I…" Kjeld blinked, then shook his head, strands of his blond hair falling into his face. "I don't know what you're talking about."

"Lady Caelian," Drake mused, thoroughly unimpressed with his general's pitiful claim of ignorance. "If she asked you to assist this morning, you could have told her no. I'm sure she would have understood if you explained you had more important, general-type things to do. Unless, of course, you *wanted* to help her."

"Why would I want to help her?" he grumbled, his trimmed beard doing very little to hide the faint pink stain on his face.

Drake shrugged with feigned nonchalance. "Perhaps you fancy her."

"I have no time for fanciful affairs. Not with a mortal, and certainly not with a fae whom I should likely never see again." Kjeld's clear blue gaze narrowed. "My duty to Brackroth, to you, comes first."

"Then you understand why I need you to stay." Drake

gestured back behind him, toward the gardens. "My contract with Lord Ariesian Starstorm includes my protection. There is no one I trust more to safeguard House Celestine than you."

Kjeld's mouth pulled into a tight line, taut with resignation. But he nodded sharply. "Very well, Your Highness. I shall do as you command."

"Your allegiance does not go unnoticed, general." Drake dipped his chin in acknowledgement, then lowered his voice. "The matter regarding the Fenmire Bogs requires my attention at once. I will be taking Svartos and leaving immediately."

Kjeld's eyes widened. "Your Highness—"

Drake lifted one hand to silence him. "I know I said I would take Lady Creslyn with me, but—"

"Take me where?" a feminine voice piped up from behind him.

Damn.

He turned slowly to find Creslyn standing behind him, curiosity etched into the soft planes of her face. Beside her was Caelian, and though she bore no expression of having heard their discussion, her gaze was fastened onto Kjeld, the brilliance of her eyes unreadable.

"Where are we going?" Creslyn asked, drawing his attention back to the task at hand.

"*We* are not going anywhere." He maneuvered around her, determined to keep his distance. The sooner he got away from her, the better. If he stayed any longer, he would undoubtedly give in to her. He was too easily swayed when it came to her.

"You intend to just leave me here?" She kept pace alongside him, practically jogging to match his long stride, her skirts of shimmering pink swishing around her. "Was this your plan all along, to abandon me without even saying goodbye?"

Yes.

Though he would not tell her as much.

Creslyn darted in front of him, blocking his path. She fisted her hands on her hips, glaring up at him, accusation coloring the deep hue of her eyes. "Answer me."

Drake grabbed both of her shoulders, lifted her off her feet, then planted her to the side, out of his way. "You are staying here with your family, while I attend to business elsewhere."

"I most certainly am not." She lurched forward, curling one hand into his leather vest as though she intended to hold him in place.

Though admirable, her physical strength would never be a match to his own.

Yet he remained still, letting her think she held the upper hand as he pinched the bridge of his nose between his thumb and forefinger. "Creslyn..."

"I am going with you." She angled her chin upward in defiance.

A dull ache was beginning to form at his temples, spreading to the base of his neck. "You must understand, *kearsta*. Where I am going, it is not safe."

"You always say that," she countered.

"Because it is true."

She shook her head, fueled with determination. "Have you ever once stopped to think that perhaps I already know it might be egregiously dangerous, and that I simply no longer care?"

Drake stared at her.

"Danger does not frighten me. Pain, suffering...that is nothing compared to how I feel when I am without you." She jabbed him in the chest with her finger, driving her point home. "I am not just your wife. I am your *mate*."

"Are you always this stubborn?" Drake muttered, annoyed by his own inability to hold his own against her. Creslyn would be his ultimate downfall. His demise. The ground he stood upon quaked and crumbled beneath the weight of his desire to please her. To see her...happy.

It was strange, this sudden sensation that had seized ahold of his heart, clutching it like a vise. Originally, he'd thought it was the bond binding them, but now he wondered if it was something else altogether.

"Only with you," she snapped, her voice tart. "Usually I am quite agreeable."

Solarius chose that exact moment to stroll past them, carrying a pile of debris in his arms. He scoffed at Creslyn's claim. "Unlikely."

She scowled at her brother, then turned that pretty little sulk on Drake. "You do not get to decide what I am capable of handling and what I am not."

Drake rolled his shoulders back, aware that every pair of eyes in the gardens were focused on them. "Perhaps we should discuss this elsewhere?"

"No, I don't think we shall." Creslyn folded her arms across her chest, glancing around as everyone watched their disagreement unfold. The sun's rays bounced off her silver, faintly rainbow-hued hair, cloaking her in golden radiance, nearly reaching the shadows of his own making. "It may not have been your intent to patronize me in front of my family, but here we are. Did you honestly think I would not care, that I would simply curtsy and bow like a good little wife, and acquiesce to your demands? That I would let you leave me *again*, even after our previous discussions on the matter?"

He gritted his teeth, roughing a hand over his face in an effort to hide his growing displeasure. "You are infuriating."

"So, now you've taken to insulting me?" She heaved a breath, her breasts swelling against the beaded bodice of her gown, and the blue of her eyes deepened to near black. "Tell me, dear husband, is this how it will always be, then? If I do not yield to your bidding, will you disparage me until I submit?"

Drake's temper flared. He bent his head low, meeting her furious glare with one of his own. "What has gotten into you?"

"Forgive me," she hissed, her voice threaded with quiet rage.

"I thought you were different, but you are not. You are just like them."

Drake stared at her. "Come again?"

He was not accustomed to being compared to *anyone*.

"I thought you saw my value, my worth. I thought you saw what others could not, that I was capable, that I was *more*." Her bottom lip quivered just slightly, and she bit it, hard enough that he thought the two tiny points of her incisors were sure to draw blood. "I learned to wield both dagger and sword, in a blasted gown no less, because you believed I could do it. Because I so mistakenly thought you believed in me. It would appear I was wrong."

Creslyn sniffed, straightening, blinking away the sheen of unshed tears. "You are exactly as you claim. A monster of the cruelest kind, who, like so many others, fails to keep his word."

Her accusation pierced him with a blinding heat, like a serrated blade shredding through him.

"Mind your tongue, wife," he growled, his fingernails biting into his palms.

"Or what? You'll cut it out?" She arched a cunning brow, her untamable wrath coaxing his own to the surface. "I do believe that was your threat when we first met, was it not?"

"It was indeed." Drake snared her by the chin, his grip fierce. When he spoke again, his voice was a menacing whisper. "Much like how you claimed you were rather fond of using it, and yet, I have seen no such proof."

Creslyn's lashes fluttered back, her lips parted slightly, and a flush bled into her cheeks all the way up to the tip of her ears.

There would be no escaping her.

Drake released her then straightened, turning to address all the prying eyes. "Lady Creslyn and I will return to Aeramere eventually, after I have conducted my business. As to when exactly, I cannot say."

With that, he released the fullness of his shadows, thick and suffocating. Then he grabbed Creslyn by the arm and dragged her into them.

He sensed her rise of panic through the bond, it simmered between them, crackling with a fierce sort of energy. Her thoughts were a torrent, a plague of confusion, mistrust, and doubt. But he did not care. If she wanted to travel with him, then so be it, but she would do so under his conditions.

They moved through the spaces of shade, the patches of darkness that spilled from beneath tree and mountain. Coldness enveloped them, and again she shuddered, but he ignored her discomfort, and that grip on his heart eased. His kindness would not extend to her now, not when she so blatantly meant to enrage him. Not until she could admit he was not the true source of her pain.

Svartos came into view on the northernmost ledge of the Moonfall Peaks, tossing his head, his bright yellow eyes tracking his master's arrival. Drake emerged from the shadows that spiraled around him, hauling Creslyn along behind him. Svartos snorted once, his breath misting before him like a heavy fog. His black scales glimmered like obsidian. His spiked tail lashed out, smacking into the wall of the mountain and sending bits of rock crumbling down. If Drake didn't know any better, he would've sworn the beast's eyes narrowed.

Of course the damned dragon would be on *her* side.

Beside him, Creslyn stumbled, tripping over a fallen stone. Drake caught her by the waist, then hoisted her into the air, depositing her unceremoniously onto the seat on Svartos's back.

"We're leaving *now?*" She rubbed her arms, the length of her silken sleeves flowing like ribbons around her. "But I did not pack. I did not get a chance to say goodbye."

"You cannot have it both ways, *solysa.*" Drake climbed up, positioning himself directly behind her. "If you come with me, we leave now. If you want to say your goodbyes, then you say them to me, and you stay behind in Aeramere. Every choice you make defines you."

He adjusted her legs, so they fell to one side, partially over his own, then he snaked one arm around her waist, the other hand taking hold of Svartos's reins. Bending forward, he placed his mouth near her ear, already knowing she would refuse to leave him.

Then he whispered, "But do not, for one moment, think you are being honest with me. I know you claimed me as your mate, I know your magic calls to mine, and I know you are lying to yourself."

Creslyn turned slightly, lifting her face to his. The shock in her gaze was fleeting, there for only a second before being replaced by something else. A plea of some kind, an emotion he did not recognize.

He stared at her, into the depths of her shadowed soul. "I have seen the darkness you so desperately try to hide from others, and I will not settle for only the pieces of you that you're willing to share. Until you embrace all that you truly are, do not *ever* attempt to scorn me again. At least I own the truth of my character."

Her eyes filled, but no tears fell.

"I gave you all of me," he continued, "volatile immorality, blackened heart, and cursed soul. It is you who are holding back, you who have yet to accept all you are capable of becoming."

Drake eased back, pulling her snugly against him, then spoke one word.

"*Vaeja.*"

CHAPTER TWENTY-FOUR

Guilt left Creslyn's stomach riddled in a tangle of knots.

She'd already been slightly annoyed by Solarius—she approached him in the gardens earlier to ask more about his lunarstorm, which he'd readily discussed at length. But the moment she questioned him for more information about their mother, he'd shut down completely. Whether he meant to protect her from the threat of any entanglement that could be misconstrued as treasonous, or he simply wished to keep her in the dark until he gathered more evidence for his claims, she couldn't be sure.

Either way, her mood was soured by Solarius's quick dismissal of her inquiry, and she suspected he still saw her as his baby sister who needed to be sheltered, even though she'd rigorously proven otherwise during Novalise and Asher's wedding. Perhaps if she hadn't been so distraught about unleashing the whole of her potential for fear of being shunned, perhaps if she'd accepted the growing shred of darkness inside her, and released the full magnitude of her power, then maybe Solarius would be able to see the scope of her strength.

After all, Drake had seen it.

He'd seen the part of her she kept hidden from everyone else, including him.

Creslyn was acutely aware of Drake's every breath, of the steadfast beating of his heart, of the way the bond continued to thrum with life despite his harsh criticism. Carefully, she leaned against him, resting her shoulder and cheek upon his solid chest. He didn't flinch, nor did he offer her any form of comfort, and for that, she had no one to blame but herself.

Because he also knew what she had done. She'd claimed him as her mate, binding their souls together. Even though his magic called to hers, she'd forced the bond, never once giving him the opportunity to deny it. Or her. Yet, he did not seem to resent her for her actions. At least he made no such claims.

But what if he begrudged her for it?

Panic washed away all remnants of guilt. What if he didn't *want* to be her mate? No, surely he did, or he would not have wasted his time marrying her. Besides, blood was as powerful as magic, was it not?

Drake ran a hand down the length of her hair, tucking it behind her ear as Svartos cut through the trees of the southern forest outlying Aeramere's border.

His deep voice reverberated through her mind, a dark melody, one where she knew the words by heart. *"I would have accepted the bond, whether or not you forced it upon me. I have wanted to claim you, to make you mine, since the first evening I laid eyes upon you. It just so happens, you did it first."*

There was a faint tease to his tone, and she sighed against him. "But Drake…"

Her voice trailed off as they approached the Veil, the shimmering shroud of gossamer that enveloped the realm.

The Veil.

"Drake! The Veil!" Creslyn bolted upright and twisted to face him, clutching both of his arms. "Queen Elowyn has not yet lifted the Veil!"

He ignored her. The arm wrapped around her waist tightened, clutching her close as he steered Svartos nearer to the sheer layer of protective magic that rippled and glistened.

"Drake, turn back!" She glanced over her shoulder, alarm firing through her as she realized his intent. "Turn back now or we'll—"

She screamed and buried her face in his chest, bracing for whatever horrors might afflict them as soon as they crashed into the Veil. But the impact never came. Instead, there was only the cool rush of air and the heady scent of earthy magic. It coated her skin, thick like honey, smelling of rich soil and over-ripe fruit. She eased back slightly, peering around as Svartos's majestic black wings glided through the Veil with ease, coasting and soaring, until he veered left toward the Arcasian Sea, leaving Aeramere behind them.

Creslyn's mouth opened and closed twice before she could form words.

"How?" she croaked. "We should not have been able to move through the Veil like that. It's impossible."

"Is it though?" Drake asked, and the arm he had fastened around her loosened, his hand sliding from her stomach to her waist. "Or have you been taught to believe your queen will keep Aeramere safe without ever questioning her abilities?"

"I..." She could not refute his claim.

Not once had she ever doubted Queen Elowyn. For the entirety of her life, Creslyn had always assumed Aeramere was safeguarded and protected from outside threats. But if Drake had been able to fly Svartos through the Veil and leave without any sort of consequence, what was to stop others from storming right in?

"How were you able to do that?" she asked, glancing up at him, and his cold green gaze slid to her.

"Fae glamour is nothing compared to the might of my power, *kearsta*."

His response gave her pause.

Aeramere bordered a human kingdom, and for the most part they kept to themselves, save for when Queen Elowyn lifted the Veil during Midsummer to allow for a fortnight of revelry and matchmaking. If Drake's magic so easily overpowered the glamour, then it would stand to reason that anyone of lesser magic, and those without any at all, should not be able to come and go through the Veil as they please. At the very least, she hoped that was indeed the case.

She stared at him then, at this man who was neither mortal nor immortal, not fae, or witch, or vampire, but simply something else altogether. Some otherworldly being who controlled midnight shadows, who was so often eclipsed by light and warmth, whose origins were a mystery to her.

Creslyn reached up, cupping the side of his face with her hand. His jaw clenched beneath her touch. "What *are* you?"

"I used to ask myself that question quite often when I was trapped in the shadow realm." He rubbed his lips together, his steady gaze focused on the eastern horizon as Svartos took them higher, across the Arcasian Sea. "The answer never came, so I stopped asking."

"Trapped?" Her hand fell away, and she frowned, confusion settling around her like a heavy cloak. "I never realized you were trapped there."

He did not look at her when he said, "One does not like to dwell on their misfortunes."

"How long?" she pressed, holding her breath as she waited for the answer.

A vein along his temple throbbed, and he rolled his neck in a slow circle. "Centuries."

Creslyn was fairly certain all the blood leached from her face. She could not imagine being imprisoned somewhere for centuries, though if she hadn't met him, the very same fate would have awaited her. She would have been confined to Aeramere for the duration of her existence, never knowing anything beyond its beautiful borders.

She toyed with the sleeves of her heavy silk gown, twisting the ribbons in her hands, and wrinkling the fine fabric. "Will you tell me about it?"

Drake watched her for a long moment. She sensed his hesitation, watched his gaze darken to the shade of a frostbitten forest as he debated how much to share with her. Not that she could blame him. She was asking for more from him, and though she would be disappointed, it would only be fair if he refused her, considering she'd kept part of herself from him.

"My first breath was in the shadow realm, the beginning of the curse set upon me by my very existence." His fingers tapped a restless rhythm against her waist where he held her. "It is a cold and empty place, filled with ancient magic and sacred prophecies."

"Prophecies?" Intrigued, Creslyn sat up straight, angling herself for a better view of him. "Are they—"

"I cannot tell you about them," he interrupted her quickly, though his voice was kind. "Even if I wanted to, I could not. The words would not come, the power of the shadow realm forbids it. All I can say is that I have seen the rise and fall of many kingdoms and worlds not our own. I have witnessed immense love, but also great loss. In the shadow realm, fortune and tragedy are a rite of passage. A burden each soul must bear."

Her shoulders dropped. How horrible it must have been to be cursed to such a place. "However did you manage to escape?"

A look passed over Drake's face, reminiscent of fondness, the sort of expression one might have when they were grasping for a memory from long ago, one that had almost escaped them completely.

"I met someone."

Creslyn's heart tumbled into the pit of her stomach. She had certainly not been expecting *that* as his answer.

"I see," she muttered. "And?"

"She was a faerie. At the time, she was a princess, but she would later become queen after the death of her parents." His Northernlands accent thickened as he spoke, as he wove a tale about some faerie princess, some past possible love that crushed Creslyn's spirit. "She lived in Faeven and was of the Winter Court."

"And she magically helped release you from the shadow realm?" she asked, focusing on the snowy white clouds they passed through as the sky blended from brilliant blue to warm gold. It was far easier to distract herself with the shifting of light than to give into the rise of envy needling away at her, prodding at her from the inside out.

"It was not so simple," Drake mused, seemingly oblivious to her inner turmoil. "For days I watched her from the shadows, though I had the distinct feeling she was always aware of my presence."

The pit in Creslyn's stomach turned acidic, roiling with jealousy. She fisted her hands in her lap, twisting the ring she wore around her finger with quiet contempt.

He'd *watched* her.

"We often had conversations, me from the permeating darkness, her crowned in the silver light of falling snow."

Bile scalded the back of her throat as the realization of his words speared through her like a sword.

Oh sweet stars, Drake had *loved* her.

Creslyn swallowed, her stomach turning. Her lungs hollowed out. She was going to be sick.

"One day," he continued, barely sparing her a glance, "she offered me a bargain. She would help me leave the shadow realm on one condition—if I agreed to return any favor she asked of me."

He lifted one shoulder, then let it fall. "So, I agreed."

"I suppose you're going to tell me she took your hand and pulled you into the light?" Bitterness tainted her tone, but she could not help it.

"As it would happen," he chuckled, and that sharpened blade of resentment wedged itself deeper inside of her. "But she fell in love with the shadows and her perception of me, and I had already born witness to the prophecy of her fate. She left me in the winter woods, and I never saw her again until she called upon her favor."

Creslyn gripped her hands together, squeezing them in her lap, and that darkness she held onto splintered open. "What's her name?"

Drake's dark brows lifted in mock amusement, sensing the shift in her demeanor. "Her name was Ciara Solasta, High Queen of the Winter Court."

The name was unfamiliar to her, and only one word stood out. "Was?"

"She died in the battle for Faeven, defending her court and those she loved."

"Oh." A wave of nauseous guilt crashed into Creslyn. Of course she'd been foolish enough to be covetous of someone who was no longer alive. Someone who had sacrificed everything. Someone who likely did not give a damn about what others thought of her. "How awful."

"Indeed." Drake gave her waist a small squeeze, inching her closer to his lap. "Jealous of my past, are you, sweet wife?"

"No." But she answered too quickly, and his mouth curved into a knowing grin.

"No need to lie to me, *sjellhert*. I find your envy most arousing." He rocked his hips forward, his hardened length nudging against her thigh. "Shall I tell you of all of my past lovers, then?"

Creslyn angled her chin, glaring up at him. Two could play

this game. "If you must but know that I will tell you of mine as well."

"Trust me, Creslyn. You do not want to see me jealous." His shadows unfurled, billowing and flexing in a show of strength. "For I am most unkind."

"Are you quite certain?" she taunted, lifting the hem of her gown to her knees, dragging one leg up and over so she straddled him. "There was a male from House Galefell who knew exactly how to make me—"

"Do. Not." Drake released the reins and grabbed her hips, yanking her flush against him. "Provoke. Me."

"Threatening me again?" A rush of longing spread through her, gathering between her thighs, sending undercurrents of desire pulsing throughout her veins. Her body hummed, set on fire by the intensity of his glare. The diamonds piercing her nipples were like ice against her heated flesh, and her breasts ached for his touch.

"Never a threat," he growled, his hands crawling up her back, making quick work of the laces there. Her bodice loosened, sagging in the front, and her sleeves slipped from her shoulders. Drake yanked it the rest of the way down so the soft fabric tumbled around her waist. His eyes were wicked dark pools of ravenous lust. "Always a promise."

Their mouths collided in an inferno, a scrape of teeth and mesh of tongues, both greedy and desperate. Her fingers clawed through his silky strands of hair, grabbing fistfuls as she rubbed herself against his stiff erection in an attempt to relieve some of the pressure already building at her core. He grabbed her breasts with both hands, squeezing to the point of tantalizing pain, flicking his thumbs back and forth across her hardened nipples, and the bite of his leather gloves against the sensitive peaks was too much.

Drake swallowed her cry, devouring her.

In the next moment, he tore his mouth from hers, breaking their kiss.

He captured her neck with one hand while the other braced the small of her back, bowing her, forcing her to arch away from him. Flashing a cruel smirk, he whispered, "I believe your breasts require my attention."

"Yes," she gasped as his hot tongue left a blazing trail across her sensitive flesh, swirling along each curve so she shuddered in his arms.

He licked and sucked, tasted and bit. Each sting of pain evaporated with a rolling rise of pleasure. His mouth discovered every inch of her, and her head tipped back, a soft moan pealing from her lips as the frigid sensation of his shadows crawled over her, forming wraith-like hands that touched, caressed, and teased. They slid down her abdomen like fingers of velvet, creeping past her navel, then lower still. She strained, holding her breath, while the inky tendrils delved beneath the folds of her gown and pressed against the inside of her thighs, spreading them wider. Her magic beckoned his own, bursts of sunlight summoning the dark.

"Tell me, *kearsta*," Drake crooned softly. "Are you wearing anything beneath this gown?"

Creslyn shook her head, her waves of hair flying around her in the constant breeze. "N-no."

"Good girl." His smile was slow. Purposeful. "Because if I ever catch you wearing anything that will prevent me from fucking you any time I please, I will make certain you regret it."

Before she could respond, one of the shadows sank itself deep inside of her.

She cried out as another entered her, and then another, until she was filled, until she thought she would break. They moved together as one, spearing into her slickness and then withdrawing, pushing into her, reaching for the apex that would send her crashing headfirst into a sea of absolute ecstasy. Darkness slithered over her flesh, touching her everywhere, leaving trails of frozen pleasure in their wake.

"Drake," she gasped, reaching for his shoulders to find purchase.

But more of his shadows emerged, tangling around her wrists and legs, drawing her away.

Panic bubbled up the back of her throat, a cruel mix of heinous fear and sensual delight as his magic continued to stroke her, to coax her closer to the edge.

Drake leaned back, unfastening the belt at his waist, slowly undoing the buttons of his leather pants one by one. His eyes were the deepest hue of evergreen, the flecks of gold icy and sharp. The corner of his mouth lifted. "Do you want me to fuck you on the back of my dragon?"

His cock sprang free, and he fisted it, pumping it with languid movements, and his impressive length swelled in his hand, the thin shadows ribbing it moving in time to the ones buried deep inside her. She whimpered and squirmed, desperate for him.

"Or..." he drawled, "shall I watch as my shadows do it for me?"

"I want..." The words wouldn't form, she was losing focus. There was only raw, mounting pressure as he jerked himself harder with practiced ease, each movement sending his shadows shoving deeper into her, so her muscles seized and her breath hitched. Her head fell back as the phantom-like cock inside her surged, stretching her wide.

Drake lifted her skirts with one hand to watch his power do his bidding. "I'm afraid you'll have to be more specific."

"You," she rasped.

He clicked his tongue, then swiped his finger along her clit. "Me, what?"

Creslyn yelped, her legs trembled.

Oh gods, if she didn't have him right this second, she was

going to come undone. And she didn't want his shadows, she wanted *him.*

"Then *say it.*" His thunderous voice sent a delicious tremor down her spine.

Her chest rose and fell in staggered breaths as she leveled him with a heated glare. If he demanded she be crude and unladylike in her desires, then she would give him exactly that and more.

"I want you to fuck me on the back of your dragon, Drake."

She lurched forward, snapping her wrists free from the shadows that held her in place. There was a flicker of shock in his eyes, but it vanished as she threw her arms around his neck, shoving the fullness of her breasts right in his face. She positioned herself directly above him until the tip of his cock prodded against her slick folds where she was already full of his shadows.

"I want to hear you roar my name. I want you to send me to the stars. Until your seed spills down my thighs. Until you can no longer recall where you end and I begin."

Then she sank onto his shaft, taking every blessed inch as the fullness of him joined the darkness that filled her.

"Fucking stars." Drake's hands captured her hips, lifting her up and down in frenzied thrusts, driving himself further inside of her than she thought possible.

She clutched at him, digging her nails into his neck as he plunged into her, and his shadows coiled into her heat, sending her higher. The bond purred to life in a heart-stopping clash of power, of darkness forged from other worlds and dazzling fragments of sunlit iridescence. Her blood hummed, her soul sang. The feel of him, the very essence of him, was a vast sea of devastating bliss, and Creslyn leapt, ready to drown in him.

"Creslyn," he groaned, and this time she grabbed his chin, forcing him to meet her gaze.

"I said *roar,* Your Highness."

Drake's gaze turned feral.

He swelled inside of her, so hard and so fast, she forgot how to breathe. She clenched around him, gasping as the orgasm ripped through her, and she tumbled into the churning abyss. On one final push, he emptied himself inside of her, and then…

Drake roared her name.

CHAPTER TWENTY-FIVE

*B*rackroth was exactly as Drake had left it.

Cold and bleak, with a steady drizzle that seemed to seep from the constant presence of looming gray clouds. The air was ripe with the scent of fresh earth, sea spray, and dragon smoke. Mist curled through the steep mountains, dense and thick like rivers of silver. It had taken most of the day to cross from where the crystalline waters of the Arcasian Sea met the dark blue waves of the Havnokk Deep. What little daylight was left remained shrouded behind the wretched conditions, already giving way to the pitch of nightfall bleeding across the eastern sky.

Drake did his best to protect Creslyn from the abysmal weather, but her skin was damp and chilled, and raindrops clung to her lashes like tiny crystals.

He guided Svartos down toward the far ledge that jutted out away from the castle and the dragon cut left, swooping low to land upon the massive slab of uneven black stone. Obsidian wings stretched wide as he hit the ground, his claws grating against the slick surface as he came to a rumbling halt. Svartos's head swiveled, those piercing yellow eyes narrowing just slightly, and he screeched once.

A warning.

They weren't alone.

Drake climbed from the seat first, pulling Creslyn swiftly into his arms, then placed her carefully on the ground so she stood just behind him.

"Stay close," he whispered into her mind, and she nodded sharply, slipping her hand into his own.

Something warm and unrecognizable burrowed into him then, something he would dwell on at another time. Because the moment he turned around, two figures emerged from the billowing mist.

Marius stood a few feet away, cloaked in robes of burgundy, his large stomach swelling over a buckle of gold. His silver crown, embellished with muddy garnets, set atop his bald head and his papery lips were peeled back into a sneer. He wore no weapons, though they would have been of little use as he posed no true threat to Drake, but his hands were tucked behind his back and his expression was one of smug satisfaction.

But it was the man who ambled toward them with a shuffling gait that gave Drake pause.

Stygg was one of his dragon riders, his leathers worn and scorched from years of assisting Kjeld with the whelps, his hands littered with the same scars as Drake's from too often being on the receiving end of a feisty whelp's claws. His wet hair slashed across his face, keeping his eyes hidden from view, and he ducked his head low as he approached. One hand, Drake noticed, was fisted at his side.

"Your Highness." Stygg bowed curtly and held out his hand, uncurling his fist to reveal a crumpled piece of parchment.

Drake released Creslyn's hand and snatched it from his grasp.

He unfolded the thick paper, grimacing as a scrawled name

inked in his own blood was smeared by the drops of rain. Rivulets of crimson spattered onto the ground at his feet.

He knew this name.

But...

Awareness caused the hairs along the back of his neck to stand on end, and a shiver of dread tingled down the bond, prodding at him.

Cautiously, he slid his gaze to Creslyn.

She was staring at Stygg, her eyes wide with an emotion akin to fright, yet her magic trembled, shuddering to life. Her teeth dug into her bottom lip so deeply, all color leached away, and he thought for certain she would draw blood.

"What's wrong?" he asked, watching as Stygg turned on one heel and slowly walked away.

Creslyn's breathing hitched, nearly imperceptible, but he sensed it as if she'd gasped out loud.

"That's him."

Ice froze Drake's veins.

Him.

That one singular word was all it took for his power to seethe with vengeance.

"He...he used one of the dragons," Creslyn continued to speak through the bond, her words hammering a frostbitten blade into his heart. *"Astrylys. That was how he was able to get to me without Kjeld or the other dragon riders noticing. It was him and two others. They attacked me in my bedchamber. He groped my breast. He was the one who threw me off the cliff."*

For Drake, there was only silence. A pervasive quiet that haunted his soul, drowning out all other sound. He was the reaping, a summoner of death. His mounting rage shifted to an eerie calm, and even his shadows stilled, shrinking in fear.

"Stygg." His voice was cold. Glacial. "A word?"

The man in question hesitated before slowly turning around to face him. Stygg lifted his chin, his traitorous gaze flicking to Creslyn before landing on Drake. "Of course, Your Highness."

"Are you aware of the punishment in Brackroth for touching another man's property?" Drake asked mildly.

"Property?" Creslyn hissed, but Drake silenced her with a deadly look.

Stygg tucked his hands behind his back.

"Ah," Drake mused, sauntering forward a few steps. "So, you are familiar with our customs. Touch what does not belong to you and lose your hands in exchange for your transgressions."

Stygg stiffened, his lanky frame resembling that of a tree preparing to be snapped in half by a gust of wind. But then the prick had the audacity to scoff.

"If I should lose my hands, then you should lose your crown for bringing her here, for tainting our kingdom with her corrupt magic. Your wife is nothing more than a faerie whore. Besides, she practically begged me for it." His vicious gaze latched onto Creslyn, and he snarled. "Isn't that right? Tell your beloved prince how much you enjoyed it when I sank my nails into the rounded flesh of your...ample bosom."

Creslyn jerked back as though she'd been slapped.

And that fissure of darkness lurking deep inside of her cracked open even wider into a gaping, endless chasm of anguish. Her rage mingled with fear and humiliation.

For Stygg's betrayal, Drake would end his life in the worst way imaginable.

He pulled the Shadowblade with ease, its leather hilt vibrating in the palm of his hand, beckoning the sinister blood-lust to life.

Stygg paled, staggered back a step.

"An insult to my wife is an insult to me." Drake twirled the midnight blade through his fingers. It hissed against the mist and hummed in anticipation. "So, let me be perfectly clear. First, I am going to cut off your hands for touching her. Then I will gouge out your eyes for looking upon her. I will carve out your tongue for even daring to speak to her. And as a final punishment for your lascivious thoughts regarding my wife, I am going to hack off your pathetic dick and shove it down your throat. The last thing you will remember before you die will be when I smile as you choke on your own cock."

And that was exactly what Drake did.

He wielded the Shadowblade with accuracy, carving at the man until there was nothing left. His screams echoed through the howling wind, but there would be no mercy tonight. The sting of another skull marked Drake's lower back, adding to the pile of death already there. A welcomed pain, like the comfort of an old friend.

The corner of his mouth lifted as Stygg choked and gagged, and then the Shadowblade stole his final breath.

Drake's grip tightened on the hilt of the dagger as the bloodlust consumed him. At some point, he'd dropped the creased piece of parchment. It was discarded on the ground, coated in a puddle of blood and grime, but the name written upon it was already etched into Drake's mind. Power emanated from the weapon in his hand, a thrum of vicious brutality that darkened his mind and twisted his judgment.

He lifted his gaze from the mess before him, his glare reaching Marius, the temptation to end his life greater than ever before. It would be all too easy to slay the swine of a king, but in doing so, Drake would forfeit his life as well, and in turn, the safety of Creslyn. A risk he was not yet willing to take.

Drake half-expected to find Marius pallid and unnerved by the sight before him, but instead the bastard maintained his callous smirk, his beady eyes fixated on something just behind Drake.

A faint whimper filled his ears.

Creslyn.

He spun around, sheathing the Shadowblade despite its

violent protest, only to find Creslyn trembling. Her shoulders quaked with each broken sob and though she'd covered her face with her hands, he could see the tears streaming down her cheeks. Not even the rain could disguise them. Her mind was a torrent of cacophonous thoughts, a tragic rush of sorrowful emotion. The mating bond quivered with every one of her shuddering breaths, and while a small part of Drake knew he should feel empathetic toward her witnessing the might of his vengeance, he was filled instead with simmering anger and mounting frustration.

Drake locked his jaw, straightening his spine. His voice was cold and detached when he said, "I must go."

The name of the man he would kill next was harbored in the darkest corners of his mind.

"No! You cannot." She shook her head, her soaked strands of hair whipping in the cold breeze. "I...please..."

"You saw what I did here tonight, and I must do it again." A sliver of remorse pierced him. "Though it will not be as gruesome."

Creslyn's head snapped up, her hands falling away to reveal a pair of puffy, sapphire eyes and damp lashes. She wrapped her arms around herself, firm resolve creasing her brow. "I am going with you."

He bit back a sigh of vexation. "You will not."

"Do not leave me here," she warned, then softer, "Not with the king."

But Drake refused to be swayed. She could not be both a damsel in need of saving and a powerful faerie who could handle herself. She would have to choose which role to play, and he had every intention of forcing the latter upon her.

"You told me you're capable of defending yourself." He threw his arms wide, gesturing toward Marius who was already slinking in the direction of the castle. "Well, here's your opportunity."

His lack of sympathy did not have the desired effect. Usually, her tongue was as sharp as her wit and sparking with the same amount of fire, but this time, he failed to ignite her indignation.

Creslyn broke beneath his lack of compassion.

"Why are you being so cruel?" Tears brimmed in her eyes once more and that plump little bottom lip trembled again—he hated being the cause of it. "I have done nothing to deserve such coldness from you."

The bond between them convulsed, and he fought the urge to pull her into his arms.

"The last thing I want is you crying over the fact that I will be forced to take another life in front of you." Drake didn't care if ice dripped from his tone, as this was not the fiery, spirited female he'd taken as his wife. Something had shifted, weakened her, and it made him grind his teeth.

"I will not cry. Not again." She lifted her chin in a show of defiance. "Now that I know what to expect."

"You think I always mutilate men until there is nothing left of them?" Drake raged, his shadows seethed. He was a monster. Cursed. Damned. Creslyn had claimed she accepted him, but that had been a lie. The truth was in the stark horror painted upon her pretty face. She would never want him. Not now. Not ever.

"I did that for *you*!" He didn't know why he felt the need to defend himself against her, he'd never been forced to justify his actions. But the way she was looking at him, with teary repulsion, wrenched open something inside of his heart he'd long since buried. "I destroyed him for *you*! For what he did, for what he *wanted* to do to you!"

Creslyn ducked her head, those damned glistening tears falling like broken diamonds down her cheeks.

He grabbed her chin, forcing her to look up at him. To face him. "Yet here you are with your miserable tears, crying over a man who deserved a far worse death than what I gave him."

"I do not weep for him!" she shouted, yanking herself from his grasp. "I weep for you!"

Drake opened his mouth, then snapped it shut, rendered speechless by her outburst.

"I am sorry that I was not enough, that my blood was not enough to break your curse." She gasped, chest heaving as she swiped at her face with the back of her hand. "And I am sorry that you are doomed to kill by that bastard's hand. I was not enough for you, and I am sorry for it."

She hiccuped and sniffled, and Zaleria's riddle replayed in Drake's mind.

Forced to kill by the hand of a king,
  Cursed in this life with a fate unseen.
  Bound to wield a blade of shadow,
  Break your oath on ground most hallow.
  Seek your freedom in the blood of stars,
  Sacrifice your heart, your soul, your scars.
  Son of rites, son of death,
  You are darkness, her final breath.

Drake cupped the back of Creslyn's neck, dragging her against him as rain fell harder, seeking the comfort of her warmth. His lips found hers.

"You are enough, *kearsta*," he whispered against her mouth. "You will always be enough."

CHAPTER TWENTY-SIX

Drake did not leave Creslyn behind in the castle to wait for him, and since his next kill was local, she trekked along beside him through the heart of Brackroth on foot.

Her hand fit comfortably in his own, and warmth seemed to radiate from her despite knowing what he would be forced to do.

Nightfall had already descended upon the city, and the oil-burning lamps lining the cobblestone paths glowed like polished amber, illuminating the winding streets in a clash of light and shadow. At one point, he supposed the storefronts and homes had been picturesque, with their richly carved wooden doors and pointed roofs. Each building was painted in a cool, frozen hue—deep navy, slate, forest green, and black. If the sunlight ever shone again, Drake imagined Brackroth would be a treasure to behold, nestled in the valley of mighty cliffs and winding rivers leading to the Havnokk Deep. Until then, however, it would remain muted and dull, obscured by heavy mist, concealed beneath a layer of gloom.

He led her toward a narrow alley, where the sloping roof of a building stretched out just enough to protect her from the elements. She'd changed her clothing after their encounter with Stygg, opting for a navy gown with long, fitted sleeves. The bodice was snug, cinching her waist, and the skirts were layers of velvet to help keep her warm. But already the thick cape she wore was sodden, the hood hanging low, shielding most of her face. A few wispy tendrils of silver hair had slipped loose from her plait, curling wildly in the slight breeze.

Drake slid two fingers beneath her chin, tilting her face up to him. "You come no further."

Creslyn's mouth fell open, ready to object.

"I know you understand that I must take another life tonight." He swallowed. "But I…"

Words failed him.

"But what?" she pressed, her sapphire eyes searching him for answers.

"But while you have accepted what I am, it does not mean that I…wish for you to see it." In truth, he'd much prefer to keep this part of himself secret from her. If he could spare her from his violent nature, he would.

"So I'm to stay here? In an *alley*?" A line furrowed across her brow. "Alone?"

"You will not be alone." His shadows swarmed, wrapping around them both, ensconcing Creslyn in a protective barrier of darkness.

She lifted one hand, palm up, and the inky ribbons of night wove between her fingers.

"No one will see you. No one will hear you. The shadows will hold and keep you safe until I return." He grasped her hands, squeezing them gently. "I know you want to come with me, *kearsta*. But please, I beg of you, stay here where you are protected, where no harm will come to you."

Creslyn peered up at him, her pink lips tugging to one side as she considered his request. His plea.

"Very well." She rose up on her toes, her mouth pressing the faintest of kisses to the underside of his jaw. "I will remain in the shadows."

He breathed in her scent, let it fill him. "I will not be long."

She nodded once, stepping back into the permeating darkness.

With one long last look at her, Drake set off to hunt down his mark.

Cold rain fell from the dense overhang of clouds in a steady pour, and despite the standing puddles, Drake's boots were soundless as he moved with practiced stealth, not a single ripple or splash left in his wake. Most of the shops were closing for the night, their wind-battered shutters drawn tight, the warmth behind glass windows snuffed out completely.

But as he rounded one corner, Elderuhn's came into view, the soft glow of swinging lanterns flooding the entrance. Elderuhn's was owned by Harald Dahlsen, a gem merchant who made a name for himself bringing some of the finest jewels and wares to Brackroth. He was another who did not deserve to die. Another skull which would be added to the collection of tattoos marking Drake's back.

He approached the shop's entrance, reached for the handle, then stilled.

Unease prickled down his spine, the sensation of being watched.

Slowly, he turned, his gaze darting between alley and street, lingering where the shadows lurked, watching for any sign of movement. His ears strained, listening, waiting, but there was only the continuous patter of rainfall. He sensed no malice, no threat. Perhaps his awareness was too keen, too amplified by his earlier interaction with Marius and Stygg. Drake reached through the bond just in case, seeking Creslyn, and was met with a calm, even heartbeat and deep, lengthy breaths.

Drake steeled his spine and pulled open the door of the Elderuhn's.

This time, he made it a point to make his presence known.

His boots thudded against the long planks of hardwood as he tucked his hands behind his back, admiring Harald's impressive collection of jewels.

Glass cases were filled with necklaces and bracelets of gold, many of them inlaid with rare, sparkling stones from other kingdoms. Rows of black velvet showcased precious rubies, emeralds, sapphires, and his personal favorite, diamonds. There was a display of numerous rings, many of them engraved with whorls and runes, while dazzling gems were set as the focal points. And then he saw a strand of illustrious pearls, perfect for draping around a particular faerie's neck. Or her thighs.

It was no wonder Marius wanted Harald dead.

There was a great deal of wealth to be made in the gem trade, and if Drake had to guess, Marius wanted full control of such a bounty.

"Your Highness," a gruff male voice called out, and Harald appeared from the back of the shop, shoving a pair of heavily embroidered drapes out of his way. "It's been some time since you've visited my store. How do you fare?"

"Well enough." Drake glanced over to Harald as he bustled behind the wide display, ignoring the call of the Shadowblade.

Harald was a stout man with shaggy auburn hair that had been threaded with strands of gray over the years. His cheeks were round and tanned from travel, and his eyes crinkled at the corner when he smiled. He smoothed both hands down the front of his vest, the leather worn and cracked in places. The smoky gray shirt he wore was rolled, revealing half a dozen braided leather bracelets studded with golden beads.

Drake inclined his head as Harald bowed. "You appear to be doing quite well for yourself these days."

He glanced around the shop once more, a smaller, nondescript display drawing his gaze. There, in a tray covered in crimson silk, sat a necklace. The silver chain was thin and plain, but it was the pendant itself that caught Drake's eye. Surrounded by a halo of black diamonds was a small, vibrant green stone, its color like that of an emerald, yet more mystical somehow.

Harald's hoarse voice drew his attention. "I have no complaints, Your Highness. Trade with other kingdoms is proving quite profitable, and now that I have Viktoria working with me, helping me select the most exceptional jewels, business has been more than fruitful."

Drake paused. There was that sensation again, the one that made his skin crawl. Like someone or something was watching him. He cleared his throat. "Viktoria?"

"Yes, yes." Harald gestured toward the back room, where the drapes stirred. "Viktoria, come out and greet your prince."

A young woman emerged a moment later, and perhaps she was the one he'd sensed watching him, because her very presence set him on edge. She was unsettling to behold, with dark teal hair that fell in unruly waves well past her shoulders. Her eyes were the color of pale gold, lined with kohl, and framed by spidery black lashes. She'd painted her lips a deep red to match her scarlet dress. The hem was dirty, the full sleeves hanging off her bronze shoulders, and a tanned leather corset was fastened around her waist.

She gathered her ruffled skirts in both hands and dipped into a curtsy. "Your Highness."

Drake nodded once, careful to disguise the line of concern across his brow.

There was something vaguely familiar about this woman, yet he was certain he'd never seen her before.

"Have you worked for Harald long?" he asked, in a casual attempt to learn more about her.

"Not long, Your Highness." Viktoria clasped her hands

together. Her long nails were painted the same dark, bloody red shade. "Only recently. Within the last season."

Her Northernlands accent was thick, stronger than most who lived in Brackroth the whole of their lives. As though she was forcing it.

"Is there anything I can interest you in, Prince Drake?" Harald asked, motioning toward the extensive display of jewelry.

The Shadowblade pulsed with power. It radiated through Drake, stirring the bloodlust churning inside him.

He would need to make this quick. And he would need Viktoria gone lest she witness his assault.

Drake strolled toward the glass case housing the silver necklace and pendant. "What can you tell me about this stone?"

"Ah," Harald murmured, coming to stand in front of him. He tapped the glass lightly with one knobby finger. "This stone is rumored to be one of power, though I find it rather plain. I'm not certain of its true name, and I've yet to see any of its apparent magical abilities, though I suppose it would depend on who was wearing it."

But Drake had seen such a gemstone before. It was a *virdis lepatite*, created by a hag who resided in the Fenmire Bogs. The very one he sought to destroy.

"All that being said," Harald continued, oblivious to the powerful stone in his possession, "its origins are unclear. It was Viktoria who discovered it and brought it to me."

At that, Drake's head snapped up, and he tore his gaze away from the necklace to question the woman.

But she was gone.

She'd vanished, possibly returning to the back room from which she came, as silent as a wraith.

Damn it. Asher was right.

If anyone else got their hands on this blasted gemstone, it would be more than dangerous. It would be the beginning of the end. Of Brackroth. Of Aeramere. Of more kingdoms and realms than Drake could even fathom.

"The pearls." Drake nodded stiffly toward the gleaming strand, fisting his hands at his side. His nails bit into his palms, breaking the skin as the bloodlust burned hot. It throbbed in time to the beating of his heart, a blinding pain that seared his vision and warped his mind. The longer he avoided its summons, the pain would only intensify further, and then he would become more violent.

"For my wife." He grit the words out through a clenched jaw.

"Ah, yes. The pretty faerie I've heard so much about." Harald bobbed his head, removing the pearl necklace from the case. He placed it carefully into a velvet pouch. "She will make a fine princess."

"Indeed she will." The guilt was agonizing. It tore through Drake, clawing at him like the talons of a ferocious beast.

Harald held out the small bag containing the pearls and raised one hand.

"No charge." He smiled, the warmth of it like a punch to Drake's gut. "Consider it a wedding gift."

"Your generosity is most appreciated." Drake accepted the pouch, tucking it away while gripping the hilt of the Shadow-blade with his other hand. "And for this, I am deeply sorry."

He was swift, ramming the blade into Harald's heart, ensuring his death was quick and painless. Shock filled the man's eyes, followed by something akin to pity. Harald's mouth fell open, but no sound came out. He drew one final breath, and the light faded from his eyes.

Drake withdrew the weapon, watched in disdain as its blade absorbed the blood of its mark. He scowled, sheathing it, ignoring the cold sting of pain as another skull was etched into his flesh. Heaving his arm back, he slammed his fist into the case, sending shards of glass scattering in every direction. He no longer cared if Viktoria heard him, if she rushed in to find her mentor dead. Drake's sole focus now was destroying the *virdis lepatite*.

But the moment he grabbed it and clasped it in his hand, the air shifted.

Dark and vile magic, unlike anything he had ever known, flooded him, whispering promises of greatness. The stone glowed a sickly green as hideous rays of light seeped between his fingers, holding his entranced gaze. Raw power was in the palm of his hand, ripe for the taking. The darkness delved into his mind, crafted feigned images scraped from the centuries of his past, taunting him with the magnitude of what he could do, of what he could become. His shadows thrashed against the assault, teeming with brutal rage.

How easy it would be to give into the gem's demand, to embrace the destruction and devastation and ruin. His limits would know no bounds. He could cast the entirety of life and existence into the shadow realm, traverse whole worlds with his excessive power, and leave a trail of wreckage in his wake.

Drake could embody the wicked and foul, he would be an entity of malevolence.

A villain of blood and shadow.

But there was something else.

Something soft and warm.

A shimmering bond tying him to another.

Creslyn.

He blinked and dropped the *virdis lepatite*, setting his shadows upon it.

Thick bands of midnight engulfed the pendant, seizing it, corrupting its power. They hissed, flaring and building until the glow of the gemstone waned. The chain melted into a puddle of liquid silver, the black diamonds turned to ash, and the *virdis lepatite*, the source of true evil, dissolved into nothing more than a heap of bones and blood.

Drake stepped away and his shadows withdrew. A prickle of

apprehension streaked down his spine, that same feeling from before, and he whipped around, half expecting to find Viktoria watching him once more.

But what he saw instead caused his blood to heat and boil.

Just outside, darting away from the rain-streaked window, was a flash of silver with ribbons of pale pink, cool blue, and lavender, cloaked in darkness.

Damn it.

Drake reached for the bond, seized it, then growled, *"You broke your promise."*

She did not answer, but he could feel the rapid beating of her heart, the spike of alarm.

"Run, Creslyn. Do not let me catch you. For if I do, you will wish to be anywhere else than on the receiving end of my fury."

CHAPTER TWENTY-SEVEN

Creslyn ran, and the shadows moved with her.

Never before in her life had she been more grateful for choosing to wear boots over ridiculous heels. Puddles splashed at her feet, drenching the hem of her gown, weighting the heavy fabric as she tried to navigate her way back to Castle Brackroth. Her heart hammered as she darted down a series of winding streets, retracing her steps. The cold drizzle of rain had turned into a steady downpour now, making it nearly impossible to see through the curtains of mist, and she was certain she'd lost her way more than once. Darkness flooded her vision in smears of gray with each step, Drake's power disguising her fleeing form from the naked eye. The hood of her cloak slipped and in seconds her hair was soaked, plastered against her face as icy rain drops slid down her neck and shoulders, chilling her. But she did not stop running.

She'd been exceedingly careful, but Drake had caught her spying upon him.

And he was *most* displeased.

Her muscles spasmed, her lungs screamed for her to stop, to catch her breath, but she only pushed herself harder.

Before Creslyn, the road lined with closed shops and store-fronts split, and neither path looked as though it would guide her back to the castle. It wouldn't matter which direction she took, Drake would follow the tug of the bond.

He would find her.

She shoved her wet hair back from her face and sprinted toward an alley laced in shadows and murky light from a low-hanging lantern.

She didn't know why she'd so foolishly decided to follow him.

The lie haunted her.

Creslyn had followed him because she *knew* there was good in him. A shred of light. And she'd seen it, right before he'd killed that poor, unsuspecting merchant. Drake had hesitated. She'd seen the mask of guilt he'd worn, the way regret harbored in the lines of his handsome face. He had not wanted to take that man's life, but he'd been bound to do so. By Marius.

Pressing her back against the rough stone of a building, Creslyn sucked in a greedy gulp of air.

She would ensure the king paid dearly for binding Drake to that damning Shadowblade.

Creslyn blew out a breath, gathered the hem of her soiled skirts, and rushed out of the alley, only to barrel headfirst into a wall that hadn't been there before.

Not a wall, a chest.

The familiar scent of frigid mountains, frosted pine, and the promise of snow slammed into her, surrounding her.

Drake.

She peered up at him through damp lashes, his predatory frame towering over her. Beads of rainwater slid from the tips of dark hair slashing across his face. His full mouth was set in a firm line, and she found herself unable to look away from the deep green of his menacing gaze. Those forbidden forest eyes of his drew her in, entranced her, and the look on his face—cruel and wicked yet eerily calm—caused even her bones to shiver. He rolled his neck, his leathers glinting like liquid obsidian in the faint light, and then he cracked each of his knuckles. One at a time.

"Creslyn." He stepped forward, crowding her, and she instantly stepped away from him. "You are not where I left you."

"No, I am not." She locked her spine into place, willing herself to stand her ground against his threatening demeanor. Jerking her chin upward in a show of obstinance, she rolled her shoulders back, refusing to cower. "But I stayed in the shadows, exactly as I promised. I just...I followed you."

He clicked his tongue. "Apparently."

Creslyn searched his face, but it was impossible to read his emotions. He was too controlled, too collected. She could not discern if it was anger he felt toward her, or disappointment, or something else altogether. But the way he moved with casual indifference and the way he spoke with measured composure left her unsettled. Her nerves frayed. The beating of her heart spiked. And her throat ran dry.

She took another small step backward, but he matched it easily, closing the distance between them once more.

"*Why* are you not where I left you?" he asked, the rumble of his voice like that of a storm brewing on the horizon.

She swallowed, her boots sloshing through puddles as she gradually retreated from him, until the cold press of stone met her backside and the icy fingers of fear played along her neck. "I followed you."

Drake moved closer, until he took up every breath of space. There was no warmth in his gaze, no humor in his expression. "You said that already."

Creslyn's chest tightened, and she fisted her hands by her sides. "Why are you looking at me like that?"

"Like what?" he mused, scraping his teeth along his bottom lip. His hand was around her throat in the next moment, his grip loose yet firm, one thumb gliding back and forth across her skittering pulse. "Like I want to kill you?"

"Drake, that is quite enough." Anger clouded her vision, and she glared up at him. She grabbed his solid forearm with both hands, attempting to pry him off of her, but he was granite and her touch was sand. "You are frightening me."

"Good," he purred, intimidation dripping from his tone. "Maybe then you will listen."

"Enough!" Creslyn shouted, releasing him and throwing her arms out wide. "Stop this at once."

Her magic flared, and beams of sunlight and fractured rainbows sparked from the tips of her fingers, sizzling against the heavy fall of rain. It welled inside of her, flowed through her veins, churning in preparation.

His shadows emerged in response, streaks of impenetrable darkness tangled with the glowing shafts of light, each one trying to devour the other.

"I warned you, *solysa*." Drake's chest heaved and he expelled a harsh breath. His jaw popped. "I told you that if I caught you, then you would regret it."

She steeled her spine, the uneven stone biting into her back. "I am growing rather tired of your threats."

"I do not make threats." His voice was low, pulsing with untethered violence. "I merely keep promises."

"Then prove it," she snapped, grabbing a fistful of his leather vest, so the power pouring from her singed the supple fabric. "Cut out my tongue, just as you promised. Make me regret following you tonight. If indeed this is how it's to be between us, then show me now what I am to deal with for the rest of my life. Show me the man who finds it amusing to terrorize his wife."

Drake flinched against her verbal assault. His shadows magnified, swallowing the iridescent prisms splintering around them. "You broke your word."

By the stars, for being absolutely brilliant, he was exceptionally dense and intolerable.

Creslyn grit her teeth. "I was worried about you."

He tilted his head, cocking a brow in feigned amusement. "I fail to see why."

"Because I love you!" The words fell from her in a burst of frustration, and that singular emotion, the one she tried to ignore for so long, swelled inside of her heart.

Drake stared at her. He did not move, nor did he speak. His grip around her throat tightened, not enough to hurt, but the tension in his touch revealed his bewilderment. He flexed his hand once and his hold on her eased.

"When I am with you, I feel safe. When I look in your eyes, I find strength. You are my anchor in the turbulent sea of my own fear, the rock which keeps me grounded when I am too high in the clouds. And I know you will never say those words back to me, just as I know in time I will make peace with that, but I..." Her whisper fell softly into the space between them. "I love you."

Slowly, Drake's hand slid from her neck to her shoulder, setting her skin on fire beneath her drenched gown and cape. He grabbed her hips with both hands, his fingers digging into her as he jerked her forward, ensuring she felt the hard press of his growing erection.

"What I feel for you goes beyond the depths of love." His voice was a scrape against her cheek. Harsh and grating. "You are correct, I will never say those words, because they will never in the span of eternity describe my feelings for you. I will burn worlds for you, I will shroud them in darkness and leave them in a rubble of despair. I will strike down every one of your enemies and defend you until my dying breath. I will sacrifice all of my shadows, my soul, all of it, for you. My *sjellhert*."

Then his voice wrapped around her mind like a scrap of velvet. "*Soul heart.*"

"Love," Drake spat the word out, dragging her against him so the warmth of his breath fanned her mouth, "will never be enough for us."

He hoisted her up, and she locked her arms around his neck, wrapping her legs around his waist, practically climbing up the length of his hard body like a tree. Their lips met in a messy, angry, rain-soaked kiss. Tongues clashed, a swirl of heat and tempered frustration as teeth scraped and bit and tugged. She twisted her fingers through his slick hair, tearing her mouth away to glide her tongue along his neck, catching raindrops as they slid down his skin. He tasted of midnight trysts during a thunderstorm, bodies tangled in cold silk, every illicit desire imaginable.

Creslyn licked a trail up to his ear, the steam of her breath mixing with the frozen, pelting rain.

Drake pitched forward, crushing her between the wall and the broad expanse of his chest. His nose grazed the side of her cheek, and he whispered, "I've decided I'm rather fond of your tongue."

"Good." She arched her hips forward, grinding against him. "Because I would very much like to keep it."

His shadows thickened, swirling like spires of inky smoke. They coiled around her like tendrils of the night, pinning her to the crumbling stone as Drake shoved her sodden skirts up her legs for better access.

"So many layers," he muttered. "Why are there so many—"

His mouth parted slightly, and he cupped her calves with both hands, running his palms up and down the supple leather of her boots.

She'd chosen them to stay warm and dry, not caring if they did not match the velvet gown she wore. The black leather was soft, and the boots rose all the way to the middle of her thighs and were studded with tiny gold beads along the back seams.

"These boots are...quite the statement." He nudged her skirts higher, following the rise of leather until the flesh of her thighs and more was exposed to him.

"Are they?" She squirmed beneath his intent assessment, watching as his dark eyes shifted from brewing anger to feral hunger. His shadows tightened their grip, anchoring her. They snatched her arms, lifting them over her head, and she linked her ankles together, digging her heels into Drake's lower back. "I hadn't noticed."

He traced the top cuff of her boots with his fingers, gradually inching them higher toward her center, and when his knuckles brushed against her most sensitive flesh, she almost came undone.

"You're looking a little wet, *solysa.*" Drake reached between them, and her teeth sank into her bottom lip as he slowly unbuttoned his pants. "Is there something you require?"

Creslyn arched against the wall, pleading with him to take her.

He chuckled, a low rumble that speared her with desire. His rough palms settled beneath her bottom, gripping her firmly as he aligned the tip of his shaft to her core, teasing her.

"So wanton," he murmured. "So needy."

She bared her teeth. "I swear to the stars, if you don't—"

Drake lifted his chin with a devastating smirk and shoved deep inside of her, filling her, the shadows encircling him sending bursts of pleasure from her toes to the tips of her fingers. Her head fell back against the stone wall as he speared her slick heat.

"If I don't, *what?*"

Creslyn gasped, clawing at only air as the shadows binding her wrists held her tight, and Drake drove into her, each thrust fierce and punishing.

"Don't," she panted, her head falling back. "Stop."

"That's what I thought." His palms molded to her bottom, squeezing so there would be bruises left in their wake.

He kissed her again, roughly, and she welcomed the aggression, snagging his bottom lip with her teeth. He groaned into her mouth and her tongue darted out, swiping at the bead of blood she'd drawn. Icy rain pelted her, but it wasn't enough to cool the smoldering heat between them. The bond throbbed, pounding in time to the erratic beating of their hearts. Swaths of shadows consumed the radiant beams of sunlight, and vibrant shards of rainbows pierced the all-encompassing night as their magic tore at one another in a display of wicked power.

Creslyn ignored the vicious sting of coarse stone against her shoulders, focusing instead on the delicious feel of Drake's length, how the ribs of darkness pulsed inside of her, causing her to clench and him to swell until she forgot her own name.

"Ever since the first moment I saw you," Drake growled, his voice hoarse. "I have wanted *this*. I have wanted to ruin you. To watch you come undone in my arms. Over and over."

"Drake," she pleaded, her breath hitching as he edged her closer to release.

"Shatter for me, Creslyn." He surged into her, covering her cries of pleasure with his mouth, only pulling away for a second to whisper, "Shatter."

And Creslyn came apart in his arms.

CHAPTER TWENTY-EIGHT

Drake did not sleep.

Not after he and Creslyn returned to the castle, not after the steaming shower they shared when he took her again, and not after she'd fallen asleep curled into his side. His eyes would close, heavy with what could be mistaken for exhaustion, but slumber was elusive. He had no need for sleep, he couldn't even recall the last time he drifted into the world of dreams and nightmares. Though he supposed it was probably for the best, as his thoughts would not settle.

He couldn't shake the uncomfortable sensation that something was going to go wrong. The mounting dread hung around him like an ominous cloud of doom. It would be a risk to bring her with him to the Fenmire Bogs, yet at the same time, he refused to leave her behind at Castle Brackroth. Marius had already tried to take her life once in Drake's absence, and he had no doubt the bastard would attempt to do so again as soon as he was gone. Unfortunately, it was more than just the journey to the bogs that occupied his mind with worry.

He had not visited Dragnott Lair in some time, and while he doubted the dragons would cause any harm to Brackroth, there was a chance they could become restless, posing a danger to the city as well as the dragon-riders. His soldiers flew them, trained them, but the majestic beasts fell under his command. And with Kjeld still in Aeramere, awaiting Drake's orders, there was no one to assist with the whelps.

His thoughts whirled, slowly descending into a storm of mild chaos.

It had been a reckless decision to assume he could bring Creslyn to Brackroth and not be faced with any sort of backlash, and while his loyalty extended far, Marius had made it quite clear that he, too, was capable of immeasurable deceit. Most notably with Stygg's recent betrayal. If Marius could turn one of his own dragon-riders against him, there was no telling how many others he had bribed or threatened to follow suit. Which brought Drake to his next conclusion—Creslyn belonged in Aeramere. And for Drake, that meant only one of two things. Abandon Brackroth and his dragons forever in favor of the security of his wife's life, or leave her in Aeramere within the fortified walls of House Celestine until he could break his curse and be free from Marius's clutches permanently.

Drake forced his thoughts to empty as wisps of shadows slinked around his shoulders, easing the burden there.

Creslyn's deep inhales and exhales kept him company as he reclined in the bed beside her, his hands tucked behind his head with her warm, naked body sprawled across his torso. He reached toward her, running his fingers through the silky strands of her hair, twirling them slowly, his gaze trained on the spitting flames of a fire in the hearth.

The gray haze of morning spilled into the room, filtered by the heavy drapes framing each window. Creslyn stirred, stretching, and the diamonds piercing her nipples scraped lightly along his chest as she eased up, rubbing the sleep from her eyes.

She blinked, her hooded gaze lingering on him and her pink lips curving at the corners. "Morning, husband."

"Good morning, wife." Drake's cock twitched but he ignored it, for once wishing he could feel the warmth, the light, that radiated from her instead of the oppressive cold that continuously enveloped him.

"Do you not ever sleep?" she asked, sliding over him, then climbing off the bed.

She sauntered toward the bathing suite, and he tracked the gentle sway of her hips.

"I haven't in years."

Creslyn stilled, glancing at him from over her shoulder. "Years? Truly?"

He lifted one shoulder, dismissing the notion. "I haven't the need."

A tiny line furrowed across her brow. "How curious."

As Creslyn freshened up, Drake dressed. He put on his leathers, stalking into the bathing suite to brush his teeth and splash some cold water on his face while Creslyn twisted the multi-colored strands of her hair into a thick plait.

"Is it a long day of travel?" she asked, leaving him to peruse the array of gowns lining her closet.

"A full day if the weather is on our side."

"And where is it we're going?" Her nose wrinkled in distaste at her options. "I think you failed to mention it last night."

"North."

She quirked a brow, planting one hand on her hip. "Further north than the Northernlands? Does such a place exist?"

"Many places exist, *kearsta*." Drake strolled over toward the chest of drawers shoved against the far wall. "But you will not be wearing a gown today."

"Oh?"

He opened the top drawer and pulled out a satchel wrapped in silver tissue, then turned and placed it upon the bed. "I had these made for you the day you trained with Kjeld and punched him in the face."

Creslyn's sapphire eyes illuminated with excitement, and she lurched toward the package, tearing it open the way a child might on the morning of Winter Solstice. But then her smile faltered and something akin to surprise, or shock even, illuminated her pretty face.

"Drake," she breathed, removing the riding leathers from the crumpled tissue. She ran her fingers over the supple leather as though it was the finest lace. "They are magnificent."

"Go put them on, I'd like to make sure they fit properly before we travel." It was a rotten excuse, but she bought it. He just wanted to see what she would look like wearing them. He already knew they would fit her perfectly.

Drake smirked, pulling on his boots and fastening the laces, her murmurs of awe and pure joy echoing from the opposite side of the room. Then he stood and tugged on his gloves, covering the scars on his hands.

"Well?" Creslyn asked.

Drake glanced over and froze.

His mind emptied of all rational thought.

Creslyn was *exquisite*.

The leather he'd chosen for her was a sleek black with a rainbow sheen, shimmering, just like her. Crushed moonstone was formed into twin eight-pointed stars on her hips, the longest point stretching down the length of her thighs. The corset was snug, cinching her waist, and studded with diamonds near the swell of her breasts. Smooth leather draped off her shoulders, covering her arms, stitched with two silver dragons, the tails wrapping around her delicate wrists.

Drake's mouth ran dry, and for the briefest of moments, he forgot how to breathe.

Her brows furrowed. "What do you think?"

"I think..." He swallowed. "I think I made a mistake."

Creslyn's face fell, crushed beneath the weight of his words.

He went to her immediately, taking her in his arms. "You

misunderstand me, *sjellhert*. Now that you've put them on, all I want to do is take them off of you."

She brightened, rising on her toes to kiss him soundly on the mouth. Soft and warm and everything he never thought he wanted.

"If we do not leave now," he muttered, pulling her close as she squirmed in his hold, "we will never make it out of this bedroom."

"Then we should probably be on our way."

Creslyn twirled away from him, her braid whipping through the air. He caught her by the woven plait, yanking on it slightly, angling her head back for another kiss.

"After you, *solysa*," Drake murmured, smacking her leather-clad ass.

☽✳☾

After ensuring Svartos was packed with bundles of extra clothing, food, and a few other provisions, Drake and Creslyn took to the skies.

They soared over Brackroth, past the jagged mountain peaks and channels of rivers cutting through them, to where the murky clouds faded into a swath of crystalline blue. Rays of sunlight bounced off Creslyn, showering her in a wash of gold, crowning her like a goddess. Yet its warmth never quite reached Drake, its radiance carefully avoiding the darkness of his soul.

He guided Svartos north, over the stretch of land known as Rivermoor, where lush valleys rose and fell, winding rivers emptied into lakes of turquoise, and small villages dotted the picturesque landscape. Rivermoor was a quiet country, one Marius had seemingly ignored for their lack of wealth, and Drake could only hope it remained that way.

The longer they flew, the colder the air became, and Creslyn snuggled back against him in an effort to block the chill of the wind.

She glanced up at him, brushing a few wisps of hair back from her face. "Where are we going exactly?"

Drake's grip on Svartos's reins tightened. "To the Fenmire Bogs."

"Bogs?" Her nose crinkled in disgust, the freckles sprinkled there taking the shape of constellations. "Whatever for?"

Drake ran his teeth along his bottom lip, debating how much to tell her. It would be useless to keep it a secret. Either she would figure it out on her own or just barrel into his thoughts through the bond. When it came to Creslyn, it was far easier to tell her the truth than to try to manipulate her with a lie.

"There is a hag who dwells in the Fenmire Bogs." He cleared his throat, keeping his gaze focused on the horizon. "She crafts a particular kind of gemstone called the *virdis lepatite*, an object of great power and destruction."

"And...you *want* this gem?" Uncertainty edged her tone, her gaze darkening with concern.

"Not exactly. The *virdis lepatite* was responsible for the very near demise of Faeven. I have seen the ruination it is capable of inflicting." Drake chose his next words very carefully. "Without the hag, no more stones can be created. Without the stones, its dark magic will no longer be accessible to the corrupt and villainous. It is my intent...to kill the hag."

"I see." Creslyn nodded, processing his words. "Is this hag the only inhabitant of the bogs?"

"She is not. The bogs are the current home of the Runes of Callievan, an ancient coven of witches who seek refuge there." He always despised this part of the story. "Years ago, after Marius took me in, he fell in love with a witch named Zaleria. She offered him power beyond his wildest dreams, something he readily accepted. But being the selfish prick he is, Marius did not remain faithful to her, and when she left him, he went on a rampage. He slaughtered and imprisoned hundreds of witches. Burned them and tortured them. Those who could, fled, vanishing into the wretched bogs as a means to save themselves from a worse fate."

Creslyn's eyes rounded like glowing orbs. "King Marius is not your true father."

It was not a question, but rather a statement of fact.

"No. He was like a father figure to me once, but that was long ago. Marius named me his heir once I was bound to the Shadowblade and his bidding, as a means of maintaining some form of control over me." It had been a damning decision on Drake's behalf. He'd craved it then, the lust for more power, to be both assassin and eventual king. "As you now know, I am not of his blood."

She rubbed her lips together, considering. One finger tapped restlessly against her thigh. "And you think this coven of witches will simply allow us to waltz into their home and murder this hag in cold blood?"

Us.

Drake bit back a grin.

"Yes, because I plan on giving them something they want." Malice curdled inside of him. "Marius's head on a stake, as payment for his crimes against them."

"But you do not yet have it," Creslyn countered, a tiny crease forming between her brows. "His head, that is."

"Not to worry, *kearsta.* I will get it soon enough." Drake bent down, pressing a kiss to her temple. "And I never break my word."

CHAPTER TWENTY-NINE

Creslyn was absolutely certain of one thing.

She did *not* like the bogs.

The Fenmire Bogs were a marshy, sodden land where spindly trees jutted up from murky gray waters, their dense canopy of dark leaves filtering out most of the early evening light. Gnarled branches stretched overhead, reaching like skeletal hands, and thick moss hung from them like discarded lace. Piles of small stones were stacked near muddied streams where black mushrooms sprouted from the damp earth. Decaying skulls were embedded into the base of a handful of trees, surrounded by clumps of braided peat and withered flower petals.

Creslyn recoiled as the icy hand of apprehension trailed one finger down her spine.

Goosebumps pebbled her flesh as she glanced around the bogs, the pungent scent of rotting, stagnant water heavy in the air. It was eerily silent, save for the rustling of leaves and the squelch of her boots against the spongy ground. This place was creepy. Unnatural.

Even Svartos seemed ill at ease, shuffling his massive weight from side to side, tossing his head, refusing to settle.

"Stay close to me," Drake murmured, pulling something from one of the satchels tossed across Svartos's back.

Drake grabbed her thigh, dragging her leg up to his waist, and she swallowed her yelp of surprise. Slowly, he removed a dagger from the leather strap across his chest, its silver blade glinting like hardened moonlight. He twirled it through the air between them, then slid the dagger into the glossy black sheath strapped to her thigh.

Creslyn's blood warmed at his touch.

It was quite possibly one of the most sensual things he'd ever done.

He released her, and she regained her balance quickly, glancing down at her new weapon. "Will I need this?"

Drake shrugged, capturing her hand. "You might."

He guided her through the swampy bogs, and the marks and signs of witches steadily increased. There were twigs bound with twine and shaped into pentagrams. Misshapen stones formed uneven altars, each of them topped with stumpy, half-melted candles and rusted bowls filled with bones. Runes she couldn't read were carved into the trunks of trees, intricate swirls and sharp lines representing a language she did not understand.

The further they trekked into the Fenmire Bogs, the more Creslyn's awareness heightened.

She pursed her lips, threading her fingers through Drake's. His gloved hand squeezed hers in return. "I feel like there is a possibility that we are being watched."

Drake lifted a low-lying branch covered in tiny white flowers and emerald spores, letting her pass under first. "We are."

A few moments later, a collection of small, rustic buildings came into view, though Creslyn supposed the proper term for them would be huts. They were constructed from dark wood, most of them hardly larger than her bedroom in Aeramere. Each roof was thatched, and gray smoke puffed out of lopsided stone chimneys, the scent of burning peat and aged wood hanging heavy in the air. Toward the center of the makeshift village was a crackling fire spitting flames into the fading twilight. Two larger logs were positioned on either side of the snapping fire. Grooves had been carved out on the top of each log to fit a long, whittled branch, and it was there a black cauldron hung, its unknown contents popping and gurgling quietly.

Unease shivered between her shoulders, and Drake drew her in close to his side as a cloaked figure emerged from one of the huts.

"Prince Drake Kalstrand of Brackroth," a sultry, feminine voice spoke from beneath a crimson hood. "What a pleasant surprise."

The female approached them, and when she came fully into view, Creslyn was shocked by her beauty. It was not a hag who stood before them, but a witch. Midnight hair fell past her shoulders, and though her skin was alabaster in color, her cheeks were flushed and rosy. Her lips were the color of ripe cherries, and her smile was laced with venom. She wore a bodice of black that hugged her waist and ruffled skirts hung around her like a waterfall of inky satin. An assortment of silver chains and charms hung from her neck, and she crossed her arms, cocking one hip to the side.

"Zaleria. It's been some time." Drake gestured toward Creslyn. "My wife, Creslyn Starstorm Kalstrand."

Zaleria.

The witch who won Marius's heart, at least until he broke hers.

Creslyn frowned, unable to keep her emotions from her face. Stars above, what this beautiful woman saw in that hideous wretch of a man was unfathomable.

Zaleria, however, did not even spare Creslyn a glance. She only had eyes for Drake.

A wedge of jealousy nestled deep into Creslyn's gut. Whether Drake sensed it or not, this witch may have at one time been on Marius's arm, but it was quite clear that she also admired Drake for rather obvious reasons.

"How long has it been?" Zaleria mused, tapping a pointy nail against her chin. "At least twenty-four years."

Drake nodded slightly. "At least."

Creslyn's gaze darted past Zaleria, to where more cloaked witches lurked in the safety of mangled trees and tiny huts. They did not come any closer, though there were quite a number of them, yet Drake seemed undeterred by their presence.

"You've traveled a great distance." Zaleria's lush voice grated against Creslyn's nerves, fraying them, like claws scraping along stone. "You and your faerie—"

"*Wife,*" Drake interjected coldly.

Zaleria's red smirk sharpened. "You and your faerie wife must be in need of rest. Won't you come in? I just brewed some tea."

Finally, Zaleria's gaze slid to Creslyn, and she almost wished the witch had continued to ignore her instead. Her eyes were the color of melted gold, heated and penetrating, framed by thick, dark lashes. She stared at Creslyn, calculating, inspecting, watching her like she was some sort of curious creature. Like a bug or insect she could pin to a wall to examine at another time. To poke and prod, to break.

Drake nudged Creslyn forward, but she dug the heels of her boots into the soggy earth. "Absolutely not."

He let go of her hand, sliding his arm around her waist. "Nothing to worry about, *kearsta*. Besides, it would be rude of us to refuse Zaleria's offer."

Creslyn scowled at the witch in question, her frustration

towards Drake's lack of concern rising as they stepped into Zaleria's hut.

It wasn't nearly as awful as she expected, given its outward appearance. Instead, the inside was oddly cozy and inviting. A fire crackled softly in a small hearth, warding off the chill from outdoors. Herbs tied with ribbon were hung to dry beside a smudged window. There was a wooden shelf filled with cracked leather books, a handful of crystals, bundles of sage, and a weathered deck of cards. Against the far wall was a bed topped with a blanket of fur and next to it was a worn chest etched with whorls and more random shapes Creslyn could not decipher. A rickety table took up the remainder of the space, with four chairs carved from different types of wood.

Drake pulled one out for her to sit, and its legs scraped against the coarse planks of the floor. It groaned beneath her weight, and she worried it might break beneath her, until Drake lowered himself into the chair beside her. He grabbed the underside of her seat, hauling her as close to him as possible, so she may as well have been sitting in his lap instead.

Zaleria lifted a bronze kettle from the hearth, pouring them each a cup of tea.

Creslyn lifted the chipped porcelain cup to her lips. The brew smelled of cinnamon and something slightly sweet, but Drake's hand darted beneath the table, and he squeezed her thigh in warning.

Do not drink it. His voice infiltrated her mind, and she plastered a fake smile to her lips, keeping her hands wrapped tightly around the cup as she set it back down on the table.

"So, tell me." Zaleria pinned Creslyn with another jarring stare. "Is marital bliss all you imagined it would be?"

That had been the last question she ever thought the witch would ask, but Creslyn had the unnerving sensation that if she showed any sign of weakness or frailty, Zaleria would not hesitate to pounce.

"I am quite content with my mate." She exaggerated the last word, laying claim to Drake, and tucking a loose strand of hair back into her braid. "We have our disagreements, as most do, but I would never choose another over Drake. For me, it will always be him."

"Mm." Zaleria swiped her tongue along her bottom lip, her eyes flicking to Drake, drinking in the entirety of him. "I lusted after a prince once. Unfortunately for me, my feelings were not reciprocated."

Drake's deep green gaze narrowed, and his grip on Creslyn's thigh tightened. *"Ignore her."*

Creslyn bit the inside of her cheek.

Easier said than done.

Zaleria adjusted one of the many necklaces she wore, drawing attention to her rather full bosom where one chain remained tucked into her corset. "What is it you seek, shadow prince?"

Creslyn squeezed the porcelain cup in her hands until she thought it might shatter. Zaleria was pushing the boundary between mild flirtation and excessive seduction, intentionally trying to humiliate Creslyn in front of Drake by making unwanted advances. She gritted her teeth, ready to grind them until they were nothing but ash in her mouth.

Drake dipped his chin, his face calm, void of any expression. "You know why I've come here, witch."

Zaleria waggled one finger through the air. "Mind your words, for the bogs are hallowed ground. I would hate for some terrible misfortune to befall you or your sweet faerie wife."

He leaned forward, propping one elbow on the edge of the table. "Where is she?"

The witch sipped her tea, eyeing him over the rim of the pale blue cup. "Who?"

"The hag, Zaleria." Anger tainted each word, and his jaw popped.

Zaleria, however, did not seem the least bit frightened or annoyed by his growing rage. "What business do you have with her?"

Drake slammed both of his hands on the table, rattling the cups so the tea sloshed over the rim and seeped into the worn wood. His shadows collected, massing like a rogue wave on an angry sea.

"Relax, Drake. There's no need for violence." She waved away his frustration, taking another sip of tea. "Yet."

Creslyn tensed, clutching her hands in her lap.

That singular word seemed to hold a hefty weight. It settled in the space between them like a threat, foreboding and sinister. The thought alone made Creslyn's skin crawl with trepidation.

Zaleria sighed heavily. "You can find her on the northern-most edge of the bogs, in the lone hut surrounded by bushes of elderberries and piles of bones. You can't miss it, the stench is intolerable."

Drake stood abruptly and held out his hand to Creslyn.

"Though I should warn you," she continued, the corner of her lips lifting slightly. "The hag does possess the sight, and she is not one to take very kindly to strangers."

Zaleria tilted her head in Creslyn's direction. "Especially those with unusual power."

"You're suggesting I leave Creslyn here?" Drake scoffed, a vein bulging alongside his temple. "With *you*?"

"Oh come now, it's not like I'm going to throw her into the cauldron." Zaleria laughed, rich and throaty. "Besides, she is far safer here than she is with the hag."

Creslyn looked up at her husband, taking in his stony expression, the way his fists were clenched tightly at his sides so his knuckles were stark white.

"Drake..." she whispered into his mind.

His broad shoulders coiled with tension as he looked down at her. *"Do you wish to come with me?"*

She gnawed her bottom lip, torn. *"Should I?"*

Hesitation held him in check. His thoughts were at war, she could feel his uncertainty tremor through the bond. He wanted to keep her safe, yet at the same time, he did not want to leave her behind. Not again.

"I have known Zaleria for many years. While I do not readily trust her, I do not think she would harm you for fear of my wrath." Drake swallowed, debating. *"This hag, however, is an unknown threat."*

Creslyn nodded once.

"Secrets," Zaleria muttered. "How darling."

"I shall stay." Creslyn straightened in her seat. She did not fear the witch or the hag. No, her concern was only for Drake.

Zaleria lifted one arm, pointing toward the door. "The hag awaits, Your Highness."

Drake pressed a light kiss to the top of Creslyn's head, then stalked toward the door, pausing only once to glance back at her, sending her one long, devastating look before leaving. When she could no longer hear his retreating footsteps, Creslyn turned to face Zaleria.

"Tell me how to break his curse."

Zaleria's eyes widened, her wispy lashes fluttering back. "My, you waste no time in your demands."

"How?" Creslyn bit the word out.

The witch considered her. She lifted the kettle, pouring herself some more tea, then eased back in her chair. Her pointy nails tapped an unfamiliar melody against the hard wood of the table. "What do you know of the prince's curse?"

"Only that he's been cursed with shadows and violence since he drew his first breath." Creslyn rubbed her lips together, remembering his story, wondering how much he withheld, trying to make sense of his burden. "And that my blood was not enough to break it."

Again, the witch's rich laugh filled the air.

Creslyn's nails dug into the flesh of her palms. "Do you wish to disclose what it is that you find so amusing?"

Zaleria sobered.

"No." She took a sip of her tea, and when she set the cup down, she traced her nail along its bumpy rim. "You realize, of course, nothing is ever free. Everything comes with a price."

So, the witch wanted to strike a bargain with a faerie. They weren't in Aeramere, so the magic of her realm would not bind Creslyn, but the magic of her blood would.

Creslyn bristled, feigning distrust. "I would expect nothing less."

Zaleria's venomous grin returned, her cherry lips stretching wide. "Very well. If I can make Drake abandon you, to break his vow to you, then you stay here with me. But…"

She chuckled softly. "If you can convince him that love is greater than power, then I will tell you how to break his curse."

Perfect.

"Done." Creslyn's blood rushed, the magic inside of her building with intensity. She offered her hand and when Zaleria accepted, a burst of sunbeams and dizzying rainbows whipped around them like a crushing gale, sealing the deal so a tiny eight-pointed star and twin crescent moons formed on the back of her hand, a matching mark covering the witch's skin.

"Foolish faerie," Zaleria snickered.

Creslyn smiled. "Wretched witch."

CHAPTER THIRTY

*D*rake did not approach the hag.

He concealed himself in the shadow realm, watching from a safe distance as the hag puttered around the outside her hut.

All he needed was confirmation.

Thinning, white hair hung past her shoulders and a twig with sprouts of leaves was tucked behind one ear. She wore a shabby cloak of soot gray, its hem frayed and the sleeves wide and gaping. In one hand, she held fast to a crooked oak cane, leaning her weight against it as she ambled through the uneven terrain of the bogs. Her back was hunched over, giving her the appearance of an old woman with ancient bones, but Drake knew better.

Every so often she would pause, then glance up at the sky with milky eyes. She would sniff, craning her neck in a different direction, then shake her head and continue muttering to herself as she hobbled toward a small fire. A scuffed cauldron sat atop the pit of flames, its bubbling contents filling the air with a foul, putrid scent. It reeked of sulfur and decaying bones and was enough to make Drake's nose burn and his eyes water.

The hag tapped the cauldron with the tip of her cane twice, then grabbed a long pair of clamps from a nearby tree stump. She dipped the clamps into the boiling cauldron, a fitful wheeze escaping her as she pulled out a green gemstone tainted with dark magic. She held it up high, inspecting it from every angle, before dunking it back into the pot and adding a pinch of powder from a tan sack tied round her waist.

She was creating another *virdis lepatite,* and it was all the proof Drake needed. He could kill her right now if he wanted, end her life once and for all, and prevent realms and kingdoms from ever knowing the power of the gems she made. But doing so would set every coven of witches and hags upon him, and while his strength and power were immeasurable, there was something to be said about being greatly outnumbered. It was a chance he wasn't willing to take, especially while Creslyn was in Zaleria's company.

Drake made the trek back to the huts, eager to return to Creslyn and make his deal with Zaleria in exchange for the death of the hag. He moved with the shadows, shifting and crawling between warped trees and disfigured branches. Power swam through him as he navigated the bogs through gloomy shades of gray.

He stepped from the obscured darkness to discover both Creslyn and Zaleria standing outside of the rundown hut. While Zaleria looked peculiarly smug, it was Creslyn he couldn't tear his gaze from. Her arms were crossed, her jaw set, and fierce determination radiated from her. In her riding leathers and with her plait of hair tossed over one shoulder, she looked positively lethal.

But there was something else.

A waver of uncertainty threaded the bond between them, but Drake ignored it. He would put her mind at ease, soothe whatever troubled her.

Drake eyed Zaleria, his lip curling at the sight of her. His fists clenched at his side, his hands itching to grab Creslyn, who was standing just a little too close to the witch. "I want to strike a bargain, Zaleria."

Her head canted to one side, and her gold eyes darkened. "Oh?"

"I want to see the hag dead, so she can no longer create the *virdis lepatite*. And I intend to destroy any of them that may currently be in her possession, as those stones are far too dangerous for this world." He rolled his shoulders back, neck cracking, as he prepared to name his price. "In exchange, I will bring you Marius's head on a stake."

Zaleria laughed, but it was apathetic and lacking its usual fullness.

"The king's head does sound like a fine treasure. And I'm certain I could find some use for it, as it seems like a worthwhile trade." She pressed her red lips together, and her forced smile faded. "No, I think I'd prefer something more...valuable."

A needle of confusion stabbed Drake in the back and his brow creased. "What could you possibly want more than Marius's head? After what he did to you and the Runes of Callievan?"

"Oh, it's quite simple, you see." Zaleria's arm shot out like a snake ready to strike, and her hand snared Creslyn by the neck, hauling her to the witch's side. "I want your faerie."

"*No.*" Drake stepped forward, but Zaleria's claw-like nails settled into Creslyn's flesh—the one area no leather protected her—drawing tiny pinpricks of scarlet.

She gasped against the assault, head falling back, her deep blue eyes wide with fear.

"No," he repeated, rage consuming him. "Not now. Not ever."

Shadows expanded like wings of nightfall, thrashing and reaching, but one wrong move, one misstep, and Zaleria would sink her nails deeper into Creslyn's neck. Or worse, rip out her throat completely. His magic amplified as swaths of darkness stretched, thick and suffocating, threatening to plunge them all into the shadow realm for good.

"Release her at once. She is *mine*. Through power and blood." His gaze narrowed. "Creslyn is not some bargaining chip."

"Now, now. Hear me out." With her free hand, Zaleria lifted one of the chains tucked into her bodice. Hanging from the strand of metal was a *virdis lepatite* roughly shaped like a large rock. "I propose a better idea. I'll even kill that old hag for you. And to make it fair, I get the faerie, and you…" She yanked off the necklace and tossed it to him. "Get this."

He plucked it out of the air with one hand, turning the gemstone over in his palm.

"Don't listen to her, Drake." Creslyn's voice was firm. Steadfast.

But the call of the *virdis lepatite* was stronger.

Dark, malevolent magic thrummed through him. It was a poison seeping into his veins, and he welcomed the rush of venom. His mind clouded, his thoughts evaporated, as the lust for power infiltrated his soul, its icy grip locking him in chains of vicious greed. The stone gripped his thoughts, corrupted his mind, snaring him deep into its ruthless hold. It was like a vise, clutching, squeezing, and the claws of its dangerous magic took root inside of him.

"Think of what you could become, more than a bloodthirsty assassin who bends to the will of a despicable king." With each word Zaleria spoke, the sickly green stone burned brighter, pulsing in his open hand, tempting him. "You would be unstoppable. Untouchable. The power you would wield could shape new worlds. Or destroy them."

One by one, he closed each of his fingers around the pendant.

"Drake," Creslyn pleaded, his name soft as it fell from her lips. "Drake, look at me. Please, look at *me*."

He blinked slowly, but staring at Creslyn was like looking at her through a foggy mirror. She was blurry, a smear of a reflection. She was there, just before him, yet out of reach. Her appearance was nothing more than a haze, unfocused and dimming. He could no longer recall the shape of her lips or the exact color of her eyes.

"Feel the bond," she whispered, but it sounded as though she was speaking to him underwater. Distorted. Muted. "Feel my heart. Feel my soul."

There was a faint tug, like a distant memory. A dull thump and nothing more.

His shadows cringed, flinching, drawing back into him.

"It isn't love you crave," Zaleria purred, her tone coaxing the darkness to life, and Drake allowed it to pull him under. "Monsters made from the dark don't need the light, they simply seek to vanquish it."

And what was he, if not a monster?

"Drake, do not do this," Creslyn entreated, but he didn't spare her a glance, his gaze once more drawn to the gem emanating its command over him. "Do not let her—"

"Make your choice, shadow prince, for I do not have all day. There is a hag whose blood I would love to have on my hands," Zaleria boomed, pushing him closer to the vile power needling its way into his soul and forcing him to choose. "The *virdis lepatite* for the faerie."

But the choice had already been made.

He was a creature of malice, corrupted by bloodlust, cursed into a realm of shadows. He was wicked. Cruel. Nothing could reach him. Nothing could save him. He was beyond any favor from gods and goddesses, the stars disowned him, the fates abhorred him. He was a blight. A plague. But more than all those things, he was *powerful*. Cold engulfed him, waves of heartless, vile energy consumed him. Overwhelmed him. The stone seized him then, fully, its potency filling him with insurmountable force.

Drake was, and always would be, the villain.

He lifted his head, meeting Zaleria's wild stare, and said, "Done."

"Drake!"

He knew it was Creslyn who screamed his name, but he was far too gone to care. If he could not break his curse, then he would embrace it, and ensure the world suffered as he had for so long.

"Kill the hag," Drake demanded, his voice dropping dangerously low. "Now."

Zaleria snapped her fingers. "With pleasure."

An explosion rumbled through the northern section of the bogs, quaking the ground so the marshy wetlands shuddered and the trees trembled, their boughs nearly snapping in half. Plumes of smoke rose from the heavy canopy of leaves, and the gust of frosty wind carried with it the scent of charred flesh. In the not so far distance, was the deafening sound of gurgling screams.

Zaleria smirked, smoothing her skirts, and dusting off her hands. "I never much cared for her, anyway."

Drake nodded once, the nefarious lull of the *virdis lepatite* luring him further into his own madness. Then he turned on his heel and strode away.

"Drake! Don't you dare walk away from me!" Creslyn's shouts were muted, silenced by a wall of foul magic. "Drake, please!"

A throaty, mocking laugh drifted through the trees, haunting him.

"DRAKE!"

Creslyn's final scream did something to him. Perhaps it was in the way her panic chilled his blood, or maybe it was the way his name seemed lodged in the back of her throat, squeezed out by a gasping sob. But he felt it through that damning bond, the absolute snap, the definitive breaking of her heart.

His footing stumbled, just barely, and he paused for half of a breath.

His chest caved, his heart torn in half.

He squeezed his eyes shut, the gem firmly clutched in his grasp, and when he opened his eyes again, he kept walking away. And he did not look back.

Drake stomped through the bogs, but his footfalls grew heavy and weighted with each step. It was like traversing through ankle-deep muck, a slog to make any kind of progress. He was tethered to an invisible rope, one that continuously jerked and wrenched him backward, and he fought against the urge to sever it completely.

By the time he finally reached Svartos, Drake's chest was heaving in pained breaths and his muscles were taut with agony, a sensation he hadn't experienced in years.

The dragon, however, was *furious*.

Svartos screeched and thrashed, rearing back on his hind legs, claws digging into the damp ground. His wings stretched in rage, the claws lining them catching on trees and branches, ripping them to shreds. He unlocked his massive jaw, displaying the fullness of his deadly fangs, and a fiery orange glow appeared in the back of his throat, sending waves of excruciating heat that slammed into Drake. Sweat lined his brow and dripped down his spine.

"Burn me, then." Drake stared up at the dragon, spreading his arms wide. "End my suffering with your inferno."

Svartos's piercing yellow gaze narrowed. He threw his long neck back, sending the deadly blaze of his power high into the sky on a howling shriek. Fire engulfed the overhang of trees, scorching the leaves and charring the branches until they disintegrated into nothing but clumps of cinders, covering the bogs in a gray blanket of ash.

"Right." Drake heaved himself up into the seat on the dragon's back, slumping as his energy continued to drain. He gathered up the reins in a loose grip, his lids heavy, his mind weary. "Maybe next time."

Svartos tossed his head, and Drake swore the beast scowled.

"*Vaeja*," he muttered, falling forward, collapsing onto Svartos's back.

The dragon hesitated, pawing at the ground, but then he was airborne and the bite of the wind was a harsh slap across Drake's face.

Drake's vision wavered as the distinctive thread binding him to the other half of his soul frayed, threatening to snap completely.

THE DREAM WORLD was not what Drake remembered, though to be fair, it had been hundreds of years since he'd slept, and his expectations were little more than a muddled memory.

At first, he thought he was in the shadow realm again, for the world around him was gray and dismal, like an opaque cloud of darkness. There were no mountains, no trees. No rivers or valleys. No earth, no skies. Just a constant, leaden mist of shadows that moved and shifted with his every breath. It was like he was in a place between worlds, where a permeating cold settled around him, where there was nothing but a vast expanse of emptiness.

Moments morphed into minutes, bleeding by in this endless state of unnatural delirium, until a collection of shadows gathered, taking the form of a figure.

It glided toward him, and Drake held his ground.

If his dream state chose to descend into nightmares, then he would welcome it. He deserved nothing less after what he'd done.

The figure approached, looming closer. A hood was pulled low over his face and a cape of ethereal mist swirled around him, never quite touching the ground. He moved with stealth, with regal silence, so much so that the lack of sound echoed loudly in Drake's ears. There was only the beating of his heart, the distant, broken thud of another, and the slow intake and exhale of air as something tightened inside his chest.

"Who are you?" Drake asked, reaching for his Shadowblade.

But his hand grasped only air.

He glanced down sharply.

There was no blade, even the sheath had vanished. His riding leathers were gone. His other weapons were non-existent. In this place, only his shadows churned around him. They rippled around his shoulders and abdomen, cloaking his legs, extending from the tips of his fingers like wisps of night.

The figure lifted his head, and the hood fell back. The face that stared back at Drake was one seemingly carved from stone. His features were sharp and chiseled, his jaw locked, his mouth set in a hard, ruthless line. Silver hair fell to nearly his shoulders, the tips of them an inky black, and the strands billowed around him in a wind that did not exist. Cool gray eyes lined heavily with kohl gazed at him with composed indifference. Potent, ancient magic swelled, the scent of it reminiscent of bleak, cold winters, overripe fruit, and decaying blossoms.

The male spoke, his deep voice sounding like it had been forged from the otherworld itself. "You know my name."

Drake swallowed, apprehension piercing through him as the realization sank in, cementing what he knew to be true, despite his lack of conviction.

"You are Aed." Drake hoped he'd come to collect. "The god of death."

"And you are Cian, god of shadow and prophecy." The corner of Aed's mouth lifted slightly. "Though I suppose Drake is more suiting. Either way, you are a god."

Drake scoffed, the notion was absurd. "Is that so?"

"If it is not, then explain to me how you wield shadows like a weapon? How you can move between realms of darkness and light? The ability to foresee prophecies is not for the weak. It is a blessing bestowed to only a god, no other being is worthy of such a rite." Aed tilted his head, analyzing Drake's outright denial before he even spoke the words. "Not even you can trace the history of your origins, yet you would be so quick to dismiss the truth?"

"You are mistaken. I am a cursed soul, tainted and vile in every aspect. Gods are worshiped and feared, statues and altars are constructed in their honor, sacrifices are made for their favor, and prayers are whispered for their blessings. I am none of those things." Fuming at his own misfortune, Drake lifted his chin in denial, his hands squeezing into tight fists. "You make a mockery of me and would have me think the damning life I've led for centuries is one of worth? And why would I dare believe such a thing?"

"Because..." The god of death's partial smile vanished, his gaze narrowing. "You are my son."

"Lies!" Drake shouted, and a wall of power slammed into him with such force, he sank to his knees in anguish.

Immense pain speared him like a blade, driving into his chest, his heart, his soul. His arms contorted, wrenching behind him. His head snapped back, sending stars dancing before his eyes. A groan of despair escaped him, his blood boiled, his magic waned—the shadows shriveling until they were just out of his grasp. He writhed in agony as his body spasmed, the pangs of torture so intense, he nearly considered begging for death.

"Call me a liar again," the god of death crooned, "and I will *end* you."

Aed's power ebbed, subsiding just enough for Drake to draw

a rough breath of air. It scraped the back of his throat and scalded his lungs.

"Your mother was Liadan, the goddess of rites, and I *loved* her. Yet, she was taken from me by the Ancient Ones." Aed's voice trembled with calculated rage. "All because she refused to give you up. They wanted you, not so much for your shadows, for darkness is easily created, but the prophecies…they are a source of greed."

"What…" Drake rasped, struggling to stand, his body still reeling from the assault. "What do they want with prophecies?"

"The Ancient Ones are fading from existence. Those who were revered in the before are now all but forgotten. Their names. Their faces. Their power." Aed moved closer, plunging them into a pitfall of impenetrable night. "They seek to restore what is lost to them, and prophecies…well, what better way to gain control of realms than by holding the secrets of fate?"

Drake shook his head, wincing as his temples throbbed and ached. "And what of Liadan? Of my mother?"

Aed's face morphed into a mask of chiseled stone. "She hid you away in the shadow realm, beyond their reach, to save your life. And as punishment, they took her from me."

Drake opened his mouth, but the god of death lifted one hand, silencing him. "I do not know if she lives, if her heart continues to beat."

"Then why now?" Drake demanded. "Why have you come to tell me this now? Why not years ago, before…"

Before I became what I am, he wanted to say.

"Your choices are your own to make," Aed's answer was cold, a hint of malice cutting through his tone. "Gods do not meddle, they do not interfere unless they are begged for assistance. And sometimes, not even then."

Drake's brows pinched together, a waver of uncertainty shuddering down his spine. "I did not beg for you."

"No." He drew the word out, opening the palm of his hand

where a fragment of golden light and shimmery rainbows swirled like a floating orb. "But *she* did."

She.

Creslyn.

Shit.

"The celestial faerie was right." Aed reached out, grabbing a hideous green gem whose glow faded abruptly in the palm of his hand. "This is not who you are."

Drake had no idea how the god of death had pulled the *virdis lepatite* into the strange dream world, and he didn't dare ask. He could only watch as Aed crushed the stone with his fist, reducing it to nothing more than blood, bones, and fumes of rancid magic.

"You are not a monster. You are a *god*." Aed sneered as he dusted the remains from his hands, and then his silver gaze latched onto Drake. "Now…act like one."

There was another burst of profound magic and Drake jerked upright, his eyes flying open. He was still seated atop of Svartos, the dragon's black wings slicing through wispy gray clouds as a sliver of moonlight illuminated their path through the night sky, and the *virdis lepatite* was gone.

He blinked once. Twice.

Either that was one hell of a dream, or Aed had indeed paid him a startling visit, and he was a god.

Drake's shadows preened at the acknowledgement.

Fuck.

He grabbed the reins, coiling them in his fists, and steered Svartos back toward the Fenmire Bogs.

Creslyn. He had to get to Creslyn.

"*Creslyn!*" Drake shouted through the bond, hoping it would reach her. "*Answer me!*"

But Creslyn did not respond, and the fraying bond remained painfully silent.

CHAPTER THIRTY-ONE

reslyn stared at Zaleria with pure contempt. With absolute loathing. She detested this witch, *hated* her, and she'd never hated anyone in the entirety of her life.

Except now, maybe, Drake.

"You knew he would leave me." The accusation struck true, and Zaleria offered a wry smile.

"Of course." The witch licked the droplets of crimson from her sharp nails, and Creslyn's hand instantly flew to her throat, her fingers coming away smeared with blood.

The injuries left behind by Zaleria were already healing, mostly in part to the magic of Crelsyn's blood, but nothing could repair the damage done to her heart.

She struggled to feel something, some emotion to fuel her resolve, but there was nothing. Somehow, she was empty. The salt of her tears had already dried upon her cheeks. That gaping, cavernous wound of Drake's betrayal had swallowed her anger, her grief, her despair. Now, there was only despondency, a shallow river of melancholy in which she would gladly drown. All of his promises, all of his proclamations of burning worlds and slaying her enemies, were a carefully crafted web of lies.

He'd tangled her in them, wrapped each thread of deceit around her so tightly that she had no means of escape. Her mate had abandoned her, traded her life without a shred of remorse, like she was of no more importance than a handful of gold. And for what?

A fucking gem to make him all powerful, like that prick needed any more of a boost to his already annoying ego that was bolstered by ruthless arrogance.

Creslyn expelled a slow, measured breath. "And did you really kill the hag?"

"Oh, yes." The fire crackled, highlighting half of Zaleria's face in a sinister warmth. She smoothed her black hair from her face, her molten eyes flashing in the play of light. "All that remains of her is dust and bone."

"I see."

Creslyn peered up through the expanse of gangly branches where shards of moonlight attempted to break through the overgrown patches of leaves. It was quite late and though she knew it would be a risk to go traipsing through the bogs at night, she couldn't very well stay here. Not with Zaleria looking at her as though she did indeed want to toss her into that bubbling cauldron. If she could just get outside of the bogs, where the sky was no longer shrouded, then perhaps she could follow the constellations to make her way back home.

No, not home.

To Brackroth. She would take Astrylys and return to Aeramere, where she belonged.

Lifting her left hand, Creslyn inspected the ring Drake had given her as a token of his utterly useless devotion. It would fetch a fine amount if she required funds, which she would undoubtedly need to make the journey. She pulled it from her finger and shoved it into one of the small pockets of her leathers.

Well, no use wasting any more time, then.

Creslyn turned and started walking in the direction where she thought Svartos had landed hours earlier.

Zaleria cackled, her lush laughter from before suddenly replaced with a heinous sort of noise. "And just where do you think you're going?"

"I am not quite sure." Creslyn huffed out a breath, and it misted before her. "I suppose I shall figure it out once I get there."

"We had a deal, faerie." Zaleria's lips twisted into a scowl, her unnatural eyes glowing like pools of melted gold. She pointed one finger in Creslyn's direction, her wickedly sharp nail aiming for her throat. "If you lost, which you did, then you agreed to stay."

"Ah, but it was you who failed to specify for how long." Creslyn lifted her hand, the mark of her house's crest fading, the magic releasing her from its binding hold. She smirked, tilting her head to one side. "Or haven't you ever heard to never bargain with the fae?"

Zaleria opened her mouth, then snapped it shut. She took one menacing step forward, her heeled boots sinking into the mossy earth. "Why, you foul little—"

"Mind yourself, witch. You forget your place." Creslyn threw both arms out to her side, summoning her magic. It spilled from the tips of her fingers in fiery orbs of sunlight splintered by brilliant rainbows. "I am Lady Creslyn Starstorm Celestine Kalstrand, and I do not take kindly to insults."

"You think I'm afraid of *that?*" Zaleria faced her head on, sparks of fire erupting in both of her hands. "Is that all you've got, then? Sunshine and pretty rainbows? Pathetic."

Zaleria sneered.

Something inside Creslyn snapped.

For so long, she'd tolerated the teasing of her power, she'd suffered the mockery of her magic. She'd taken every jab and taunt in silence, with a strained smile, refusing to unleash her full potential for fear of the repercussions. She'd cared too much about what the nobles of Aeramere might say, she agonized over what her family might think if they found her out. Her magic was not of the stars, it was a fury of the sun's blinding intensity, a mesmerizing maelstrom of illustrious splendor, a sunstorm of chaotic delight flawed by a harrowing sliver of darkness. Of fallen loveliness.

But she was not the pretty little faerie anymore.

She was the wicked beauty.

Creslyn reached for that darkness, that chasm she'd attempted to seal for far too long, and ripped it open. She embraced it, welcomed it. Her hair unraveled from its braid, and the strands whipping around her morphed from silver to inky black, the same streaks of icy blue, lavender, and frosty pink now vibrant and blinding. She stretched one arm out in front of her and pulled the other back, the storm of her creation more catastrophic than ever. Sunbeams shot around her in an unhinged sphere, each rainbow sharpened to a fine point, ready to strike.

Zaleria's eyes widened, but the fire in her palms crackled and spit, sending a rush of heat forward in warning.

Creslyn's sphere shuddered but held firm. She eyed the witch as they paced around each other in a slow circle. She was vaguely aware of other witches in the bogs who cowered behind huts and disfigured trees, watching the impending battle unfold before them. Their fear was palpable, the smell of it reminded her of freshly tilled earth and crushed herbs. Though whether they were afraid of Zaleria or her, she could not tell.

For their sakes, she hoped it was *her.*

Zaleria struck first, her fiery ball of fire aiming right for Creslyn's head.

Creslyn whirled away from the attack, launching a hissing beam of sunlight flanked by honed shards of shattered rainbows. She moved like fluid music, remembering every move, every instruction of Kjeld's constant demands. She spun and dodged, mindful of her footwork on the soggy earth, sending glaring sunbeams in Zaleria's direction as the storm around her continued to strengthen.

The witch launched another fireball. This one singed Creslyn's shoulder, and she hissed in pain as the smell of her own burnt flesh filled her nose.

"He'll never love you. The Prince of Brackroth will always choose power over you. Over anyone." Zaleria matched her, carefully crossing one leg in front of the other as she stepped, her ruffled skirts hindering her movements in the steady wind. "The blade drives him with bloodlust. It fuels him. The more he uses it, the more it owns him. Controls him."

She ducked low, narrowly avoiding a blast of sunlight, then popped back up, her lips stretched into a feral smile. "Quite the curse, don't you think?"

Creslyn faltered.

The Shadowblade.

It was the Shadowblade that cursed Drake, and it was all Zaleria's fault.

"You." Creslyn's arm shot out, and a rain of dagger-like rainbows assailed the witch. They pierced her clothing and flesh, lodging dangerously close to her heart. "You did this to him. You hated that he didn't choose you, that he didn't *want* you."

"I was not enough for him. And you...you will not be enough for him either." Zaleria staggered forward, gripping the iridescent shard protruding from her chest. She attempted to yank it out, her hands sliding over its keen edges, slicing her palms until they dripped with her own blood. "What use was a prince, anyway, when I could have a king?"

"A king who could not afford you the decency to remain faithful." Creslyn inched closer as Zaleria's knees slammed into the soft earth.

Her body swayed, rocking back and forth, before she

slumped over completely. She rolled onto her back, the vicious light in her eyes slowly dimming. Her pallor waned, the rosy hue of her cheeks fading as a trickle of scarlet slid down her chin.

Zaleria was dying.

Creslyn hesitated. She'd never slain anyone before, even if it was done to protect herself. Her stomach turned sour with remorse, and her magic ebbed, hovering at the tips of her fingers. She never imagined what it would be like to take a life, certainly not while her own was threatened, yet all the emotions she expected one would experience—horror, shock, utter bewilderment, panic—failed to rise to the surface. She found herself overwhelmed with a strange kind of understanding of who she'd become, of the world around her. Her perception shifted as she stared at Zaleria, whose blood loss was staining the patch of mossy ground beneath her fallen body. If war truly was coming to Aeramere, it would be like this from now on. There would be death and loss, and she would be a damned fool if she resorted to her former beliefs that her realm, her home, were untouchable.

But that did not mean she should withhold compassion. The witch's death would weigh heavy upon her conscience, become a festering burden of regret unless Creslyn found some means in which to save her.

Creslyn knelt beside Zaleria, carefully grasping the rainbow-hued shard with both hands. She was a lady of House Celestine, and she knew every Starstorm before her to be both loyal and merciful.

She would be gracious enough to show mercy to the witch who cursed her husband.

"Surrender." She spoke softly, her grip around the shard tightening, preparing to tug it free. "And admit you cursed the Shadowblade out of jealousy and spite, dooming my husband to a lifetime of servitude to that bastard of a king."

Zaleria scoffed. Choked. The blood trickling down her mouth and chin was thick, and a horrible metallic scent lingered in the air. "I would rather succumb to my wounds than ever admit anything to you."

"Very well." Creslyn released the shard and stood, wiping her hands on her leathers. "So be it."

Zaleria sucked in a gasping, garbled breath. "He will *never* love you."

"You're wrong, witch." Creslyn's lips pressed into a hard, fierce line. "Drake's heart is *mine*. And whenever I see him again, I shall carve it out."

A tremor wrecked Creslyn's body, causing goosebumps to pebble all over her flesh as the bond warmed and a low, familiar voice entered her mind.

"Your blade...or mine?"

CHAPTER THIRTY-TWO

*D*rake stared in awe of Creslyn, of the sheer magnitude of her.

When she spun around to face him with those sapphire eyes so dark of a blue they were nearly black, he almost didn't recognize her. Firelight danced off her features, highlighting the planes of her furious face. He could barely make out the smattering of freckles across her nose, the ones that reminded him of a dusting of constellations, because the dwindling embers cast half of her in shadows. A tiny line of rage creased her brow, her lips were pressed into a hard line of resolution, and her hair—gods, her *hair*—he wanted to fist it in his hands.

Gone were the waves of silver, they'd been replaced by strands of midnight silk. And those ribbons of pale blue, cool pink, and lavender seemed to glow, banishing the night.

He reached out to touch her hair, curious if it would feel the same as before.

Creslyn jerked back, away from him. Her chest heaved, her burning fury simmering down the bond between them.

"Kearsta—"

"No." She lifted her chin, her jaw set in challenge. "I am not your *kearsta*. Or your *solysa*. And I am most certainly not your *sjellhert*."

She spoke each word with such loathing, leaving him captivated by her. She had mimicked his accent so perfectly that a spear of lust shot straight to his groin, and his lips twitched in amusement.

"Creslyn," he tried again, careful not to provoke her. He knew she was seething and hostile, knew it was entirely his fault, but she was also crestfallen. He'd broken her heart, the one that bled for him, and now he was left to pick up all the jagged pieces, hoping they would fit back together. "I must tell you—"

"Do not speak to me. Do not look at me."

He moved closer, just a step, and a gust of chilly wind blew her hair behind her. It was then he saw her shoulder, the skin raw and pink. Burnt yet healing. Vengeance consumed him and he bared his teeth. He would kill whoever was responsible, but he'd watched Zaleria die by Creslyn's hand, and his desire for retribution ebbed. Unsure if he should be proud or offer her some form of comfort after taking her first life, he reached for her again.

"You're hurt."

She threw up one hand, halting him. "Do *not* touch me."

His gaze dipped to her bare finger, the lust he felt earlier cooling instantly. Something cold and frigid settled deep in his gut, freezing him from the inside out. A sickening sensation roiled in his stomach like hot acid. His chest was hollow. Gaping and empty. Perhaps Creslyn had already carved out his heart.

"Where is your ring?" he demanded.

She lifted her injured shoulder, then let it fall, dismissing him. "I must have lost it."

"Do not lie to me." He had no right to lose his temper with her, but his own guilt was sending him into a spiral of unfathomable turmoil. Seeing her without his ring was tragic proof of how deeply he'd wounded her. It was like being caught at sea in the midst of a violent storm. She was the steadfast shore, and she was disappearing beyond the horizon.

He wouldn't be able to reach her.

"I will do as I please! I owe you *nothing*. Not after what you did to me." Creslyn wrapped her arms around herself, her windswept hair lashing around her. "Every choice you make defines you, does it not? I believe those were your exact words."

She stalked past him, and though he knew he might suffer for it, he grabbed her arm to stop her, dragging her toward him. Resentment flashed in her indigo eyes. She fought to break free of his hold, but he refused to release her.

"Creslyn, please hear me out." He needed her to listen. He was never one to ask for forgiveness, it wasn't in his nature. Yet he needed her to understand. To hear him. To see him. To believe him. "I am not what I thought. I regretted leaving you the moment I walked away."

"Your regret is not enough for me," she spat.

"Damn it, Cres!" He captured both of her arms, pulling her flush against him so her feet dangled off the ground. "Will you let me speak?"

"No." Her tone was severe, but there was a quiver. And he didn't miss the way her bottom lip trembled before she bit it hard. "Nothing you could possibly say is of any interest to me. I warned you, Drake. I told you that if you broke my heart, I would break yours in return. You made your choice, and now you must live with the consequences."

She kicked in an effort to free herself, the toe of her boot hitting him directly in the shin.

"Fuck." His hold loosened, and she wrenched herself free from his grasp. She stomped through the bogs, and he bolted after her.

"Creslyn, wait!" He lunged for her once more. "I cannot!"

She turned to face him abruptly, and in the fading embers of the fire, he saw the full devastation of what he'd done. Damp lashes. Flushed, tear-stained cheeks. Eyes that reflected so much sorrow, so much grief, he wasn't sure he would ever feel the warmth of them again. Worse than all of that was the bond.

All her emotions thundered into him, stealing his breath.

Drake had done more than break her heart.

He'd fractured her soul.

"You cannot *what*?" Each word dripped with bitterness.

"I..." Pinpricks of panic prodded along his neck. "I cannot live without you."

Creslyn stared up at him for one solid minute, and as those seconds gradually ticked by, he thought his declaration had been enough. Until she spoke.

"Then perhaps you should have thought of that before you abandoned me in the bogs." The stinging wind howled around them, and though she shivered from the cold, the look she gave him was full of so much fire, she could start an inferno if she so dared. "Though I suppose I should thank you for it. Your betrayal pushed me to finally accept who I am, which is what you've always wanted. Unfortunately for you, it's too late."

Drake stood there as she walked away, each step she took driving a blade of desperation right into his useless heart.

Mine.

No, he would not let her leave. She was his fucking wife, bound to him through blood. He may have made a damning mistake, but she belonged to him. Whether she liked it or not.

He ran after her, catching her by the hand, forcing her to face him. There was a sheen in her eyes, but the tears no longer fell. And the bond shuddered in warning.

"Creslyn. Forgive me. I will do anything you ask of me. Anything to prove how sorry I am for walking away from you. For leaving you."

Because he was sorry.

Drake had plenty of fucking power, the only thing he was missing now, the one thing he needed, was *her.*

"It is too late for apologies, Drake. I never should have claimed you as my mate." She shook her head, glancing down at the sodden earth. When her gaze lifted, it was empty. Every emotion had been buried away. She'd locked him out. "I prayed to any god or goddess who would listen as you walked away from me. Begged them to make you *see,* to make you realize there was goodness in you. I should have known my love would never be enough to save you. It will be the greatest regret in my life that I so foolishly bound myself to a monster."

"I am not a monster!" Drake roared, and she startled, her lashes fluttering back. He snared her by the waist, hauling her close, then grabbed her chin so she had no choice but to hold his gaze, to see the truth in every word. "I am Cian, the god of shadow and prophecy. Born of Aed, god of death. And Liadan, goddess of rites. I was hidden away in the shadow realm by my mother, and the Ancient Ones took her from my father as punishment."

Creslyn didn't even blink.

"I am not..." He swallowed hard, took a steadying breath. "I am not a monster."

Surely that would be enough. His admittance, his apology, his willingness to do whatever possible to piece together her heart, to have it belong to him once more, would be enough.

In the penetrating darkness of the bogs, with nothing more than shafts of diluted moonlight to see, Drake witnessed Creslyn's eyes soften.

But every muscle in her body tensed in his arms.

Her voice was a hoarse whisper in the frigid night air. "Lucky for you, a god has no need for a wife."

"Creslyn!" Drake shouted her name like a curse. He threw his arms wide, letting her go, and she stumbled back a step.

"No! You ruined me! My heart beats solely for you. I would

bleed and die for you, yet you showed no remorse as I screamed for you to choose me." She shoved him then, hard, and though he swayed, he didn't lose his footing. Her finger jabbed him squarely in the chest, and the erratic beating of her heart echoed in his ears. "You truly want my forgiveness, Drake?"

The space between them was growing colder. Thinner.

She was slipping between his fingers.

He never thought to lose her forever.

"Yes." Drake nodded once. Knowing this would be his moment, the only chance she would ever offer him for redemption. "More than anything in this life."

"On your knees, god of shadow and prophecy." The way his title rolled off her tongue was like sin and stardust. "And *grovel* for it."

Drake did not hesitate.

He dropped to his knees upon the miry ground, resting both of his hands on her waist, and gazed up at the feral beauty before him.

"I will never forgive myself for the choice I made here tonight. And you are right, an apology will never be enough. My remorse will haunt me for the remainder of my life because I yearn for you, ache for you, every hour of every day. My soul is restless when you are not near." He slowly reached for her arms, letting his hands glide down the length of her leathers until he captured her hands. He placed a kiss upon each of her knuckles. "You are a sea in which I would gladly drown, a storm I would let destroy me until there was nothing left. When I am with you, I remember what it means to live, to feel. You are my eternal breath. Through shadows and sunlight, prophecies and fate, all I want, all I long for, is you."

A single tear rolled down Creslyn's cheek, like a drop of moonlight, but Drake didn't dare move to catch it.

"You have my forgiveness." There was a catch in her voice, the slightest of tremors. "But you do not have my trust."

Drake rose, squeezing her hands in his grasp. "Then I will earn it."

Moments of tense silence spread between them as they stared at one another. His movements slow and precise, Drake ran his fingers through her silken strands of midnight, marveling at her transformation once more. "I like your hair."

Creslyn huffed out a breath. "Now is not the time for flattery, husband."

He bit back a smile. "Whatever you say, wife."

Drake linked their fingers together as he led her back to Svartos, who patiently waited at the edge of the bogs. "Shall we return to Aeramere?"

"No." Her tone was icy, like the northern mountains. "To Brackroth."

Apprehension stiffened Drake's spine and his muscles tightened in response. "Brackroth?"

"Yes." Creslyn smiled, malice lacing her perfect lips. "I have business with the king."

CHAPTER THIRTY-THREE

*H*ours passed, and still Drake could feel Creslyn's anger radiating from her.

They sat atop Svartos as the dragon glided through the midnight sky, yet she refused to lean against Drake's chest as she so often did when they were flying. Her back was straight, her body stiff and stoney. Though she'd forgiven him, there was an underlying current of crossness pulling tight along the bond between them.

Worse, however, was the scent of the air.

Drake inhaled deeply, breathing in the smell of rain and heavy storm clouds. The glow of the moon had vanished, disappearing behind a swath of blanketed darkness. Lightning splintered across the sky, piercing through the pitch in a vicious pattern. Thunder cracked, the sound of it so loud it caused his ears to ring. Creslyn jumped, then lurched backward, curling into him, and the rush of her unease flooded him. He wrapped one arm snugly around her waist, gripping the reins tightly with his free hand as icy rain began to pour from the black heavens.

It soaked them thoroughly in seconds, slashing against them with such force that Svartos loosed a screech and pulled back, slowing his speed. He tucked his wings, swooping lower, dodging masses of clouds and avoiding the strikes of lightning that shattered the night.

"This is quite the storm," Creslyn called over the howling wind, and it carried her words away from him. She shivered, tucking herself closer into his body. "Are we going to fly through it?"

"Not if I can help it." He scanned the earth below, but it was impossible to see anything. Between the blinding flashes of lightning and the intense rainfall, his visibility was slim. "It will be safer if we can land and find somewhere to wait it out."

Landing Svartos in this wretched weather would be another feat entirely.

The dragon had a keen sense of sight, but he also fell under Drake's command. It would be up to him to guide them to a place where Svartos could land without too much trouble, preferably somewhere without trees but large enough for them to seek shelter from the storm.

Drake gritted his teeth together until his jaw ached. He clenched the reins and tugged, steering the dragon lower.

If only he could fucking *see.*

Without warning, beams of brilliant light flowed from Creslyn's hands. She shot them downward like rippling waterfalls, illuminating the ground below. Sunlight cut through the dense clouds and pelting rain, bouncing off a thick grove of trees and a desolate mountain range. Land, thankfully, that was familiar to Drake.

They were flying along Brackroth's most northern border, an uninhabited stretch of the kingdom littered with rugged mountains and impassable valleys. There were a few caves nestled into the side of some of the higher peaks. Many of the witches from the Runes of Callievan sought refuge there in the early days of Marius's assault against them. They'd been long since abandoned, the king's army sniffing the witches out like hunting dogs on the prowl.

Creslyn's magic coated one of the ledges in light. The small gray cliff jutted out over the tops of the trees, its surface covered in small rocks and boulders. But just beyond it was a darkened entrance of nothingness.

A cave.

The ledge was barely large enough for Svartos to land. It would be a tricky maneuver. One wrong move—if his wings hit the mountain face or his claws grasped only loose rocks—they would go right over the other side. Drake aimed for the ledge, sensing the dragon's hesitance. His wings stretched wide in long, slow beats, bringing them closer to the mountains.

Stiff gales knocked them slightly sideways, but Drake maintained his grip on the reins. Strong and steady. But there was something else, a soft murmuring, barely audible over the deafening roar of the wind. Through its mighty call, Creslyn's gentle voice reached him. She bent forward, wet hair falling around her, sticking to her face and neck. Sunbeams burst from one hand while she ran the other along Svartos's gleaming scales, soothing the dragon.

Drake's heart strained for her.

Guilt riddled his conscience once more. He did not deserve her. No one did. She was far too wonderful for this world.

Svartos swept down, tucking his wings, and Drake gripped Creslyn tightly as the dragon touched the ground, his claws scraping against stone as he grappled for purchase. He let out another screech, his body pitching forward then rearing back as he came to an abrupt halt on the rain-soaked ledge. Creslyn fell back against Drake, her head smacking against his shoulder, and she hissed in pain as her magic snuffed out.

"Are you alright, *kearsta*?" Drake attempted to lift her into his arms, but she swatted his hands away.

"Fine." She shoved her drenched hair from her face and huffed out a breath. "I'll be fine."

Drake jumped out of the seat on Svarto's back, turning to help her, but she was already climbing down on her own, those legs of hers dangling like they had the first time he'd left her to get out of the dragon's seat by herself.

The memory scorned him.

He should have taken more care with her.

Drake blinked, shrugging off the burn of shame as she touched the ground. He moved past her, grabbing the pack of supplies strapped to Svartos's back.

"There." He nodded toward the abysmal looking cavity on the side of the mountain. "We can seek shelter here until the storm passes."

"A cave." She stared into the penetrating darkness, glancing back at him, her full mouth pressed into a hard line. "We're going to sleep in a cave?"

He arched one brow. "Do you have a better idea?"

Drake tossed the pack over his shoulder and marched into the cave's entrance. It was small, more so than he anticipated, but at least it was dry. He unloaded a bundle of kindling, a thick blanket, some food, and two fur cloaks. There wasn't much else, just enough for one night of travel. He rolled out the blanket then set to work on situating the kindling for a fire, only to realize that Creslyn wasn't with him.

Looking back at the opening of the cave, he caught sight of her silhouette. She stood there, shivering in the rain, refusing to move.

"Creslyn, come in here and get out of the weather." It was one thing for her to still be pissed at him, it was quite another for her to be so stubborn that she'd rather catch a cold than share the same space as him.

"But it's dark. I can't see anything." She raised one arm blindly. "I can't even see you."

He cocked his head to the side. "Last I checked, you were more than capable of creating light."

She held out both arms, and Drake watched as sparks of sunlight flickered, then faded like dying embers. "I have nothing left. I've not ever used that much of my power before. My magic is not an endless supply, unlike yours. I'm tired, Drake."

Weariness pained her voice.

Drake abandoned the pile of kindling and went to her side. Sliding one arm around her waist, he walked her to the far side of the cave, then whispered, "*Fierys.*"

Svartos rose, angling his long neck, his yellow eyes latching onto Creslyn before he faced the cave. He opened his mighty jaws and flames erupted, catching fire to the stack of twigs and branches in the center of the mountain's mouth. Heat blazed to life, engulfing the whole of the cave, casting light upon the hollowed space made of carved rock and uneven stone.

The dragon's nostrils flared, and he pulled his wings in close, curling up outside of the cave, effectively barricading them, protecting them, on the inside.

Creslyn's wide-eyed gaze slid from the dragon to the fire, then back again. "I've never seen…how did he—"

"I'll teach you." Drake stalked closer to the glowing fire, tugging off his gloves. "But first, remove your leathers, *kearsta.*"

Her awe was instantly replaced by a scowl.

"Fine." He shrugged, removing his vest and tossing it to the ground. He continued to discard various pieces of clothing, watching as her gaze tracked over the length of his body and color bloomed in her cheeks. "If you wish to be cold and soaked to the bone, that is your choice."

Drake grabbed one of the fur cloaks and fastened it around him, ignoring her as he quietly prepared them something to eat. There were a few strips of dried, spiced meat, a ripe pear, a red plum, and a flask of water. He debated asking her if she'd rather have the pear or the plum, then thought better of it when her disgruntled mutterings reached his ears.

Removing soaked leathers could be quite the task, and since she'd yet to ask for his help, he continued to busy himself as she struggled to undress. He didn't watch, knowing that would likely further incite her anger, but a smirk tugged at the corner of his mouth as she mumbled off a swear foul enough to make a grown man cringe. He listened as the wet leather slid and slapped against her skin, biting back a smile each time she hissed in frustration.

When the crackling of the fire was the only sound in the cave, Drake finally shoved up from his crouched position with an offering of food to hopefully appease her.

Creslyn sat upon the blanket, facing the fire, her knees pulled up to her chest. Her arms were wrapped around herself, her chin resting upon them, firelight reflecting in the depths of her sapphire eyes like the darkest part of the ocean set aflame.

"Are you still angry with me?" he ventured, setting some of the food beside her.

Her burning gaze darted up to him. "Yes."

"Fair enough." Drake grabbed the other fur cloak, this one a soft gray, and gently draped it around her bare body. "You should eat. I know it's not much but—"

"Thank you." She snatched a piece of dried meat, tearing off a hefty chunk, and chewed quietly, her eyes once more trained upon the orange flames spitting into the cavernous ceiling.

They ate together in silence until Drake could no longer ignore the one question that had been plaguing him since they left the Fenmire Bogs. He bit into the plum, its refreshingly sweet flavor coating his tongue, and said, "Tell me, *solysa*. Why do you really want to return to Brackroth? I thought you would be eager to go home to Aeramere."

She did not look at him. "I intend to kill King Marius."

Drake almost choked. He slammed his fist into his chest,

forcing down the bite of plum that had lodged itself in the back of his throat at her admission.

"Do not try to stop me." She licked her thumb, popping it out of her mouth. "And do not stand in my way."

"Creslyn," he began, but she shifted abruptly, holding up one hand.

"No." She sucked in a deep breath, the steady beat of her heart pounding through his veins. "I am going to make certain that no matter what, you are never forced to use the Shadow-blade again."

Drake shook his head, raking his hands through his damp hair. "After what I did to you, why would you want to help me?"

She rolled her eyes to the cave's ceiling, releasing an annoyed sigh. "I am fairly certain you already know the answer to that ridiculous question."

Right.

Because she still loved him, even after he betrayed her heart.

Creslyn eased back, lying upon the blanket on her side, the cloak falling open, exposing her fully. She tucked one hand beneath her head, watching him, calculating each breath he took. Her other arm fell lazily over her hips, her finger tracing slow circles along her upper thigh. The diamonds piercing her sparked with tiny rainbows, and the glow of the fire seemed to caress her skin. She was lush and warm, and though a slight frown crinkled her usually smooth brow, her nipples pebbled beneath the intensity of his gaze. He missed the feel of her satin flesh beneath his roughened palms, just as he missed the searing pain of her teeth when she marked him out of greedy lust.

Desire surged to his cock, pulsing through him with fervor.

Drake reached for her, and she swatted his hand away.

"You may look." She raised her knee, taunting him while she spread her legs, her own fingers drifting dangerously close to the source of all her pleasure. "But you may not touch."

He gritted his teeth, his fists clenching the plush blanket beneath them. "You intend to deny me indefinitely?"

"I intend to do as I please." She shot a pointed look at where he strained for her. "And right now, I am thoroughly enjoying watching you ache for me."

The wisps of shadows around his cock coiled tightly, squeezing, and he swallowed a groan. "Wicked little faerie."

She dismissed him with a wave of her hand. "Another time, perhaps."

"Will you not let me worship you?" He bit the words out.

Creslyn pinned him with a look of sheer boredom, as though she couldn't be bothered with his inner turmoil. "You mentioned nothing of wanting to worship me."

Drake snarled. "You know I do."

"Could have fooled me." She splayed her hand over her abdomen, her fingers daring to skim even lower than before. "Given your recent behavior, I would have thought infinite power was far more enticing than bejeweled breasts and the silky wetness between my thighs."

Despite being torn between crushing need and mounting frustration, Drake's lips twitched. "Such shocking words from a lady of Aeramere."

She sat upright, and the gray fur of the cloak nearly swallowed her. "Do I disappoint you, Your Highness?"

"On the contrary." His hand darted out, capturing her chin. An emotion flashed in her eyes, a tantalizing mesh of annoyance and longing, but she banked it quickly, replacing her expression with a mask of indifference. "I find you most enchanting."

Creslyn snorted, throwing one arm out and gesturing to Svartos's back. "It's rather difficult to be enchanting when one is stuck on the side of a mountain in the middle of a thunderstorm. Ballrooms are enchanting, caves most certainly are not."

Drake stood, his black fur cloak billowing around him. "You can't hear the music?"

Her head canted to one side, and she arched a suspicious brow. "No…"

"Listen."

The distant rumble of thunder was a dark melody. The whistling wind played the harmony, each howling gust another striking chord while the constant rainfall carried the notes of a lulling refrain.

He offered his hand to her. "May I have this dance, my lady?"

Reluctance gnawed at her, and the bond hummed with her uncertainty.

"I won't bite," he promised. "Yet."

Creslyn pursed her lips, then accepted his hand, letting him pull her to her feet. He slid one arm around her bare waist, and the feel of her against him was like being home. Drake lightly cupped her elbow, running his fingers up to her wrist before he clasped her hand. Heat simmered between them, heavy and decadent, and he breathed in the intoxicating scent of her.

Fresh rainfall and delicious citrus.

In one fluid movement, he whisked her around the cave in a series of intricate steps. Creslyn stumbled in his arms, her footwork a confounding sequence of missteps. At one point he was certain he could hear her counting under her breath, her knee bumped into his shin, and then she stepped on his foot.

Drake glanced down at her. "Are you intentionally trying to hurt me?"

"No," she ground the word out, tripped again, and her brow furrowed in exasperation.

"Are you certain you've waltzed before?" he asked, teasing.

He spun her away from him, then pulled her back in, and she blew out a breath, sending wisps of her hair fluttering. "I can manage well enough."

Moving his hand to the center of her back, he hooked the other one under her leg and lowered her into a steep dip. "You, my lady, are a terrible dancer."

"There is a reason I was always without a partner at balls." She glared up at him, clinging to his arms. Her cloak slipped from her shoulders, and her breasts were so close, he could almost capture one with his mouth. "I am hardly perfect at anything. I lack skill in the arts and needlework. I'm not at all proficient with any musical instrument. But I perform well enough in bed and that must count for something."

Drake's mouth opened, snapped shut, and then he laughed.

Full and loud.

He grinned, sweeping her off her clumsy feet, and lifted her into his arms. But she surprised him by capturing his cheeks with both hands. Her lips parted and the look in her eyes was one he'd never seen before.

"You're smiling." The words were barely a whisper, she spoke with such reverence.

His brow lifted. "I've been known to do so a time or two."

"No. It's different. It's *real*." She shook her head. "It's the first time I've ever seen your smile reach your eyes."

Then Creslyn's mouth was on his, warm and wonderful. Full of a kind of intimacy that was almost unfamiliar to him. Their tongues met, soft and slow, as though they were tasting each other, discovering each other, for the first time.

Creslyn sighed, pulling away just enough so they could breathe the same air.

"If a real smile is all it takes to earn a kiss from you..." Drake pressed his forehead to hers, savoring the moment, hoping the bond, the kiss, would heal the wounds he'd left behind on her heart. "Then that is gladly how I will spend the rest of my days. Smiling at you."

CHAPTER THIRTY-FOUR

Brackroth had not changed in the least—it was still dismal, dreary, and damp.

Creslyn missed the sunlight and sparkling blue skies of Aeramere. She missed the warmth of the sun upon her skin, even when there was a chill in the air. Here, there were no seasons. It was cold and wet, then colder and wetter. There was no escaping it. How anyone could choose to live and even thrive in Brackroth was beyond her. She once thought herself capable of ruling here alongside Drake, but the cost to her own peace of mind would have been great. Its morose aura, its gloomy climate, begat misery and despondency.

It was a good thing Drake had promised to return with her to Aeramere once she was done with this bloody business of murdering a king. No crown was worth such a spiritless existence.

Svartos touched down near Dragnott Lair, further from Castle Brackroth than Creslyn would have liked. She had hoped to have the element of surprise, even if perhaps a small one, on her side. But now, King Marius would undoubtedly know they'd returned before they made it back to the castle.

Drake reached up, his large hands capturing her waist as he lifted her from the dragon's back. She pinned him with a knowing look. "I told you I had business with the king."

"And I have business with my dragons." He took her hand, leading her toward the wide opening of a tunnel carved deep into the rugged mountain's face.

"Dragons," Creslyn repeated as they passed at least a dozen dragon riders, none of whom dared to glance her way. They kept their heads down, their eyes averted, murmuring hushed greetings as Drake strolled further into the lair. "We're going to see the dragons?"

Torches lined the jagged walls, casting the uneven ground in a fiery orange glow, much like the flames Svartos controlled. Despite the frigid cold of Brackroth, it was almost excessively warm within the lair. Beads of sweat slid down Creslyn's neck, rolling along her shoulders and slipping down her spine. Tapered spires of curving stone plunged down from the high ceiling, where drops of water dripped from their sharp points, spattering against the rough path in a puddle of steam. Her stomach fluttered, fraught with nerves.

"It's time I paid them a visit." Drake guided her around a corner, away from the high-pitched screeches she could only assume were the cries of the whelps. "Besides, how else will you choose one of your own?"

She drew up short.

"Choose one?" She practically squealed, clamping one hand over her mouth as the sound of her excitement echoed through the lair. "You're giving me a dragon?"

Drake's full lips curved into a slow smile. "Why else would I put you in leathers if not to give you a dragon of your own?"

Creslyn threw her arms around his neck, rising on her toes to whisper into his ear. "And here I thought you merely enjoyed the way I looked in them."

He grabbed a handful of her backside, giving her bottom a firm squeeze. "That, too."

"Now," he continued, tucking a lock of hair back behind her ear, "dragons are capricious creatures, you must—"

"I've already made my choice."

"You have?"

"Yes." She nodded once with absolute resolution. "I want Astrylys."

"I thought you might." Drake tucked her arm into the crook of his elbow as they ventured further into the winding tunnel.

"How long have you commanded the dragons?" she asked, curiosity piqued. He spoke so rarely of them, of their origins, yet he seemed to have quite the fondness for them. "And what will become of them when we leave for Aeramere?"

In the haunting glow of torchlight, his forbidden green eyes darkened, taking on the color of a somber, silent forest.

"The dragons were here long before man laid claim to this land. Before Marius, before the bloodline predating him took its first breath. When I arrived, all that stood was the castle, built with stone capable of withstanding immense heat. Or fire. There are rumors surrounding its creation. Some claim the witches used magic so that the dragons could not burn it to ash, others believe it was the will of the gods." Drake chuckled, low and unamused. "I doubt Valorahan had anything to do with it."

Creslyn peered up at him, squinting in the dim light. "What is Valorahan?"

"It is where the people of the Northernlands believe they go once they die. A place of revered respect, an afterlife for those deemed worthy, where they wait for their souls to be reborn." There was an edge to his tone, a layer of doubt.

"Oh yes, Kjeld spoke of Valorahan to me when we first met. It sounds much like an eternal paradise for souls of the brave and gallant. Like the fae have Maghmell." She glanced up at Drake. "You do not believe such a place exists?"

"What I believe does not matter. There is only what is, and what is not." He lifted her hand from his arm, pressing a featherlight kiss across her knuckles that sent her pulse skittering. "The shadow realm has shown me many things. What are gods, stars, and fates if not ancient stories woven by folklore and myth, then shaped to fit the beliefs of one society?"

"Yet here you stand before me, a god of shadow and prophecy." She threaded their fingers together, tucking their joined hands beneath her chin. "Far more real than a story."

"In time, *kearsta*, I too will be forgotten." His lips brushed over hers. Once. Twice. "We all will."

Before she could object, he continued speaking, his cadence almost musical, his accent heavy.

"The dragons do not fear me, perhaps because they recognize me for my true self." He shrugged, but the movement was stiff, wrought with tension. "When we leave this place, we will take only Svartos and Astrylys to Acramere. If the dragons wish to follow us, they may. If they choose to reclaim their homeland, then I will not stop them. Their wisdom spans centuries. Either way, they will know that I will not return to Brackroth."

Creslyn's heart twinged, ached for the dragons who might be left behind, the pang growing more severe as she thought of the citizens who would be left to fend for themselves once she took Marius's life. "What of the people?"

"They are of no concern to me." His voice was cold. Leaden. "I am not their prince, nor their god."

They approached a den of rubble and what appeared to be a large pile of shimmering diamonds.

"Here she is." Drake gestured to the waking dragon. "Your Astrylys."

Creslyn held her breath as the magnificent beast rose, stretching her fibrous wings that gleamed like crushed moonstone. Astrylys sat up, shifting in such slow, fluid movements that her silver scales looked to be crafted from moonlight. Each flicker of torchlight cast her in a glow of iridescence, from her long neck to her onyx claws, and her piercing blue eyes with horizontal obsidian slits for pupils latched onto Creslyn.

Astrylys inhaled deeply then huffed, the heat of her breath sending Creslyn's hair flying behind her.

From beside her, Drake murmured, "Easy, girl."

Creslyn would not be so bold as to assume she could simply claim a dragon as her own. She imagined the bond between rider and dragon would need to be mutual, a kinship would need to be formed, a binding between one of magic and one of fire.

She carefully held out her hand, palm up, hating the way she could not keep herself from trembling.

Astrylys angled her head, bending lower, sniffing her open palm.

"You saved me once," Creslyn whispered, and the dragon's ears twitched. "You heard my pleas, and you saved me. I owe you my life."

She stared into the startling blue eyes and did not blink. Did not falter.

"I choose you…if you'll have me."

Astrylys lowered herself even further, nuzzling the side of her head against Creslyn's outstretched hand. Her scales were smooth yet rough, and cool to the touch. Her hand was so small, so slight, compared to the majestic creature.

She ran the pads of her fingers across the glimmering scales once more and smiled. "My Astrylys."

Creslyn looked back over her shoulder to where Drake stood nearby, watching the interaction with an expression of subdued pride. Her husband had set her free. Though it was painstaking and devastating, he'd helped her unleash all that she wished to embody, all that she longed to become. And now, she would do the same for him.

Drake held her gaze, then dipped his head.

It was time.

CRESLYN STALKED through Castle Brackroth with Drake by her side, its dank halls eerily silent. No doubt King Marius had been informed of their arrival, and if she had to guess, he was preparing for a fight. Unfortunately for him, it would be his last. There were no servants, no guards, no hushed whispers or muttered conversations. Only the pattering of rain against the grimy windows could be heard, that and the measured timing of her breathing. She inhaled with purpose, exhaled with vengeance.

Drake had armed her with a sword, and she kept one hand wrapped tightly around its hilt as they strode toward the throne room.

The arching double doors carved of rich oak stood before them, and Drake paused, taking her arm. "A king is not so easily slain."

She met his imploring gaze, unable to discern if he was attempting to sway her mind or warn her of their impending battle.

"I am aware of such matters." She glanced toward the arched doors, anticipation firing through her. Rolling her neck, she loosened her shoulders, connected with the hum of magic coursing through her veins. "He deserves to feel my wrath."

"And how, exactly, do you plan on doing this?"

She clasped one hand over her heart, feigning shock. "I am surprised you did not think to ask me sooner."

Drake's brows furrowed and his jaw popped. Most of his hair was pulled into a knot on top of his head, but a few strands fell loose, and though she itched to smooth them back, she kept her hand firmly planted on the hilt of her weapon.

"I'm asking now," he ground out.

"It's quite simple." She tugged her arm free, then gave him the most sinister of smiles. "I will make him think he's won."

Without another word, without a backwards glance, she marched into the throne room.

Creslyn heaved the doors open, the aged wood groaning on its hinges as they swung wide, creaking loudly, drawing the attention of every soul in the room.

And there were *many*.

Dozens of soldiers filled the throne room, each of them decked in full armor of black with blood red sashes wrapped around their waists. They lined the walls in a multitude of rows, swords drawn and at the ready, helmets covering most of their faces so only the fierceness of their eyes could be seen. At least twenty stood before the dais, the rest were positioned by windows and other doors, barricading every exit, every means of escape.

Regrettably, Creslyn had not taken that into consideration.

King Marius stood from where he lounged on his throne, his round frame teetering as he ambled forward. His wrinkled face was twisted into a sneer, the crown sitting atop his bald head sagged, revealing spots of age and scraps of gray. He gripped his belt with both hands, likely to support the weight of his protruding stomach, as he descended the gray marble steps. His boots clicked noisily against the polished floor, and though her stomach clenched in disgust at the sight of him, Creslyn did not step back.

She sensed Drake directly behind her, found strength in the bond binding them together. It made no difference if every weapon in the room was aimed at her, if she could feel the burn of hate seeping from each soul who tracked her with guarded eyes. She had come here with one purpose, and she had no intention of leaving until King Marius's body was lifeless on the ground, his blood staining her hands.

"Drake." The king's beady gaze drifted beyond Creslyn, then refocused on her. His mouth stretched wide in a hideous grin, displaying rotten, yellowed teeth. "And your faerie bitch, too. How lovely."

He sauntered closer, appraising her. His black eyes roved over every inch of her, lingering on her hips and chest, and the sick bastard adjusted his belt once more.

Creslyn's stomach soured. Her blood boiled.

"I see you've outfitted her in riding leathers." The king licked his thin, cracked lips, and from behind her, Drake growled.

"Mind yourself," he warned, his voice low and lethal.

But King Marius paid him no mind.

"Finally bending her to your will, are you?" he mused, breathing heavily, and the stench of stale alcohol and rot assaulted Creslyn's nose. "Tell me, pretty little faerie, did he break you?"

She stiffened, steeling her spine. Her magic raged to the surface like an angry tide, but she tempered it, crushing its furious swell. "No one can break me."

"We shall see about that."

The king snapped his fingers, and Creslyn pulled her sword, but the soldiers were on her with lightning speed.

Metal clanged in her ears, the clash of weapons sending tremors down her arms. Her mind raced, reliving every move, every instruction Kjeld had taught her. She dodged and parried, stepping into each attack, swinging her sword with deadly accuracy. Her blade struck true, but where one guard fell, another quickly took his place. The tip of a dagger sliced across her shoulder, and sudden, stinging pain tore down her arm. Sinking her teeth into her bottom lip, she spun away from the threat, only to find another guard rushing toward her. Her muscles ached and her head was spinning. Blurs of black and bloodied red were everywhere, their grunts and vile shouts a cacophonous noise that drowned out the sound of her own thoughts.

Creslyn kept her elbows up, using both hands to guide her weapon. Another streak of pain lanced across the back of her thigh, and she lurched forward, gasping as the cut of a blade sliced through her flesh. The healing property of her magic heated her blood, tending to the wounds on her arm and leg, but if she continued to take hits like this, she would fall too quickly. And she couldn't very well kill the king if she was already dead.

Guards swarmed her, flashes of swords blinded her, but she continued to fight, each strike becoming more punishing than the last.

Off to her left, she could have sworn Drake shouted her name, but his voice was lost to her.

Something warm and sticky splattered against the side of her face, and she staggered backward, the metallic tang of blood filling the air.

Blood that did not belong to her.

Shadows swarmed the throne room, plunging into chaos around her, forming a pit of eternal darkness.

It was a cloak of velvet nightfall writhing with the promise of death. Shades of gray colored her vision as the shadows moved like serpents, snaring soldiers by their legs and arms, tearing their limbs from their bodies. Harrowing screams reverberated through the throne room as Drake's power cleaved through the space, rendering them silent.

She squeezed her eyes shut, and Drake's booming voice split through her mind with such force, the bond quaked.

"Use your magic!" he demanded. *"Now, Cres!"*

Creslyn shook her head violently, blocking him out.

Not yet.

She had a plan, she had to make King Marius think he'd

brought her to heel. And the only way to do so was to fall directly into his hands.

Pitching herself forward, she feigned a misstep, tumbling right into one of the guards closest to the king.

"I've got her!" the guard shouted, taking a fistful of her hair and yanking her head back. Splitting pain scoured her neck, streaking down her spine. "I've got the faerie!"

The edge of his finely honed blade pressed hard against her exposed throat, threatening to cut clean through her skin, so cold it burned. A whimper escaped her, and her sword clattered to the ground. She clawed at his forearm in a desperate attempt to free herself, but the soldier only tightened his grip, his sword dangerously close to breaking her skin.

Drake roared, his magic amplifying until the screams of the dying were too much to bear.

King Marius grabbed her by the upper arm, dragging her so close his scraggly beard scraped her cheek. "Cease your insufferable darkness at once, or I will end her pathetic life."

The shadows evaporated, leaving behind a messy bloodbath in their wake.

In the center of it all stood Drake.

His eyes were wild, crazed with bloodlust. In one hand, he held the Shadowblade, in the other, a severed head. He dropped it at once, and Creslyn grimaced as it rolled across the sleek floor, smearing it with a trail of crimson. Chest heaving, he stared at her, and they both knew—one wrong move, and the king would slit her throat.

"That's better." King Marius released her arm and let out a low whistle. "Quite the mess you've made, Drake. I suppose I should have your wife clean it up…then again, I imagine I could find other ways for her to be of use."

Drake snarled, and a vein along his temple pulsed in rage. His fury thundered down the bond and left her breathless. He sheathed the Shadowblade in one quick movement, his fists clenching by his side until his knuckles whitened.

"*Trust me,*" she pleaded. "*You must trust me.*"

He bared his teeth.

But the king was no longer looking at him, he was looking at *her*. "As for you, fae bitch…"

The remaining soldiers laughed cruelly, as though they already knew what was coming, like they were in on some wretched secret. The one who held her captive angled her head back further, his sword digging into her throat, so she was forced to look up at the king. She sucked in a painful breath.

King Marius stood before her and gave her a poisoned smile.

He dragged his rough knuckles across her cheek, and they came away scarlet. "If you wish to spend the rest of your days with my son and not with your head upon a stake, then I suggest you prove your loyalty."

Creslyn swallowed the knot of trepidation lodged in the back of her throat and met him with malice of her own. "Drake is not your son."

"Ah, he told you the truth, did he? That he's nothing more than a common bastard?" King Marius chortled, his large stomach jiggling as he ran a hand down his beard.

"He is more than you will *ever* be."

The king snatched her chin, squeezing so hard with his gnarled fingers, tears spilled down her cheeks. "On your knees, faerie whore. And prove your loyalty to your king."

Drake roared.

King Marius reached for his belt again, except this time he unbuckled it. For one horrendous moment, she thought he meant to whip her. Until his knobby fingers reached for the top button of his pants, and it was only then she realized with absolute horror the act with which he intended to force upon her. The bulge in his pants caused her stomach to heave.

Creslyn spat on him. "A fae kneels for no man."

Her magic exploded in a catastrophic sunstorm. The soldier holding her hostage screamed, releasing her as he fled. She aimed all her power, all her might, at the king. Radiant beams of sunlight shattered his hideous body, scorching him, scouring him. His screams brought her solace. Thrusting both of her arms forward, she channeled that fury, that raw darkness she'd come to accept, directly at his vile soul. Sharpened spears of rainbows blasted from within, and she drew on the well of magic, siphoning all of it in his direction until the stench of charred flesh hung heavy in the air. Light erupted in the room, swerving around her in an impenetrable sphere, in a flurry of tumultuous beauty.

Guards ran, clambering over one another to flee from her, lest they be burned to death. Their shouts and fearful screams were deafening, filling the throne room until her head pulsed and pounded.

"Creslyn!" Drake shouted as he leapt over dead bodies, sprinting to her side. But she ignored him.

Streak after streak of magic blasted into the king's burnt, lifeless body. His flesh was all but melted from his skin. His clothing was nothing more than soot and cinders. Bones protruded from the singed remains, crumbling to ash. Exhaustion clawed at her and her arms dropped, her knees wobbling. Though her body swayed, she managed to remain upright. To hold her ground. Finally, once she had nothing left, her magic waned. Tiny shadows crept into the sphere, soothing the anguish, calming the storm. They cocooned her, wrapping around her so she grew limp.

So tired.

So weary.

"Creslyn." Drake remained motionless. He did not reach for her. He did not offer his hand. He simply waited for her magic to subside, waited for her to come back to him.

She tore her gaze away from the dead king at her feet and looked up into a pair of mesmerizing eyes.

"Drake?" Her throat was scratchy, rough like gravel and stone.

"Yes, *kearsta?*"

She shivered. "I'd like to go home now."

Drake said nothing. He scooped her into his arms, and she collapsed into the strength of him, her head lolling against his shoulder.

She inhaled softly, breathing in the comforting scent of frozen mountains and the promise of snow.

"*Rest now, sjellhert.*" His words were a lullaby, a balm to her soul.

Her eyes closed, weighted with fatigue. She would not think about what she had done. She would not think about the permeating reek of blood or the lifeless eyes of the dead. No, she would allow none of those things to haunt her. She would fall into a dreamless sleep, in her husband's arms, and only one thought would stay with her.

"*I love you, Drake.*"

Creslyn could have sworn he said something in return, something she did not understand, and his voice faded as she slipped into a peaceful abyss.

CHAPTER THIRTY-FIVE

"Creslyn...your hair." Caelian stared in shock, glancing down at her own silver locks, then looking back at her twin. "What happened?"

Creslyn sighed, folding her hands in her lap. It was a long story, and a difficult one, and she debated how much of it to tell. She was seated on a sofa with Drake to her right and Caelian to her left. Kjeld stood just behind her twin, his arms folded across his wide chest, his shoulder propped against the wall, included in the conversation yet distant at the same time. Were it only Caelian in the room with her, she would likely disclose everything, but as she glanced around the sitting room with nearly her entire family in attendance, words seemed to fail her.

Ariesian was across from her in one of the high-back leather chairs, his legs kicked out with one ankle crossed over the other, his fingers strumming a careless rhythm against the smooth fabric. Asher occupied the matching chair and Novalise was perched on his knee, her teeth worrying her bottom lip. Sarelle and Narissa sat on a plush velvet settee and Solarius lounged against its curving wooden arm, his silver gaze glancing cautiously out the arching windows where the Moonfall Peaks stood in the distance.

"I think her hair looks lovely." Solarius pushed off the edge of the settee, tucking his hands behind his back. He strode toward the window, looking back at Creslyn from over his shoulder. "But I find myself much more fascinated by the fact that she has a *dragon*."

"Astrylys." Creslyn nodded in confirmation. "She and Svartos will be staying with us. Along with General Holtstrom's dragon, Odryss."

Considering the dragons couldn't very well traipse through the gardens of House Celestine, Drake had suggested they work on building them a lair of their own within the Moonfall Peaks. Apparently, Astrylys would be in need of a den, and quite possibly a nest, as Drake believed the female dragon was pregnant and would require a well-protected place to guard her eggs. And as it would happen, Svartos was Astrylys's mate.

Fitting, all things considered, and Creslyn found herself absolutely giddy at the prospect of baby dragons.

She hoped they all had blue eyes like their mother.

"Staying?" Caelian bounced in her seat and clutched Creslyn's hand. "You're staying here? In Aeramere? Permanently?"

Warmth spread through the bond, a comforting reminder of Drake's approval.

"Yes." Creslyn met her twin's hopeful gaze with a smile. "Permanently."

"And what of Brackroth's crown?" Ariesian asked. He rested one elbow on the arm of the leather chair, running his thumb along the pad of his fingers as he studied Drake. "Should the heir not reside in his own realm?"

"I suppose that would be appropriate," Drake mused, angling his head to meet her brother's intimidating gaze. "If I were the heir."

Ariesian's hand coiled into a fist. "You are not?"

"It's an amusing story, actually," Creslyn interjected, trying to diffuse the growing tension between the two males. "As it would happen, Drake is not a prince."

She lifted her chin.

"He's a god."

Her announcement was met with a few gasps and some choice words from both her brothers and Asher. Only Kjeld looked no less surprised by the proclamation. Caelian lurched back, letting go of her hand, gaping in shock.

"A...god," Sarelle repeated, wringing her stardust-coated hands in her lap, smearing the glitter on her gown. "As in, an actual god?"

Creslyn peered over at her husband, and a rush of pride left her beaming. She laced their fingers together, enjoying the way the softness of her skin fit easily into his callused palm. "Cian, god of shadow and prophecy, to be exact."

Solarius laughed, then shook his head, raking a hand through his silver, black-tipped hair. "Well, that certainly explains a lot."

Ariesian, on the other hand, looked more displeased than ever. His brow was knitted in concern, deepening his scowl. "What says the King of Brackroth about this sudden revelation?"

"Nothing." Drake squeezed Creslyn's hand, steadying her confidence. They both knew where this conversation would lead. "King Marius is dead. Slain in his own throne room."

Ariesian jolted upright. "By whom?"

Creslyn swallowed hard, her stomach tangled in knots of dread. This was her moment, when her family would realize the truth of her nature, when they would see what she had become. She could only hope they would not scorn her for her actions, but instead grant her the peace of understanding.

On a shallow breath, she met Ariesian's unnerving stare and said, "Me."

The answering silence frayed her nerves. She counted each breath, each heartbeat, waiting for someone, anyone, to speak. As the agonizing seconds bled by, Solarius cleared his throat.

He roughed a hand over his face, the corner of his mouth lifting. "Well done, sister."

"Oh, Cres." Novalise's face softened, her pretty features etched in faint lines of sympathy. "Are you well?"

"As well as I can be, given the circumstances." She did not yet know if what she'd done would haunt her, if she would wake from nightmares drenched in a cold sweat, or if she would lock them away in the darkest part of her heart and forget them. Either way, there was only one path going forward for House Celestine, for all of Aeramere, and it would not be so easily won. "The stars never lie, Nova. War is on the horizon and we must prepare. Our house has already come under attack once, and it is our duty to protect it. We must be ready for the bloodshed that will inevitably follow."

"Wise words, my lady." This from Asher, who was gently rubbing Novalise's back. "A bit grisly, but wise."

Ariesian leaned forward in his seat, his elbows resting upon his knees, fingers steepled together. "So, the throne of Brackroth sits empty?"

"For now." Drake did not seem at all concerned by this notion, despite Ariesian's growing temper. "I have no doubt someone will lay claim to it eventually."

"And if they pose a threat to us?" Ariesian demanded, gesturing wildly in Creslyn's direction. "If they seek retribution against my sister for the death of their king?"

"Then we will do whatever is necessary to end that possibility before it begins." Drake's response was glacial. A frozen promise, never a threat. "No harm will come to Creslyn. Ever."

Solarius strode across the room, shoving one hand into his pocket while he clamped the other on Ariesian's taut shoulder. "You worry too much, brother."

Ariesian spared him a withering glance and muttered, "At least one of us does."

"Solarius is right." Asher nodded in Drake's direction, wrapping an arm around Novalise's waist. "Brackroth's future king or queen is of little concern at the moment. There are far more crucial matters at stake, many of which require our immediate attention."

Ariesian sighed, dropping his head into his hands. Stress seemed to seep from his very bones, the heaviness of it caused his shoulders to sag. He wore his responsibility to his family like a crown of granite, its burden a constant weight. For so long, he had been the one to protect them, to look after their wellbeing, to keep them in line. It was a role he was forced into after the untimely death of their father, and though he'd never outright complained, Creslyn always wondered if maybe Ariesian wished his life had been one of his choosing and not one of obligation. She knew he never wanted his siblings, especially his sisters, involved in any kind of court unrest. Yet now it seemed unavoidable, and it was a struggle, a kind of inner turmoil Ariesian had not quite overcome.

"Indeed," Novalise murmured, toying with the delicate lace of her violet gown. "Granted, there have been no more attacks since you left, but the rumors of rebellion and uprisings continue to circulate."

"Mistrust grows easily." Ariesian sat back, his head falling against the stiff cushion of the chair. He yanked on the collar of his shirt, loosening it. "Doubt lingers."

"In some more than others," Solarius added, pretending to adjust the rolled cuffs of his sleeves.

Creslyn did not miss the look that passed between her two brothers. It reeked of animosity and resentment.

"The gift of prophecy has afforded me an advantage." Drake shifted, straightening to address the room in its entirety. "Unfortunately, there is only so much I can see, so much I can say. While I am able to confirm Lady Novalise's star reading regarding the alignment of the constellations and what it means for the future of Aeramere, I cannot discern who is at fault. Prince Aspen…or Queen Elowyn."

"The queen?" Caelian's eyes flashed with disbelief. "You think the queen is behind the rumors surrounding her own ousting?"

Drake lifted one shoulder, dismissive. "It remains to be seen."

"Absurd." She waved one hand through the air. "Positively outrageous. Prince Aspen must be at fault. Everyone knows he is wretched and cruel. A most wicked prince if there ever was one. All of Aeramere is aware of his foul reputation, as well as his desire to claim the crown for himself."

Sarelle bristled, smoothing the pleats of her gown that were now covered in stardust. "He isn't entirely horrible."

"You're only saying that because he saved your life," Caelian shot back. She gesticulated as she spoke, a dramatic waving of her hands. "What if his actions were nothing more than a front, a trap, to win you over? Especially with Mother attempting to arrange your betrothal to him."

Sarelle ducked her head, her cheeks flushing pink as she wrung her fingers together, further wrinkling her skirts.

"Speaking of our mother," Creslyn interrupted, not wanting her sisters to tumble into a full-blown spat. "Where is she?"

"She remains at court with the queen." Ariesian tilted his head, brushing his knuckles along his jaw, his curious gaze drifting to her. "Though I am surprised she is not here to welcome you home. I assume she would have been sent word when you requested passage through the Veil."

"About that…" Creslyn winced.

Oh, this was *not* going to go over well.

"Passage was not requested." Drake's mild voice did little to soothe her anxiety. "As it was not required."

Ariesian stilled, his expression vacant. "What?"

"The Veil is only a glamour, Aries." Creslyn used his nickname in the hopes that it might make the news she was about to share slightly less shocking. "We flew through it quite easily when we left Aeramere and did the same upon our return."

"*What?*" Novalise cried, her starlit eyes widening in horror.

"Fucking stars." Solarius dropped onto the arm of the settee by Narissa, muttering to himself as he loosed a stream of offensive swears.

Narissa, who had been oddly silent since Creslyn's arrival, finally spoke. Her voice was melodic, her demeanor as calm as the waves that kissed the shoreline of House Azurvend. "You are saying our realm, our homes, are protected by nothing more than a simple glamour?"

"The word protected is a bit of a stretch, my lady." Drake leaned back against the sofa, the cushion groaning beneath his weight. He draped one arm around Creslyn's shoulders. "More like hidden away from mortal eyes. It is unlikely any humans, witches, or even vampires could move through it at will, but a fae of any kind, most especially ones of great power, could certainly do so."

Narissa's golden, rosy pallor faded.

Solarius quit fiddling with his rolled sleeves and glanced down at Narissa, whose complexion continued to wane. His hand flinched, but he offered her no comfort.

"Whether the Veil is a glamour or not is of no consequence." Ariesian's gaze lingered on a streak of sunlight pouring in from the windows, its haze catching the toes of his boots. "Not when the perceived threat is coming from within our own borders."

"So, what do we do?" Novalise asked, her voice pitched with anxiety.

Asher collected her in his arms, stroking her hair in calm, slow movements to lessen her panic.

"We shall continue on as though nothing is amiss." Ariesian

commanded the room with an air of authority. "On the outside, we will maintain appearances. Host balls, attend parties—"

"Marry off siblings," Solarius grumbled.

Ariesian cut him with a look of scorn. "Do our duty to our house. But on the inside, where prying eyes cannot see, we will train with our magic. Each Starstorm will learn to wield a weapon of their choosing. I will form alliances as needed, just as I've done with the former Prince of Brackroth and now Lord Reif Marintide, to ensure House Azurvend stands with us when the need arises."

Sarelle clasped her hands together, her deep blue eyes alight with excitement. "I've always wanted to use a bow and arrow."

Ariesian pointed one finger in her direction. "Not you."

"But Aries," Novalise rose from Asher's lap. "That is unfair. Why not Sarelle? You just said—"

"I know what I said." He lifted one hand, giving her pause. Then he looked at Sarelle with purpose. "If you want to learn how to use a bow and arrow, then you will need to convince Prince Aspen to teach you."

Sarelle blinked in confusion. "Whatever for?"

"Because, darling sister, since our mother and the queen have deemed you an appropriate match for the prince, then I am going to use their intentions to our advantage." Ariesian settled back into his seat, and the pieces of the puzzle he laid out gradually fell into place.

"You intend to have Sarelle spy on the prince?" Solarius stared at their eldest brother, bewildered. He stood, paced the length of the room, then circled back, shaking his head, anger simmering with every step. "No. It's too dangerous, Ariesian. If she is found out, the punishment will be death. I won't stand for it."

Ariesian arched a brow, a look of bemusement settling over his previously stern features. "You won't be found out, will you, Sarelle?"

"Ariesian, I agree with Solarius." Creslyn chewed her bottom lip. Preparing for war was necessary, true, but sending their sister directly into harm's way was a terrible risk. "I don't think we should ask this of her."

"I will manage just fine." Sarelle's lips were set in a hard line, but her eyes gave her away. They reflected worry, doubt, fear of the unknown. "If my siblings can make sacrifices for our family, then so can I."

"But Sarelle," Novalise pleaded, kneeling before her. "Prince Aspen is—"

"I said I will manage." Sarelle's voice was frosty. She remained steadfast in her decision, despite the treacherous task set before her. "If Ariesian wishes me to play this part, then I shall."

"Fear not, dear sister. You must only gain his favor, learn what you can of his plans, and convince him you're his perfect match." Ariesian stood from his chair and moved toward Sarelle, covering her hand with his own. "If by chance he proposes, you will accept. And I swear it now on our father's grave, I will not allow any such marriage to take place."

He offered her a small, rare smile. "Just don't fall in love with him and you'll be fine."

Sarelle looked as though she might be ill. Her skin turned a sickly green shade, and she swayed in her seat. Narissa reached out, gathering her into her arms to steady her.

Creslyn blew out a low breath, hating that her sister was so distraught, that she would be put in such a predicament as to act as though she truly sought the Prince of Aeramere's affections.

"And..." Creslyn swallowed, a lump forming in the back of her throat. "And what of Tovian and Nyxian?"

"They should return to Aeramere before winter's first breath." Ariesian released Sarelle's hand, his gaze trekking to the window, where the Moonfall Peaks formed a barrier, where the sea would carry them home. "Just in time for Solarius and Narissa's wedding."

Stallions neighed in the distance, announcing the arrival of a coach.

Solarius stepped back, his voice dropping an octave. "Mother's home."

"Disperse at once," Ariesian ordered, rolling his shoulders back. He straightened his shirt, smoothed his sleek silver hair so it fell to one side. "No one mention a word of our discussion here to her."

As though he sensed some form of objection, Ariesian lifted a finger, placing it near his mouth. "Not. One. Word. I love our mother, but her willingness to pair Sarelle with Prince Aspen is an avaricious reach for power that I will not tolerate."

He met the gaze of each soul in the room, ensuring his orders were to be followed. "As of now, she is not to be trusted."

Everyone nodded, and one by one, they left the sitting room as they went in search of other pursuits, the secrets they shared fading in their absence.

Creslyn looped her arm through Drake's as they strolled toward the courtyard. She stole a glance up at him, daring to ask the question she feared an answer to the most. "Do you think my family is afraid of me?"

"Not at all, *kearsta*." He bent low, pressing a kiss to her temple. "I think they are most impressed by you."

She certainly hoped so. While she was grateful they had some semblance of a plan moving forward, she knew one obstacle remained in her way. Overcoming it would not be for the faint of heart, and the task alone fell to her, for none of her siblings could be the one to free Drake of his curse.

If she wanted her god of a husband to truly be hers and belong to no other, then there was only one thing left to do.

Creslyn must destroy the Shadowblade.

CHAPTER THIRTY-SIX

*D*awn came early for someone who was never in need of sleep.

Or a god.

The early mornings in House Celestine were quiet, and Drake roamed the decadent halls where the floors glittered like the night sky and star-shaped lanterns glowing with faerie fire floated overhead, illuminating the walls of rich navy and gold. He passed under archways lined with gleaming selenite and stained glass windows depicting constellations of varying forms. Outside, the clouds were heavy and gray, as though the gloom of Brackroth had followed him to this place.

Creslyn was still asleep in bed, her warm and supple body buried beneath a thick layer of velvet. He'd stoked the fire in the hearth to ward off the autumn chill that had crept into the room, then set about wandering, knowing he would eventually make his way to the courtyard to train.

The previous night's events continued to replay in his mind as he descended the staircase.

He supposed he would have to grow accustomed to family dinners with the Starstorms.

Between the constant chatter, the banter and bickering, it had been almost impossible to keep up with the flow of conversation. Though he had to commend the siblings in their efforts to remain aloof while keeping their mother in the dark about their scheming. Not once were there any moments of strained silence or caustic tension. They were cordial if not amusing, oftentimes teasing one another over some joke Drake did not understand.

It was a strange feeling, he realized, being absorbed into a family that loved each other so fiercely.

Save for their unpleasant mother.

Lady Trysta Starstorm was downright loathsome. Pompously snide, she was derisive in manner whenever she spoke to any one of her children. It almost made him wonder why she felt inclined to bear offspring at all. She was appalled by Creslyn's hair, claiming it looked as though she'd soaked the strands in black ink.

It had taken every ounce of self-control for Drake to not reach across the table and throttle the damned female.

Not only that, but she seemed rather perturbed by his and Creslyn's unannounced arrival. She excused herself from dinner quickly after barely eating anything at all, no doubt alerting the queen that they had traveled through the Veil without raising any kind of alarm.

The matriarch of House Celestine possessed many faults, yet Drake remained unsure of her loyalty to her family. Though she'd manipulated star readings for her own gain, in some cases outright lying about them, she had not done anything terribly malicious in nature. Nothing truly evil or sinister.

At least not to his knowledge.

Perhaps she was just a shitty mother.

"Ah, there you are, Your Highness."

A male voice sounded from his right, and Drake turned to find Lord Asher Firebane walking toward him.

"Or god of shadow and prophecy." Asher raised the cup of coffee he held in greeting. "I'll be quite honest, I haven't the slightest idea of how to address you."

Drake inclined his head. "Drake will do."

"Noted." Asher ran a hand over his rumpled hair, the silver streak falling right back into his face. "I've already spoken with Ariesian, but I figured I would inform you as well."

Drake's brows rose.

"Novalise and I will be returning to Emberspire tomorrow. I need to fortify my house, while also protecting my wife, sister, and servants."

"A solid plan." Drake nodded, his thoughts drifting. House Celestine was safe for the most part, but at some point, he and Creslyn would require a home of their own. Preferably a place where he could ravish her without having the entirety of the house being made aware of their affairs. Maybe they could find somewhere in the city, or build a house in the mountains, closer to their dragons.

He quite liked the idea.

Asher's voice pulled his attention, drawing him back to the conversation at hand. "Celestine will have our unwavering support in every endeavor."

"Good." He watched as a servant scurried past them carrying a tray of food. Mouthwatering scents of freshly baked rolls and crisp beef lingered in the hall. "They will have mine as well."

Asher leaned around him, making sure the servant was well out of earshot. He stepped forward, lowering his voice. "Is it done?"

"It is done." Drake glanced over his shoulder, his gaze skimming the double staircases, searching for any sign of eavesdropping. "The hag is dead. The *virdis lepatite*...destroyed."

"I sense some hesitation." Asher sipped his coffee, his face a mask of indifference.

"It is a long story, and one I do not wish to relive." Drake rubbed his temples, remembering all he nearly lost. "But to put it mildly, that gem almost ruined me. Almost ruined everything."

"I see. According to my research, it has been known to have quite the number of undesirable effects. Especially on those who resist its power." Asher went to take another drink of coffee, but then his gray eyes widened, his back snapped straight, and he almost dropped the cup completely. "I beg your pardon. I hate to cut our conversation short, but if you'd excuse me, it would seem my wife requires my immediate attention."

"Ah, yes." Drake smirked. "The mating bond."

Asher's cheeks colored slightly, but he smiled in return. "See you around, shadow prince."

Drake nodded once. "All in good time, fire fae."

With that, Asher made haste to the bedchambers he shared with Novalise, and Drake found his way to the courtyard, his muscles longing to be put to work.

He expected to be alone for the duration of the morning but was genuinely surprised to discover his training space was already occupied by none other than Creslyn, her twin sister, and Kjeld.

Caelian stood toward the center of the courtyard in a simple dress of pale blue and silver lace, a fur cape fastened at the nape of her neck. Kjeld stood opposite her, dressed in his favored brown riding leathers, the ones that had seen more battles than Drake cared to admit. But it was Creslyn, always Creslyn, who drew his eye.

She was leaning against the stone wall outlying the court-yard, the corners of her mouth lifted in a barely there smile as she watched her twin face off with the general. Her skirts fell from her waist in waves of deep rose, covered with an overlay of gilded lace. The bodice was snug, hugging her in layers of gold, and the sleeves were long, dipping off her shoulders and flowing down to her wrists. Loose waves of black hair tumbled around her, completely unbound, the facets of color glinting despite the fact that the sun remained hidden behind a wall of clouds.

She was ethereal in every sense of the word.

And he *longed* for her.

"I still don't see why I must begin with a wooden sword." Caelian waved the carved weapon around, its sharp point just missing the side of Kjeld's face. He swiftly ducked out of the way, and she gave it another bored twirl. "It looks like a child's toy."

"All warriors begin at the same level, then rise through the ranks," Kjeld stated calmly, his patience never seeming to wane.

Caelian gazed up at him and fluttered her lashes. "Do you really think I can become a warrior?"

Drake's general took a decisive step backward, away from the threat of a simpering smile.

"Your sister learned quickly. Perhaps it will be the same for you." He tapped her wooden sword with one of his own. "Again."

Caelian lunged forward, but her footing was all wrong. She twisted, tangled in her skirts, and tumbled to the ground.

Creslyn covered her mouth, disguising her laugh.

Kjeld made no move to help her up. "Or perhaps not."

The lady scowled, and he knocked her sword once more. "Again."

Crisp autumn air drifted through the courtyard, carrying the scent of fresh rain and sweet citrus. Of Creslyn.

Drake's gaze slid to the wall again, and she sauntered over, having caught sight of him watching their session. She flipped her sword with ease, as though she'd been born with it in her hand, and aimed its shining tip towards his heart.

"Fancy a wager, god of shadow and prophecy?"

His blood stirred, he enjoyed it immensely when she was feisty. "Are you challenging me, wife?"

"I am." She tucked her sword behind her back and rose up on her toes, placing a kiss underneath his chin. Her warm breath fanned his throat and filled him with insatiable lust. "Afraid you'll lose?"

He flashed her a vicious grin and nipped her bottom lip. "Not in the least."

"Name your terms, whatever you want, you can have...but only if you win." She arched her arm, her weapon slicing through the air, so the flat side of her blade landed with a resounding smack against her open palm. "Then I shall name my prize for *when* I win."

"Very well." A low, rumbling laugh escaped him, and he bent low, pressing his mouth to the tip of her pointed ear, so the words he spoke were only for her. "If I win, I want you. Naked and restrained by my shadows in your bed, so that I may do as I please to your body."

She shivered and the bond heated, warming him.

Creslyn drew back, just slightly, one eyebrow raised in question. "For how long?"

"Until moonrise."

Her gaze flicked to the overcast skies and her lips twitched. "Seems reasonable."

"And your demand, *solysa*?" he purred, enjoying the way goosebumps pebbled across her flesh.

"If I win..." She straightened, edging away from him, and her smile vanished. "I want your Shadowblade."

Drake blinked, unsure he'd heard her correctly. But her words sank into him, chilling him to the bone. He shook his head. "No."

"Yes." She slapped her sword against her palm again, this time with more force. "If I win, the Shadowblade is mine."

The weapon in question hummed to life in its sheath, sensing the tension, craving the possibility of spilled blood.

"Absolutely not." He backed away from her, withdrawing. "It is far too dangerous for you to use."

"It is *cursed*, Drake." She advanced on him, refusing to yield. "You will give it to me so that I may destroy it. Once and for all."

This time, he held his ground. Her eyes, those fearless orbs of damning sapphire, were nearly black. She was fierce. Dauntless. Rapture in the making. But she was also wrong.

"The blade is not cursed, nor am I." Even as he spoke, there was a summons. A calling. His hand spasmed, fighting the compulsion that beckoned him. "It is a weapon of my choosing, and it belongs to me."

"You are mistaken. Zaleria told me of its power before her death." The wind grew colder, more violent, and Creslyn shoved her hair back, her gaze never once leaving his face. "She was the one who cursed it, and she did so because you refused her."

Lies.

Drake staggered, putting space between them. He couldn't believe it, couldn't believe her. The Shadowblade was only dangerous when Marius inked a name in blood, binding Drake to assassinate any victim of his choosing. It was not cursed. It was a powerful, reliable weapon. It never missed, it always struck true. He had no intentions of giving it up or seeing it destroyed. Certainly not out of petty jealousy stemming from his wife.

Creslyn's dislike and envy of Zaleria had been evident since their first introduction. Now she sought to punish him for something beyond his control—the misconstrued feelings of a witch.

Drake shook his head. "No, *kearsta.*"

"You think I'm lying?" She swung her sword in a slow circle, stepping closer. "Does it not call to you even now? Its coercion is one of bloodlust. The more you use it, the more it controls you."

"Back away, Cres."

"Never."

She attacked him.

His fucking *wife* attacked him.

"Damn it, Creslyn!" He pulled his own sword hastily, blocking her assault, but not before the tip of her blade scored the leather armor covering his chest. She was stronger than he gave her credit for. What she lacked in height, she made up for in sheer force. "I did not agree to the terms."

He lunged to one side, dodging her next strike. The clang of metal echoed through the courtyard, drawing the attention of Kjeld and Caelian. His general shifted forward, planting himself directly in front of Creslyn's twin sister. Though a wide berth of space separated them, Drake stole another glance in Kjeld's direction.

His brows were drawn, his stance taut and at the ready.

He knew the fight between them was serious.

"Fail or succeed," Drake warned, shoving her backward as their weapons clashed. "I will not yield the Shadowblade to you."

She huffed out a breath, kicking her skirts behind her as she gripped the hilt of her sword with both hands. "Then I shall be forced to take it from you."

The angry heavens opened, and cold rain fell from the somber skies, the continuous drizzle soaking her gown. Raindrops clung to her lashes, sliding down her cheeks like tears. She lifted her sword, swiping the back of her hand across her forehead. Her pink lips parted, each breath she took filled the bond with fire. With determination. She flexed her fingers, stretching them out, then curling them back around the leather-wrapped hilt, her knuckles draining of color.

Her intent was clear.

"You're making a mistake," he warned.

Drake took one step back, planting his feet, his knees bending just slightly as he prepared for her next assault.

"No, Drake." Beams of sunlight poured from her fingertips, wrapping her in ribbons of gold. "I am merely doing what must be done to free you."

"We're bound by blood, *solysa*." At the mention of the word blood, the Shadowblade pulsed in its sheath, and he gripped his sword tighter. "You magic cannot harm me."

"Maybe not." Creslyn lifted one shoulder, then let it fall without care. "But my weapon can."

She launched herself at him in the next moment.

Drake had expected her to aim high, but instead, she dove for him. The hilt of her sword slammed into his chest, and he gasped as all the air was pushed from his lungs. She charged for his abdomen, driving home another insufferable hit, using her momentum to knock him off his feet. His back collided with the stone courtyard, pain lancing from the base of his neck to his lower spine. He grimaced, gnashing his teeth together as blackened stars and murky sunlight danced across his vision. Creslyn's weight settled upon him, her thighs spread across his waist, the cold, flat edge of her sword planted firmly against his neck.

His cock throbbed. Swelled and ached, completely undeterred by the weapon poised at his throat.

Creslyn straddling him with the intent to inflict harm was quite possibly one of the most provocative things he'd ever endured.

She leaned over him, beads of rainwater sluicing down her neck and breasts, dripping from the tips of her hair onto his face. He stared into her eyes, into those endless pools of damning sapphires framed by full, damp lashes. Her skin was flushed from exertion as currents of magic continued to ripple around her. She was devastating in every sense of the word. She wrecked him. Owned him.

The bond heated and tugged, pulling them together. It secured around their hearts, anchoring them to one another.

Her gaze slid from his mouth to his eyes, then back to his mouth again. She bent lower, applying just enough pressure to her weapon splayed across his throat that Drake had to fight back the urge to groan in approval. Her pink tongue darted out, sliding along his bottom lip, like she only wanted a single taste.

Fuck that.

Drake dropped his sword, didn't care as it clattered loudly against the stone ground. He reached up, fisting both hands into her wet, silky hair, and dragged her mouth to his own.

She opened for him readily, their tongues meshing in a furious kiss as they sought to devour one another. A noise escaped her, a faint whimper that caused his cock to thicken even further. He swallowed the sound, wanting all of it. Every soft whisper and gentle moan, every breathless sigh and cry of his name. All of it, all of her, belonged to him.

He wanted to flip her over, to bury himself inside of her while Kjeld and Caelian watched.

And he would have done it, too.

If Creslyn hadn't chosen that exact moment to reach for the Shadowblade.

The noise that tore from his chest was inhuman. Ungodly.

It did not belong to this world.

Creslyn scrambled off of him, her face contorted into one of pure horror as Drake pulled the blade from its sheath and aimed it straight for her heart.

Power overwhelmed him as the Shadowblade vibrated in his grasp, seeking death. Bloodlust blinded him with bitter rage, stealing into his veins. It was like a festering disease, a rot that plagued him, a dark magic beyond his command. He raised his arm, preparing to strike, and any restraint he had left was suffocated. His control slipped, his mind emptied, and he staggered forward, compelled by the call of the blade to spill blood.

The blade consumed him, its predatory nature knowing only death. His arms burned, struggled as the weapon urged him to strike.

In the far-off distance, a female cried out. Her panicked cry lanced through the air.

Drake lunged and Creslyn screamed.

The Shadowblade sang as it met flesh, sinking deep as he plunged it into a beating heart.

"No!" Caelian wailed, and Kjeld collapsed, his body dropping to the ground at Creslyn's feet.

A final sacrifice.

Drake blinked as his vision blurred in and out of focus. A fist struck his jaw, snapping his head to the side, and the metallic tang of blood coated his tongue. He lurched to the right, tripping over his own feet, and then Creslyn was there. The expression on her face was unreadable, her eyes once again near black in color.

She wrenched the Shadowblade from his grasp, throwing it high into the air. The sunstorm whipped around her, a seething vortex of bright light and prismatic rainbows. Her magic shoved him backward, sent him stumbling away from her, from the blade. Beam after radiant beam were launched skyward in frenzied bolts, hissing through the rain in a trail of steam, thrashing the blade as it whined, plummeting back toward the earth.

Creslyn threw her arms out before her, and in one final burst of violent magic, thousands of shattered rainbows struck the Shadowblade down. Its midnight blade turned gray, splintering from tip to hilt, disintegrating into nothing more than a pile of chalky dust and decayed bones.

He stared at what was left, as clumps of ash dissolved into

the rain, leaving behind plumes of smoke, filling the air with the rancid stench of sordid magic.

Slowly, Drake's gaze fixated on where Creslyn and Caelian kneeled next to Kjeld's unmoving body, where crimson pooled beneath him, mixing with puddles of rain, creating a small river of red.

Drake looked down at his hands, his throat closing tight as he whispered, "What have I done?"

CHAPTER THIRTY-SEVEN

Creslyn grabbed a handful of her sodden skirts and tore, her nails digging deep into the fabric until the sound of ripping satin filled her ears. Her heart hammered wildly, and her body was wrecked with tremors as she tried to focus, to save the life draining before her eyes. She bundled the smooth cloth together, pressing it firmly onto the wound in Kjeld's chest. His blood soaked through it in seconds, staining her hands and seeping through his leathers. All the color drained from his tanned face, and his summer blue eyes listed toward her.

"My…" Kjeld sucked in a garbled breath. "Lady."

"I'm here."

Her heart tumbled into her stomach, and the tears that slid down her cheeks were lost to the rain washing away his blood. It weakened her, paralyzed her, seeing a man of his strength and fortitude succumb to such a horrid fate. There was nothing she could do, nothing she could say to reverse it.

She continued to press the bundle of cloth to his wound, knowing it wouldn't make a difference, knowing she would be unable to save Kjeld's life.

Caelian clutched his worn leathers, her nails digging into the stiff fabric of his vest. She did not cry, but her eyes roved all over his body, wrought with worry. Gnawing on her bottom lip, her gaze darted to the overcast heavens, then back to Kjeld.

"I can save him."

Her voice was soft when she spoke, and Creslyn wasn't entirely sure she heard her correctly. She stared at her twin whose eyes were alight with resolution.

"He's losing too much blood, Caelian." Creslyn's lungs hollowed out and she fell back, the blood-soaked scrap of her gown soiling her lap. The rain continued to fall, the cold drops running down her back like the fingers of death. She pressed her lips together and looked upon Kjeld, whose eyes had closed, whose pained, wheezing breaths were thick and rasping. There would be no saving him. Not even a general of dragons could survive the Shadowblade. "A wound from the Shadowblade has no cure, Cae. It takes every life, every time."

Caelian shook her head, her hair sticking to the sides of her face like streaks of liquid silver.

"No. I can do it." Caelian cupped Kjeld's face with her pale hands, running a thumb along his beard in gentle, comforting strokes as his chest rose, then fell for the final time. Her voice broke as she said, "I cannot let him die."

But it was too late.

Kjeld Holtstrom, General of the Brackroth Dragon Legion, was dead.

Creslyn tilted her head back, sniffling, and lifted her face to the misty gray skies. Her tears were hot, the rain was cold. The Shadowblade was gone. Her mate was free, his curse finally broken.

But the cost, oh sweet stars, the *cost*.

Kjeld had forfeited his life for hers without hesitation. He'd shoved her out of the way right before Drake struck, taking the blade to his heart. Searing pain flared through her and her lungs squeezed at the memory. She would never forget the blinding terror she'd felt when Drake fixated on her, his pupils so large and crazed that they obscured the green of his eyes. In that one frightful moment, the bond had fallen silent, as though it had been severed completely.

Even now, she was hesitant to reach for it, to even look upon him for fear of what she might see.

But she could not be afraid anymore.

She could not be afraid ever again.

Creslyn felt for the thread of her heart, and it vibrated softly in return. Still there. Still intact. But it was empty and lacking warmth, as though the soul bound to hers was utterly defeated. Wrecked and damaged. Desolate. A husk of a life.

Daring a glance over her shoulder, she sought Drake and almost fractured at the sight of him.

It was worse than she ever could have expected.

Drake stared where Kjeld laid motionless on the wet ground, each sharp inhale shuddering through him as though it hurt to even breathe. His face was pure agony and the vacantness in his eyes almost broke her. He stood with his arms limp by his sides, his gaze harboring all those restless emotions he fought so hard to control. Creslyn had never seen him in such a state of despondency.

This was *Drake.*

He was cool, calculating, and cutthroat. He was a god.

And he was breaking.

"Kjeld." His hoarse voice stole through the courtyard, gravelly and tinged with suffering. He blinked, his gaze sliding to her, and a rush of emotion trembled through the bond. Sorrow. Remorse. Guilt.

"The Shadowblade." Drake swallowed, his mouth opening and closing as though he couldn't get the words out. "I didn't believe you. I...I didn't trust you."

He stumbled forward and dropped to his knees beside her, bowing his head.

Creslyn grabbed his hand and squeezed. His palm was like ice, clammy and cold.

"I killed him. My general." He lifted his gaze, and his throat worked as he tried to fight some unreadable emotion. Misery carved the handsome planes of his face. "My…friend."

"It wasn't you." Creslyn's voice caught, pleading with him to understand. The guilt he carried was torturous and suffocating, so heavy she felt herself gasping as she said, "It was the blade. It was cursed."

"You," Drake choked out, searching her face for something. He grabbed her by the waist and hauled her into his lap. His arms curled around her, locking tight, his fingers gripping her sodden gown as he held her close, refusing to let her go. He drew her into him, clutching her like she was the only thing keeping him from drowning in a volatile sea of despair. "I tried to kill you."

"It was the blade, Drake." Creslyn despised the way her voice quivered. She threaded her fingers through his dark hair, soothing away the tumultuous emotions coursing through him. The side of his face came to rest against her heart, and she whispered, "Not you. Never you."

His fingers molded to her back, like he was trying to compress all the space between them, like he needed her to breathe. He held her firmly in his fierce grip, all the while murmuring two words over and over again.

Forgive me.

Forgive me.

Forgive me.

To her. To Kjeld. To the gods, and the stars, and the fates.

Creslyn squeezed her eyes shut and held him, pouring everything, all of her, into the bond they shared. She gave him her strength, her comfort, her love. All that she was, belonged to him. She calmed his mind with her own thoughts, embraced his torment as though it were her own. Her soul strained, reaching, pulling him from the fathomless pit of torment. She cradled his heart in her hands, warming the stone until it was soft and pliable, wiping away all traces of ash.

Until finally, Drake's rumbling voice gently caressed the walls of her mind.

"Kearsta."

"Here." She pressed a kiss to the top of his head, unsure she would ever be able to release him. *"I'm here."*

But magic simmered along Creslyn's skin, and her eyes flew open.

A startled cry escaped her as dozens of stars tumbled down around them in streaks of glittering silver, slashing through the rain and wind. They whistled as they fell from the sky, tinkling like broken bits of glass as they bounced off the hard ground of the courtyard.

It was then she noticed Kjeld was glowing.

He loosed a pained groan, a golden aura coating his body as he swallowed an impossible gulp of air. The tanned hue of his skin was suddenly more vibrant, a flawless bronze. Wondrously radiant. The wound from the Shadowblade had healed, disappearing as though it had never been there at all. Blood still stained his leathers, but the slash in them was gone. His fingers twitched, and while his eyes remained closed, his brows were drawn into a frown of discomfort.

Kjeld was alive.

The same...yet different.

His blond hair shone like spun gold and his features were sharper, chiseled and angular. The scar that marked his bottom lip was slightly more pronounced, more visible as the color returned to his lips. He'd been solid before, yet now he looked to be forged from granite, every inch of him hardened muscle. The tattoos of runes crawling up his neck looked freshly painted, the ink a glossy black. Even his beard, short and well-trimmed, seemed to highlight the striking planes of his face.

He rolled his head to one side, away from Creslyn, and she clamped one hand over her mouth in shock.

Where his ears should have been round, they were now long and pointed.

Kjeld was *fae*.

Creslyn gaped at her twin, shock ricocheting through her.

Impossible. What Caelian had done was somehow unimaginable, and yet…Kjeld continued to draw air. To breathe. To live.

"How?" she croaked.

Caelian sat back, tucking her bloodied hands beneath her. The skin beneath her eyes was sunken and she hung her head, her silver hair falling around her like a curtain.

When she spoke, her words were a scrape of sound against the wind. Tainted by exhaustion. "I made a wish."

Creslyn could only stare, watching as Caelian's magic receded and the shooting stars fizzled out completely. Whatever she did to revive Kjeld, the cost would be great.

Dangerous magic that…wishes upon stars.

WEEKS LATER, Creslyn found herself doing exactly as Ariesian instructed—acting as though nothing was amiss and dancing at a ball.

Or at the very least, she was *attempting* to dance.

Drake was obscenely patient, having offered to teach her how to waltz. Unfortunately for her, she was far better at fighting with a sword than she was being twirled around a ballroom. She could dance just fine on her own, letting herself ebb and flow to the sound of the music. But as soon as she was in his arms, she turned into a stumbling, awkward mess of a lady who could not keep time if her life depended on it.

Tonight, they were at House Emberspire, as Novalise and Asher were hosting a ball to celebrate Embernyte, when the decadence of the autumn season was at its most illustrious point. Nearly every noble in Aeramere was in attendance, dressed in their finery, dazzling with exquisite elegance. While Asher donned more formal attire, a simple suit of black and silver, Novalise wore a gown that looked like it was on fire. Scarlet silk swirled around her like flames and the bodice was covered in gold crystals that shifted in the light, mimicking the glow of burning embers.

Couples swirled across the obsidian floor of the ballroom in a kaleidoscope of colors, moving in time to a melodic symphony. Gilded leaves of topaz, citrine, and ruby dripped from the ceiling, some of them falling to the ground, making it seem like they were dancing in an autumn forest. Golden trees overflowing with sprigs of berries and jewel-toned leaves were clustered into corners and the mirrored walls reflected the radiance of warm faerie fire that sparked like orbs in chandeliers carved from ancient branches. Music and laughter filled the breathtaking space, and the heady scent of spiced wine and cinnamon hung heavy in the air.

While Creslyn tried to follow Drake's lead, she couldn't quite seem to tear her gaze away from Caelian.

Her twin stood in a lonely corner, her hands clasped together, her gaze downcast. She fiddled with the sleeves of her navy satin gown, tugging at the gold crystals lining the cuffs. Every so often she would scan her surroundings, her eyes filled with dreadful yearning, before she once again retreated into herself. It was dreadful to think of Caelian as a wallflower, for she dearly loved to dance, but her sister had refused every male who asked for her hand thus far.

Likely because the one she longed for the most, a stunning fae who rode a dragon, was currently ignoring her very existence.

Creslyn stole another look at her sister as Drake guided her into a confusing series of steps around the ballroom. "Why is Kjeld so mad at her?"

"Remember how I told you the story of Valorahan?" Drake asked, lifting her by the waist to spare his feet from being stepped on yet again. "Kjeld is a warrior, *solysa*. He made the ultimate sacrifice to save your life, and for him, there was no nobler way to die. For him, Valorahan was his fate. His destiny."

He carried her off the dance floor and set her down by a table filled with various forms of pumpkin and apple desserts.

"Caelian brought him back to life. She made him fae. Gave him magic. None of which he ever wanted."

Drake sighed then, and a line formed across his brow.

Whatever he was going to say next would not be kind.

"Caelian robbed him of his destiny." He slid an arm around her waist, leading her out through one of the arching doorways to the gardens beyond. "Kjeld will not be so quick to forgive her for it."

"But she saved his life," Creslyn countered.

Drake slid one finger beneath her chin, his eyes warming. "It was not her life to save."

As much as she didn't want to admit it, she knew Drake was right. While it seemed like Caelian was acting out of a noble cause when she'd brought Kjeld back, her actions had also stemmed from a place of thoughtlessness. She'd mistakenly assumed the general would be grateful, and now he wanted nothing to do with her.

Outside, the air was brisk, and while the moon had graced Aeramere with the fullness of its dark side, the stars twinkled as bright as diamonds. Out here, in the solemnity of the night, the rest of the world seemed so very far away. The music was distant, a whispering refrain, the laughter and voices no louder than the strumming of a harp.

Creslyn turned in Drake's arms, admiring the way he grinned down at her, the way the smile she loved finally reached his eyes.

"I have something for you," he murmured.

Her brows lifted. "Is it something sparkly?"

His smiled widened. "Perhaps."

Drake reached into his pocket and pulled out a strand of glittering pearls. "I meant to give them to you before, but you were rather furious with me."

"Mm." She lifted her hair from her neck and turned, allowing him to drape the pearls and fasten them in place. "I believe it was well deserved."

"Indeed it was." He chuckled, clasping the strand around her throat. His mouth grazed her ear, his whisper full of dark lust. "How do they feel?"

She leaned against him and sighed. "Lovely."

"Then later tonight, I will show you how much better they will feel between your thighs."

Shivers of delight raced down Creslyn's spine and heat bloomed low in her belly in anticipation of his sinful promise. She spun in his arms. "I have something for you as well."

"Is that so?" Drake crooned.

"Yes." She pulled a small velvet pouch from her gown and emptied the contents into the palm of her hand.

Two rings tumbled out.

One belonging to her, the one Drake had given her, the one she'd claimed to have lost. She slid the black diamond ring back onto her finger, admiring the way it fit so perfectly. Like it always belonged there. The other, however, was a simple band that sparkled softly in the night. She'd had it made especially for him.

"It's made of black opal. Both dark and light." Creslyn held it out to him. "To remind you of me. Of us."

Drake took the ring and rolled it between his fingers.

"I know it's not much—"

He kissed her soundly on the lips. "It's perfect, *sjellhert.*"

Drake put the ring on his finger, then captured her waist, drawing her close. His other hand cupped the back of her neck, his favorite spot, and he lowered his head so his mouth brushed hers once more.

"*Vai levska dey,*" he whispered softly against her lips.

"And what," Creslyn asked, swaying into his embrace and melting into him, "does *that* mean?"

His forest green eyes danced as he said, "You'll figure it out."

Creslyn smiled, weaving her arms around his waist, letting his kiss take her to the stars...because she already knew.

EPILOGUE

Solarius skated his teeth along his bottom lip.

At one point, balls and festivals had ranked quite high on his list of favorite things, mostly because of the ladies who attended, with their pretty dresses and simpering smiles. Recently, however, the parties had become a tedious drone of mediocrity. He swore a cloud of doom grew ever closer with each passing event, dampening the gaiety. The impending storm of his own demise.

He kicked his legs out, crossing one ankle over the other as he sat alone, watching the opulent splendor of Embernyte unravel around him.

Perhaps his disdain toward such festivities stemmed from his own roguish behavior. He'd lost count of the number of beds he'd slipped from in the predawn hours after a night of revelry. The faces and names of the females whose company he sought had begun to bleed together like a messy watercolor painting of soft lips and flushed cheeks. He could no longer discern one from the next.

Propping his elbow on the table next to him, he swirled his

glass of applefire whiskey and took a hefty swig. Its fruity, spicy flavor coated his tongue, burning the back of his throat.

Or maybe the reason he could no longer stand attending these wretched parties was because his eldest brother had seen fit to marry him off to Lady Narissa Seaborne, the only female in the whole of Aeramere who despised him with every fiber of her being.

Solarius's scowl deepened.

To be fair, she probably wasn't the *only* female who could not stand the ground upon which he walked. There were likely a few who cursed his name, clutching their broken hearts, even though he'd been clear with his promises. Or lack thereof. That being said, Narissa certainly had no qualms about making her sentiments regarding her strong dislike of him widely known.

As if by some divine intervention, Narissa appeared in his line of sight, despite his best efforts to avoid her for the duration of the evening.

One thing Solarius could not deny was her excessive beauty.

If a goddess of the sea were to walk the planes of this world, it would be Narissa Seaborne.

She stood across the crowded ballroom near a cluster of faux gold trees with his sister, Sarelle. Tonight, Narissa wore a gown of sea green, reminding him of the cresting waves along Azurvend's coast. The satin scooped across her full breasts, skimming her hips, and dipped dangerously low in the back, putting entirely too much of her sun-kissed skin on display. Her golden waves were piled high on her head, the tresses pinned in place by white pearls and crystals of aquamarine. A few pieces of her hair had fallen loose, curling around a rather kissable neck. Pearlescent beaded earrings hung from her ears, and she wore thin golden rings on nearly every finger, some of them were shaped like waves, others were embellished with tiny blue gems.

Solarius found the one she wore on her thumb oddly attractive.

Fucking stars.

He tugged on the collar of his shirt. This ballroom was too warm. Damn near suffocating.

He slammed his empty glass on the table and reached for another, having learned it was best to always have two drinks in hand for such occasions.

Sarelle must have said something amusing, because then Narissa laughed. Her smile illuminated the whole of her face. But it did not reach his ears over the music and conversations floating around him. In truth, he'd long forgotten the sound of it.

"Cheer up, Sol." Lord Reif Marintide pulled out the chair across from him and dropped into it. His own beverage, a blazing red liquid with gold flames, almost sloshed over the rim. He tipped the drink in Solarius's direction. "She's not so terrible. Narissa is positively delightful, so long as you don't piss her off."

Solarius shook his head and muttered, "She fucking hates me."

"And you hate her," Reif countered, with far too much mirth. The lord of House Azurvend grinned broadly, raking a hand through his windswept hair. He leaned back in his seat, his eyes filled with amusement. "Sounds like a match made by the stars, if you ask me."

"I'm not asking." He ran one finger around the rim of his glass, his patience thinning.

"What is it that plagues the two of you with loathing, anyway?" Reif asked, his brows pinching together in thought. "I can hardly remember what set off the years-long quarrel between you both."

Solarius remembered.

Clearly.

But he had no desire to rehash such memories with Reif. Or anyone, for that matter. "It isn't worth discussion."

The corner of Reid's mouth curved into a knowing smirk. "I heard it was because you were shit in bed."

Solarius scoffed and his jaw popped, rage filling him at the unbidden memory. "Wouldn't know, to be honest. Some other noble bastard got his cock inside of her before I got the chance."

Reif's face hardened, all traces of humor vanishing. His expression sobered and his gaze turned cold. "Mind your tongue, Lord Solarius. That is my cousin you're speaking of. Narissa is a lady of House Azurvend, and it will do you well to remember it."

It was impossible to forget, since he would be marrying her soon enough.

Still, a stab of remorse needled him, and he dipped his head in acknowledgement. "Apologies, my lord. It was not my intent to insult her reputation."

Reif studied him a few moments longer. Then he stood abruptly, and as he bowed before taking his leave, he said, "Either way, might I kindly suggest you pull your head out of your ass and go ask your betrothed to dance?"

Solarius lifted one brow. Dancing with Narissa would not be on his agenda this evening. "And why would I do that, Lord Marintide?"

"Because I don't trust Lord Calfair Skyhelm further than I can spit."

Solarius's head snapped up, and he jerked upright, scanning the ballroom. Sure enough, Calfair Skyhelm had Narissa cornered by one of the doors leading out into the darkened gardens. His hands were planted on either side of her, pinning her against the wall. If he managed to coax her outside, there was no telling what that prick of a fae would try, and knowing Calfair, he'd succeed.

"Fuck." Solarius downed the rest of his drink and stood, wincing as the ballroom seemed to tip to one side.

Reif clicked his tongue and slapped him soundly on the back. "Atta boy."

Solarius stalked toward them, uncaring as he shoved his way across the floor, barging through couples who were mid-dance. The alcohol he'd consumed this eve only served to fuel his frustration, and he rolled his sleeves as he went, preparing for a fight. Though whether his fist would meet Calfair's smug jaw in a satisfying crunch or he would be forced to endure another verbal sparring match with Narissa, he couldn't quite be sure.

For Calfair's sake, he hoped it was the latter.

"Well," he drawled, glowering at the both of them. "This looks cozy."

Calfair startled, edging away from Narissa only slightly. He gave Solarius a condemning look. "Ah, Lord Solarius. I did not realize you would be in attendance tonight."

Solarius rocked back on his heels, running his tongue along his teeth. "So, you figured you would take it upon yourself to corner my future wife?"

"I didn't see the harm in it, especially since you'd rather spend your time with applefire whiskey. Lady Narissa deserves affection and decent company, both of which I am more than willing to provide." The damned noble grinned, a silent dare.

"I'm sure." Solarius grabbed Narissa's arm and hauled her to his side. "I can assure you, Lord Calfair, she is having a most enjoyable evening. One that will be spent in my arms. Not yours."

With that, he dragged her out onto the floor of the ballroom.

His hand found the small of her back, and he hated the way the feel of her bare flesh caused his blood to burn. Still, he pulled her close, capturing her other hand as he led her into a dance, ignoring the way she moved so fluidly against him despite the absolute rage reflected in her eyes.

Eyes, he thought, which had always been his undoing.

They were pale green, frosty and cold, but right now they resembled an ocean set on fire.

"I could have handled him on my own." Her tone was dismissive, and she turned her head away from him, leaving him no choice but to inhale the scent of her.

Exotic florals. Sandalwood. A hint of the sea.

Solarius's mouth watered, and he gritted his teeth.

"Because you were doing such a good job of it." He lowered his head so his mouth grazed her ear, and her entire body stiffened in his arms. Her earrings tinkled softly, reminding him of music. "One more minute and he would've had you alone in those gardens with his hand beneath your skirts."

He pulled back just in time to see the rosy gold hue of her cheeks pale.

"Just leave me alone, Solarius." She attempted to break free, to abandon him in the middle of a dance. A most insufferable offense. "You're drunk."

"Mildly intoxicated," he corrected, and her fiery ocean eyes flew to him once more. "Not in the mood for my company, Rissa love?"

"Don't call me that."

"But I enjoy it so much."

An honest truth.

As far as he knew, he was the only one who ever called her Rissa. It was a nickname he'd given her some years ago, and while she'd been fond of it then, now it only seemed to infuriate her.

Which was another form of pleasure altogether.

"Besides," he crooned, spinning her away from him, then hauling her back into his arms. "I rather like it when you look at me like that."

Anger simmered beneath her flawless skin.

"Like what?" she spat.

"Like you want to gouge out my eyeballs with some pointy seashells."

Narissa flicked her gaze to the gilded leaves falling around them. "I shall be sure to find some and put them to good use. Though there are other means. The beaches of Azurvend have more than sharp seashells as weapons. Syrenshade, for example. They're deceivingly lovely flowers that grow beneath the light of the moon, and their purple petals contain the most interesting toxin. If you were to crush them with a mortar and pestle and add some fern berries to the mix, then you'd have a perfect poison."

Stars above, she was brilliant.

Solarius chuckled. "Such a naughty midnight siren you are, crafting toxins born of the sea."

His comment only incensed her further, and her gaze narrowed.

"I do not want this any more than you do, my lord."

Of that, he had no doubt. Yet there was something so utterly pleasing about taunting her.

He guided her around the ballroom, the alcohol in his blood emboldening him as he said, "Not looking forward to sharing my bed, my lady?"

Her lashes fluttered back in shock, but she recovered quickly, her nails digging into his shoulder. His cock throbbed in response.

"I do not even care to share the same air as you, my lord."

He moved deftly, snaking his arm further around her, so the pads of his fingers slipped beneath the silky fabric of her gown, and gripped her bare waist.

Narissa gasped, and he hauled her so close, the tips of their noses almost touched.

"That makes two of us." His hand dipped lower, grazing her hip, a current of unwanted desire rippling through him as he realized she wore no underthings of satin or lace. His jaw locked, and he ignored the flood of lust coursing through his veins. "Don't worry, I plan on being thoroughly smashed after we marry. Should make it rather easy to get the necessary deed over with, should it not?"

She reached back to slap him, and he caught her wrist with his free hand, squeezing tightly.

"Your despicable habits will be the end of you," she hissed.

"Shall I be worried about you poisoning my drink on our wedding night?" he mused, his thumb tracing small circles along the inside of her palm. "You seem rather adept in the art."

"No." Narissa smiled, her glossy pink lips drawing his attention. "If your wine was poisoned, I would gladly drink it myself. If only to spare me from ever having to spread my legs for the likes of you."

Solarius dipped her roughly, hooking one hand beneath her knee, and hiking her leg to his hip. Her eyes widened and she clutched at his arms, as though she truly feared he might drop her. The beaded strap of her gown slipped down her shoulder, revealing the golden curve of her breast. He was half tempted to lower his mouth to her right then, to swipe his tongue along those perfect swells. To make her pay for her transgressions against him.

"Unfortunate for you, then." His voice was rough with vexation as he stared down at her. "Since I prefer whiskey over wine."

He yanked her upright as the final note of music carried through the ballroom. To anyone watching, it might appear as though they were a breath away from kissing, her mouth was so close to his own.

But Solarius knew better.

He released her, his hands falling to his side.

Narissa dropped into an elaborate curtsy, piercing him with a look of revulsion that cut straight through him. "My lord."

He bowed, never taking his eyes off her. "My lady."

She whirled away from him in a flurry of satin, and Solarius roughed a hand over his face. His future wife would rather drink poison than fuck him.

Lovely.

He stomped back over to the table he'd previously abandoned, his foul mood brewing and souring his stomach. Another glass of applefire whiskey was already there, waiting for him, and he knocked it away with the back of his hand.

Solarius slumped into the empty chair.

Of course Narissa didn't want him.

No one wanted him.

But fuck if he didn't want her.

ACKNOWLEDGMENTS

Well, you were starved for Drake and Creslyn by the end of All the Chaos of Constellations, and since you finished All the Sacrifice of Shadows, I can only hope I delivered. They were so much fun to write, I loved fleshing out their characters and diving deeper into their stories. Bringing them to life on paper is a whole other kind of satisfaction.

I'd love to thank my Brainstorm Spiral discord chat for not only helping with Creslyn & Drake, but for also helping me plan out the next few couples of our beloved Starstorms. To Ashley, Sasha, Stephanie, and Kelsy, thank you for keeping my secrets and for helping me make my books the best they can possibly be. Sorry not sorry for the thousands of messages, it was worth it.

To my patrons, thank you SO much for your support. Words can't even describe what an honor it is to know you actually like me that much.

A HUGE thank you to my beta readers for their valuable feedback and suggestions. You ladies are such an asset to my whole process and I am so grateful for each one of you.

To my lovely cover designer Lexie, thank you for always understanding my nonsensical ideas and turning them into something beautiful. To Elayna, map artist extraordinaire, I am always in awe of your talent. Thank you so much for coming on this journey with me. My eternal gratitude to my editor, Emily, for reading and loving each of my books, and for never making me feel stupid when I make the same mistake twice. Or three or four times. It's fine, she gets me.

QoC. You know who you are. Thank you for adopting me into your chaos.

To Vanessa, Jaclyn, Nicole, AJ, Jessica, VB, Alexis, Jenny, and Renee, thank you for being my tribe. I love you all with the whole of my heart. To Margie, for helping me with all the things. I love you!

Thank you to my family for putting up with my antics, to my husband for taking an even more vested interest in my work, so much so that he's started spraying the edges of my books and his IG algorithm is now all bookish people. To my daughters, my darlings, my two broke best friends, I love you fiercely.

And finally, for my amazing readers. Without you, the world of Aeramere and beyond would likely be nothing but a dream. Thank you for reading, for loving my stories, and for always waiting for whatever comes next.

ABOUT THE AUTHOR

Hillary Raymer is a fantasy romance author. She's a wanderer, a storyteller, and the founder of BohoSoul Press.

Hillary has always been a dreamer, and lucky for her, she turned those dreams into stories. She has an unfinished Bachelor's Degree in English because she ran off and married a Marine halfway through college. She has an affinity toward plants, loves the mountains, and enjoys scoping out metaphysical markets for crystals. Wanderlust comes to her naturally, and she's doing her best to instill the same wild and free values in her daughters. When not writing, Hillary can be found attempting to do yoga, buying more makeup she doesn't need, or discovering small businesses on Etsy.

Join her Court here https://discord.gg/EfHVy93Gvz

ALSO BY HILLARY RAYMER

The Faeven Saga

Crown of Roses

Throne of Dreams

Realm of Nightmares

Void of Endings

The Starstorm Series

All the Chaos of Constellations